D1132930

THE CUSTOM HOUSE

The central event of this novel is a savage and seemingly inexplicable murder: about this hub revolves a panorama of life in contemporary Japan impressive in its complexity and insight. *The Custom House* is in some ways a saddening book, with its recurrent misunderstandings between West and East and its picture of people forever straining to rise above their limitations: the missionaries above their spiritual limitations, some of the Japanese above their intellectual limitations and others above the material limitations imposed by overpopulation and poverty. Yet since the book is like life, in that it is never solely tragic, it flashes throughout its length with passages of delightful wit and humour.

In his central characters—the English teacher, Knox; the pathetic Australian missionary, Welling; Sanae, the Japanese girl with whom he falls in love; Setsuko, one of the 'new women' of Japan, and her uncle, head of a vast cartel and an amateur painter—no less than in a host of subsidiary characters—students, servants, journalists, police-officers, bar girls and strip-show girls—Mr. King once again displays that penetrating knowledge of motive and character for which he has so often been praised. This book gives not only a thrilling and intensely vivid picture of post-war Japan, but is a work of art which digs deeply into universal experience.

By the same Author

Novels

TO THE DARK TOWER
NEVER AGAIN
AN AIR THAT KILLS
THE DIVIDING STREAM
THE DARK GLASSES
THE FIREWALKERS
(under the pseudonym Frank Cauldwell)
THE WIDOW
THE MAN ON THE ROCK

Short Stories

SO HURT AND HUMILIATED

Poetry

ROD OF INCANTATION

THE CUSTOM HOUSE

FRANCIS KING

LONGMANS

LONGMANS, GREEN AND CO LTD
48 GROSVENOR STREET, LONDON W1
RAILWAY CRESCENT, CROYDON, VICTORIA, AUSTRALIA
443 LOCKHART ROAD, HONG KONG
PRIVATE MAIL BAG 1036, IKEJA (LAGOS)
44 JALAN AMPANG, KUALA LUMPUR
ACCRA, AUCKLAND, IBADAN, KINGSTON (JAMAICA)
NAIROBI, SALISBURY (RHODESIA)

LONGMANS SOUTHERN AFRICA (PTY) LTD
THIBAULT HOUSE, THIBAULT SQUARE, CAPE TOWN

LONGMANS, GREEN AND CO INC
119 WEST 40TH STREET, NEW YORK 18

LONGMANS, GREEN AND CO
137 BOND STREET, TORONTO 2

ORIENT LONGMANS PRIVATE LTD
CALCUTTA, BOMBAY, MADRAS
DELHI, HYDERABAD, DACCA

PRINTED IN GREAT BRITAIN BY
NORTHUMBERLAND PRESS LIMITED
GATESHEAD ON TYNE

In front of the custom house
a woman, just landed from a boat, says
'Here we are in Japan, my dear.
Japan starts from here.'
Her little daughter replies in the sooty wind:
'So this is Japan!
Japan is dark, isn't it, Mummy?'

THE CUSTOM HOUSE *by Saisei Murou* (1889-   )
Translated by I. Kono and R. Fukuda

ONE

I CANNOT and do not wish to sleep again and so, for want of
anything better, I have taken up this diary, neglected since I
came to Japan, and am hunched over it in the *roka*, the glassed-in
porch which separates my quarters from the garden. The wicker-
table and chair are both too low so that I have to sit with my
knees simultaneously brushing my ears and clamping the table
between them. Oh, the discomfort of living native in a scantily
furnished doll's-house! Even those hideous Ministry of Works
three-piece suites in the houses of the Osaka consular officials
now seem enviable in comparison.

A gong has just sounded, some dozen times at intervals of three
or four seconds. Peculiarly lacking in resonance, like an amplified
footfall on grass, it appears to be thumped in the road just beyond
the garden; and yet the nearest temple must be that of Hyakuman-
ben, at least half-a-mile away. Four o'clock. And now that
melancholy wail on a conch announces the noodle-man. There's
the rattle of his cart, a rickety sedan-chair on wheels with a
string of lanterns swaying across it. Again the dying wail. Who
buys from him at this hour? Workers returning from a night-
shift? Students preparing for examinations? Insomniacs like
myself? Or the labourers for whom the day, sweat-soaked and
dust-stifled, is just about to begin? (Sometimes I hear another kind
of conch-wail, spasmodic and throaty: the blind masseur, led by
a hydrocephalic tot of indeterminate sex who, perhaps in an effort
to appear less minuscule, teeters on stilt-like *geta* at least a foot
high.)

What, I wonder, was the cause of this night of jumbled dreams
and waking panics? The dinner for the visiting Archbishop at
the Miyako Hotel; the car-accident; or the death of the puppy?
(I must remember to tell Endo-San to bury it tomorrow—or, rather,
today.) Of the dreams I can remember little, but an impression of
walking, insect-like, along a black fissure between immensely
elongated moon-lit buildings (New York? but I have never been
there) which gave the impression of streaming down on either

1

side of me, twin cataracts of concrete. The panics I can remember better, since I have experienced them often. One wakes with some small sensation of discomfort—a burning behind the sternum; the collar of one's pyjama-jacket drenched in an acid sweat; a rawness of the throat when one first swallows; or a faint, throbbing pain above one groin—and an immense sensation of despair and dread. The first onset of a long-drawn, fatal malady whose teeth are just closing on one? Tuberculosis, cancer, who knows what horror? Slowly the panic is put to rest; by sips of lukewarm water, a sleeping-tablet, Alka-Seltzer, aspirin, or the brief re-reading of a newspaper or magazine one has already read from one end to the other. One sleeps again. Dreams again. Wakes again, in the jaws of the same incubus. Far better to stay awake entirely.

My first impulse had been to refuse the invitation to the dinner; but I know that the 'Caucasians' (as they describe themselves when they do not say 'Westerners') will soon cease to think of me as 'shy' and 'retiring' and will decide that I am 'stand-offish' and 'stuck-up'; and so, reluctantly, as part of a new policy of Friendship to All and Enmity to None (a recently enunciated slogan of Prime Minister Kishi), I made up my mind to go. Friends are always surprised to learn of my dread of entering rooms where either I know no one or, far worse, I know two or three individuals so little that I wonder if they will recognise me. 'You shy!' They laugh at the seeming affectation; the shyness no more evident to them than the nerves of an actor on a first night.

In exchange for my invitation I was given a label to pin to my lapel—'Mr. W. Knox, C. of E.' How did they guess the 'C. of E.' I wonder? No one ever asked me; but perhaps somewhere, in the town-hall or the central police-station, all such information about foreigners is available. 'Next floor, Mr. Knox, to the dining-room.' The Japanese in the clerical collar had tiny, seemingly ineffectual hands, like the paws of a new-born rabbit, but it was with astonishing speed and dexterity that he scrabbled among the labels in his box to pick out the right one.

I mounted the stairs behind a broad pair of shoulders and the curly back of a bony head. 'Hello, Marion . . . Jack . . . Ikeda-San . . . Hello, there, Mrs. Crawley . . . Well, Ito-San, how did your sale of work go?' How pleasant to be able to imitate that jovial voice (a trace of Cockney accent?) and to go round pumping the hands of the surprised, politely-bowing Japanese. But Marion, Jack, Ikeda-San, Mrs. Crawley, Ito-San: none of them is known to me. Look friendly; look benevolent; look as if you were spilling over with the milk of human kindness instead of this sour distrust of yourself and others. . . . Well, I must have succeeded. The man turned round, squinted at my label, and said: 'You're Mr. Knox! I've heard of you, Mr. Knox. Now let me see, Mr. Knox . . .' The hand that enveloped mine was large; the dry knuckles protuberantly knobbly, the palms strangely fleshy and moist in contrast. 'Let me see, Mr. Knox . . .' (It is usually Americans who repeat names like that; a device to remember them.) 'University teacher, Mr. Knox?' I nodded; the guess was easy. 'Well, now, come and meet some of these charming people. You're a newcomer, aren't you?' 'Charming' people; you must be no less charming. Marion and Jack, who are obviously American, will expect a grin and brisk shake of the hands; for Ikeda-San, who wears glasses fitted with lenses that tilt upwards, like miniature skylights, on hinges—one hand is tilting them now—a deferential bow and a small, sardonic, Japanese-style smirk will be required. Yes, exactly. You seem to be bowing and smiling to your own image in a distorting mirror, legs foreshortened and face like a crushed persimmon. 'How d'you do, Mrs. Crawley.' Shake hands, not shake hands? Better shake. The voice is pitched low, the tone confidential; after all, we are compatriots in a country where the English, because they are vastly outnumbered by the Americans, therefore tend to despise them and huddle together against them. Ito-San (fifty, sixty, seventy?) is exquisite in Japanese dress: her face, the chalk-white skin of which is stretched as taut as if an over-zealous plastic-surgeon had just lifted it, is set at a slant on a pole-like neck. Is the woman winking at me as I bow deeply to her? No, a nervous tic.

The worst was over. I hurriedly and, I hoped, unobtrusively glanced at the label of my introducer. 'Rev. M. C. Welling, C. of E.' Groups of people were drifting towards the tables and I began to drift with my own group. Ito-San soon detached herself and taking those small, tottering, yet determined steps of elderly Japanese women (Setsuko for whom something always symbolises something else says that they symbolise their lives: the timidity and seeming ineffectuality of the movement forward belying an unfaltering certainty of aim) made for the table on the dais at the far end of the banqueting-hall. Obviously someone of importance; and, like most Japanese, aware of the exact degree of that

3

importance, no more, no less. The rest of us seated ourselves in humbler positions.

'Tell me, Mr. Nott——' Welling, who had begun to devour his roll before any food had been placed before us, leant across the table towards me, chewing vigorously.

'Knox.'

He took no notice. The face, so close to mine, looked attractive, but unintelligent: the eyes, blue and set a trifle too close together beneath the bushy, sandy eyebrows, seeming strained, as if he had spent all day out in the sun. The nose was straight, the nostrils faintly marbled with minute mauve and purple veins. A drinker, perhaps. Everywhere there were freckles, thickest on his forehead and the backs of his massive hands.

'What's your subject at the University?'

'Phonetics, chiefly. Dull, I'm afraid.'

'Whew! I wonder what you make of my accent?'

'Your accent?'

'Yes, this ugly Australian'—he exaggerated the vowel intentionally—'accent of mine. Do you think you could do anything about it, Professor Higgins?' It was like the jokes made by patients to their doctors ('Perhaps you'd better chop off a bit of the other leg to make them equal'; 'Now, Doctor, I don't want any instruments rattling about inside me to frighten the wife when I next make love to her . . .').

'It doesn't sound as if much needed to be done about it.'

'The perfect diplomat! I know just how an Australian accent sounds to your ears. It's not only *different*, like an American one, it's hideous. Everyone says so. You're not going to kid me into thinking that you *like* the sound of my vowels.'

I said no more: it seemed better to leave the subject. We had just dipped our spoons into our green-pea soup—the surface of mine split open as if it were a stagnant pond—when a loudspeaker cracked above us: 'Your Graprr! Ladies! Gentlemen!' It was the Japanese bishop welcoming the Archbishop, welcoming us, members of the Anglican communion, welcoming our fellow-workers in Christ, welcoming our friends of the Press, welcoming, welcoming . . . Somewhere a spoon rattled on a plate; a glass tinkled. But those around me—Marion, Jack, Ikeda-San etc. etc.—seemed to have been jerked up into a region where considerations of whether soup was hot, lukewarm or cold had ceased to be relevant. I touched my spoon twice but on each occasion lost my

4

nerve and did not dare to raise it. The wound in the pond-surface slowly began to knit itself together again.

Introduce, introduce, introduce . . . 'Members of the Church of St. Peter and St. Paul of Omi-Maiko.' Some people at the table opposite to us exchanged glances, looked at the youthful Japanese clergyman seated at their head, and then, at his nod, rose to their feet, turned towards the Archbishop and bowed. 'The Church of St. Luke of Sanjo.' More risings and bowings. 'Our Canadian visitor from the Viatorian Mission of Takamatsu.' A quick bob and the tossing back with one hand of a hank of white hair from a bushy white eyebrow. 'The Church of St. John the Divine of Gojo and Shijo.' Marion and Jack got to their feet with a number of other Westerners and a few Japanese, obviously prosperous and English-speaking. The list ran on. All round me people kept rising : some eagerly, like dogs in expectation of a walk or a feed, others with as much self-conscious reluctance as guests surprised into appearing in a Christmas Party charade. I began to wonder if my neighbours noticed that I myself never had occasion to rise; surely they must? The thought made my heart throb faster and faster, as the list extended itself; my cheeks were on fire.

Other speeches followed; but they aroused in me not that same agony of embarrassment but another agony of boredom . . . 'Put our hands to the plough . . .' 'Japanese hospitality, renowned throughout the world' . . . 'Let us not be found with our talents hidden in a napkin' . . . 'Your city which seems to me comparable only to Florence in beauty and culture' . . . 'A light unto the Gentiles . . .' '. . . Have in common the same precious thing—a sense of humour . . .' '. . . Bear witness together . . .' The expected ramshackle phrases were either wheeled out apologetically, like rusty penny-farthings, for our inspection (the latest thing in bicycles to the eye of faith) or were ridden impudently around the room with all the assurance of the trick-cyclist who manages to propel himself on no more than a single bent wheel attached to a length of scrap-iron. What seemed to me the saddest feature of all was the way the Japanese, the sedulous apes of the world, executed exactly the same manœuvres as their Western counterparts. I found myself speculating on the subject of boredom : a disease of which the incidence seems highest in Western Europe and lowest in America and the East.

At last it was over. Mrs. Crawley turned to me (the yellow, rucked skin on the backs of her hands was in no way different in colour and texture from the skin on the leg of the chicken at which she had been hacking) and asked: 'Are you a Church of England man, Mr. Knox?'

Her label had already told me that she was what I suppose I must call a Church of England woman; had she not looked at mine? Perhaps she was short-sighted; though those brown eyes seemed remarkably sharp and far-seeing.

'Yes,' I said.

'Oh, then, Mr. Knox, you must join our Breakfast Club.' Marion (pretty; snub-nosed; glossy and neatly-bobbed brown hair) had turned to me on my other side. A Breakfast Club? It seemed to be the kind of absurdity possible nowhere but at Oxford or Cambridge. ('Only stupid people are brilliant at breakfast'— wasn't it Wilde who said that?)

'A Breakfast Club?'

'Yes, we meet every Sunday morning after Holy Communion at St. John's. Do join us. We take it in turns to go to each other's houses. We each contribute one-hundred-and-fifty yen and for that you'd be surprised what you get! Mrs. Crawley actually produced *kippers*—can you imagine? We've no idea where she got them and she's not telling us, but we expect that she made love to the chief cook on the *Himalaya* the last time it berthed in Kobe.' The idea of Mrs. Crawley making love to anyone, especially for a kipper, seemed to me highly improbable.

'My kippers are nothing in comparison with your waffles and maple-syrup.'

'Do come, Mr. Knox!'

What was I to say? Oh, but I don't go to Holy Communion? Oh, but I'm not really a member of the Church? Then why are you here? they would answer. Or wouldn't, being far too embarrassed and polite to do so.

'It sounds a wonderful idea. And I'd certainly like to try Mrs. Crawley's kippers—not to mention your waffles and maple-syrup.' It's only later, in recollection, that the falsity of this kind of adroit side-stepping makes one want to puke. 'But I always try to get away from Kyoto at a week-end. The place has a slightly claustrophobic atmosphere and I think it's good to break free when I can.'

They are nice people, all of them, oh, far nicer than I; and I expect that they believed me. They asked me where I had graduated ('Oxford! Ah, the boat-lace . . .' mused Ikeda-San)

6

and whether I was married ('No, I'm a widower . . .') and how was I enjoying Japan? As so often with missionaries I felt that we were shouting and waving to each other from the roofs of houses on either side of a busy thoroughfare: the sounds and gestures were friendly enough, but no real communication was possible.

Welling taught at the school run by his mission and he now turned to me for advice. '. . . I can make out with the mathematics and the science—that's up my street—but as a teacher of English I'm a fraud, there's no other word for it.' I have often caught myself out seeking advice which I don't need from people incompetent to give it, merely out of motives of flattery. But I don't think that there was any such guileful desire to please in Welling. He was genuinely worried that his students might be learning to say 'Naow' instead of 'Now' or that he might be passing on to them his own confusion about the rules governing the use of 'shall' and 'will'.

'You should really take your problems to Mrs. Crawley.' This was no flattery to the small middle-aged woman, dressed in black, with bunions ill-concealed by flat-heeled strap-shoes. I had met former students from her mission and their knowledge of spoken English had astonished me. 'She's the expert, not I.'

'Well, you're the University lecturer, aren't you? The Oxford graduate? The master of phonetics?' Welling seems to have acquired the Japanese faith in diplomas; in my case, as I know, of so much less real value than the experience of people like Mrs. Crawley. Perhaps this faith accounts for his deference to me; I almost expected to hear him call me 'sir'.

When we rose from the table and began to disperse, Mrs. Crawley touched my sleeve and asked: 'Have you met the Archbishop?'

'No, I haven't.'

'Oh, do come and be introduced. Come! Don't be shy!'

I muttered something about having to get home before nine-thirty; some students; a seminar . . . (Coward! Coward!)

'But it seems such a pity to come to a dinner like this and not meet him.' The remark was as penetrating as her gaze.

Welling followed me down the stairs. 'Where do you live?'

'Kitashirakawa.'

'Then let me give you a lift in my old bus.'

'Do you go in the same direction?'

7

'Practically.'

'But I don't want to take you out of your way . . .'

I made the usual protestations, secretly glad that I should not have to endure a prolonged and painful bumping in the tram. (A few days ago a woman next to me started her labour-pains outside the Imperial Palace. The event did not surprise me as it seemed to surprise our fellow-passengers.)

The 'old bus' turned out to be a green M.G., almost brand-new. Welling obviously thought he ought to apologise for it; perhaps some of his colleagues had suggested that it was a vehicle un-suitable for a missionary. 'It sounds silly, but I really chose this kind of low-slung, racy affair to please my son. I bought it when I came into a little money. Mind you, it's not the luxury it may appear. I take Bible Classes in Otsu and Ishiyama—and even as far as Ashiya—and I can buzz back and forth in no time at all. Watch your knees. . . . Yes, the boy loves this car. It's the age, nineteen. . . . No, he's not out here, he's studying medicine in Sydney. Maybe he'll enter the mission field, that's what his mother and I hope. Maybe. But for the moment he doesn't seem to feel any vocation for it. Well, for that matter, mine came late.' As he drove, expert and relaxed, and talked to me, I noticed for the first time that, in profile, he had the kind of slit-mouth, a horizontal gash, which I so often find in people I dislike. Avarice; intolerance; asceticism; prudery. . . . That kind of mouth seems to be saying all those detestable things. But, strangely, so far from finding Welling repellent, I felt attracted to him.

'Is your wife in Japan?'

He sighed and then there was a silence before he made his reply. (Some confession will come: 'No. Well, you see, my wife and I . . . You'll understand how it is . . . The best of friends still . . .') At last he began: 'She's back at home, in Austraïlia. She was ill off and on for a year and then they told her that she ought to have this big op.' (The abbreviation made me wince.) 'You know, one of these women's things. Nothing serious, you understand, but drastic, pretty drastic.' In short, a hysterectomy, I decided. 'The op. is over now and she came through it pretty well. She'll stay at home during the boy's summer vacation—we can't afford to bring him out here this time—and then she'll return to Kyoto. They say it's not only a question of the physical recuperation; there's something psycho-logical, mental . . . Have you heard that—about that kind of

8

op.? She's got to adjust, that's what the surgeon told me. Top man. In Austraïlia, I mean.'

It was at that moment that the accident happened. God knows that the Japanese roads are narrow, ill-made and ill-lit; but the woman had only herself to blame. She was talking to another woman and each of them had a fluffy white Spitz, so common in Japan, on the end of a leash. Our headlights picked them out as we roared up between the avenue of maples; and simultaneously one of the dogs hurled itself at the other. Jerking it, the woman backed into the road—I remember that her vast, black shadow seemed far more real than herself as it wriggled out before us—and then there was the vain swerve and the screeching jolt and shudder as Welling applied the brakes. 'I hit her! I hit her!' I had the door on my side open and was about to jump out when the extraordinary thing happened: the car lurched forward twice and then suddenly again began to gather momentum.

'Shut that door!'

'What on earth are you doing?'

'I hit her, I hit her!'

'Stop! Stop, you fool!'

And then he stopped: some two hundred yards from where the woman must be lying.

'Turn back.'

'I can't. You go. Please! Please!'

I got out and began to run back. Damn you! Damn you! You bastard! I was too near to losing my own nerve to have any sympathy with the loss of his. Fortunately it was dark; nothing would look so bad, I told myself, one would not see all the details —the particles of smashed bone; the brains mashed to a grey porridge; the all-pervasive blood. The woman lay in a whimpering heap in the road, and the other woman knelt whimpering beside her. One dog had bolted, while the other also whimpered on the end of its leash, from time to time tossing its head in the air and rolling its eyes. Thank God, there was no blood to be seen; and people were collecting, many people. Usually when there is an accident in other countries, no one seems to know what to do; but here no one had a doubt. A man in Japanese style underpants, resembling pyjama-trousers snipped short below the knees (I recognised him as one of my University colleagues from another department) said to me in English: 'We must not move her.' Cars were swerving to either side of the group in the road; some of them stopped, but only a few. Hearing the English, a woman in a kimono came over: 'Yes, we must not touch her. We must wait for the police.'

'They must take measurements,' the man explained.

'Photographs,' the woman added.

'I've telephoned for them,' said the man.

'One must always leave the body exactly as one finds it.'

'But she's not yet a body! Supposing another car should hit her!'

The woman gave a giggle behind a raised sleeve. I often tell myself that there is no more reason why one should weep at a disaster than that one should giggle at it—it is solely a matter of custom—but nothing irritates me more than what Wilfrid Owen, if he had been Japanese, would have had to amend to 'the eternal reciprocity of titters'. ('Titters, idle titters, I know not what they mean . . .')

'That's the law,' the man said.

But at that moment the victim herself decided to disobey the law and got slowly first to her knees and then to her feet. Were the crowd encouraging her to rise or urging her to stay where she was? They all talked fast at once; impossible to tell. She hobbled to a tree and leaning against it drew a handkerchief from her pocket and wiped it back and forth across the tip of her nose. The nose seemed undamaged. Someone pointed to her leg and then everyone began pointing and muttering. She looked down and gave a little scream. The stocking hung in tatters and blood was trickling down. But the wound on examination proved to be only superficial; soon the crowd were drifting away. . . . I decided that I had better go back to reassure Welling; but as I moved in the direction of the car, I saw that he was already standing, some twenty yards away, half-concealed behind a tree. . . .

When we were at last able to resume our journey (the police had been courteous; the woman had admitted that the fault was hers) I noticed that, though it was a sultry night, Welling's teeth were chattering. 'You need a drink. Come back to my place and I'll give you one.'

'Thanks. But I want to get home.' He sounded not merely ungracious, but angry with me. I remember thinking at the time: Well, hell, what have I done? But the answer was obvious: I had done the things which most other people would do in the circumstances and he had failed to do.

Silence: thick and prickly, like a blanket pressed against the mouth. Then: 'Well, where do we go from here?' The car came to a stop. A notice-board flared in our headlights, on a high, Japanese-style gate: 'The Anglican Mission of St. Luke.'

'Oh, I can walk. It's no distance at all. Just three or four hundred yards along the river.'

'Is that all right?'

'Yes, perfectly.'

I was making the conventional protestations, with no real intention of getting out of the car; but he, I suddenly realised, did not propose to make the conventional response. ('Don't be silly! It's far too late to walk. I can drive you there in a jiffy.')

I made an effort to be amiable, though I did not feel it. 'If there's any trouble about that business just now, don't hesitate to get in touch with me. Here's my card.' It is so difficult to find a house in Japan that many people have cards printed with a map on the reverse side. 'It's even got a pretty little picture'—I showed him—'to help you to get there.'

'Thanks.' He took the card and placed it in the car-pocket beside him.

I wanted to say: 'Why put it there? I'm not a garage,' but I merely bowed stiffly (a habit one acquires) and said, 'Thank you.'

'Not at all.' He was fumbling with some keys to open the gate and did not look round at me. 'Good night, Nott.'

'Knox . . . Good night.'

I gazed back twice and on each occasion he was turning the bunch of keys over and over in his hands. Any passer-by might have thought he was fuddled with drink.

Although it was still only early May, I began to break into a light sweat as I walked up the road to the bridge. Ten twenty-five. And the whole city seemed already to have subsided into a profound, humid torpor. I thought of the people all around me, sleeping one family to a room, in houses that elbowed each other for space and even climbed on to each other's shoulders or burrowed under each other. Like the privacy in the separate cells of a honeycomb, there was a visual privacy, created by paper-screens and mud-and-wattle walls and fences of bamboo, but there was no privacy of sound; and the snores, yelpings of dogs, creakings of those making love, screeching of ill-fed babies, turn-

11

ings of the sleepless, all the noises, however faint, that betrayed human activities, however intimate, seemed to mingle together in a concert as dreadful and saddening as human existence itself. You can never see the whole of Japan in a lifetime; but you can hear it, any night of the week.

A grey path, squirming worm-like between dusty clumps of sallow and myrtle—they looked, in the moonlight, as if they had been splashed with whitewash—took me down to the river. I had never attempted this short-cut before, but I knew that my servant used it. Gnats buzzed in my ears; the stench was appalling. Garbage lay everywhere: in mounds great and small, or scattered as though in a deliberate effort to contaminate as large an area as possible—here a wooden *geta*, its strap rotted away, there the refuse of some kitchen, further on a trail of ragged garments left there as though their wearer had hurriedly stripped, flinging them to all sides, and had then plunged into the oily water to be lost to the world forever. Excrement, of course; one is never far from it in Japan. Sometimes I passed a solitary walker with a dog. Sometimes, though rarely, I came on a couple, seated decorously side by side with physical contact confined at most to a touching of hands or an arm about the waist. How could they bear to watch the river, certainly beautiful in the moonlight which played on its sluggish ripples, in this miasma of decay? Yet I remember how, when I first visited Kinkakuji and a dead leaf had been blown on to the sand-garden, an ancient gardener had at once appeared with an implement which looked like an immense pair of bamboo sugar-tongs and had removed it from sight. How cross, too, I make Endo-San when I go out of the house and then run back in, having forgotten something, in my outdoor shoes! In Japan there is a place for order and cleanliness, and a place for chaos and dirt: and the order and cleanliness are usually artistic or ritualistic, seldom hygienic.

All at once I was brought up short. There was a towering pile of garbage, tipped presumably from some truck, right across the path, and sprawled at the foot of it, almost across it, was a body. This woman was far, far deader than the woman I had supposed that Welling had killed; and to my horror I saw in the bright moonlight that the face was already swollen and flies had settled on it. One leg was twisted under the thigh of the other, like a snapped twig, and a hand, resting against the mound of refuse, had the fingers open (the nails long as talons) as though to clutch at something in a dying spasm. The smell here was far worse than anywhere else and I thought: 'This is the smell of death, of human death.'

Well, I must do something. And as I decided that, the mouth suddenly opened and a stream of something black poured out of one side of it. Then the rigidly prehensile hand closed, opened, closed. The figure sat up and squinted at me crossly; and then began to screech incomprehensible words—imprecations, I suppose. Not a woman but a man in a *yukata*; not a corpse, but a drunk. I giggled to myself as I hurried away (the tousled, vomit-stained figure yelping hoarsely at me now), but I still felt my scalp tingle and my heart thud from my first discovery.

It was almost at the house that I found the litter of puppies— my last adventure of the night. There were four of them: three moribund and one whining feebly in a cardboard box which had been placed neatly on a newspaper (God knows why) under a bush. Many people here feel restrained by their Buddhist faith from themselves destroying the life even of a blind kitten; and so they throw out their unwanted animals to perish from hunger, exposure or the depredations of animals stronger than they. Setsuko has a terrible story of seeing an ancient, sick dog, hardly able to stand from the ravages of disease, being set on by a pack of starving pariahs who began to tear it to pieces before her eyes. 'What did you do?' 'What could I do? I fled. I was alone.' I remembered being faintly shocked by that admission; but what indeed could a single woman have done? Risk infection with rabies for an animal already beyond all saving?

I was walking on as I remembered this; and then I thought: 'You were quick enough to feel reproach for her. But what about these puppies? How typical of you and your holier-than-thou attitude!' I went back. I should keep one, I decided, and it would be the whimpering one, since it seemed the one most likely to survive. The others I must drown in the river. I removed my choice from the box and put four large stones in the place where he (for I discovered that it was a he) had lain crushed against his siblings. At that, he at once began to squirm away, his paws small, ineffectual paddles in a sea of grass and nettles, and his whimperings becoming a series of high-pitched, prolonged screams. I myself was looking for something with which to fasten up the box. I turned over the refuse around me with a foot and eventually found a broken blind from which I was able to wrench off the

13

cord. The box made a splash; the grey waters split open like an overripe grape and then closed again, ripples lapping to my feet. It was done. So easy; and yet few Japanese would find it easy.

Putting the surviving puppy under one arm, I walked on, talking to him as I did so. 'Well, you're the lucky one. I wonder what were the odds that anyone would find you before you died of hunger. And who, finding you, would be likely to take you home? Oh, you're lucky all right! You're lucky!' But the puppy's only response was to discharge on to my sleeve something which, warm and glutinous, could only be one of two equally nauseating alternatives. 'Blast you!' I smacked his head, eliciting another high-pitched scream followed by a renewal of whimpering.

Back at home, he lapped greedily at the saucer of milk I gave him, grunting from time to time and scrabbling with his paddle-like feet. As I stroked him, I felt something knobbly under my hand and had to remove a tick between my finger-nails. When, at last, the little wretch had stupefied himself with food, I placed him in a box in the outhouse where I keep my wood and coal and began to undress for bed. Whimpers. Then a screeching, like a child's when its finger is caught in a door. He would quieten down, I told myself. Just a matter of time. Since he had no teeth, he must be very young; and therefore missed his mother. The screeching went on. I heard the sounds of paper-screens being pulled back in the houses behind and on the left of mine. There was a general unease—one could sense it and even hear it—growing among my neighbours. It would be a long time before anyone complained; perhaps no one would complain at all. But each of them would remember and when they next were discussing all the things against me—'He was sun-bathing in his garden in nothing but a pair of drawers', 'And she wasn't even sober, I could tell at once'. 'It's odd that someone of his age is *still* not married'—they would discuss that too. ('And that terrible night when none of us could sleep because . . . Do you *really* think that it was only a *dog*?')

As I imagined all this, the unexpected happened: someone actually shouted: a man, in the kind of voice, high-pitched and plaintive, which neither seems to expect nor manages to receive the consideration for which it begs so abjectly. I took no notice of him. It was no doubt the middle-aged clerk from the Post Office who has a bobbing Adam's apple and rides to work on a high, old-fashioned woman's bicycle, with a black-and-white check cap

14

on the back of his head. But then a woman started—perhaps the ferocious dam with which he lives?—and that upset me. A woman to protest—in Japan! I should have to do something. Wearily I got out of bed ('I ought to have drowned the lot, damn fool thing to do') and carried the box back into my bedroom. I stroked the puppy for a while and he grunted, attempted to get my little finger into his mouth to suck, and then at last fell silent.

But that was only temporary. Again the whimpering; again the child-in-agony screeching; again the stroking; again the silence. I had the sensation, in my extreme tiredness, of a wheel which turned ceaselessly and at a certain foreseen stage in its revolutions unfailingly struck a stone and brought me to a jolting stop. Half-awake, half-asleep, I saw the wheel: the wheel of Welling's car, screaming as the brake was jammed against it: a wheel that was now crushing my face into my pillow; that was rolling (the paper-screens were once more being jerked angrily along their slots) on all sides of me . . . 'Shut up!' I sat up and shouted. It was what my neighbours were also shouting by then. 'Can't you hear? Shut up! Shut up!'

On and on the wheel turned. I got up and fetched myself a sleeping-tablet (a barbiturate acquired, without prescription, at any chemist's) and then, as I was about to put it in my mouth, an idea came to me. I broke off a corner and offered it to the puppy. He sniffed at it, wailed and then let out a single howl, followed by snivelling. 'Eat it! Go on, eat it!' One reads from time to time in the newspapers of mothers who have suffocated their infants or fathers who have punched them to death. 'The little bleeder never let us get a wink of sleep,' explains the father —inadequately, it used to seem to me. But how well I can now understand that mood of crazed exasperation. I grasped the puppy, forced open his mouth and pushed on to his tongue the fragment of the tablet. He squirmed, shook his head and spat the fragment out. This time I thrust it down his throat and pinched his nose to ensure that he swallowed it. Then I waited.

The wails came at greater and greater intervals; there was no longer the same note of insistence in them, they sounded disheartened, even despairing. Then they were replaced by a drowsy whimpering. Grunts. A brief scrabbling of the little paws against the side of the box. Silence. Thank God! And now my own share of the tablet.

I awoke, as I supposed hours later but in fact after less than an

15

hour and a half. Still silence. I do not know why, but some impulse made me lean over the side of the bed to look down at the puppy. He lay on his side in the moonlight, his paws stretched out before him, and something in the position—too rigid, unnatural—made me reach for the light-switch. A yellow froth, flecked with blood, had seeped from his mouth and nostrils on to the copy of the air-mail edition of *The Times* I had spread for him to lie on. I touched him, tried to move him. Dead. I cannot myself now believe the extraordinary chill of fear and remorse that came over me. 'You've killed him. You've killed him. You did that. . . .' I took him up in my arms; the coat was as wet as if he had been left out in the rain. . . . Now I've just gone back into the out-house to look at the little corpse. A blue-bottle had somehow got in and began to buzz round me angrily as once again I touched the poor wretch. Stiff. Cold, as anything ever is cold at this season. And again I felt that self-accusation—'Look what you did!' . . . Of course this is irrational. After all, I felt no qualms about throwing the other three puppies into the river. And think of all the Japanese who kill themselves daily in the most uncomfortable or excruciating ways because there are too many of them —just as there are too many puppies. Death by barbiturate—that's the *de luxe* way. The puppy was lucky.

Yes, I know, I know; but the arguments make no difference. This was the puppy I picked out; this was the one which I decided should survive; this was *my* puppy.

The idea of a Chosen People is not really as absurd as I've sometimes thought it.

16

THAT gong! Something ought to be done about it, Welling muttered to himself. There'd be the hell of a fuss if they started to ring their own chapel-bell at four o'clock each morning. His bony feet, protruding out of the end of his bed where the sheets had come untucked, felt unpleasantly cold and stiff; for some time now he had been making ineffectual efforts to get them covered again without having to rouse himself. First he drew his knees up; then he burrowed with the toes of one foot and tried with the toes of the other to drag the top-sheet over. Hell! He said the word aloud; Mary, had she been in the bed beside his own, would at once have reproved him. (God, Hell, Damn: they still shot from him when he was in one of his brief rages, directed as often against himself as against someone else.)

Then all at once it hit him: *he had run away.* In the prison-camp he would often waken like that, drowsily happy and at peace until, seconds or even minutes later, memory would also waken with the realisation: this was not the beach-house at Omi-Maiko; that was not Mary who had just moaned in sleep beside him; and there was no point in deciding (as he had just done) that he would continue to drowse until Sakai-San brought him his cup of tea, for no tea would come. *He had run away.* It was not the first time that he had made that reproach to himself; indeed there were times, as on this early, oyster-grey, oyster-clammy morning when his whole life seemed to him to be an endless, headlong flight away from the things which people (Mary was one of them) never ceased to assure him were 'not as bad as they seemed'. But he was wiser than that. He knew that they were not as bad as they seemed merely because they were worse. . . . And now he was drowning in the whirling horror of blood-spattered water, flailing arms and murderous saw-teeth; yes, lying there, his cheek pressed to the pillows and his pale-blue eyes fixed intently on the carafe on the bedside table, he was gulping down the bitter, flecked waves: salt of the sea, salt of the life-blood of

17

the brother he had deserted, an abject manikin, six-foot-three of youth and muscle reduced to nothing more than headlong footprints in the sand of the illimitable Australian beach and an open mouth howling for the help that he knew was not there. It was Mary, his fifteen-year-old cousin, who had plunged in beside the dying boy-hero of the sports-field (how often had Welling thought that he loved him so dearly that he would give his life for him) and it was she who had somehow, no one knew how, dragged what was left of him (a leg gone, face lacerated beyond recognition) back on to the beach where his life had broken out of him, over her, in a terrible crimson spasm on spasm. She had known then; but she had never said anything, either to Welling who was to become her husband four years later or to anyone else. Often since he had told himself that they (women were often 'they' to him) loved a man for his weakness; and, in her own way, she certainly loved him.

He almost moaned out aloud now as, thick and fast, other recollections thronged to pluck him hither and thither and then fling him, face averted and hands outstretched to shield himself, against those hidden rocks which were always there, blunt as sacrificial-stones or sharp as spears, however much the sea smiled under the perfectly smiling day. The boy-soldier was screaming; Welling could hear him scream (Help me, Help me, Help me, Mike) and, turning, he could see or thought that he could see (one could never be sure what was truth and what imagination) the body jerking like some giant fish in its ever-expanding scarlet net, until some fucking little Nip in a tree (but one called them 'brothers' now) diverted a splutter of machine-gun fire to stop the threshing agony from which he himself had run in ignoble, animal panic. Well, but he was done for, anyone could see that; so it was only commonsense to leave him to get on with his dying, while one got on with things more important. Like saving one's own skin? Again the desire to moan overcame him.

And what sort of opinion would Nott have of him now? (He still thought of him as Nott, not Knox.) He had liked 'Nott' and he knew that at first that liking had been returned. But after he had knocked down a woman, knocked down a woman and made a bolt for it——! Oh, God, God, God! He threw himself about on the bed. Nott would probably say nothing to anyone; like Mary after that—well, no more of that business. He was a decent sort; a real gentleman. (How Knox would have winced at those

18

phrases.) But in his heart of hearts, he must despise him, how he must despise him!

As always after such self-laceration, Welling soon felt an abject sort of contentment: the spiritual counterpart of the physical sensation which had so baffled him after each of the half-dozen occasions when he had been beaten-up in the prison-camp. One seemed to have fallen from a great height; and the two facts that one had fallen and yet survived and that one could fall no farther seemed to produce their own kind of euphoric calm. He shut his eyes again; he almost slept. What did it matter? His upper lip had been split by a shattering blow from the fist of one of his guards; he had run away when a shark was tearing his brother apart. His back smarted from the weals raised on it in ridges; a friend, abandoned, had died kicking convulsively against his own guts. It would be days before he could walk properly on the blistered soles of his feet; he had driven on after almost killing a woman. Each of these events seemed to be at one moment of equal importance and at another moment of no importance at all. To hell with it, to hell with it!

Often these mornings he woke early with the same sensation of discomfort, throbbing and not unpleasant: a reminiscence of early wakenings at the beach-house when, a thirteen-year-old boy, he lay watching Lake Biwa slowly brighten and expand in the first flickering gleam of summer dawns. Odd. Perhaps he needed Mary; but when Mary was there, there was little enough of 'that' (as both of them so often called it—'Oh, not "that" again, dearest', in the first years; and 'All "that's" so unimportant really', in the later). Perhaps, on the other hand, this was one of those physiological changes of which one sometimes read in the newspapers ('Peer accused of indecent assault. Not fully responsible, says Harley Street specialist.'). Welling got out of bed and padded in his slippers to the lavatory. The sensation of gorged congestion having been relieved by the emptying of his bladder, he could drop back into sleep. But only briefly. When he next woke, it was with him again. He turned over on his back and raising his knees so that the sheet made between them a valley, rose-pink in the first flush of the sun, he began dreamily to run his fingers through the reddish hair that sprouted on his chest and extended in a narrowing line down to his navel. In the days when they were children, living either at Kobe or, in the summer, at the beach-house at Omi-Maiko, it was not unusual for older

Japanese women of the working-classes to leave their breasts bare. He remembered now someone of whom he had not thought for God knows how many years: the nurse from whom he had learned his first words of Japanese. Other images were carried back on this same tide of memory (his right hand still dreamily moving in a rhythm through the thickly-matted red hair on the lean yet muscular chest): she was stooping above him—what was her name? He would remember it in a moment—and he, a child of seven or eight, was putting out a hand. She laughed, displaying her broken, discoloured teeth, and then groped beneath the bed-clothes to pinch his thigh. Laughed again. Laughed . . . Welling shifted his position; patted the pillow back into shape; and then drew from under it a handkerchief. There was a girl who used to come to the Bible Class (God, he had the Bible Class this morning; he had only now remembered it). She had come three—no, four—times and then she had disappeared. It was when she got engaged, someone had told him, that she had given up the Class. Why? But that was the kind of question to which one could rarely be sure of getting the true answer in Japan. She always wore Western-style clothes; he remembered one day of intense, clammy heat when she had on a white silk shirt which the sweat made cling to her softly-rounded shoulders and the exquisite channel of her back-bone. The sun was shining through a skylight onto the place where she sat and when she got up to draw the blind, struggling with the knotted cord (of course, none of the male Japanese students offered to help her), he could see, as her raised arm drew the shirt tight across her right breast, the dark aureole of her nipple. Eventually he himself had come striding across the room to help her; and as he took the cord from her, he realised all at once, in horror and shame, that he had begun to betray the physical excitement which her nearness induced in him. Could she have seen—or guessed? For it was after that that she had vanished.

The men of old Japan found the most titillating part of a woman's body to be the back of the neck. That was why in a geisha every part of the body was curved inwards, he supposed: the knees, the feet, the shoulders, the elbows. Odd. In the West everything was thrown open. Open. Ah, that girl, with the faint shadow-halo under the damp silk, and the clammy compression of his own garments. . . . The sun had now wholly risen and a ray through the slit between the two paper-screens fell across his freckled forehead on which small globules of sweat were glistening. Beneath, in shadows, his pale-blue eyes, staring at the light-bulb suspended from a hank of frayed flex, had turned a dark-violet. The slit-mouth which Knox had so much disliked was parted, as though in a rixus of agony, to reveal large, white, perfectly-shaped teeth. His chest, the nipples standing out pink against the tousled hair, heaved convulsively.

Soon after, he sprang out of bed and knelt down, burying his face in a corner of the sheet. But he could not 'connect'—the word he often used to himself; what he tried to say was meaningless and, worse, no one was listening to it. Instead he could only think of an incident from his adolescence in Sydney: one which he did not wish to remember, least of all when on his knees in prayer. As a boy of twelve or thirteen, his mother already dead, he had somehow (he had never discovered exactly in what fashion) betrayed to the aunt who now had care of the children that he was indulging in what she described to his father as 'disgusting habits'. His father, a business-man who had probably had more true vocation for a religious life than his elder son, was less vehement in his condemnation. He spoke kindly to the boy, explaining that what he was doing was both unhealthy and, far worse, a sin. 'Now, Mike, when you are next in bed and feel the temptation come upon you, I want you to put on your dressing-gown and slippers and come down to me in my study. Together we shall then pray to God to help you to put such thoughts from you.' For a while Welling did as his father said; they would kneel down together, on either side of the table at which his father often worked late on the ever-growing ramifications of his business, and his father would say a prayer: 'Dear God, inasmuch as this child of thine, Michael, is troubled by thoughts of the flesh, we beg thee in thy mercy . . .' and Welling would murmur 'Amen'. Sometimes the prayer was effective; sometimes it was not. Then the winter came and a night so icy that when the dreaded temptation assailed the boy, it seemed preferable to accept it rather than to have to leave the warmth of his bed. A few days later, the same experience was repeated: the bed was so cosy, the air outside so cold . . . And so the weeks passed. Until one evening, his father came into his bedroom, sat down on the end of the bed, and said: 'Well, Mike, it's a long time since you had to come down to the study, isn't it?'

'Yes, Daddy.' It was, in fact, exactly two months; the boy

21

knew the period, adding day to day in the way that only prisoners and children accumulate them. Having said that, he waited in dread. ('It's no use lying to me, Mike. I always know'—his father had so often said that, that the boy had come to believe it.)

'In fact, it's exactly two months—to the day. I've kept a note of it.' One of the large hands closed on his ankle through the bed-clothes. 'Now, get out of bed, there's a good boy. Here, put on your dressing-gown.'

(A thrashing hurt so much more through one's pyjamas; but afterwards it was easier to go straight back to bed than to have to get through a whole interminable day.)

'Come along, hurry up. Come!'

The boy clambered down from his bed; his teeth were already beginning to chatter from mingled cold and fear.

'That's right. Now kneel down beside me.' Uncomprehending still, the boy knelt. 'Dearly beloved father,' intoned his father in his special 'prayer' voice: deeper, softer, less crude than that which he used for everyday, with 'God' pronounced, inexplicably, 'Gud'. 'We thank thee for thy goodness in as far as thou hast put away from thy son, Michael, those temptations which once would assail him . . .'

Welling leapt to his feet in even more acute shame and self-loathing. He had never learned the truth that most people's secret actions are often worse than their open ones and that their thoughts are sometimes worse than either. He imagined, on the contrary, that he was an exception, a monster of vice and hypocrisy, from whom his fellows would turn away in horror if they but knew the whole truth about him. Perhaps they would, indeed, do so; but in the case of how many people would a knowledge of the whole truth not evoke the same response? He dashed into the shower—if the spout from which lukewarm water dribbled down on to his head could be given that name—and began to soap himself all over, in such a frenzy to be clean that he even managed to rub the suds into an eye. But he welcomed the smart as though it were some cauterisation. Energetically he then dashed a tooth-brush first across, and then up and down, his teeth; the peppermint-flavoured lather cleansing his mouth of its sour taste and, like the shower, taking on the significance of some kind of liturgical purification. Lastly he shaved with an electric razor, before he dressed.

Each night he would empty all his pockets and set out the things they contained: coins in little piles, according to their denominations; black-ink pen, red-ink pen and two propelling pencils set out horizontally, the one below the other, with the largest at the top and the smallest at the bottom; two bunches of keys; wallet; diary, address-book and pocket account-book; letters. Each object had an appointed place on the scratched plastic top of the table at the foot of his bed; although Mary was not there, he did not use her dressing-table. She would laugh at this obsessive tidiness because secretly it disturbed her. 'I believe if you were going to be executed the next morning, you would still go through the same ritual!' she had chaffed him more than once; and 'Yes, I'm sure I should', came his unsmiling reply. When he had dressed, the 'ritual' was repeated in reverse; in this case each object being picked up and stowed away on his person in an immutable order of precedence. His wallet, loose coins and pocket account-book were always left to the last. He would seat himself before them at the table and first count his money and then set the figure calculated against the figure in the account-book. He was 'close' and knew it and knew that people said it about him. But, like many people who are close, he preferred to think of himself as careful. ('Well, yes, I don't like to *waste* money. I hate any kind of waste; and I haven't enough of it to waste anyway.') What was unusual was that his money-meanness was offset by an extreme emotional generosity. He would scruple to make an expenditure of sixpence on a friend; but he would expend himself without stint even on someone he disliked.

The servant, an old, limping, bilious-skinned woman in Western clothes, brought him a cup of tea and, to his horror, stopped to pick up the soiled handkerchief which he had inadvertently left lying on the floor by his bed, having dropped it there in disgust. She was both deaf and half-blind (though some of the mission-staff had reason to suspect that she exaggerated both of these defects) and there had been repeated discussion of pensioning her off. Clutching the handkerchief in one arthritic hand, she muttered and wheezed as, with the other, she gathered up the shoes he had been wearing the previous night. She was a Christian and had, indeed, been one of the first converts of the mission in Japan (taking the name Sarah); but no one could decide how 'good' a Christian she was. One of the Japanese teaching-staff declared that, at the time of the Bon Festival of the previous year, he had seen her set off for the cemetery with a basket in which she had concealed the traditional offerings for the dead; and when her eldest son was dying of tuberculosis there had been gossip that, though he was a patient at the mission-hospital, she herself was paying visits on his behalf to a 'witch' in a village somewhere on the further slopes of Mount Hiei. As Welling gulped his tea, she glanced at him briefly from under drooping lids which seemed to be exactly duplicated by the brown purses of flesh under each of her eyes. Pressing the back of the hand which clutched the handkerchief into her side (she had some indeterminate pain there, presumably nothing serious since it had been with her for years), she then spoke. Japanese is an ambiguous language, and with an intentional or unintentional ambiguity, she phrased her sentence so that it could mean either 'You slept badly last night' or 'I slept badly last night.'

Welling suspected that she intended the former meaning, but he preferred to choose the latter. 'Oh, I'm sorry to hear that.' Some of his colleagues were less gentle and considerate than he with the servants: either because they were unaccustomed to dealing with servants at all; or because they were following the example of their Japanese friends; or (most usual) because the exasperation which the country induced in them could be worked off on such victims more unobtrusively than on each other or their congregations. 'Why don't you ask them to give you something at the hospital?'

She muttered something about sleep being the gift of the Good God and that man must wait for it as the earth waits for the rain: one of Sarah's 'utterances' as they called them at the mission.

He cut short the conversation to hurry to the Bible Class since it was two minutes to half-past seven and he was as obsessive in his punctuality as in his tidiness. This class met three times each week and was composed, not of students of the school, but of anyone who wished to come. The hour had been chosen to conflict neither with office-hours nor with classes at the University. Mary and he had divided between them a duty which was generally unpopular, since it meant getting up early and putting in an hour of work before breakfast with people who were usually themselves also sleepy and hungry. It was impossible not to admire the power of the Japanese will. Regularly they came—with coughs in winter, with fevers in summer, grey with fatigue, blue with

24

cold, red with prickly-heat. They lost their parents or their jobs, had to walk the distance because they could not afford to travel by bus or tram, rumbled with hunger or a gaseous diet of beans and rice. But still they came. 'Well, one must hand it to them,' many of the missionaries said; and 'it' meant not love nor even liking or sympathy, but a grudging admiration. First Welling said a prayer with them. The floor of the class-room was dusty and it was therefore recognised that they should not kneel, but remain seated in their places. One woman, however—middle-aged, tiny, grubby—would invariably take to her knees and, screwing her eyes tight shut like a child who has been told not to look in a game of hide-and-seek, would sometimes even join her voice to Welling's in the prayers. (The others confined themselves to a muttered 'Amen'.) When she rose, she would make a token gesture of dusting-off the hem of her skirt: always the same skirt, a mottled blue, which seemed each time to become further saturated with the detritus of the class-room.

Usually Welling did not look at the faces before him during the prayer, even on those occasions when his repetition of it was accompanied by as little concentration as required by a yawn or a scratching of one's ear; but he knew that it was customary for each pupil to stare down at the top of his or her desk with head bowed forward and hands clasped together. Some pupils even covered their faces with one or both hands. This morning, however, he was aware that someone at the back was staring fixedly at him; though, his own eyes lowered, he could not be sure who it was, or even guess at the sex or age. '. . . Forgive us our . . . For thine is . . . power and the . . .' He wished that *that* woman (as he always thought of her) would be silent; though, as he hurriedly reminded himself, she had as much right to repeat the Lord's Prayer aloud as he had. But 'harrowed be thy name', 'dairy blead'—and in that loud, over-assertive voice, issuing from the paradoxically small, pinched mouth in the small, pinched body . . . Well, he had to look up: a glance so swift that he was sure that no one, except of course the person at whom it was directed, could possibly notice it.

It was a youth whose attendance at the class had been erratic; indeed Welling doubted whether in the course of the four months since he had first joined he had put in more than five or six appearances. He had an air of fatigue and ill-health (but then so many of them had) combined with what had struck both Welling and his wife as a quiet, unshakeable arrogance. Often they had thought that he was not attending as he fiddled with a pencil, excavated with a finger-nail the splintered surface of the wooden desk before him or merely gazed out of the windows at the tennis-court where, at that hour, no one was playing; but if they put a question to him, he invariably knew the answer. In the winter he had suffered from chilblains; now, in the early summer, his high, bony forehead had broken out in a rash of small, yellow pustules. Probably the Japanese would have said that he was good-looking since he had both the long nose and the 'Caucasian' eyelids which they admire. Even in the sultriest weather as today, he always wore the same shabby dark-blue linen suit and a black tie, the knot of which was small, hard and frayed. Welling now resolved to find out his profession from the records the moment the class was over.

To hear most of them read was agonising even to someone of Welling's limited sensibilities and it was a relief, therefore, to come to the boy. His voice was devoid of all expression; but he pronounced each word approximately as it ought to be pro-nounced and gave the impression of understanding, even if not greatly caring about, what issued so monotonously from between his chapped lips. But paradoxically Welling found after a time that it had exasperated him less to hear what was, after all, one of the most beautiful texts in the whole Bible garbled and gobbled into nonsense by the other students rather than to have it thus presented, as flat, terse and tedious as a weather-forecast on the wireless. The boy was reading the Sermon on the Mount.

'. . . Ye have heard that it has been said, Thou shalt love thy neighbour and hate thine enemy:

'But I say unto you, Love your enemies, bless them that curse you. Be good to them that hate you, and pray for them which despitefully use you and persecute you . . .'

Welling, who had been watching with a mounting annoyance, noticed that at this point the boy paused in his reading and drew down the corners of his mouth in what could only be distaste. Then he sniffed and resumed: 'That ye may be the children of your Father which is in heaven. . . .' But at that Welling inter-rupted him. 'What do those last verses mean to you?' He knew, as soon as he said this, that he had made an error. Long ago he had learned the folly of asking his students questions: for to extract an answer was, as Mary had once put it, as difficult as pulling teeth. According to the Japanese academic tradition the *sensei* or teacher must be assumed to be infallible and it is the duty of his disciples to support the fiction of this infallibility in silent respect. Often, of course, being human, the *sensei* makes a mistake; but no one points it out, even if everyone is aware of it. 'Well? Well?' He looked round the class-room, challenging them to voice some view, however absurd. 'Then let's read those two verses again. Verses forty-three and forty-four please. Listen, please, as I read them to you.' It was a long time since he had allowed this deadness of response to rile him; after all, it was something to which every teacher eventually had to inure himself in Japan. He read the two verses and then the verse that followed, his voice betraying an odd tremor as he came to the last words '. . . and sendeth rain on the just and the unjust . . .' Suddenly the full beauty of the words had once again been revealed to him : an intermittent occurrence which he could never predict or analyse. 'Well? What does that say to you? Put it into your own words. What was Christ telling us to do? Well?'

Silence. Their heads lowered in embarrassment as much for him as themselves, they stared down at their Bibles. 'That woman' was nibbling at her lower lip and at the same time scratching her shin as though it had just been stung by a nettle : the only overt sign of the tension which each of them was feeling. 'Well, look at it, look at it!' (But that was exactly what each of them was doing.) Putting on that falsely jolly voice of schoolmasters and clergymen (after all he was both) who are near to a loss of patience, he now cried out: 'Come, come; it's not as hard as all that. Goodness me! What's the matter with you all? This chapter contains all that is most important in the teaching of Christ. The Sermon on the Mount. You know that, don't you?'

The boy at the back had suddenly looked up; and though this was at last the response which Welling had been trying to provoke, it brought him, not relief, but a constricting sensation of dread. 'Yes?'

'The verses seem to me nonsense.' Having delivered this verdict, the boy once again stared down at his desk and resumed his picking at its surface with the nail of his little finger.

Welling could feel the suspense tightening and tightening about him; though no one else had moved or even glanced up. The unprecedented had occurred; the *sensei* had been contradicted, and in a sentence as brief and brutal as a blow to his face. Well,

27

this was what he wanted, Welling told himself. He had asked for it, hadn't he? Complained, hadn't he, to his colleagues that he never got it? But if it had only come from someone else—from 'that woman' for example! He did not care for this opponent; he feared already that he was hopelessly outclassed.

'Nonsense?' He forced himself to smile and the result was oddly like that rixus of seeming agony which had appeared on his face earlier that morning. 'Do you mean that you can't understand what those verses mean?'

'Oh, I understand O.K.' (Not looking at him; the nail still excavating.)

'Then . . . ? . . . But how can you call nonsense one of the most sublime statements ever made on this earth? How can you——?'

'I don't get it,' the boy cut in: in the same flat, terse voice with which he had read the passage. ('O.K.'; 'I don't get it'—the slang seemed to make his opposition even more graceless.) 'Sorry,' he added, as casually as if he had bumped into someone by mistake.

'Well, we all have a right to our opinions. This is interesting. What don't you—don't you *get*? Tell us.' (Again that rixus of seeming agony.)

'This business of loving your enemy and saying thank you very much to those who starve you or kick you in the stomach.' The accent was more transatlantic now than when he had been reading from the Bible; 'G.I. English' the missionaries, both British and American, called it. 'That's no good. That's what made things as they are. That's for slaves, not men.' His long face was slowly growing crimson. He seemed to be in a fury; but really it was nervousness.

'But that's the whole basis of Christ's teaching.'

'Yes.' A splinter from the desk suddenly broke off under his nail. As he tried to pick it out, holding his hand up to the light from the window and peering at it, head on one side, he went on: 'Though Christians only want it put into practice when it suits them.'

'I don't understand you.'

'Well, when there's a war, nobody thinks about that sort of thing, do they? So you drop bombs. So you drop an atom-bomb. But when the atom-bomb has fallen, then the people it hits must say "Thanks for the present"—those that are still alive to say

28

it—and "We love you, even if you are our enemies and do these things to us—for our own good, of course" . . .'

'Let's leave the bomb out of this.' (Soon they'd be arguing about the treatment of prisoners-of-war, Welling thought.)

'O.K. But I guess you know what I mean. Anyway, it's not just the *bomb*: that's an example. That's all.' He had at last managed to jerk out part of the splinter; now he was worrying at the rest. 'We should *hate* those which despitefully use us and'— he glanced down at his open Bible—'persecute us. Fight them. Kill them. Otherwise things will never be any better, here or anywhere else. That's what's wrong with us. Buddhism, Christianity . . . It's the same story.'

'But as a Christian you can't refuse to believe what is something—something basic . . .' Welling was suffering the humiliation of knowing that he could express himself less fluently in his own language than the boy could in a foreign one.

'I'm not Christian, sir.'

'Then why—what on earth are you doing in this class?' No answer. Like any other Japanese faced with a question he prefers not to answer, the boy sat motionless, his head bowed. 'Well?' He would have to repeat the question. 'If you're not a Christian, I can't understand why you——'

'For the same reason that most of them come! To practise English.'

'Oh, so you come here just to practise your English!' The boy nodded.

'But this isn't an English class. It's a Bible Class.'

'English classes cost money.'

'Well, this is interesting, very interesting.' Welling's face was twitching, the skin seemed unnaturally tight; he gave the impression of having laid back his ears, like some animal when it picks up a hostile scent. 'Very interesting. And how many of you come to this class just—just for the English?'

No answer, of course.

Growing paler still, he stepped down from the dais on which his desk stood: 'Well, let's put it another way. How many of you come to this class for the Bible?' He repeated the words as slowly this second time as if he were giving a dictation. No answer.

'Well, does *anyone* come here for the Bible?'

Surely at least 'that woman', so ostentatious in her grovelling

29

on her knees in the dust and her lisping of every prayer, would now speak out. But even she was silent. There had set in that peculiar Japanese paralysis caused not, as in the West, by fear, but by embarrassment. All seemed to imagine that if they sat still enough and silent enough, then the room would absorb their presences, as it absorbed the grubby sticks of furniture, into the anonymity of things.

'Well?' But even Welling now knew that the infinitely delicate machine which regulates all intercourse in Japan had become inextricably jammed. No one except the boy would answer any question he cared to put; and the boy was the one person in the room from whom he did not wish to hear anything further.

He strode on to the dais and faced them (their heads still lowered) to announce in a cold, clear voice: 'Then the lesson is at an end. Thank you.' He felt that he was leaving a room of corpses: no one stirred, no one looked up; each rigidly sustained pose suggesting that death had come to them simultaneously and instantaneously, as with the atom-bomb of which the boy had talked.

Because he had left the class-room early, no one was in the two rooms, lounge and dining-room, between which the sliding-doors were always left open. Some of the members of the mission lived in small houses or apartments in other parts of Kyoto; but the American director and his wife, the Japanese house-surgeon, the English matron, the Deputy Director (Welling) and his wife and three unmarried teachers all had their quarters on the premises. They ate communal meals; but it was significant that they seldom used the communal lounge except for prayers or their weekly staff-meeting. In consequence this room had the disused, derelict air of a waiting-room at a suburban station. The two sofas and the seven chairs, all pushed back against the wall, were made of rattan, with lumpy cushions covered in olive-green rep to serve as upholstery. A harmonium stood in one corner below a picture of the founder of the mission, his handsome, cross-looking New England countenance defaced by a number of wart-like blotches caused by the all-pervading damp.

In the dining-room Sarah and one of the two houseboys were laying the table in silence. They both moved with a grave and unhurried absorption, standing back from time to time to review the alignment of a mustard-pot or a fork and knife, as though this duty were not one which they performed every day. One of the male unmarried teachers was the first to arrive. A pale young American, prematurely balding and with a receding chin and watery eyes, he was the possessor of a surprising physical strength which he developed by playing basketball and baseball with the students and spending hours on what he called 'the bar'. (One elderly Japanese visitor had misunderstood the phrase and spread the word that much of the unfortunate man's time was passed in solitary drinking.) He nodded perfunctorily to Welling and, taking a letter out of his pocket, began to read it by the window, moving his lips with the words. Since it was too early for there to have been any post, it was presumably the same letter he had read before evening prayers. 'Good morning, good morning.' First the young girl and then the middle-aged woman, both American, who taught the kindergarten, clattered down the uncarpeted stairs. The young girl, with her broad hips, capacious bosom and untidy, mouse-coloured hair, was endowed with a natural vitality which her senior gave the impression of trying valiantly but unsuccessfully to emulate. The older woman smoked without ceasing once she had reached the privacy of her room and it was her constant dread, in spite of the use of a holder and a pumice-stone, that her colleagues (who, in fact, knew all about this 'vice' as they knew everything else that was discreditable about each other) should see tell-tale stains. It was she who played the harmonium, though her hands were so small that it seemed impossible that she would ever be able to stretch an octave. Now, as she walked to the window next to that at which the young man was leaning, she began to sing: 'Oh, what a beautiful morning, Oh, what a beautiful day, tra-la-la-la la la la . . .' in a surprisingly deep, vibrant contralto.

'You seem very happy, Miss Rosenthal,' the young man looked up to say.

'Yes, Frank, I am. Aren't you?'

The young man did not answer, but merely folded up his letter and pushed it back into his trouser-pocket.

'A love-letter?' the young woman queried.

'M'm, m'm.' The young man shook his head; then he tittered: 'My, Norah! So inquisitive!'

'Yes, I know. It's my besetting sin.'

'Well, there are worse,' Miss Rosenthal put in. 'Aren't there, Mr. Welling?' she queried archly.

Miss Pinter, the English matron of the hospital, now

31

descended the stairs, making them creak under her heavy, brooding majesty. Her face was large and flat and had a strange, greenish luminosity, with tight reddish curls, like lacquered shavings of wood, on either side of it. She always wore black strap-shoes and each step in them suggested that they hurt her. She was followed first by the English Director, Ambleside, a raw-cheeked, portly, jolly figure who was often to be seen in shorts reaching to knees oddly lean and knobbly for one of such bulk; and then by Watanabe, the Japanese house-surgeon, a young man whose ambition to pursue his medical studies in America had been the secret reason for his joining the mission. Mrs. Ambleside, an American, was always late and they never waited for her.

She arrived, as usual, in the middle of the last prayer: smiling vaguely at the bowed heads around her and fastening a brooch, a cross of seed-pearls, to the white organdie collar of her dark-blue silk dress. Her complexion was yellow and spongy from years spent in climates far worse than that of Japan; so that the white hair piled untidily on top of her head gave an impression of whipped cream surmounting a madeleine far from fresh. Miss Pinter, who had known her many years ago in India, had said that in those days she was 'as pretty as a picture—with all this lovely gold hair and a porcelain complexion'. Now, in her sixties, she was still handsome: stiff and sinewy, with a long, straight nose and splendidly arched, if over-thick, eyebrows. Welling, like many other members of the mission, never felt wholly at his ease with her. She was careless both about time and appearances and about the remarks she let fall: remarks apparently innocent of all malice but wounding none the less. Though she rarely said anything overtly critical of anyone, people seemed to become more wary in her presence, especially if new to the mission. She was the gynaecologist of the hospital.

'I had to take a look at that Caesarean and that's why I'm late. Rendering unto Caesar the things which are Caesar's instead of rendering unto God the things which are . . .' Her voice trailed off as she raised a cup of tea to her lips, cradling it in her large, bony hands. Her witticisms—if they could be called witticisms—invariably involved some play on words and seemed to be as involuntary as the spoonerisms of others. Every morning she made some such excuse for her unpunctuality.

Miss Pinter grimaced as she sipped her own tea. 'This chlorine!'

32

'Oh, it's always like that once the rainy season starts. They have to be careful,' Ambleside said.

They all munched and gulped in silence until the chinless young man, Frank, cleared his throat and announced: 'Yesterday I saw the new movie-equipment which the Viatorians have been sent. They never seem to lack funds.' He sounded aggrieved. 'A mobile theatre. And last year they put up that gymnasium.'

'Well, good luck to them,' said Ambleside reprovingly. It was his policy to banish all uncharitableness and envy not only from his own thoughts but from those of his staff. But none the less he could not help feeling a momentary pang. On his last journey to America he had succeeded in financing only half the projects he had at heart.

They all, with the exception of Welling, now began to discuss the financial position of their rival or—as they would have put it—'brother' missions, unchecked by an occasional reminder from Ambleside that each labourer must till his own part of the field and not concern himself with the labours of his fellows. But they were all careful to accompany any implicit criticism with some words of explicit praise: 'Of course, there's no denying that they're doing a splendid job . . .' 'Her work with that choir is a wonder to me' . . . 'A first-class man, absolutely first-class . . .' '. . . and you could have eaten off the floors of the wards . . .'

'You're very silent, Mike,' Mrs. Ambleside suddenly said to Welling. 'What's the matter with you?'

'Oh, nothing.' But, since Mary was not there, he had to tell someone else, though he had resolved not to do so. 'Just that Bible Class,' he muttered; loud enough, unfortunately, for Frank to hear.

'Oh, that crowd,' the young man took up. 'Yes, I'm not surprised they depress you. When I had them that time you were in Tokyo, I couldn't get a single word out of them.'

'Is that anything unusual?' queried Norah. 'In Japan, I mean.'

'It was more than just *silence* this time,' said Welling.

'Sleep?' suggested Miss Rosenthal, crunching toast between her long butter-coloured teeth.

Welling wished now that he had told Ambleside or Mrs. Ambleside after the meal was over. But once started, he could not now turn back without making each of them suppose that what he checked himself from saying was far worse than the reality. Haltingly he told the story. '. . . Not one spoke up, not a single

33

one! It knocked me sideways, I can tell you. Made me ask myself exactly what, in fact, we achieve here.'

At first they were stunned; then, a moment later, acutely embarrassed; and then, almost as soon, each began to make light of the incident. No one cares to think that his life has been a failure; and even if he thinks it, he prefers not to hear that it has been a failure from others. To each of them, even to Miss Pinter whose monumental self-satisfaction might on occasions be chipped but could never be wholly shattered, there had come hours when, inexplicably, the wells of life had seemed choked-up and out of their brackish waters a voice had boomed, muffled and remote, to ask: 'What's it all about? What are you up to? Is it worth-while?' One heard the voice in solitude; and, as about so much else that happened to one in solitude, one said nothing about it.

'Oh, but that means nothing!'

'A typical Japanese reaction . . .'

'Probably the boy himself was only showing off . . .'

'You can't expect them to behave in such circumstances as we ourselves might . . .'

'Nothing to worry about at all!'

'. . . A consciousness of self far more acute than we Westerners experience . . .'

'Oh, put it right out of your mind, right out of your mind!'

And they all at once proceeded to put it out of their minds, except for the Amblesides. Mrs. Ambleside, as soon as they had all started to discuss some other topic, turned back to Welling: 'But who was this youth? Who was he?'

'I haven't a clue. I must look up the register.'

'What's he look like?' Welling tried to describe him. 'Oh, that one!' she then exclaimed. 'Arai or Asai or some such name.' She had an astonishing, if erratic, memory for names and faces. 'His mother is one of those Out-Patients who become almost In-Patients, one sees them so often. A Bad Lot, I'm afraid. And the daughter seems to be becoming a Bad Little.' Welling, like the rest of them, never knew what to make of these verbal twitches. Was one expected to laugh? Usually he compromised with a vague smile (for the possible joke) and a turning away of the head (for the seeming affliction). 'Yes, that must be the family. Poor woman, one must not be hard on her. Husband killed in the war, I believe; or missing for years, was it, and then turning up

34

and dying almost at once on her? I really can't remember. Yes, she's got pluck—of a sort. One can't judge her for taking to a life of that kind. Given the circumstances, it might have gone as hard with us too, don't you think? ' She was a genuinely kind woman, spilling over with the desire to commiserate, forgive and shoulder the burdens of others. But if there was nothing to forgive and no one with whom to commiserate, and the burdens were as light as her own? Or her 'lame dogs' (as she called them) denied that they were lame and tried to bite her hand as she hoisted them, willy-nilly, over stiles they had in any case no wish to cross? What then? This was her problem; and it often caused her to sigh and say that one must do a good action for its own sake and not expect any gratitude. For it was not always that people felt gratitude for the efforts, kindly intended and efficiently executed, which she made on their behalf.

Miss Rosenthal had been discussing an American journalist who, having abandoned his wife, was living with a Korean girl in conditions of squalid seclusion. 'And she was such a lovely person, I just can't understand him putting her aside like that. And now he looks so *awful*. Well, I could tell at once he was drunk, and it was barely eleven o'clock in the morning and there he was outside the Kyoto Hotel, clutching on to a tree, can you imagine, a tree in the parking-lot, and I guess that he was just about to throw up . . .' At this Mrs. Ambleside turned hurriedly from Welling.

'Now, Ruth dear, he may very well have just been taken with a bad turn. I heard that he was suffering from an ulcer—gastric or duodenal, was it? Of course, one shudders to think what kind of food she gives him. . . . Yes, I agree with you, it's tragic that a mind like that should go to *waste* in that way. He was such a brilliant man when Harry and I met him just after the war—though even then one sensed some kind of *instability*. I really must call round to see him. Mrs. Crawley told me that he was almost rude to her but, as I told her, I'm sure that's just a defence-mechanism. He's got to be coaxed out of his shell like a *child*—or like my poor pussum who won't leave the linen-cupboard when the dogs have been teasing him. I do feel that we oughtn't to abandon him now; after all he is one of *us*, isn't he? And I dare say that girl is quite a good sort. One knows, of course, what people say about the Koreans but, according to her own lights, she has stuck by him and for that I take off my hat to her . . .'

Ambleside watched his wife with a faintly sardonic weariness. It would be wrong to say that they were a couple who always saw through each other; for that would suggest a far greater degree of hypocrisy and a far lesser degree of love than, in fact, existed between them. It would be truer to say that they always saw into each other. He, himself, was one of those men so oddly made up of altruism and ambition, otherworldliness and shrewd practical sense, that those with whom they come into contact tend to regard them as either saints or charlatans, when in fact they are at once neither and both. Welling idolised Ambleside; but others, like Miss Rosenthal or Watanabe, took a maliciously disingenuous pleasure in showing up each of his small impostures.

When they had all risen from breakfast, Ambleside came over to Welling and placed a hand on his shoulder. Like many people whom an unsuspected shyness inhibits, Ambleside was given to establishing physical contacts in place of emotional ones. He would lead a man away into a corner by a linking of arms; he would pump the hands of even those old-fashioned Japanese who shun the slightest touch of another; he was always patting knees, squeezing biceps or thumping backs. 'Now you must not go on worrying about that business.' The large hand slid from the shoulder to Welling's elbow. 'That kind of thing is disturbing, I agree. As if all those women my wife treats suddenly told her that not one of them had got any benefit from her. . . . Well, the others are partly right—some of that class *must* be believers. Some. Two, three, four? The one who always insists on kneeling—she's a certainty. Some. Not all, of course not all. They're silly to think that. . . . But let's suppose, Mike, that *none* of them is a Christian. Let's suppose, as that boy suggested, that they *all* come to the class just to improve their English. Well, so what? Is that really so terrible?' His hand moved up again and massaged Welling's shoulder. 'If we can make them do the right thing for the wrong reason, then perhaps in the end they'll come round to doing the right thing for the right reason. That's the point. Do you suppose many of our patients are Christians? And the children who attend the school? Oh, I know that they're *supposed* to be Christian, but how often do the parents send them here merely because they know that English is going to be useful to them in later life? . . . No, don't worry. The grain of mustard-seed, the grain of mustard-seed. That's our work here.'

He wandered off, leaving Welling full of gratitude and admiration. It was an effect he could produce in some. Others said that he was a fraud, and turned away in disgust and even imitated his booming nasal voice in private to those who shared their view of him. Welling also imitated him; but with no intent to mock. Certain phrases; a certain modulation of the voice from a bawl to a sudden, dramatic whisper; certain gestures, like the holding out of the meaty hand, palm upwards, for emphasis or the rubbing with forefinger and middle-finger, of an invisible spot on the chin: to an observant eye all these were discernible, in faint copy, when Welling took the pulpit or made some other public appearance.

Miss Rosenthal and Norah were mounting the stairs ahead, and, still ruminating on Ambleside's words of comfort, Welling caught only snatches of their conversation.

'. . . Waterbrash . . . every single morning . . .'

'. . . My aunt . . . charcoal cookies . . .'

'. . . A tongue like a chow's . . . yoghourt . . .'

'. . . Bishop . . . lives on it, they say . . .'

'. . . Badminton, at *his* age . . .'

They went into the bedroom they shared and closed the door behind them. Welling continued down the passage to the apartment which was his and Mary's: a bedroom, a living-room with an alcove which they had curtained off so that he could use it, unseen but not unheard or unhearing, as a study, and a lavatory and shower (cold). As he entered the bedroom, he remembered that what with his haste to get to the class on time and Sarah's interruption, he had failed that morning to complete his daily check of his money and accounts. He would have to do it now. . . . That was odd. Again he counted; again he totted up the items for the previous day. Ninety yen were missing, there was no doubt about it. He got up, went to the wardrobe, and ransacked the pockets both of the suit he had worn in the morning and of the other suit into which he had changed for the dinner. How stupid of him! All at once it came to him. He had bought two air-letters at forty-five yen apiece, one to send to Mary and the other to the boy. But it was odd of him not to have noted down the purchase; something, or somebody, must have interrupted him. Ah, yes! That post-office clerk who was upset because his daughter had failed her mathematics examination. . . . In his round, immature hand, with the o's and a's never properly

37

closed on top so that they both looked like u's, he now made the entry. It took him some time, for he wrote at the speed of someone who is not used to a pen. Then, having finished, he jumped up and strode over to the window, at the same time stowing away in his pockets fountain-pen and account-book. He had experienced a sudden elation for which he now tried dimly to guess the cause. The discovery of his error? Too trivial. Ambleside's advice to him? More likely. His moods tended to change from one moment to the next, as though some invisible hand were perpetually turning a switch on and off; and the flow of his vitality, irresistible at its flood, seemed to suffer the same inexplicable checks and spurts. He stretched himself out on the window-seat, placing an old copy of the *Church Times* under his shoes, and gazed down into the garden. He had nothing to do for an hour, and, for once, so far from feeling his usual restlessness, he wished to do nothing. The humidity of the last days, a kind of pervasive green catarrh which formed the mould on one's shoes, the slug-trails on the walls, the moss on the doorsteps, the rash of vegetation on the tennis-court and even, it seemed, the gummy, clogged consistency of all one's mental processes, had miraculously dried out. The air, thin and clear, reminded him of the desert of Australia. In the garden below, Frank was busy at his callisthenics. He wore newly-laundered running-pants and vest; even his gym-shoes appeared to be pipe-clayed every morning. Self-absorbed, he was taking a series of leaps in the air, drawing knees up to chin and smacking the soles of his feet with his hands. On and on he went, the chinless face, anonymous in its plainness, set above the body equally anonymous in the perfection of its beauty.

'Hiya, Frank!' Welling shouted in his exuberance, waving a hand.

Frank stopped momentarily and squinted up at the window. 'Hi,' he gasped perfunctorily. Then he was off again in a series of hand-springs around the lawn.

'Silly ass!' thought Welling; but he felt an unbounded benevolence towards him, towards Ambleside, towards 'Nott', towards every member of the mission, yes, and even towards that boy in the class this morning. He breathed deeply, putting a hand inside his shirt and scratching under an armpit. Usually the hills around Kyoto at this season were no more than humped shadows, seen, immensely far, through that catarrh-like haze. But now how near they had come, and how green. Again he stretched and breathed the clear, invigorating air, deep, deep into his lungs.

Everything seemed to smile, perfect under the perfectly smiling day, and he had no thought of the rocks which so often waited for him, treacherously hidden.

THREE

ENDO-SAN had just buried the puppy. In an obvious, super-stitious horror of having to touch it, as though it were death itself, and not disease, that is contagious, he had made up a vast parcel, composed of innumerable layers of newspaper, with the dreaded little kernel at the centre, which he carried by the string into a corner of the garden. With that seeking after per-fection which makes Japanese servants forget time and every other task except the one in hand, he first put down his burden and then surveyed all possible sites for the interment. Under the maple-tree? The roots would interfere. By the wall? The ground was too stony. Behind the outhouse? The septic-tank was some-where there. Finally he chose the farthest end of what I call the lawn: an expanse covered with couch-grass because I am too lazy to cover it with anything else, and too poor to pay a gardener to do so. I always think of Endo-San as an old man, but like many Japanese 'old' people he might be any age from forty-five to seventy-five. His face is unlined, because whatever emotions he may feel are seldom allowed to line it; his hair has the crispness and colour of wire-wool; he is thin to the point of emaciation (in the West, one would assume that he was the victim of some fatal malady) so that the sinews stand out, with a kind of poignant beauty, on the frame of bones and skin. Like many servants in Japan, he is the 'perfect' servant: not because he is ambitious (why should he work for someone as unimportant as myself?) nor because he is laying by money for some little business of his own (I pay him a pittance) nor even because he likes me (I am sure that he regards me with a total indifference) but because of some dedi-cation to the vocation of servant far more intense than mine to the vocation of teacher or, probably, Welling's to that of missionary.

While he dug, I myself was writing in this journal at a table I had set up on the terrace. A day such as this has been, the air as clear as in Athens in April, changes all one's feelings about Japan; changes all my feelings, at any rate. One ceases to feel that some vast, clammy parachute has enveloped these islands, the intricate cobweb of telegraph-wires and telephone-wires and electric-cables over one's head mercifully keeping it from descending altogether to smother the life out of God knows how many ever-breeding millions of people. At last one can smell something other than sodden earth and the sodden ordure spread to fertilise it. At last one can see something other than a sepia haze or rain.

'Isn't it a perfect morning?' Setsuko came into the garden, which we share, to cut some flowers. My little stick-and-paper bungalow (God help me in a typhoon) faces the house in which she lives with her aunt, and they own both it and the two houses on either side. I never discussed directly with her aunt the division of the garden—we have discussed few of the terms of my tenancy directly—but I learned through Endo-San, from whom I usually learn the things that Mrs. Furomoto wishes me to learn, that my share of it runs from here to here, takes a turn here, includes that bush, excludes that pond, then here, then here, etc., etc. There is no visible indication of our boundary, but we never cross it without asking each other's permission. Sometimes I think that my relationship with Setsuko follows the same convention.

'Perfect,' I said, laying down my fountain-pen. Untidily dressed as usual, she wore a blue-and-white check shirt, torn under one arm (torn for as long as I can remember), and a pair of navy-blue slacks and sandals. She is one of the few Japanese women whom slacks do not suit; but then, as I am always reminding her, she is not really Japanese. Her thighs and hips are heavy and have none of that boyish slenderness and fragility common among Japanese girls; she is unusually tall; and her breasts, beautifully uptilted, are large and firm. Sometimes I wonder if I should find her sexually so exciting if I were to meet her in Rome or Paris or London. In the East the sexes seem much closer to each other, the boys looking like girls, the girls looking like boys. So when one meets a woman like Setsuko about whose appearance there is nothing equivocal or androgynous the effect is overwhelming. On me, at any rate.

'Does a day like this make you feel any better disposed to us?'

'To them—yes. As I am always telling you, Setsuko, you are not one of the Japanese.'

'Then what am I?'

'God knows. A Russian mother. School in Shanghai. Two years at Vassar. I've no idea.'

'Nevertheless, I am Japanese.' She speaks a perfect American English; her voice is deep and (again rare among Japanese women) always audible. If she seldom laughs—I suspect that she is lacking in humour—at least she never giggles behind a raised hand, or indeed giggles at all.

She began to walk about the garden, briskly cutting flowers and throwing them into a basket. Sometimes I have watched her aunt, Mrs. Furomoto, engaged on the same task; and what a difference there is! Shoulders hunched and head drawn in, she takes her infinitesimal, tottering steps from rose-bush to rose-bush, selects now this bloom, now that, and then, having severed the stems, stoops to lay the flowers gently on a bed she has made for them of foliage, ferns or moss.

'For your aunt's flower arrangement class?'

'Yes. . . . Tell me, Bill—frankly—do you think there's anything in it?'

'Sometimes I think yes, sometimes no.'

'A rose stuck on a spike, with a lily floating beside it, and a sprig of cow-parsley as a garnishing? It's just hokum: like so many of the things I detest in this country.'

'Such as?' I had got up and was walking about the garden with her.

Her scissors hissed angrily as she ravaged the bushes. 'Oh, Zen. Tea-ceremony, Sand-gardens. All that nonsense. It's not Japan.'

'No, but it's a part of Japan.'

'A small part, such a small part. But these ridiculous tourists imagine that that is Japan, that and nothing else.'

'Only the more ridiculous of the ridiculous tourists.'

She paid no attention. 'One afternoon you must really come and see my aunt's class. Last year, you know, all the foreign cows were crazy about ceramics. They unburdened their misshapen abortions on to each other at Christmas and that put an end to it; they knew that the time had come to call a halt.' I laughed, but she had intended no joke. Savagely she continued: 'Now they all take lessons in flower arrangements. As you know, it's important to belong to the right school. My aunt belongs to one of the most famous and so she's very much in demand—especially as there is the additional advantage that she refuses to be paid.

. . . Well, I think that ought to be enough for them!' She surveyed the flowers in the basket. 'I tell my aunt that she should tell them to bring their own flowers. Why should we strip our garden for them?'

'Where do all these foreign ladies come from? One never seems to meet them in Kyoto.'

'Well, you never meet any foreigners anyway. . . . Oh, the wives of the various consular officials; missionaries, married and unmarried; teachers and the bored wives of teachers. Two of them come from the mission down the road. An English woman, called Pinter, who is always reluctant to take off her shoes—perhaps she's afraid she won't be able to squeeze them on again—and the wife of the director, Mrs. Ambleside. *She's* all right.'

'I met one of them at the dinner for the Archbishop yesterday evening.'

'Really, the things you let yourself in for!'

'He was called Welling.'

'Oh, poor Mr. Welling. I've just been hearing about him and his Bible Class from a young man who was waiting to see my aunt. Have you met Asai-San?'

'Who?'

'The boy who's been teasing Mr. Welling. No? Then come and meet him now.' I followed her up the step of their house: not because I had any wish to meet Asai-San, but because I so rarely receive this kind of invitation and see so little of her. 'He's much more the real Japan than flower arrangements, or sand-gardens or tea-ceremony.'

'And no doubt far less attractive!'

In that I was right. He and Mrs. Furomoto were seated on the *tatami*; and she, with that pretence of deference which she showed to any male, even if as young and unimportant as Mr. Asai—or, indeed, myself—was pouring out some green tea for him at the moment that I entered. Unless young, Japanese are almost always plain, if not ugly; this boy was young, but he had none of the buoyancy or sheen of youth and so he was plain.

When we had been introduced (he got to his feet scowling and gave me a curt, jerky bow), Setsuko remarked: 'I see that my aunt has tied up your finger.' I had already noticed that he had some sticking-plaster around the index-finger of his right hand.

'Yes, I managed to get out the splinter.' Mrs. Furomoto wore

43

Japanese dress, a heavy dark-blue silk with an *obi* (sash) of her own design and weaving, and the white *tabi* or bifurcated socks. She is even smaller than the average Japanese woman of her generation; and it may be this smallness of physique which makes her features, nose, eyes and mouth, and her hands seem so unnaturally large. Her nose is especially impressive as it descends, in a bony, aquiline ridge, from between the black, hooded eyes. The total effect of her face, with its glossy hair parted in the middle and brushed straight to the point where, just above the lobes of the ears, it is cut in a straight line, is one of severe masculinity and strength; but every movement she makes and every phrase she utters suggests some dim-witted, fluttery schoolgirl.

'I have been telling Mr. Knox that you have been baiting the missionaries.'

'Baiting? Please?' She translated into Japanese. With a shocked look (Oh, their literal-mindedness!) he at once protested: 'No, no. That is wrong. I have to speak the truth. He asks me a question and I have to speak the truth. Isn't that right? It was like this, if you listen, please . . .' It seems that many people attend Welling's Bible Class, not to study the Bible, but to learn English; and that Asai exposed this unwelcome truth, to Welling's annoyance and pain. Poor Welling! I have no doubt that Asai's picture of him, flustered, incoherent and at a loss for a retort, is an accurate one; and yet I wish that it were not.

'Oh, these missionaries!' exclaimed Setsuko. 'They really are insufferable.'

'Welling isn't. He's rather likeable, as a matter of fact.'

'But you can't approve of them, surely?'

'Well, that's a difficult question. I don't like organised religion; and I see no reason for them to be here. Japanese hospitals are quite as good as theirs——'

'Better,' put in Setsuko.

'And so are Japanese schools, except for the English teaching. Why should they introduce our Western conception of guilt to people who are mercifully free from it? In the end, it will prove far more destructive than the syphilis or tuberculosis we brought to the South Seas. So to that extent I disapprove of them profoundly.'

'But?'

'But.' I paused. 'Well, I admire people who are single-minded; who endure discomfort—I hate discomfort myself; who sacrifice

44

all worldly ambition; whose ideal it is to make life a little more tolerable for their fellow human-beings . . .'

The boy giggled (that dreadful raising of the hand to the mouth) and Setsuko laughed; Mrs. Furomoto smiled, one beautiful, heavily-ringed hand reflected in the lacquer of the table.

'I must say you have some illusions about the missionaries! They are not half so noble and self-sacrificing as you seem to imagine.'

'Some of them are, I feel sure. Anyway, more noble and more self-sacrificing than I am myself.'

Again the boy tittered. It annoyed me and I continued with greater vehemence: 'I don't like their cause, in short. In fact I don't like any causes. But I admire people who sacrifice everything to a cause. From time to time I even wish I could be like them.'

Suddenly I realised that something in these last words had caught the attention both of the boy and of Setsuko, and had impressed them. They gazed at me in silence, from either side of the table, while Mrs. Furomoto contemplated the reflection of her hand in the table-top. I felt embarrassed as one does when, inadvertently, one sets off an alarm-clock, and I asked myself—as I still ask myself—how I had done it.

After that moment (for it was, in fact, only a moment) when I was aware of creating an effect at once greater than, and different from, the one I had intended, Setsuko changed the subject. 'Asai-San used to be employed in my uncle's factory at Takatsuki.' Mr. Furomoto, from whom Setsuko's aunt separated soon after the end of the war, is one of the great industrialists of Japan and his empire, a cunning federation put together to avoid the anti-cartel laws, is said to be second only to that of Mitsubishi. He owns factories, hotels, cinemas and two newspapers.

Setsuko and Asai began to tell me, antiphonally, how the boy had lost his job. He had worked as an engineer in the Furomoto Factory for transistors and had there set about organising a trade-union: something forbidden by the Furomoto organisation. Eventually he had been approached by the man in charge of his department. His work, he was told, had made the most favourable of impressions, it was obvious that he was eventually destined for a position of authority—for, as he knew, in the Furomoto organisation merit was the only measure of fitness for promotion. The tasks on which he had been engaged so far were simple and

45

tedious and were unlikely greatly to extend his resources of intelligence and skill. It had therefore been decided to offer him a transfer to the office in Tokyo where he could at once use his knowledge of engineering and acquire a familiarity with the workings of the whole Furomoto organisation, essential if (as they hoped) he was eventually to assume an important position. The salary would, of course, be considerably larger than the one he was now receiving. That was the way it was, wasn't it? White-collar workers were always better paid than the men at the bench. Well, he must think about it. No need to hurry a decision. Take a few days.

Asai refused.

Not long after he was summoned to the office of the Personnel Manager, a vast, sleepy-eyed man, apparently a sufferer from alopecia arida, from whose lolling head the hair had fallen out in tufts to leave patches as pink and shiny as the surface of a skinned rabbit (Asai dwelled on this physical detail as though to humiliate, in retrospect, the man who had humiliated him). The Personnel Manager came (unusual in a Japanese) at once to the point. The Furomoto organisation did not tolerate trades-unions since it saw no need for them. Workers of the organisation were cared for as well as any in Japan (this, indeed, was true) . . . Recreation centres; hospitals; old people's homes; sickness benefit; family allowances—the Personnel Manager enumerated all the advantages of working for the organisation in a drowsy, clogged voice. The Japanese tradition in industry was one of benevolent paternalism; and it was one which the organisation intended to maintain, un-contaminated by influences from America.

'America!' Setsuko laughed.

'And then? What did he say then?' I asked.

'Oh, then, he tell me to lay off—to get on with my work and to stop meddle in "politics", as he called them—or else . . .'

'Or else?'

'I am fired.'

'And now they have fired you. But how can they do that? Isn't there such a thing as unlawful dismissal in Japan?'

Asai bared teeth, many of which were capped with silver, in a humourless grin. 'Oh, the organisation can work that O.K.' A few days later some parts which were missing were discovered, wrapped up in a pair of his dungarees, at the back of his locker. Three fellow-workers were brought to confront him and, eyes lowered, mumbled their evidence; one, elderly, with grandchildren of whom he had often spoken to Asai, even declared that the boy had tried to persuade him to join in the theft.

'How I despise them, how I despise them!' Setsuko exclaimed. 'How can things ever be better when people behave like that to their comrades? Didn't they understand that you were trying to help them, help all of them?' I like Setsuko least at such moments when, cheeks aflame and voice strident, she works herself into a state of impassioned rhetoric over some issue like equal pay for women or the revision of the treaty with America. 'Didn't they see what they were doing not only to you, but to themselves —themselves, and their families?'

Mrs. Furomoto poured out some more tea into our three cups, holding the pot high above them so that the liquid hissed and then gurgled as it descended. She had given the impression of listening to no part of this recital; as though it were not for her, a woman, but for men and this man-woman who was her niece.

Asai resumed: 'So I am given the choice. Get out and never come back here and we won't—won't——'

'Prosecute,' Setsuko supplied the word he did not know.

'Persecute? Persecute?'

'Prosecute.'

'Ah, pro-se-cute.'

'Or else, if he made a fuss,' Setsuko completed for him, 'they'd take him to the courts.'

'And is he going to make a fuss?' I asked. 'Has he seen a lawyer? And how strong, in fact, is the evidence against him?'

'Well, that's what—that's why . . .' Suddenly Setsuko broke off; I thought—but could not be sure, cannot even now be sure— at a tiny movement of Mrs. Furomoto's hand on the lacquered table. (The hand had been resting, palm downwards; suddenly she flicked it over on to its side, then, seeing me gaze at it, began gently to massage the heavy gold-and-diamond ring on her wedding-finger with her thumb.) 'Well, I suppose you must think about that—get advice on it—Asai-San?'

The boy nodded; oddly silent after the volubility with which he had just been pouring out his tale.

Mrs. Furomoto rose from the floor and, her knees close together, gave a series of small, abrupt bows to us. 'If you will excuse me, I am doing some wax-dying. It is to be a present for a friend whom Setsuko and I must visit tomorrow. Excuse me. *Arigato gozaimashita . . . gozaimashita . . .'* She repeated to Asai the phrases which even the most perfunctory courtesy demands in Japan and then once more turned to me : 'Thank you, Mr. Knox . . . Thank you for coming . . . Thank you. . . . Goodbye . . . Goodbye . . .' The bows became more and more rapid as, almost imperceptibly, she backed away from the table and eventually disappeared into the next-door room.

Asai at once declared that he must return to his home and, having made obeisances to me almost as elaborate and extended as those of our hostess, went out into the hall, accompanied by Setsuko. For a long time they talked out there, in low voices, in Japanese. Impossible for me to understand even though, inquisitive as I am, I at first shamelessly tried to do so. The room, being in the Japanese style, presented little for me to examine while I waited for Setsuko's return. Upstairs she has a study of her own where, so she has told me, she keeps her books; but I have never been invited into it. I looked first at the *kakemono*, an immensely fat man riding a donkey the size of a large dog through a wintry landscape of bamboos, weighted with snow. I had heard that it was by one of the early Kano painters and was valuable. Next to it was one of Mrs. Furomoto's flower arrangements. I stared for a long time at it. Hokum or not? I could not be sure. On a shelf there were some back-numbers of English and American periodicals : *Encounter, The New Yorker, The Economist, Time* magazine. I picked up the copy of *Encounter* and out of it fell a card to announce an exhibition of painting. Probably I should not have done more than glance at the abstract design in orange, green and black if my eye had not been caught by the name FUROMOTO. (The card was printed in both French and Japanese.) ART INSAISSIBLE, I read; and below, a list of painters, FUROMOTO first in large, orange letters and then, in smaller, black letters, another eleven surnames including one, presumably English or American, COLETHORPE. Without capitals the announcement then concluded : 'nous ne serions que des marteaux ou des drilles, perçant le mur qui empêche l'apparition de l'inconnu. furomoto.'

I had just read this brief declaration of purpose when, the card still in my hand, I turned at Setsuko's return. 'I had no idea that your aunt also painted.'

'Oh, that's not my aunt. That's my uncle.'

'Which uncle is that?'

'*The* uncle. The one we've just been discussing.'

48

'The tycoon?'

She nodded. 'He took up painting when he was locked up for a few months after the war.'

'Good?'

'As good as intelligence, taste and will-power can make an artist. Not good enough. He has his "group", because every considerable artist in Japan has a group and artists here, as you've probably noticed, like to huddle together.'

'Everyone here does.'

'And just as the cameras turned out by his factory are almost as up-to-date and almost as good as the Leicas and Rolleiflexes of which they are imitations, so the works of the Art Insaissible painters are almost as up-to-date and almost as good as the most recent Dubuffets or Capogrossis. Almost but, unfortunately, not quite. . . . Would you like to see the exhibition? You can come to the "vernissage".'

'It might be amusing. And even more than the exhibition, I'd like to see your uncle.'

'Yes, he's worth seeing. He's no imitation. He's entirely himself.'

We agreed to meet the next afternoon. Setsuko accompanied me into the hall, and as I sat on the door-step and put on my shoes, stood beside me, her legs apart and her arms crossed under her breasts. How beautiful are Japanese feet (she was barefooted); no wonder that the Japanese tend to keep their eyes lowered in company. I put out my hand on an impulse and encircled one of her ankles, trying to make this appear a casual movement by saying simultaneously: 'That was an odd boy, wasn't it?'

'Which one?'

'Asai. . . . How did he come to see you? Had you known him before?'

She moved out of my gentle grasp and jumped down into the sunshine of the garden. 'Oh, I think my aunt was the one who got him the job. Although she and my uncle are divorced and never see each other now, they are quite friendly, you know, and he often does little favours for her. Yes, I think that's how it was. His mother came to my aunt and asked her to do something for him. So much in Japan is still arranged like that, influence is still important.' She spoke with an unusual vagueness, at the same time tugging at some weeds that had come up between the jagged fork of a rose-bush.

49

Am I falling in love with her? An oriental skin, with its incomparable smoothness and luminosity, makes any other seem crude. I still seem to feel between my fingers that momentary contact with the flesh of her ankle and now, as I think about it, renew my sensation of a pleasure so abrupt and acute as to be almost a physical malaise.

FOUR

ASAI'S finger was throbbing. Perhaps it was infected? He tore off the sticking-plaster which Mrs. Furomoto had placed on it that morning and, getting up off the floor, examined it under the window. Red, shiny where the splinter had entered under the nail of his right forefinger. He squeezed and squeezed again, exerting all his force, until first a minute yellow bead of pus and then a crimson bead of blood broke through the skin. He picked a grubby handkerchief off the table, wiped away the discharge, and then put his finger to his mouth. Scowling solemnly, like a baby, he sucked and sucked. It would be just his luck if the whole hand got poisoned. . . . Damn that bitch! Looking out from here into the dismal yard, with its three rusty cages of hens, piled one on top of each other, its huge mound of empty cans (the Korean never remembered to come to collect them) and the broken sink which no one wanted enough even to carry away for nothing, he saw that she had gnawed through her rope and was scavenging in the wooden box which served as their dustbin. The same colour as the mud in which she lived out her days, mangy (Asai thought with disgust of the patches of raw skin on the Personnel Manager's head), her dugs swinging loose and shrivelled as she tottered along and her long ears swinging with them, she had been trained to be a good watch-dog by the Japanese methods of starvation and perpetual confinement. The last time she had got free she had taken herself off, in heat, for the best part of the day and had subsequently littered four puppies which Asai had had to carry down to the river in a string-bag only last evening, in order to dispose of them. He had wanted to push their heads under the water in a bucket (far less trouble) but his mother and sister had set up such an outcry at the suggestion that he had eventually fallen in with their wishes. Sentimental fools! And yet hadn't he once wept when, as a child, a cat or dog had overturned the cage in which he housed a pet rat and devoured all but a few blood-stained tatters of fur? His mother and father had laughed at him then; as if the house were not infested with rats enough! . . . He now

51

watched, without pity, as the dog curled its tongue around the jagged edge of an empty tin of corned-beef (when had they eaten that?) and then, having rummaged again, pulled out its head from the box with a fish-tail dangling from between its jaws.

He had read nothing, written nothing, done nothing except go to that Bible Class, for the last four days since the transistor-parts had been ' discovered ' in his locker. Hour by hour he lay stretched out on the floor, nagging or being nagged by his mother and sister, until in exasperation as much at himself as them, he wandered out along the river. At last, goaded by his mother, he had agreed to call on Mrs. Furomoto. ('Oh, those two just play at being on our side! What do they understand? What do they know? They've never wanted for anything. It's a game to them '—all his resentment and envy, directed against these two women who, for a moment, seemed all the more hateful precisely because they had always been good to him.) And what had he got in return? They would discuss his problem with ' friends'; some talk of a lawyer; of course if he needed any immediate help—financial help . . . But he wasn't going to touch their money, oh no! That was making things easy for people of their kind; it helped to soothe their consciences.

The bell which was attached to the front-door tinkled faintly as the wood rattled along its groove. Then a cough. Then his mother's voice, repeating the phrases of greeting as though they were incantations the true meaning of which was unknown to her. *Takahashi!* He could all but hear the obese professor wheezing and grunting as he stooped to remove first his galoshes (oh, no doubt he was wearing galoshes even in this weather) and then his shoes. His mother would now kneel with the slippers and he would thrust his huge feet (the socks soggy) into them as, once again, he coughed with a rattle of catarrh. Four—or was it five?—
—children; three grandchildren: and yet he paid these visits at least once a week. Asai had heard that foreigners thought him ' charming' and ' amusing'; with his quotations from Thackeray and Browning and his stories of the well-known Americans and Englishmen whom he had met during the last half-century. A distinguished scholar : that was how the Furomoto niece had described him. But all his mother's connections were ' distinguished ' !

' Ah, Asai-kun ! I am sorry to hear that you're not well.' Asai had ordered his mother to say nothing to anyone of his dismissal. ' The climate before the rainy season is always treacherous. One must take care. Yesterday evening I took a stroll beside the river and now I'm wheezing and coughing—there, you can hear me ! ' Again the phlegm rattled in his long, sinewy throat, until his face under its untidy bird's nest of greyish-green hair became flushed and damp. 'The mist, the mist,' he got out between barks. 'Gets —into—the lungs ! '

His mother had slid aside the doors which separated the two rooms and was waiting, hands clasped low and head bowed, for the great man to pass in. She looked like a girl of twenty now that, with a coating of liquid white paint, she had filled in the faint wrinkles that had started to crack the glaze of the skin about her eyes. She did not care for these conversations between the professor and her son, dreading that the older man would one day suspect the savage irony behind every phrase that the younger addressed to him. But here she underestimated the professor. He was fully aware of the hostility of the boy and it pleased him to bait him, without appearing to do so.

'And how are you passing your enforced leisure? Have you been writing any more of those charming little poems your mother once showed to me? I am afraid that I am too much of a reactionary fully to appreciate them—I belong to the age of the " haiku " and the " waka "—but I found in them certain—certain flashes of illumination.'

'I am glad to hear that. I was afraid that they might totally fail in their effect. . . . No, I have written no more of the poems which you are kind enough to find " charming ". And you? The long essay—or was it a book?—on " The Yellowplush Papers "? '

'Alas, not even an essay ! Merely a few notes to aid my students.' Bowing, he went through the conventional ceremony of leave-taking before going into the other room; and the young man gave the appearance of executing the same ceremony in the subtlest of parody. The doors rattled and hissed back. But if he wished (did he so wish? He still was not sure) Asai had only to lie down on the *tatami* beside the screens, to hear every sound in the next-door room. The professor had evidently made some joke —one of his elaborate puns, no doubt—and now his mother was squeaking like a bat with feigned amusement while the old boy wheezed, chuckled, wheezed and finally guffawed. Oh, it was too tedious; he had heard the whole performance so often before ! If it was not this professor, it was the other—the one who was a Christian and taught Theology; and if it was neither of the professors, it was the curator of the geological museum or the business-man who imported office equipment or the lawyer. All old, all creaking and catarrhal, all dust-impregnated, jocular, patronising, rich. And all, of course—one must not forget—all, all 'distinguished'! In disgust Asai flung himself down on the floor by the window and, lying on his stomach, his head propped on his elbows, began to drum with his heels on the *tatami*. One, two, three, four . . . One, two, three, four . . . Then after a while, he altered the rhythm: One *two*, three *four*, One, *two*, three *four* . . . His mother sliding back the door, one naked arm still struggling with the sleeve of her kimono while the other arm attempted to hold it over her breasts. 'Now stop that noise at once. At once, do you hear? You're a very naughty little boy to be awake so late. I told you to go to sleep long ago, long ago. That's enough of all that, quite enough!' Then the hateful, drawling voice—ironic, really, that he should himself so often be told that he spoke G.I. English—saying 'Oh, c'mon, Belle, c'mon!' (horrible travesty of his mother's name) and the great, hairy arm at her shoulder. Afterwards the twelve-year-old boy staring up at the ceiling (rats could be heard scratching and thudding behind it and, like an echo of them, came the sounds from the next room) and swallow, swallow, swallow, he forced himself, swallow the tearing sobs, the desire to retch, the disgust, the jealousy, the loathing, swallow . . . Oh, father, father, father! And the eyes tried to blink away simultaneously both tears and the picture of tattered rags mouldering in the jungle about a corpse from which innumerable ants (that was how he always saw it) slowly shredded away the putrescent flesh. . . .

Asai sprang to his feet. Ah, but she disgusted him! He pulled his tie over his head like a noose (he never unknotted it) and then jerked it tight. Once again he could hear that bat-squeaking followed by the ho-ho-ho. His jacket pinched him under his arms—he had had it since adolescence; his finger was again throbbing and now his head had also started to throb. When he went out, he jerked the door back and forth so savagely that the bell on its spring bounced up and down and back and forth with a lunatic jangling. He had no idea where he would go or what he would do.

As he passed the bus-stop, he saw his sister step down off the bus. Her bobbed hair was tinted the colour of a tangerine and she wore a dress which was in fact made of raw silk but looked as if it were made of sacking. Like many young Japanese girls, she resorted to cups of foam-rubber to simulate a Western bosom and was invariably drenched in a perfume of a rank, even nauseating sweetness. Asai pretended not to see her, his head turned as though in examination of a shop-window in which were displayed an astonishing variety of dusty implements of irrigation, bulbs, nozzles and tubes; but she called out to him: 'Oni-chan!'

'Ya.' He stopped in his tracks, but did not cross the road.

'Where are you going? It's almost time for supper.'

'Oh, I don't think supper will be ready yet awhile. Mother has other things to occupy her.' He was kicking with his shoe at a lamp-post, each kick seeming to jar both his inflamed finger and his temples.

His sister laughed, without disapproval. 'I must get to the cinema by seven-thirty,' she announced.

'The German?'

'His name is Max.' She had repeatedly asked him not to refer to him as 'the German'. He was a student of Japanese whom she had met two weeks ago at the German Institute where she worked as a library-clerk and Asai guessed that already she had become his mistress. One always knew—in some peculiar way women always smelled of it; and, besides, she had suddenly lost her natural ill-temper and laziness. 'He wants to meet you,' she said. 'I've told him a lot about you. Often, you know, he asks me questions about Japan and the Japanese and I just can't answer them. Yesterday he got on to Zen'—she giggled behind her tiny, raised hand, from the wrist of which dangled a gold bracelet ponderous with charms—'Can you imagine, asking me! I told him that you were the clever one.'

'Thanks. But I don't want to meet him.'

'Why not?'

Asai shrugged and did not answer. 'I must go,' he said at last.

'When will you be back?'

Again he shrugged. 'Goodbye.' He marched on, his hands deep in his trouser-pockets and his feet kicking out intermittently at stones in his path. Like mother, like daugher, he thought. And where would it get her? She was pretty, but not pretty enough; calculating in the small things, but without the larger shrewdness that would enable her to make a success of such a life. She said that the German had 'masses of money'; and compared with any Japanese student, of course he had. But it was a measure of her essential silliness that because he sometimes took her out to dine in Western restaurants and even, occasionally, to dance in a cabaret, she should imagine that he had a fortune. And anyway, even if he were rich, there was not a chance of his marrying her. Like her mother, waiting week after week for her 'Tex' to be demobilised and send her a summons to Dallas, she was one of nature's dupes. 'What does he say?' he used often to ask his mother when a letter arrived from the American; and she used to frown and fidget with her *obi*: 'Ah, there are all sorts of delays, things always take longer than one expects. Anyway, he's sent us twenty dollars, that was good of him . . .' But the American Express cheques soon came with the same irregularity as the letters. Then there were three or four letters with no cheques at all. Then silence. Eventually when he used to ask her 'What does he say?' she would snap 'Attend to your own business!' Or 'Just let me read in peace without your perpetual questioning.' He knew that it now hurt her to have him probe; and hurt her even more that she should have to admit that her American lover had been only a 'Butterfly'. (The Japanese, by an understandable confusion, call a Pinkerton a 'Butterfly'.) But he had wished to hurt her and always persisted in his questioning. Then, at last the photograph of Tex, lower lip stuck out truculently in his uniform of a military policeman, disappeared from its place in the *tokonoma* and Asai found it in the dustbin, the cheap frame bent and the glass smashed, as though, in the impotence of her rage, she had stamped on it with her *geta*. He extracted the photograph, criss-crossed now with white lines and with an edge torn off at a corner, and locked it away with his most treasured possessions, he could not have said why. He hated the man; but the image of him, lying among sea-shells, used postage-stamps, picture-postcards and pinchbeck souvenirs of holiday-trips with his school, seemed to give the boy a certain power over him, as nail-parings, head clippings or faeces give primitive peoples power over each other. That hairy carcase could now do them no more harm, he told himself.

Asai was passing the coffee-bar, misnamed LE GLAND SALON, where many of the young intellectuals of the University tended to congregate. He felt in his pockets: since he just had the price of a cup of coffee, he might as well go in. Even on a day as sunny as this, the interior, an enormous shiny black tube upholstered in shiny red, gave the impression of a tunnel at the far end of which could be glimpsed a Japanese garden, exquisitely minuscule in perspective. The espresso-machines and emulsifiers for fruit-juice gleamed under flower-like lamps, black or red, the stalks of which could be bent this way or that at will. In another room were the turntables of the hi-fi equipment which now filled the whole vibrating cylinder with the music of Bach's Double Concerto. A girl sat alone, sucking at the straw in her empty glass, with a hand over her eyes: she was sobbing, either at the music or at some private disaster. Two youths were arguing. Fools, thought Asai, as he took a seat behind them. Neither listened to what the other said: Camus, Bertrand Russell, Sartre, Ruskin, Whitehead, Gandhi, Heidegger. . . . The names were spewed out one after the other; but they had no closer connection with thought than a vaccination-mark has with an actual attack of small-pox . . . That was the Japanese, Asai told himself savagely. They did nothing (except grub for a living) and thought little. Just talk, talk, talk: an endless game in which they passed back and forth the same tinny counters which could never be redeemed for real money.

Kanizawa, a friend of his from his days at the University, entered, clattering in *geta*, with a pile of books under one arm and his jacket over the other. He had the face, lined yet wholly innocent, of a new-born baby, with a nose which seemed lacking in cartilage, gums that were almost toothless, and a bulging fore-head. He was said to be an excellent scientist and worked in the same laboratory as the Furomoto niece. He greeted Asai and sat down beside him. Unusual in a Japanese, he always gave out a sourish odour, like a dish-cloth that needs to be boiled, thus creating in others a vague exasperation which his natural kindness and goodness would eventually overcome.

The two friends often sat together without talking and they did so now after the most perfunctory of enquiries as to each other's well-being. Kanizawa read a newspaper; Asai stared moodily at the garden where the last rays of the sun were turning the leaves of a maple-tree from emerald to gold, as though in some sudden, premature autumn.

All at once Kanizawa exclaimed: 'Really this case is extra-ordinary!'

'Which case?'

'This painter who managed to exterminate twenty-two people.'

'I thought he'd been executed.'

'No, he's still appealing against his sentence. It'll go on for another two or three years.'

The case, which they now began to discuss, had created more stir than any other since the war. The murderer was an elderly painter in the Japanese style of flowers, animals and birds, who had passed all his life with his two sisters in a small house in a suburb of Kyoto. He was mild and infinitely courteous, with a narrow, straggly white beard which flowed from his chin on to his chest, a large nose and large, knobbly hands and feet in their *geta*. It was therefore to the astonishment of everyone in court that medical evidence had been called to prove that he had been suffering from syphilis for years, apparently with no effort to be cured. Near his house an office was being constructed, and one morning, at a time when there had been one or two isolated cases of cholera in the town, he had appeared on the site and announced that he was one of the health officers of the municipality. He wished to learn whether any of the workmen had been drinking the water from the well in one corner of the site; being told that many had, he had shaken his venerable old head and muttered: 'That's bad, bad, bad!' A test of the water, he explained, had shown that there was an astonishingly high concentration of cholera bacilli present. (They knew what bacilli were?) The ignorant workmen were terrified and some even broke into noisy lamentation. At once the old man calmed them: there was no cause for alarm, since science, in its wonderful advance during recent years, had discovered a simple prophylaxis. (They knew what prophylaxis was? Well, no matter. Science could save them.) At this he raised the clasp of his Boston bag (his elder sister's, it later transpired) and took out a bottle and a number of paper cups purloined from the railway-station buffet. As though he were host at a party, he handed a cup to each of the workmen and splashed into it two fingers of the fluid. 'Now,' he beamed, 'one swallow and you will all be all right.' The men swallowed; and immediately screamed out, writhed briefly and were dead. The old man had subsequently offered no explanation for this holocaust and none could be extorted from him. The defence, needless to say, had suggested that he had suffered an acute congestion of the brain due to his disease.

Now, as the two friends went over the gruesome details, Asai began first to giggle and then to roar with laughter until Kanizawa and then everyone else in the bar began to stare at him in amazement. At last he somehow managed to control himself: 'I'm sorry,' he gasped. 'But you will agree that, in a way, it's wonderfully funny. Ne?'

'Funny?' The baby looked as if it were about either to puke or to burst into a wail. 'Funny? I think it's absolutely horrifying. Horrifying.'

'Oh, it has that side too. But what a splendid parable of life in Japan—or, indeed, anywhere in the world. Ne? The pseudo-official arrives from this or that government department and no one thinks of questioning his right to tell them what's wrong with them and what they ought to do. " You're doomed! " he tells them; and of course they believe him since, after all, he is the expert and they are not. " Never mind," he then adds. " I can save you." At this they are all delighted and sit up and beg like dogs for his cure. He produces a bottle and they all grin from jowl to jowl, yelp their pleasure and run to slobber over him. He administers the draught; joyfully they gulp it down. And hai! All of them are dead. Well, in a sense, he has done what he promised. Ne? He has solved their problems in the best of possible ways.' Again he was shaken by mirth, rocking back and forth and rubbing at his eyelids while the other gaped at him.

'No, but seriously'—again getting himself under some semblance of control—'I'd love to do something similar. What did he use? Cyanide? A cocktail-party for all the Caucasians! Gentlemen, ladies—a toast! To Queen, Fatherland, Liberty, Equality and President Eisenhower! A sensation!' The baby-face was being pulled this way and that, as though an invisible hand were squeezing a sponge. 'You look alarmed. What's the matter? You're not Caucasian, are you?'

'I don't like that sort of joke.'

'But it's not a joke. I've never been so serious in my life.' Again he tilted his chair backwards and shook with laughter. 'Now you must help me out. I rely on you.'

'Help you out? What do you mean?'

'When I give my little cocktail-party, I shall ask you to provide the most important ingredient.' The baby was looking at him as though it had swallowed a marble: face turning scarlet, Adam's apple bobbing up and down, and eyes rolling convulsively. 'The cyanide, you idiot! From that laboratory of yours. Or can you procure me some cholera bacilli? That might be even better.'

The baby seemed, at that point, to cough up the marble. A gasp

59

followed that threatened to lengthen into a wail: 'But—but why? Why?'

'Why? Do you ask me why? How many people are slithering and crawling over each other on these islands, like maggots on a rotting hunk of meat? Ninety millions, *ne*? No wonder they most of them have too little to eat and either work like termites or have no work at all. Wouldn't half of them be happier dead? And wouldn't it be better for the other half if they *were* dead? . . . No, don't laugh. I'm not joking. Sometimes I think it would have been better if the Americans had dropped, not two atom-bombs, but twenty!' Again he tilted his chair back, revealing his unattractive teeth—discoloured, silver-capped, irregular—in a grin. 'Well, that's reason number one. Reason number two? Well, I like the idea of power—people like us have so little of it. If I had in my pocket a bottle of cyanide—or a bomb—or a revolver, I shouldn't feel so—so shamefully impotent. . . . Eh? Don't you ever feel that, too?' He got up and rummaged in his pockets for the coins—one yen, five yen, ten yen—which he hoped might add up to the price of his cup of coffee. He pushed the pile across to Kanizawa: 'That's all I've got. Make it up for me, like a good friend.'

Kanizawa blinked and again seemed to choke.

'Now don't take me too seriously! I'm only teasing you. Don't you understand? I'm teasing.'

At that the baby gave a gurgle and a croak. 'You idiot! Asai, you idiot! For a moment I thought—I thought you'd gone right out of your mind.'

But had he been only teasing? As he strode down the street, Asai asked himself the question. These fantasies were like his boyhood fantasies of killing Tex; but whereas those had occupied him only on the nights when he had lain awake, hearing his mother and Tex on the other side of the paper sliding-door, these seemed to come to him with greater and greater frequency and vividness, whatever he might be doing and wherever he might be placed. When, for example, that morning he had argued with the missionary and declared that, so far from forgiving those that 'persecute and despitefully use us' we should, on the contrary, fight them and kill them, his mind had at once whirred off down its secret familiar groove, until it struck a picture: Welling, hands and feet tied with wire, screaming under a lash (wire too) which was tearing the flesh off his face in slivers and gobbets. The

60

remembrance now nauseated Asai; he had been nauseated almost as soon as mind and picture had met in lurching impact. But he knew that some time, perhaps even today, he would view that scene again, not in horror, but with an Olympian indifference: a God whose scheme it was that men should suffer in the vain belief that their suffering made them dearer to Him.

He turned down a pathway which led to the river, grimacing fastidiously at the stench and squalor all about him. Such were the lives of these people (in his mind he was not one of them), tipping their garbage out pell-mell to breed flies which in turn would breed the disorders which sapped their energies and wills. If they made this hideous waste of what should have been a retreat for them of coolness and greenness, why be surprised at the mess they made of existences whose potentialities were so much smaller? How he hated them! Maybe Kanizawa had been right when he had told him that it was not love of the people, but hate of them, that drove him to try to improve their lot. Perhaps if their lot was improved, then they, too, would improve—that was his faith! But would they? Probably the only real solution was a fresh start: the twenty atomic-bombs which the Americans had failed to drop. Bang! Flash! Twenty bangs, twenty flashes. And then something good might crawl on its hands and knees out of the rubble . . .

This, he suddenly realised, must be the place where he had left the puppies, neatly tied up in a parcel, to take their chance of death or life. Yes, he remembered that vast pile of rotting rags; the bush from which other rags fluttered like the prayers scribbled on paper and tied to trees near Shinto shrines; and that one shoe, yes, he remembered that, because he had wondered how people managed when they abandoned just one shoe. . . . But there was no sign of the puppies, huddled together in a fly-blown heap, as he had expected to find them. So someone had taken pity on them! So even in this world, cracking at the joins like an ancient nightsoil bucket piled too high with excrement, someone had found room for them! A miracle! Welling should be told about it.

Then, somewhere in the recesses of his brain, he heard that curious whirr and rattle-rattle-rattle as the small cage shot down its groove. (He was in the cage.) He licked his lips and smiled vaguely at the huge pile of rags. One by one he picked up the puppies (little bastards!) and one by one he held their heads under the water. They gurgled, they kicked convulsively, one even managed to make an audible whimper; but it was quick, easy.

And then, all at once, it was Welling's head that he was pressing down into the bucket, crying: 'Die, *chikusho*, die! Die! Die!' But the arms that flailed out in an impotent effort to shake off the all-conquering assailant were not Welling's, but another's: long, hairy, muscular . . . 'Die, *chikusho*, die!'

An ancient rag-picker, appearing from the other side of the heap, her whole face shrouded as though to conceal a disfiguring leprosy and one hand searching for fleas in the recesses of her bodice, stared at the young man who was muttering to himself, legs apart and head thrown back, with a look of exultation on a face the forehead of which was covered with a rash of yellow pimples.

FIVE

In the taxi on our way down into the town for the exhibition Setsuko seemed deliberately to sprawl out in such a way that our two bodies must touch. Admittedly the taxi was small; but that was because she had insisted that we should take one that started at a tariff of sixty yen, rather than at seventy or even eighty. Setsuko is not usually parsimonious. I could feel her knee against mine and the warmth of her bare arm through the thin sleeve of my summer suit. Was she not conscious of a contact that brought to me that peculiar sensation of weakness—knees and loins aching, heart thumping, body drenched in sweat—which, paradoxically, also accompanies a vomiting attack? Yet the Japanese are said to be even more sensitive than the English to human touch and to shrink from it in disgust; and certainly, on previous occasions, when I have deliberately put an arm through hers or around her shoulder, she has at once found some pretext for moving away from me.

I now tried an experiment which, at the time, seemed to demand as much concentration and daring as edging oneself slowly out over the wafer of ice which covers a lake in winter. I first put my hand, palm downwards, on my knee (disagreeably hot and tacky, I found, even through my trousers); then slowly, I extended the fingers, as though I were suffering cramp, until my little finger made contact with her thigh; finally I allowed the whole hand to slide, like some inanimate mass, over and over and down until not the one finger, but my whole fist was resting on her, my knuckles pressing into her flesh. Astonishing! She made no response, whether of approval or reproof; she did not move away, she did not move nearer. Instead, she merely went on, tranquilly, with what she was saying. Emboldened, I now again turned my hand over, so that not its back but its palm pressed on her thigh. I exerted a tentative pressure (would the ice hold me?); increased it; and then moved the hand gently up and down. '. . . When the Japanese are working in some traditional mode, their taste is always exquisite. But once they stray outside that . . .' Her cold, beautifully-modulated voice ran on, like water under the ice which, I felt sure, would at any moment split open in a grin of ferocious derision.

But already we had arrived.

'I'll do it,' she said, opening her bag.

'Don't be silly.' In my confusion I pulled out handkerchief, keys, letters, and a number of coins which cascaded to the floor of the taxi. Setsuko laughed:

'Much better to have let me pay! Look at the mess you're in.'

Oddly, she did not clamber out of the taxi, but remained seated, so that I had to scrabble about between her legs, with my cheek on more than one occasion brushing against her legs and even her thigh.

'All right?'

'All right.' (Dusting off my suit and attempting to smooth down my hair with my hands.)

'Now you have a smudge on your nose!'

'Hell.'

'A little to the left. . . . Yes, now you've got it.'

The exhibition was on the second floor of the municipal gallery, and as we mounted the stairs, we were halted by two marmosets, dressed in Japanese-style underwear, who were scampering, with thin squeals and sudden grins, around a huge canvas at which, from time to time, they would make a rush to tug briefly and impotently in an effort to extricate one edge of the frame from the banisters. Above a voice was giving directions in Japanese. We waited. Until both marmosets suddenly crawled under the canvas, heaved it up, rocked it from side to side, and then shoved it up, and downwards to crash into the hall below. The marmosets peered after it between the railings, their small faces twitching with fear; while the voice above grew louder and even more staccato as it scolded them for their folly.

'Are we late?'

'Perhaps we've arrived on the wrong day.'

The man who had been shouting from above now came forward to greet us. He was small and thin, in a brown suit the trousers of which were cut unfashionably wide, and black stub-toed shoes. His green woollen tie was hanging loose around his neck and he was making ineffectual efforts to knot it as he approached in a series of small, jerky steps each interspersed with a bow. Setsuko returned his greetings and then, careless as usual about introductions, said my name, but not his. 'Nothing is ready,' he gasped distractedly in English. 'The food and drink have arrived, but they do not know where to place them because Miss Yamaguchi is putting together one of her constructions on the only three tables. She wants to leave the construction there, but it must go on the floor.' He drew a handkerchief out of the pocket of his jacket and crushed it over his face and then the back of his neck, letting out a sigh that was almost a groan. His hand, which seemed unnaturally small even for someone of his stature, had short, thick fingers two of which were orange with nicotine-stains. The eyes, veiled by lids which resembled scales, were as brilliant and dead as fragments of mica. 'Anyway'—he gestured and bowed—'please go in. Things will arrange themselves. Please.'

The first gallery presented a scene of confusion astonishing in a country as orderly as Japan. Trays of food had been set down on the floor among pictures, screws of paper holding picture-hooks or nails, carpentry-tools, tins of paint, a pair of wooden *geta*, a bucket awash with some substance that appeared to be liquid mud, a mop, a broom and a trowel. Waiters in white jackets squatted in corners, puffing at cigarettes or giggling at each other and the disorder around them. At the far end, three long tables had been placed together and a diminutive woman in black toreador pants and a red turtle-neck sweater, her hair closely cropped, was assembling, with the aid of two elderly men and a girl of eleven or twelve, an immense construction of plaster-of-Paris, twisted wire and many-hued electric-light bulbs. Others, men and women, were perched on ladders, hanging pictures, were dragging pictures behind them or were tottering beneath their weight; while a few people, as formally dressed as ourselves, dodged hither and thither with smiles of mingled apology and embarrassment. From the next gallery could be heard the sound of someone whistling 'Roll out the Barrel'. It was towards this jauntily rendered tune that we now picked our way.

A tall, flaxen-haired girl was at work there and it was she who was whistling. COLETHORPE, I decided; the Anglo-Saxon name in black capitals on the card of invitation. Around her were ranged buckets containing liquid mud like that which I had just seen in the main gallery, pebbles of various sizes, sand of various shades, cinders and ash. In a tin kitchen-basin lay an assortment of seashells. She was tipping these ingredients out on to an aluminium sheet and then either scraping them into piles or scattering them broadcast with a rake and a trowel. As she bent over, her vast buttocks, on immensely thin and long legs, stuck up in the air like pumpkins and her pumpkin-breasts hung down, thus establishing between them a perfect equilibrium. A Japanese girl stood and watched her.

'Hell!' Colethorpe grunted. She had handled a bucket too energetically, sending pebbles rattling across the floor to our feet and knocking her aluminium sheet sideways. She tipped her snub-nose up at us through strands of blonde hair and grinned: 'How do you like my Japanese sand-garden? The Director of the Gallery kicked up an awful fuss about it—as though one could make these barracks any more untidy and filthy. It's because of him that I have to use this aluminium sheet. . . . Give me that bucket, Sanae—the cinders.' The Japanese girl relinquished the pose—feet together, hands clasped before her and head on one side—which she was maintaining with such an obvious self-consciousness and made feeble efforts to lift the bucket. Had she wished, I felt certain that she could have tossed it, without ado, on to the aluminium sheet itself; but that, for her, would have been 'unwomanly'. At last, raising it a few inches off the ground, she began to totter across with it; watched by the other woman and by Setsuko with a certain good-natured irony. I hastened to help. 'Thank you' then came out in a feeble little gasp as though it were beyond her overtaxed strength to say it properly. She looked down at her hands in a seeming surprise that they were not lacerated, and then, slipping them into the sleeves of her kimono, assumed a pose as decorative and even more self-conscious than the last. To many men the whole performance, calculated with such a nicety and executed with so much grace, would have been irresistible. But it exasperated me, as it has so often exasperated me in the past. I do not want the fragile, helpless, innocent girl-wife of a Victorian novel, even though every Japanese man and every other American man wants her. But this girl with her pallor, high cheek-bones and immense, liquid eyes was certainly beautiful.

'Thanks.' Colethorpe took the bucket from me. 'I'll be finished in a jiffy. How long is it after the time of opening?'

'About ten minutes,' Setsuko replied.

'Golly! And I've simply got to change before the big wigs start to arrive. I must look a mess.'

66

'Not at all. Though you could do with a wash,' Setsuko added, smiling.

I strolled on into the next gallery and then realised that Setsuko had not followed. She was still talking to Colethorpe and her friend and was even handing Colethorpe the buckets as she needed them. The man who had first greeted us now hurried over to me: 'You must forgive all this—this delay and untidiness. We artists, you know, are always unpunctual. . . . You like that?' His gaze followed mine to one of the pictures.

'H'm. Quite good. Yes.'

'Then you must meet the artist. Fukuda-San is an elementary school teacher whom I discovered last year. I think that he has a very real talent. He has understood the importance of cutting one-self free from this tradition that strangles us in Japan. In Japan everything is tradition. Well, tradition has its place, of course. But we of this group are trying to create an art that has no tradition and therefore has no nation. The beautiful that has been ignored and the—astonishment that one feels when one encounters it—all this made concrete—you understand?—in a—a matrix which is the idea that one carries within one, like an—an egg, when one is born. From concrete existence must spring the idea which will—will incarnate itself in a newer—deeper—different reality . . .' The hand with the nicotine-stained fingers was being wagged, palm open, in an increasingly rapid rhythm as the words, presumably often repeated, clanged on to my head, blow on stupefying blow, and a yellow froth was generated at either corner of his mouth seemingly by the mere friction of the dark lips against the darker teeth. 'Ah, I am afraid in English, it is difficult for me!' He broke off, his hand letting fall the invisible hammer when he saw that he had belaboured me into a state of semi-consciousness. 'You will understand our aims when you have heard Madame Mollet. You speak French?'

I nodded.

'Good, good. So many Americans do not.'

'But I am not American.'

'You are not——? Then you are not Mr. Nixon?'

'No, I'm afraid my name is Knox.'

'Ah.' Suddenly his face assumed the expression of someone who has put a coin in a slot-machine and failed to get anything out of it. I knew that he wanted to shake me in rage and even bang on me with his fist. 'So you are not Mr. Nixon?'

'No.'

'We had a telephone-call from the American Cultural Center that Mr. Nixon wished to visit our exhibition.' (Surely not the Vice-President?) 'We were of course delighted. Madame Mollet has made our works known in Paris and some of my own works and Miss Yamaguchi's have also been shown in Barcelona and Torino. But none of us has ever exhibited in America.' The mica-eyes glittered in a face which now seemed to be carved from yellow sandstone: and suddenly it came to me—Of course? How stupid! This was Furomoto himself. 'Mr. Nixon is very important. Your Herbert Read is more important perhaps. But he is not connected in the same way with a gallery—and such an important gallery . . . Excuse me, please.' Obviously he had no further use for me.

I wandered on; and since the rooms led one into the other to make a quadrilateral, I eventually returned to the food, drinks and the waiters. Miss Yamaguchi's construction was now on the floor but owing to some faulty wiring the bulbs would not light up. First one of her ancient assistants tried and then the other; until, in exasperation, she pushed them both aside and, going down on her haunches, fiddled with the wires and flex herself. As so often in Japan, what had been a confusion that seemed to require at least twelve hours to sort itself out, had vanished in a moment. The pictures were hung; the ladders were being dragged away; and to the three tables, separated now and covered with white cloths, the waiters were already carrying plates of food, glasses and bottles. The guests stood either singly or in groups of three or four, eyeing now the pictures on the walls, now each other and now, with greater pleasure, the refreshments; while a carp-faced photographer wiggled and darted among them, emitting sudden flashes. Only one person had so far had the hardihood to help himself: a vast foreigner, his silver hair cropped close, in a distended, and, no doubt in that weather, suffocating suit of purple tweed. One of his hands, as swollen and purple as the sleeve from which it emerged, was clutching a glass, while the other was spread over the mouth of the bottle he was nursing under his arm as though in fear that the beer remaining in it might either evaporate or froth itself away. 'Help yourself,' he suddenly said to me, motioning towards the table with his glass. To my surprise his accent was not English but American. 'Go on, go ahead.'

68

'Thanks. I'll wait a moment.'

'Hopeless mess,' he went on. 'They ask one here at four-thirty in a heat like this and then it's past five o'clock before one can get a drink in one's hand. A moment ago that goddam picture over there all but crashed on to my head. Broke at least fifty glasses, but what does that matter? I dare say Furomoto manufactures them. . . . What do you think of this junk?'

'I've seen some things I like.'

'I wish I had. And I've got to do a piece on the exhibition. God knows what I'll say.' He belched. 'Pardon me. If there's one thing I like it's sage-and-onion stuffing but it always does this to me. . . . Go on, help yourself, help yourself! No need for party manners here! Go on!' Reluctantly I poured myself out some whisky, intending to wander away from him. But when I turned, I found him at my elbow: 'It's not bad, this Japanese Suntory. Wish I could drink it. But my liver won't stand up to spirits now. They bring me out in blisters—blisters, imagine! Each the size of a silver dollar. . . . Here, I'd better introduce myself. Ed Schneider.' The purple hand was thrust out and simultaneously the bottle tucked into the crook of his arm crashed to the floor, beer frothing out of it. 'Leave it, leave it. Let one of those goddam apes pick it up. Plenty more where that came from. I dare say old Furomoto owns a brewery.'

Ed Schneider? The brilliant American journalist who had 'gone to seed' or 'gone to pieces' or even 'gone to the bad'? I had heard about him. Korean mistress; or was it a wife? An alcoholic. Knew Japanese as well as any foreigner in the country. The phrases of gossip came back to me.

'I'm Bill Knox,' I said.

'Ah yes, I've heard about you. And I bet you've heard about me.' (Let that one go.) 'Well, how are you enjoying things out here?'

'Very much—if you mean things, and not people.'

He brayed with laughter. 'Oh, they're a lovely crowd, a lovely crowd! I was a prisoner of theirs, you know. Civilian prisoner. That means I had it good. But my cell-mate hanged himself while I was asleep one night—funny thing, that—and two of my pals went clean off their heads. Well, that could have happened anywhere, I suppose. Oh, they're a lovely crowd, just lovely.' His speech was beginning to thicken, a film descending over his small,

69

pale blue eyes as he swayed before me. 'But you be careful! Just a friendly warning, but you be careful! When you're up—when you're up there on top—well, then they're fine to you, they love you, see. They'll do anything to help you. Such nice, gentle, good people. Got it? But wait till you're down. Then it's a hearty kick in the teeth—or the crotch, if you're unlucky—and your head is in the gutter. . . . Oh, I know what I'm talking about. I know all about them. One day you'll remember what I've told you.'

Fortunately at this point Furomoto clapped his hands, there were cries on all sides for silence, and I was able to slip backwards and away. Furomoto began to introduce Madame Mollet, a tiny, muscular woman who, in her grey jersey and tight grey skirt, with her grey hair worn short and flat in a fringe, had the appearance of a midget footballer. She kept glancing impatiently at Furomoto as though he were a referee and she were waiting for his whistle to take a penalty-kick and even the fulsome compliments he paid to her—'le rencontre de Madame Mollet avec notre groupe a provoqué une emotion dramatique', 'elle a donné un solide fondement esthétique a l'Art Insaissible', etc., etc.,—elicited from her no more than a tremor of her bullet-head, a twitch of the lips and a sniff.

I had heard of her gallery, because one of my English friends had once exhibited some pictures there; and I even knew of her friendships with Jackson Pollock, Kline and other American painters associated with them. She was said to be an Alexandrian Greek who had married a French 'colon' from Algeria and it was in Levantine French that she now addressed us:

'. . . cette ambiance créatrice irrationelle tout a fait dans la tradition du Ten vécu . . . une qualité innée . . . leur mot de passe est créons l'étrange' . . . Ten . . . l'unité la plus intime de la matière et de leur rhythme de vie . . . Ten . . .'

I blinked; coughed; realised that my calves and the small of my back had started to ache; then noticed that the prongs of her fringe had the bluish, metallic sheen of a fork which has come into contact with egg.

'. . . une groupe d'individus qui s'emparent donc de toutes les techniques et matières possibles . . . un autre monde silencieux et vide, qui se reconnaitra plenitude . . . Ten . . .'

How fortunate that I had given way to the urgings of Schneider and helped myself to a drink! And how equally fortunate that

70

if I took a single step backwards I could lean against the wall!

But the step landed me on to someone's foot: a sandalled foot, a downward glance informed me. 'Oh, I'm most terribly sorry! I'm so sorry!'

'Bitte! Bitte sehr!'

The tall young man with the fair hair flopping on either side of his girlishly pink face managed eventually to transform his grimace of agony into a smile.

'. . . Ces choses insupportables se heurtent contre la matière et se font visibles . . . Avec aussi peu de complexes que n'en avait Picabia . . . Ten . . . mon ami Pollock . . . érudition stérile . . . mon ami Kline . . . Ten . . .'—the ball dribbled down this endless field was at last near the goal, the midget footballer braced herself to shoot, I wanted to cheer—'Klee, Furomoto, ma chère Lee Krasner . . . Furomoto . . . Pollock . . . Furomoto—ART INSAISSIBLE!' Smack! Success! Relief! Everyone at once burst into a clatter of applause.

The man on whose foot I had trodden bent himself double, as though on a hinge, and massaged his bruised toes. Looking up at me, he asked: 'What did you think of that manifest?'

'It's hard enough to say anything that's worth saying about literature, as I well know when I have to prepare a lecture. It's next to impossible to say anything that's worth saying about art.'

'She is wonderful! She made so much clear to me! And her emphasis on the connection with Zen—that for me was especially interesting.'

'I'm afraid that the connection still seems to me obscure.'

'I wish that I had brought my tape-recorder. This was something I wish to hear many times again. Such a manifest cannot be understood immediately.' He belonged, I realised, to that not uncommon group of people who put questions to others merely in order to answer them themselves. He stroked his straggly blond moustache and then cupped his equally straggly beard in his hand as he announced: 'I have very much interest in Zen. I live in a Zen monastery.'

'Ah, then you are Herr Hultberg.'

'You know my name?'

'I've heard about you.'

'How so?' He at once became alarmed, fidgeting and squinting at me with an odd, paranoiacal intensity.

'Doesn't everyone hear about everyone else here?'

'But why should you hear about me? Yes, I am Max Hultberg, but I do not understand. How should you know my name?'

'Someone mentioned it to me. Isn't Professor Makabe a friend of yours?'

'Ah, so, so. Yes, yes.' At once he relaxed. 'Let us eat something. A plate?' I shook my head. Taking one himself, he darted a long, bony arm hither and thither through the people jammed about the table and snatched at sandwiches and canapés with which to pile it high. 'I seem to take too much?' He gnawed at a chicken-leg, holding it in a fist and dragging it across his teeth so that the skin stretched like rubber. 'In our monastery we live off rice. And sometimes ice-cream,' he added.

'Ice-cream?'

'Yes, our abbot likes ice-cream. Sometimes he sends into Kyoto for ice-cream. Naturally our monastery has no refrigerator.' Again the chicken-skin twanged like a catapult beneath the long, rose-tipped nose. 'Now I am worried,' he got out between mouthfuls. 'Every morning for six days my *sensei* puts to me the same question. I get up at four o'clock, I go into him, and he says to me: "Is a dog possessed of Buddha-spirit?" Sometimes I reply this, sometimes I reply that. Then he says gently: "You are wrong, please to leave the room", or he shouts "Idiot, get to hell out of here", and today he raises his stick and hits me on the shoulder. This is a *koan*, you understand? "Is a dog possessed of Buddha-spirit"—this is a *koan*.'

'Yes, I see.'

'Now I think to myself: "Max, how will you answer to-morrow?" I do not know.'

'Perhaps you should say "Bow-wow".'

'Or "Wang-wang", which is Japanese for bow-wow.' Setsuko was behind us.

'You think so?' He eyed us, half-impressed and half-suspicious.

'Worth trying,' said Setsuko. 'You never know in Zen.'

The German surveyed the sandwich he had already half devoured. 'Perhaps you are right,' he said at last. He practised it: 'Bow-wow!' Then, head on one side: 'Wang-wang!'

'Yes, that's right,' Setsuko encouraged him.

'Wang-wang,' he repeated.

Setsuko turned to me: 'Shall we go?' she asked.

'Yes. But first I must see some of your uncle's work.'

'It's over here.' We left the German, still muttering 'Bow-wow' and 'Wang-wang' to himself through a barrier of half-masticated sandwich.

Furomoto's paintings, of which there were six, covered the whole of one wall; and the wall was the best-placed and best-lighted in the gallery. All of them were in black and shades of grey and brown and all employed the same motif, endlessly repeated, now miniscule and now huge, to make up patterns of an extreme ingenuity and sometimes even of power. Setsuko's reference to Capogrossi became immediately intelligible.

'Interesting,' a voice slurred behind us. 'That little character, repeated over and over again, as though it were a nervous *tic*. The mad sometimes paint like that. I know, because I was once with them in a Sanatorium.' It was Ed Schneider. 'You know what the *kanji*—the character—means, don't you?'

I shook my head.

'In Chinese it's "wang"—the character "wang". Means a king. Get it? I wonder if Furomoto chose it consciously or not.'

'Wang-wang again!' Setsuko laughed. 'We can't get away from it.'

The American eyed her through his film of drink. 'No, young lady, you can't get away from it. "God save our glorious Wang" . . . But he doesn't really need God to save him. He's always with us, my dear, always with us—in one form or another.'

Setsuko had begun to move away and I followed her, so that these last words were shouted after us.

'I knew him once,' she said. 'But he doesn't remember me. And I don't want to remind him.'

'When did you know him?'

'Oh, during the occupation. We worked together.'

'What kind of work?' From time to time Setsuko has referred to her work with the Americans, but she has always been reluctant to give me details. Perhaps it was something so menial that she would prefer me not know.

'Oh, office-work.'

'Interesting?'

'Fascinating!' She laughed. 'I'll tell you all about it someday. If I'm not giving away State—or State Department—secrets. . . . He was fun then, you know, even though he'd already started to drink. I liked him. It's a pity he's become so—so disgusting.' She spoke the last sentence with a vehement distaste. Unlike her compatriots in so many other ways, she is also unlike them in her puritanism, acquired, I have always assumed, during her stay in America. 'He's got this Korean girl, you know—quite a beauty. But they say that he's often to be seen lurching around the town with the lowest type of prostitutes. We're too tolerant to people like that. Why don't they take away his residence-permit and send him back to America? A guest should behave himself.'

'But, Setsuko, he is a *paying* guest—which is different, surely? He is not living here free, you know. And when one is in a hotel or a boarding-house, one is not under the same obligations as when one is——'

'Well, but he does live here free—or almost! All sorts of people give him loans—which he never repays—and even presents. My uncle does, for one.'

'And you know that if a Japanese gives a present or a loan, it is usually because he expects something in return.'

'What could my uncle possibly want in return?'

'Schneider is to do an article about the Group for some American magazine. He told me so. It'll probably be a favourable article, don't you think?'

Our argument ended at this juncture, since Colethorpe and her Japanese friend had come in sight, accompanied by Mrs. Ambleside from the mission. Mrs. Ambleside and I are no more than nodding acquaintances; but Setsuko she greeted as an old friend: 'Hello, my dear. I'm late again, I'm afraid. One of my patients—eclampsia—set in quite unexpectedly. A Korean, such a pretty little thing, you really ought to see her.' One large bony hand fiddled with the cross of seed-pearls fastened to the vee of her mauve-silk dress, as her eyes, under the mobile, hairy-caterpillar eyebrows, darted hither and thither. 'She'd attempted an abortion herself—so foolish, when such things can be done for practically nothing in this country—and then decided to go ahead and have the child after all. I know what people say about these Koreans, but I feel so *sorry* for them. They use our little hospital a lot, you know, because they sense that we make no difference between them and the Japanese . . . Well, here I am, running on with my shop, when I really came here to look at all these lovely pictures.' She grasped Colethorpe's arm: 'Now, my dear, show me your

74

work. And please be patient with someone whose tastes have never had a chance to go far beyond Whistler's Mother. I want you to explain to me *exactly* what you had in mind—and what all these other clever people had in mind. Will you do that? ' Colethorpe looked unhappily dubious; suspecting, as I was suspecting, that Mrs. Ambleside was far cleverer than most of the ' clever ' people whose work she had come to see.

'Do tell me'—suddenly the long straight nose was all but inserted into my ear as she whispered—' isn't that man over there Mr. Schneider? ' I nodded. 'Oh, I must go and have a word with him. People are so terribly unkind—and *unjust*—about him, aren't they? If he's taken to drink—and, from all accounts, to even worse—then, as I always say, there must have been a *reason* for him to have to do so. . . . Excuse me, will you? I'll be back in a moment.' She touched Colethorpe's arm. 'Excuse me, dear.'

'He'll make short work of her,' Setsuko said.

'I fancy it'll be the other way round.'

Setsuko turned to the English girl: 'Then it's Friday at half-past two? Are you sure you can find the house? '

'Well, if I can't, Sanae can.'

The Japanese girl lowered her eyelashes to make stiff fringes of shadow on each of her waxen cheek-bones and gave a small bow and an even smaller smile.

'Good.'

As we were saying goodbye, Mrs. Ambleside returned, shaking her long, distinguished head at us as though in kindly reproof: ' Poor man ! He's very far gone today, I'm afraid. I couldn't get a word out of him—or, rather, the words I got out of him were hardly for female ears ! Well——' she sighed, raising a hand to her froth of white hair whipped up on top of her head—' it's all very sad, very sad indeed. . . . Now, my dear, did you make this *interesting* affair, over here? ' She pointed to Colethorpe's 'sand-garden'. ' I'd just love to know what passes through the mind of an artist like yourself when you are *creating*.' (The word brought back to me memories of nursemaids: ' Now what are you creating about, Master Bill? ') ' I feel that you lucky people belong, as it were, to another order of *creation*.' (She stressed the word and followed it with a gay laugh, so presumably the pun had been intentional.) ' Oh, these shells ! Aren't they pretty? ' she exclaimed with the gaze of an enraptured child at the seaside, her large hands clasped together under her long chin. 'Did you find them in Japan? You must tell me where!'

After such an occasion a post-mortem is inevitable.

'Well!' I threw myself, exhausted, into the recesses of the taxi. (Eighty-yen: no chance of the same accidental, unnerving, exhilarating contact of body pressed to body.) 'How on earth does your uncle manage to run his empire when he seems to be totally incapable of running an art-show?'

'Oh, he could run an art-show with a clockwork efficiency if he wished. But he doesn't wish.'

'Doesn't wish?'

'Of course not. My dear Bill, you know as well as I do that the Japanese are the most brilliant imitators the world has ever known. My uncle has become rich and powerful because he has that ability to imitate others to a remarkable degree. His factories produce sewing-machines that are almost Singers, cameras that are almost Leicas, and cars that are almost Austins or Fiats. He himself is almost an American tycoon, and he is as ruthless and capable and daring as the best—or, if you like, the worst—of them. But today it was another drama; and so his act had to be changed. We all know that the great artists are hopeless about practical matters. They paint pictures so huge that they can't get them up the stairs into the gallery where they're supposed to be exhibited. Nothing is ever ready on time. And though they remember to order the food and drink, they forget that some tables will be required on which to place them.'

'So you really think all that confusion had been deliberately planned.'

'Planned, yes, but planned in that twilight between the conscious and the unconscious where so much is planned in Japan. If you challenged him—if you *dared* to challenge him, I wouldn't —he would be sincere in his indignation. Up to a point,' she added.

'He's so unimpressive.'

'Not always.' And I remembered, at that, the eyes glittering like fragments of mica in the sandstone face: of course she was right.

'What did you think of the Colethorpe girl?' I next asked.

'Typical.'

'Typical of what? An artist? or an English woman?'

76

'Well, it's pretty obvious that she must be "one of those".' I did not grasp the colloquialism until she continued: 'Anyway she's found herself a very attractive little piece, don't you think?'

'Do you mean——? Oh no, I'm sure you're wrong.'

'Of course I'm not wrong.'

'But what on earth makes you think that——'

'Oh, women have an instinct about each other. You probably have the same instinct about other men.'

'Yes, but in this case, there's nothing to suggest——'

'There is, if you use your eyes.' She laughed. 'But otherwise she seems to be a nice enough girl, intelligent and not unattractive.'

When we arrived, I offered a cup of tea. Setsuko hesitated: 'Oh, Bill, I've so much to do. I ought never to have taken this afternoon off. We're understaffed in the laboratory and in any case the boy who is my assistant is so slow that he's really no use at all.'

'You always seem to be in a hurry. The only Japanese who is. Come on,' I coaxed.

'Well, for ten minutes. But really for ten minutes.'

Although the house, when I took it, was furnished throughout in the Japanese-style, I myself bought two wicker-chairs, a table, a desk and some bookcases. I now wished that I had a sofa. It would be impossible even to sit on one of the arms of the wicker-chairs without its snapping beneath my weight.

'You make excellent tea,' Setsuko smiled up from the cup from which she had just sipped.

'I'm glad to hear you say so. Most Japanese assume that they are the only people in the world who know how to make tea; just as they assume that they are the only people in the world who know how to lay out a garden.'

'I wish you weren't always so critical about us.'

'Yes, it's a fault, I know. I've become such a cross-patch since I got here. Temperamentally I'm not suited, I suppose. I'm quick, and restless, and blunt, and short-tempered: all things which the average Japanese is not. When I'm angry, I want to show it and then forget all about it. But I can't do that here. If I show my anger, I may forget all about it, but others won't.'

'Oh, I expect they make allowances for you as a foreigner.'

'And therefore as someone inferior?'

77

'Well, as someone different, let us say.'

She cupped her tea in both her strong, capable hands and stared down into it. 'But you're right that there's a great deal that must be changed in Japan. We are clever at changing the names of things so that the things themselves appear to have changed. But they don't change all that easily! The Americans gave us a brand-new constitution, full of beautiful words like peace and equality and freedom. But they are only words; the *things* remain the same. Just as syphilis remains syphilis even though we Japanese call it " the flower-willow sickness ".'

'More tea?'

'I'd love another cup.'

When I returned from the kitchen, I remained standing beside her chair instead of going back to my place opposite to her. 'Tell me, Setsuko, about your work with the Americans. I think you must have had a bad time. You seem to dislike them so. Or did you come to dislike them when you were at Vassar?'

'I don't dislike them,' she retorted sharply. 'It's hard to dislike children. The other day there was a panic in Kyoto because some children of five or six had stolen from a doctor's car a container of radio-active needles. Terribly dangerous, of course, for them and for others. But one couldn't dislike them for it. Could one?'

'I don't agree with that view of the Americans. They are neither so unintelligent nor so innocent. It's the superior person's view, of course—and the view commonly held in Europe. . . . But tell me about your work with them. What did you do?'

She hesitated. 'Well, shall I tell you or shan't I?' She put the cup down on the table, still deliberating.

'Is it something of which you are so ashamed?' I asked, in joke.

Seriously she replied: 'Yes, I am ashamed of it now. And I'd like to forget it. . . . You've heard of the Cannon organization?'

'Oh, one sees mention of it in the Press. I thought that it was probably invented by some Japanese journalist who had seen too many Hitchcock films.'

'No, it existed all right. Probably it still exists, but under another name, and without the same co-operation of the Japanese authorities—the same open co-operation at any rate. Well, I belonged to it.'

'I see. Yes, I can understand that you would be useful to them,

78

with your knowledge of Russian and Chinese. But how did you get in? That's a thing that always interests me—the recruitment for these Intelligence groups.'

'I had an American friend. I thought this—this friend worked at the Embassy. We were—well—very attached to each other. And then, one day, the suggestion came—would I like a job? I had my degree in chemistry already, but the firm for which I was working was paying me practically nothing, and my uncle's property had been confiscated and he himself was in prison. So it seemed a good offer.'

There was an air of long-delayed confession about the manner— tense, eyes averted from me, jerky—in which she brought out all this. Obviously the memory of what seemed to be a job more interesting than some but of no particular consequence filled her with embarrassment and even shame and remorse. Yet years must have passed—seven, eight, nine?—since she had ceased to work for the Americans. And suddenly I thought—perhaps I am the first person she has ever told! In a way it was flattering to believe that; but it was also disconcerting.

'How long were you with them?'

'Two-and-a-half years. Then I was paid off with the scholarship to Vassar. I think that they had begun to realise that my heart was not really in the work.'

'And your colleagues—what were they like?'

'Oh, nice enough, I suppose, when they first went into the game. But that was the trouble—it *was* a game to them. They had to do some pretty low and even vicious things; and to do them and yet not to become corrupted by doing them, they had to believe that what they were doing served some noble purpose. But none of them believed that. The end could never justify the means they used—trickery, treachery and even torture of a subtle kind—because they had absolutely no end in view.' This was not rhetoric now; she was speaking with a sober intensity which I found extraordinarily impressive. 'I'm not saying, you see, that cruelty and even, well, yes, murder may not sometimes be necessary. But if you get a taste for those things for their own sake— then it's terrible. I was often used to interrogate people, as assistant to a man—well, I don't have to tell you his name. He used to rave about these "goddam Commies", but he could never produce any rational reason for having to hate them. He had none. He just had to hate—as—as an animal has to make love when it's on

79

heat. If one tried to ask him what he was offering instead of communism—and it was not easy to ask him a question like that, after all, he was my boss—he'd either say "Oh, hell!" or he'd start on the usual stuff about democracy and the American way of life. Perhaps he believed in hell; but in democracy and the American way of life, no.'

'Yes, I know the type. When I was in Salonica shortly after the war, a dainty little man turned up, a Polish refugee, who wore beautiful hand-made shoes and hacking-jackets tailored in Savile Row. He said that he was a tobacco-merchant; but many of my friends were in the tobacco-trade, and it was easy enough to see that he was not really one of them. He believed in nothing but intrigue and mystery and violence. In the end, whenever I was with him—and he sought out my company because, as he used to put it, I was "the one congenial soul in the place"—I used to get a peculiar sensation of oppression, sometimes so acute that I could not eat a thing. . . . Poor Setsuko.' I stepped close to the chair. 'It must have been horrid for you to have to work for such people, day in and day out.' I placed my right hand on the back of her chair. 'But I think that in all our lives there are periods which each of us would like to forget. Don't you?' My hand moved to her shoulder.

At once she leant forward to put down her cup of tea. Then she looked at her wrist-watch and jumped to her feet: 'Heavens! I've stayed much longer than I intended. Thank you for listening to me so patiently.'

'Won't you let me listen to you a little more?'

She went out into the hall, as though she had not heard this sentence. Slipping her feet into her low-heeled shoes, she looked up with a smile to ask: 'Do tell me—what is "eclampsia"?'

'Eclampsia?'

'Yes. Whenever Mrs. Ambleside is late, she always announces either that she has had to perform a Caesarean or that "eclampsia has set in". I'd love to know what it is. I've never dared to ask her.'

'I like the word. Perhaps she invented it?'

'Yes, after the spleen, the vapours, hypochondria and angst— eclampsia! . . . Well, goodbye, Bill. See you soon.'

I wanted to say 'Yes, but when? When, when, when?' But already she had waved, jumped down into the garden and made off rapidly towards their house. I went back into the sitting-room, sat down in the chair in which she had been sitting, and stared at the *kakemono*. Two birds on a snow-covered branch, I had acquired it during my first week in Kyoto and had since come to hate it for its Disney-like 'tweeness' and 'charm'. Suddenly I got up and jerked it off the wall.

There was no doubt that eclampsia was setting in: a violent attack for which Mrs. Ambleside would be no use at all.

SIX

FUROMOTO'S relationship with the former sumo-wrestler who was his valet, bodyguard and frequent companion would have seemed odd in any country but Japan, with its tradition of the *daimyo* and his faithful comrade-slaves. Nakatani was a giant, with vast, pendulous breasts, a belly in which the navel appeared the size of a wine-glass, huge hands and feet, and a total absence of any hair except on his head. He had no life but his life with Furomoto : sleeping in a cubby-hole off Furomoto's own bedroom, waking up before him and going to bed after he had helped him to undress. Sometimes, when the two men had been drinking together, he would turn on his master, liquor eroding the crust of his habitual taciturnity, and would mutter at him : 'You're a dog, that's what you are. A dog. How many years have I been with you? Seven, eight? And what have I gained from it? You don't even pay me properly, in spite of all your riches. And do you know the reason? It's not because of your stinginess—though everyone knows about that—but because you're frightened that if I save up a bit of money, I might go and leave you. That's it, isn't it? Dog!'

It is not unusual in Japan for master and men to gather together to drink from time to time, and for the men, their tongues loosened, to pour out their complaints and troubles. Like a benevolent but severe father, the master listens to his 'children' at this hour of confession, and that he should do so with equanimity and even a show of sympathy serves to bind them closer to him. So, on these occasions, Furomoto would never lash out at Nakatani, as he so frequently did when, in the course of his duties, the giant either neglected to do something or did something wrong. Instead he would listen, the scale-like lids half-covering his eyes, in complete impassivity until, Nakatani having at last voiced all his pent-up grievances, he would make some sardonic remark like : 'Noisy here, isn't it?' or 'We must make you drunk more often.' The others present would admire this detachment : the true mark of an aristocrat, they would tell each other afterwards.

That evening, after the opening of the exhibition, Nakatani was, as usual, in the hall of the house high up among the hills near Ashiya, when the company car, a Cadillac, swished up the drive; and as usual he stooped to unlace his master's hideous, stub-toed shoes and then held out the slippers for his feet. The chauffeur was waiting for his instructions; but Furomoto did not hurry to give them, although the man had been on duty since half-past seven that morning. 'If I want to go out again, I'll use the other car,' he said at last to Nakatani who, in turn, nodded his huge, close-cropped head at the driver in dismissal.

'Messages?' Furomoto asked, going down the hall into his bedroom where he began to remove his clothes and hand them to Nakatani.

'Yes. Three calls, sir.'

'Well, where are the notes?'

'Shall I get them now, sir?'

'I asked for them.'

As Nakatani hurried out, Furomoto sank down on the edge of his Western-style bed. Wearing a long-sleeved silk vest and silk under-pants which flapped about his calves, he ran a hand, two of the stubby fingers orange with nicotine, over his face. He was tired, tired, tired. He lay back on the pillows, four of them, against which Nakatani would have to prop him when he had one of his attacks of asthma; and then, incapable of relaxing, made a cat-like crawl and a leap to the dressing-table. He took two mauve, heart-shaped pills from a bottle, threw them one after the other into his mouth as though he were a monkey catching nuts, and then gulped them down without water. He would feel better soon.

'Here you are, sir.'

An apology from the manager of the advertising agency which handled his commercials on television; an invitation to a dinner he had no intention of attending; and a cryptic message from Oku-San. 'The chair which Furomoto-San wished to see had been delivered. The age and the shape were both as advertised, but it might need some polishing before Furomoto-San would wish to buy it.' What a fool the woman was becoming! He had told her time and time again that Nakatani was entirely discreet and that she could therefore dispense with this childish kind of code. In any case, such tricks were too blatant to fool a woman as shrewd as Lisa. He remembered now, with discomfort, his wife's cool disdain as she had told him one evening when he returned from

83

the office: 'You will be glad to hear that your bow-fronted book-case has arrived. You will have some pleasant literary evenings ahead of you, I can see.'

'The time?' He turned to Nakatani who was waiting, motion-less, his hands holding out the *yukata* he would wear down to the bath.

'The time, *shacho-san*?'

'The time. Yes, the time. What time did this message come?' The time was immaterial to him, but he wished to vent his exasperation with Oku-San and she was out of reach—at least until the evening. He extended the sheet. 'It's written here—"Time". Perhaps you've never noticed? That's where you're meant to write in the time when you receive a message.' He spoke as quietly as if he were explaining this to the servant for the first time.

'It was about eleven o'clock. After the mistress's bridge-party had begun.'

'The guests were punctual?'

'Eh?'

'I said, "The guests were punctual?"'

It was like prodding some ancient, half-blind bull around the ring: no sport at all. But to do it had become for Furomoto an action as semi-involuntary as scratching a mosquito-bite. The scratching did not relieve the irritation; and it certainly brought no pleasure with it.

So the interrogation continued while Nakatani administered to his master in the bathroom; until, as the two pills began to take effect, Furomoto's mood of weary brutality freshened into joviality. When, the bath over, the sullen giant (himself now stripped, with a towel about his loins) began to massage him, Furomoto could even discuss the evening ahead. 'We might go and look at this girl of Oku-San's. From Hokkaido. Only fifteen. Oku-San says that she's a virgin.'

'Oku-San always says that. If you ask me, she has a doctor-friend who is clever with his needle.'

Furomoto's body, beneath the vast, muscular paws, was sinewy and lean; the brown skin rucking up, like a pelt, as it was squeezed and pushed hither and thither. From time to time he gave an involuntary groan.

When he emerged from the bathroom, he walked down the corridor to the quarters of Lisa, his second wife, a German.

'Come in.' She was lying in bed, on her side, neither reading nor sleeping nor watching the television.

'How are you feeling?'

She yawned and stretched; holding her bony arms up above her head so that the sleeves of her silk nightdress fell away to reveal the pallid, wasted flesh. Something was wrong with her, but the doctors—Japanese, American, Swiss—had never agreed what. There were times when she made up her mind that she was dying; and times, less frequent, when she even persuaded Furomoto that it was so. She was a woman in her late forties who had been first the wife of an Argentine diplomat and then, after his death, the mistress of one of the highest-ranking of the American generals of the occupation forces. Furomoto felt for her a tenderness which he had never felt for his first wife who, to appearance at least, seemed to need tenderness so much more; and Lisa repaid this tenderness with an off-hand, humorous affection such as a teacher might feel for one of her charges.

'I thought of getting up. The dizzy spell has passed.' She swung her legs out of the bed and reached for the wrap thrown across the bottom of it. 'No, don't ring for that slut.' Her Japanese was almost perfect; but she used few of the polite circumlocutions customary for women. 'How was the exhibition?'

Furomoto seated himself beside her and, drawing down her nightdress, kissed her bony shoulder. He was a man usually immune to pathos, but her fragility never failed to stir him. She gave no response, sitting hunched with her fingers clasped between her knees and her large, pale blue eyes, under lids that had an almost metallic sheen, staring at the dressing-table.

She repeated the question: 'How was the exhibition?'

'Oh, I think it was a success. Nixon never came, in spite of all that telephoning from the American Cultural Center. I must see that he comes tomorrow, before he leaves for Manila. I've discovered that he's at the Miyako Hotel, so it should be fairly easy.' He gave his peculiar, falsetto chuckle. 'But when that crowd next want a trophy for a Speech Contest or anything of that kind, they can go to someone else. . . . Old Mollet was magnificent; said exactly what had to be said and got an ovation. At first she thought the lacquer plate was modern, by the by, and was obviously dissatisfied. But there was a German youth there who began to rave about it and then she brightened up.'

'You're very clever, *Liebchen*.' He could never be sure whether she was being ironical at his expense or not; but the uncertainty seemed only to add to her attraction.

Even his oldest cronies would have been amazed to see him now, as he helped Lisa off the bed and set about dressing her. Sometimes she teased him about this habit. 'I remember,' she had stated on one occasion, ' that when we were in Alexandria, Arturo ' —this was her first husband, the Argentinian—' showed me some photographs he had bought off a pedlar near the Bourse. There was one of a lascivious young couple, seated naked at a dinner-table, while behind them stood an elderly moustached man, in a maid's black uniform and a cap with "Marie" embroidered across it.' To that, however, his only reply had been, 'But I'm not yet elderly, *my dear*—and I've never worn a moustache, let alone a cap with "Marie" embroidered across it'; so that having failed in this first attempt to nettle him, she had given up for the time being. Most of all, he liked to brush her hair; though, having lost its former blonde beauty, it was now as dry and faded as hay.

Alone they next knelt down to their Japanese-style dinner, served by two maids in kimonos, one a harridan who had once been his nursemaid and the other the 'slut'.

'Did you enjoy your card-party? '

'Well, I won.'

'You always do.'

Years of diplomatic life had made an expert bridge-player of her.

They continued to discuss the events of the day; but already, before the meal was over, he started to feel restless. It was those pills, he decided. Stupid of him to take them; one was supposed never to take them after two o'clock. It was peculiar : he cared for Lisa more than anyone else in the world—perhaps, indeed, she was the only person for whom he really cared—and yet so much of his time was spent in plotting to get away from her. Sometimes, in moments of rare self-knowledge, he wondered if he could only love someone whom he betrayed. The same pattern had been followed in the case of his first wife; but she, superficially so docile and inwardly so tough, had soon refused to stand for it, and both his love for her and their marriage had come to an abrupt end.

He glanced twice at his watch, he hoped without being noticed;

86

but nothing escaped her. 'What are your plans for this evening?' she asked him.

'Oh, I said I'd call in at the club. I must speak to Yamada about that contract—the government one. If I let him beat me at a game of billiards, it will be easier. Honestly, I think it would give him more pleasure to be club champion than to be made Foreign Minister. . . . But I can see him some other day, if you'd like me to stay with you. Would you?'

She yawned. 'Oh, I have a book I must finish. And then I'll take a pill to make sure of a good night's sleep.' Both he and she were always taking either sedatives or stimulants. 'I'll try that new Ciba thing.'

'Sure you wouldn't like to go to a cinema? Or come to the club with me,' he added, as an afterthought.

'No, I don't feel well enough to go out.'

'In that case . . .'

As he left the house, after having kissed her unresisting but unresponsive mouth, she called out after him: 'I hope that Yamada fulfils your expectations. Try not to be too generous to him!'

Of course she had guessed; and mingled with his annoyance that she should have done so, was an inexplicable elation.

Oku-San had been his mistress for a brief period, and like many other women who had served him in this capacity, she had been paid off with a bar of her own. Now, when exhorting some reluctant country-girl to submit to him, she would never fail to cite her own example: 'In those days he was little more than a boy. You're much luckier—he's a distinguished man now. In my case, it lasted for only five months. It seldom lasts even that long. What's five months out of your whole life? And then he'll give you a place of your own and you'll have no more worries. Look at me! I'm all right, aren't I? How do you think all these foreigners find their way here? The porters in his two hotels are told to send them, that's how they come. And it's the foreigners who have the cash. . . . But for a long arrangement, foreigners are no good. With them, it's a large salary but no pension at all—ne? Whereas a man like Furomoto—he makes sure that you're all right for the rest of your days.'

It was in such terms that she was now exhorting the snivelling child who had arrived, only two days ago, from a farm on the northernmost tip of Hokkaido. The child herself was in a state of terror, not so much because of what Furomoto would do to her, but because she was conscious of her own inadequacy. Why should such a great man want a girl like herself? He would expect from her all the little tricks and accomplishments of a *maiko*, and of these she was wholly ignorant. Probably he would get angry with her; and then Oku-San would throw her out, and how was she to manage?

Oku-San guessed all this; for such fears were common to almost every country-girl who passed through her hands.

'You're young and you're pretty and you've got the kind of figure he likes. He doesn't like them too full.' Oku-San had herself grown enormous, her kimono cascading over the twin hillocks of her bosom and the greater hillock of her stomach in such a way that her pudgy little feet, in their white bifurcated socks, were visible only when she was seated. 'You don't need anything else. "The best rice requires only pickles,"' she added in quotation.

Soon after this she hurried away to deal with a drunken English naval officer who was bawling out obscene songs ('It was the good ship Venus . . .') in one of her upstairs rooms. What did he think this was? A brothel?

'Yes, she'll do,' Furomoto nodded, after the girl had been brought into a private room for his inspection and was then sent away again, pending a decision. But he had experienced none of the expected excitation when Oku-San had at last succeeded in coaxing the giggling little fool to undo her *yukata* and display her body to him. The breasts were as he liked them, pubescent, and the thighs were those of a boy; her skin had an astonishing bloom, almost luminosity. It was a pity that the hands, also like a boy's, should be so ugly; manual work had done that to them, and the savage way in which she had gnawed at the nails. But, all in all, she was an excellent specimen and he wondered at his apathy.

When they were alone, the girl first attempted a parody of the graces of the *maiko* or apprentice-geisha : emitting a tinkling, unreal laugh at everything he said, bowing her head and glancing sideways at him from under her eyelashes, and coquetting with a fan which her mistress had lent her. But as soon as he began to undress her (she had been re-attired before she was sent back to him) there was an end to this theatre and her teeth began to chatter, her ugly hands to tremble, and her small rabbit-face to

88

twitch and screw itself up preparatory to tears. On other occasions this would have sharpened his enjoyment; but now it filled him with irritation and even disgust. He had himself slipped from his Western suit into a *yukata*, but he did not remove it as he sat on the bed and began to caress the bare, shivering carcase beside him. Once he pinched a nipple too savagely and she let out a little squeal; but for most of the time she remained huddled in a gloomy indifference.

It was too boring! He drew her to her feet and motioned to her to get dressed again. Sensing failure, she at once began to whimper; and then, as she was pulling up her drawers, broke out into torrential weeping.

'Don't be an idiot,' he said, not unkindly. 'What's the matter with you? That was all right. An old man doesn't want what the young fellows want. I'll see you again.' He drew his wallet from the breast-pocket of his jacket and extracted two notes. 'Here, you buy yourself something pretty to wear.' She had not expected to be paid directly by him at all and now, smiling up at him through her recent tears, hesitated whether to accept the money or not. Oku-San might be angry; after all, she had gone to pains to explain the system—'And, remember, you must never ask one of the gentlemen for his present. That is always arranged by me."

'*Dozo*, take it. *Dozo!*' Divining the reason for her slowness, he reassured her: 'I'll settle with Oku-San as well. This is just a small secret between us.'

The girl left the room almost in love with him. Oku-San was right. A distinguished gentleman like that was better than any boy; and she thought with hatred and distaste of the clumsy young peasant-cousin who had caused her flight from home.

Soon Oku-San burst in, her white-plastered jowls quivering with perturbation. 'Wasn't she all right? Wouldn't she do what you wanted? I hope she was clean—I made her go down to the bath with some of the other girls less than an hour ago.'

'Oh, I'm not in the mood. She's all right. You've found yourself a good investment. But get her to stop biting her nails.'

'Yes, I've already scolded her about it. It's when the poor child is frightened. . . . I remember an American who came here once and asked for a girl with bitten nails. Can you imagine? Of course I hadn't one on the premises.'

'But I bet you told one to go into another room and bite her nails down to the quick to oblige!'

The jowls and the slack mouth quivered at this sally; in fact, on that occasion, she had sent someone out into the streets to find the type desired.

'What's Nakatani doing?'

'Oh, he picked on that Russian Jewess—the one with all the hair. And only yesterday I was telling her to take it off.'

'The attraction of Yo and In for each other!'

'Do you want to peep? I've shown them into that room.'

Unknown to the giant, Oku-San and his master were often the amused witnesses of his laborious frolics in a room for which he always asked because every wall was faced with mirrors.

Furomoto pulled a face; but when he had fastened his tie and slipped into his jacket (the first dingy, the second ill-cut) he followed her down the passage into what had been a room for the Tea Ceremony when the bar was a private house. They found the Jewess engaged on a task comparable to executing the Appassionata on a penny-whistle; while her victim-instrument threshed about like a stranded whale, groaned and either bit on his enormous knuckles or thrust them into his eyes or the sides of his abdomen. The girl was obviously aware that she might have an audience and deliberately exaggerated both the satire and depravity of her performance; even, on one occasion, glancing up from a labour that was causing her whole lithe body to stream with sweat, to wink at the intervening glass.

Oku-San shook with silent mirth and had the utmost difficulty in not betraying their presence. From time to time she would whisper to him some comment—that on a narrow road a small Japanese car was better than a large American one, for example— since she knew that, like most Japanese men, he was amused by such bawdiness. Furomoto watched motionless, with his usual sardonic smile: one hand on the glass in front of him and one deep in his pocket. Now at last he was feeling the growing excitation which the girl, in all her childish beauty, had failed to produce. Eventually he broke away:

'Oh, it's too boring!' The words were an echo of the phrase he had repeated under his breath when he had stopped his perfunctory love-making with the girl.

'Really he looks like a baby having his bottom wiped,' Oku-San tittered behind a paw.

When Furomoto and Nakatani were driving away in the car, Furomoto still felt an excitement, almost a perturbation, which made it impossible for him to return home so soon. There had been many other evenings like this. Every place to which he went seemed equally savourless; and every face, however young, beautiful or exotic, was equally powerless to arouse his desire. 'Oh, it's too boring!' But he could not break it off, any more than he could break the chain of cigarettes which followed each other, one after another, to be briefly puffed and then flung aside. Suddenly, as he stared morosely out into the rain which had begun to fall in large, warm drops, bringing no coolness but only an intensification of the temperature, an idea came to him. 'Drive to the Colethorpe woman's.'

'Where, *shacho-San*?'

'You heard.'

Nakatani tended to ask for every statement to be repeated to him at least one, if not twice; but if his master merely replied 'You heard', it usually transpired that he had indeed heard.

'You don't want that one, do you?'

Furomoto gave his falsetto chuckle. 'My palate isn't quite as jaded as all that, thank you. But I'd like to inspect her friend once again.'

'Her friend?'

'Yes, her friend.'

'Oh, her friend. That one.'

'Yes. That one.'

Furomoto had seen Colethorpe's room-mate three times in the last week and his concupiscence had on each occasion been vaguely aroused. She was older and far more sophisticated than the women who usually appealed to him; but such considerations seemed secondary to the perfection of both her features and figure. In a sense it was he who was housing her; since the shack (it could not be called a house) in which Colethorpe lived and worked was attached to one of his properties in which he had long ago placed his mother and two aunts. Sometimes he wondered if the English girl were charging her companion rent; she paid none herself. Nor was this her only debt to Furomoto. The materials for each of her enormous canvases cost twenty or thirty pounds and he had told her to charge whatever she needed to his own account at a store in Osaka. From time to time he would buy one of her pictures,

91

to be stacked with so many others by members of the group in the basement of his house; and on such occasions she would always urge him to accept the work for nothing. But he insisted on paying, deriving from her obligation to him, as from the obligations of all the rest of the group, a gratifying realisation of the extent of his wealth and power. One day when he learned that she had paid out of her own pocket for some of the ping-pong balls she had recently begun to use to create a three-dimensional effect, attaching them to the canvas and then daubing them with paint, he had said to her chillingly: 'You know very well, Miss Colethorpe'—he always spoke to her with an extreme formality—'that you have little money. If you spend it on things like ping-pong balls, how will you eat? And if you do not eat, who will pay for you when you are ill and have to go into hospital?' He did not speak the answer to the second of these questions, which was—as Colethorpe well knew—'Furomoto'.

She had been washing her hair (a rare occurrence, Furomoto fastidiously surmised) and came to answer the ring at the bell in a dressing-gown with a towel wrapped about her head. She never felt at ease with him; partly because it is seldom possible to feel at one's ease with someone to whom one is perpetually indebted and partly because, as she used frankly to put it, 'he's right out of my class'. Now she suffered an excruciating confusion. 'Oh, golly! I'd no idea . . . Do come in. My hair got so dirty preparing the sand-garden that Sanae told me that I must wash it at once.' She sneezed. 'I hope I'm not going to get one of my colds. Sanae! Where are the slippers?'

'It's quite all right, please do not bother. Like this, in my socks, I hope I am not disturbing you.' He had left Nakatani out at the wheel of the car. 'I was passing and I thought that I'd call in. I wanted to hear how you thought the opening had gone off.'

'Oh, I was really too busy with that awful sand-garden to notice much. But we got a good crowd, didn't we? Your niece bought one of my pictures, you know—the one I call *Hiroshima*.' She hesitated: 'I feel I ought to give it to her.'

'Why? No need to give it at all.' Her face crimsoned under the towel at the icy rebuke. 'She's quite able to pay you for it.'

'Well, yes . . . but . . . I'd . . .' She said no more. 'Come and sit down and I'll get you some coffee. Or perhaps you'd prefer a drink?'

'Have you a drink?'

'Yes, I *think* we have some saké. And there may be some whisky—Japanese whisky, I'm afraid.'

'A cup of coffee will do very well.' He lowered himself into one of the two battered armchairs, shifted in it from side to side until it creaked so loudly that Colethorpe feared that it would collapse beneath him, and then said: 'I'll send a carpenter tomorrow to fix this. Why didn't you tell me about it before?'

'Oh, really, it's such a small thing. I didn't want to bother you . . . Sanae! Sanae! Do come and talk to Mr. Furomoto while I make him some Nescafé. Sanae has just returned from work,' she explained as the girl slipped into the room.

The two Japanese bowed ceremoniously to each other, Furomoto drawing in his breath with a sharp hiss at each inclination of his body. Colethorpe hurried out. Golly! Jumping Jehoshophat! Crikey! All the exclamations which she habitually used to express alarm or consternation seemed inadequate on this occasion. Yesterday they had had two other unexpected guests, Frank Ryan from the Anglican Mission in Kyoto, and a diminutive, square-shaped Japanese youth who had partnered him in a tennis-tournament at the Kobe Y.M.C.A. Then it had all been easy. Frank had helped her to prepare a supper of scrambled eggs, salad and fruit, and afterwards they had all played Mah-Jhong until the two men had had to race off down the hill to catch the last train home. She shook the kettle and, finding it half-full, placed it on the gas-ring. But when it began to boil and she poured it on the Nescafé she discovered to her horror that the liquid was not water but green-tea. She had repeatedly told Sanae not to make tea, Japanese-fashion, in the kettle. Oh, Lord! Oh, Crippen!

Meantime, in the other room, Furomoto was exerting all his charm in a conversation at once ceremonious and replete with slily flattering overtones.

'Did I understand correctly that you've been working until now?'

'Yes, you understood correctly.'

'But it's nearly eleven o'clock.'

'Yes, you are right.'

'It's never pleasant to have to work so late in the evening. Especially if one has also had to work during the day.'

'Fortunately, I do not have to work during the day.'

'That, then, will explain why you are still so fresh.'

'You do not look tired yourself, in spite of the opening of the exhibition.'

'Ah, but I am tired! I am no longer young and it's easy for an old man to overtax himself!'

She turned her head aside and tittered behind her raised hand. 'Old man!' she exclaimed.

'And may I be permitted to ask what is the work that keeps you so late?

'It is of no consequence or interest.'

'I can't believe that.'

She hesitated. 'I work in the theatre.'

'Ah, yes! Yes!' he exclaimed, as though this were not a new fact but one he had forgotten. 'At Takarazuka?' (The famous Girls' Theatre.)

She shook her head. 'My small talents would not gain me employment there.'

He sensed an increased tension as he asked about her work, even though, to the outward eye, there was no change in her pose of smiling relaxation. Probably she was employed in a burlesque-show or even one of the strip-shows where the girls, devoid of all artistry, pranced and postured grotesquely for an audience that consisted as much of women as men. If so, it was natural that she should be ashamed to admit it to him. He would ask Colethorpe sometime later.

He now enquired about her *obi*, the sash worn about the kimono. His discerning eye knew at once that it had come, mass-produced, from one of the department-stores, but he pretended to believe that it was a product of the famous Ori-Dono, and she did not contradict him. He thought no less of her for the attempted deception; though he decided that the next morning he would order to be sent to her an *obi* which really came, hand-woven, from the Ori-Dono—an action which would satisfy both the generosity and the cruelty of his divided nature.

The coffee was disgusting; and now that Colethorpe had returned, there was really little point in remaining anyway. For a few minutes longer he engaged the English girl in perfunctory conversation about the exhibition; noticing, as he did so, innumerable small details about her appearance—the hair trailing in dank ringlets about her broad face and her neck, the press-stud undone at the side of her corduroy-slacks, the faint down of blonde hair along her upper lip—which filled him with exasperation against

94

her. She was never content to talk about everyday matters, but was always straying off into vast, vague generalities: a habit which irritated him further.

'. . . I thought Madame Mollet's remarks awfully interesting. I wish I really *understood* Zen. There was a German there with whom I chatted for a while and he said something—I hope I can get it right, because I felt that it was so important—about the mind being like a cinema-screen and our thoughts being like the moving-pictures projected on to it. . . . No, that was not it. No. . . . The projector is our minds—yes, I think I've got it now —and the screen is our consciousness. . . . Would that be it? I'm sure that you and Sanae, being Buddhists, know far better than I do what he was driving at.'

To this Furomoto paid no attention at all. Putting down his coffee cup as far away from himself as he could reach across the table, thus indicating beyond any doubt that he had no intention of drinking from it, he decided to call a halt to her nonsense.

'It was interesting'—his voice was like a knife cutting into fudge—'to see all your work of the last six months hanging in one room.'

'Oh, gosh, I felt awful when I saw it! It seemed so little after all the labour I'd put into it.'

'It convinced me of what I had before only suspected. This three-dimensional stuff is no good.'

'No good?'

'As an experiment, it was interesting. Necessary perhaps, also, to your development as a painter. But I think that now you should stop it.'

The expression of dismay on Colethorpe's face spurred him to a further cruelty.

'You're worried about all those ping-pong balls! Don't worry. I'll buy them off you.'

She had indeed thought momentarily of the boxes of ping-pong balls piled on top of each other on the floor of her bedroom cupboard; but they had been the least of the reasons for her consternation. Until Furomoto had spoken, she had been convinced that, at last, she was on to that 'line' of her own which he was always urging her to discover. And now he proclaimed it a mistake! Suddenly she felt rebellious: sitting hunched forward, her knees apart and her hands dangling down so low between them that they all but touched the *tatami* floor-cover at which

95

she was staring. As if he had a 'line' of his own! It was lucky for him that hardly anybody in Japan had seen the work of Capogrossi. And it was those reproductions she had brought with her from Italy that had started him off, she was sure. But if she quarrelled with him? Once before, in Spain, she had had to present herself, penniless, at the British Consulate with the request to be sent home. 'A distressed person' they had called her; and by the time they had finished with her, she was certainly that. No: she must have her one-man show first, sell some pictures and make some money; then she would be free of him.

'Perhaps you're right, perhaps I *am* on the wrong tack,' she got out with the monotonous inflections of a child who says that she is sorry and she won't do it again and, please, may she be forgiven?

'I'm sure I am. You were far better off before that idea took you.' He smiled at her now with a paternal benevolence as he rose to his feet. 'Everything else in the house all right—I mean, everything except this chair? Is the geyser working? . . . Good.' He looked round the room and, noticing the books and magazines stacked in untidy piles in every corner, added: 'You need a bookcase. We've probably got a spare one stored away somewhere. I'll send it over with the carpenter tomorrow.'

Colethorpe mumbled her thanks, tossing the damp cork-screws of hair away from her face and then fiddling with the undone press-stud. 'Sanae, give me a hand.' The Japanese girl, herself so neat in her kimono and *obi*, with her upswept hair glistening as though it were lacquered, came forward and squeezed the studs together.

'I think that these slacks are too small for you.'

'You mean that she's too large for them.' Furomoto gave his brief, falsetto laugh. 'Well—thank you for my coffee.'

'I'm afraid it was pretty beastly.'

He did not contradict her.

In the car he sat slumped morosely, most of his body resting, not against the upholstery, but against the door, so that he was looking at Nakatani's profile: the bruiser's nose, the full curve of the lip that in a woman would have had a voluptuous beauty, the small, glittering eye set slantwise under the absence of both eyebrow and eyelashes. He thought for a while of the little country-slut and then of Sanae: what a contrast for one evening. But wilfully, of its own accord, his mind kept veering back to the ludicrous, yet oddly appetitive scene glimpsed from the confinement of the tea-ceremony room: the hairy Jewess, teeth bared, grappling with this overblown baby like one of the rats which (so one read in the papers) from time to time devoured a neglected infant in its cot.

'Did you like her better?' Nakatani asked.

'Who?'

'That one. The one you've just seen.'

Furomoto did not answer. He knew that he was now due for one of his 'depressions'; an attack as disabling as one of asthma and one which he would always fight alone, without the aid of doctors or Nakatani. Probably, he had decided, the two maladies derived from the same cause: physiological or psychological, who could decide which? Certainly a prolonged use of the preparation of dexedrine and amytal seemed to precipitate them. He would go straight to bed with a pill, or even two—'the Ciba thing', he might try that—and then, if he were lucky, he would wake up in the morning, himself again.

Himself again! But how he hated that self! Almost as much as his employees must hate him. (But there he was wrong: he was a man as scrupulous in his obligations to them as he was exigent in his demands from them, and for that they felt for him admiration and even a grudging affection.) He almost groaned out loud now as he thought of the series of labour crises which he had surmounted by a mingling of cunning, brutality and bribery. He preferred to be ignorant of the details—it was more dignified, more comfortable and safe—but he knew that, from time to time, his subordinates would arrange for the closure of a mortgage, an eviction-order or even a mysterious beating-up. Since the war, each week seemed to bring with it some report of unrest in his empire. One could no longer rely on the government, the police or the law-courts, whatever the size of the 'gifts' or the favours. Of course it was chiefly the fault of the Americans—and their labour troubles were worse, far worse. The old system had worked, whatever its defects and shortcomings: a man had lived his life concerned with two things—his employment and his family—and between them they had circumscribed most of his rights and obligations. About his fellow-men, if they were neither fellow-employees nor relations, he rarely concerned himself. Of course the employer, like the head of the family, was often exacting and even harsh; but, also like the head of the family, he protected his own. There were literally hundreds of employees in the Furomoto organisation who were engaged on doing nothing at all merely because, if they were dismissed, Furomoto knew that they would find no other jobs. And only yesterday one of his sub-managers at the Takatsuki factory had come grovelling to him because the fool had gambled away his monthly salary at the bicycle-track and had no idea how he was to feed his family. And what had Furomoto done? He had given the man an envelope in which were two five-thousand yen notes, without saying a word in anger or reproach. How many American bosses would do that?

But what was it that that agitator Asai had said to the Personnel Manager? Ah, yes! 'It's not a question of whether the father is wise or benevolent or generous or not. All that's irrelevant. Eventually one reaches an age when one no longer wishes to live in the paternal shadow—however much one's father is loved.' Something like that: Oh, the usual Euro-American claptrap about individualism which was really another word for egoism. Well, they'd licked Asai as they'd licked the others; kicking them either upstairs or down into prison or the gutter—whichever proved the easier. But what about the man after Asai? And the man after him? Could they go on doing it? Suddenly he saw himself not as the General marching victoriously at the head of his conquering Army but as the head of a beleaguered garrison, food scarce, ammunition running out and most of the wells poisoned. The pathos of it moved him; far more than the pathos of the shivering country-girl with her scrubbed hands, the nails bitten to the quick, her tiny, hard breasts and the beautiful, boyish thigh on which some insect—mosquito, bug or flea?—had left three weals.

They had arrived.

'I can manage alone.'

'Sure you don't need me, *shacho-San*?'

'Quite sure.'

It was only with an effort that he controlled himself from saying: 'Yes, I need you, I need you. I'm afraid, I'm lonely, I hate myself. Stay with me. Hold me. Comfort me.' He had never said such words to anyone; he would never say them. *He would rather die.* Yes, it was in order not to say them, that men like himself killed themselves in Japan.

'Good night, *shacho-San*.'

'Good night.'

As Furomoto lay fully-clothed on his bed, smoking cigarette after cigarette and staring up at the ceiling, he could hear first the giant lumbering about his cubby-hole next door and then his grunting and snuffling. Like a dog, thought Furomoto, like a dog in its kennel: contented, unthinking. If only one could stop all thought!

SEVEN

JAPANESE 'politeness' has as little connection with consideration for others as Japanese cleanliness has with hygiene: both
are ritualistic. This aphorism, as true and as untrue as any
other aphorism, has been suggested to me by the events of this
morning.

A few days ago Mrs. Crawley, the elderly English missionary
to whom I was introduced at the dinner for the Archbishop,
telephoned to enquire whether I was interested in some part-time
lecturing at Ibaraki University. I was surprised that she had remembered me; and even more surprised that she should have gone
to this trouble for someone she had met only once. Since in Kyoto
we all learn everything about each other, she has no doubt been
told the exact sum which my University pays me each month
and has even heard, at second, third or fourth hand, my complaints of chronic poverty. Still, it was good of her. I wonder
how many of my Japanese friends would have bothered to do as
much?

The University is some two hours' journey by train and bus from
Kyoto, and like many other private 'universities' created since
the war, is not really a university but a college. Notorious both
for the lowness of its academic standards and the highness of its
fees, it is patronised chiefly by the sons and daughters of rich
business-men in Osaka and Kobe. As I walked up from the
railway-station in a heat so humid that I was soon drenched in
sweat, cars perpetually passed me containing my future students.
Since none of them could guess that I was their future teacher, it
was perhaps unreasonable of me to curse them (as I choked on
their dust) for not stopping to give me a lift.

I had met the Dean of the English Faculty briefly, over a cup
of stewed Indian tea in Mrs. Crawley's flat, when we had discussed the terms of my employment. (A Christian: 'one of our
little flock', Mrs. Crawley explained.) He was evidently now
watching for my arrival; or, perhaps, had told some minion or a
student to watch for it. 'Ah, Mr. Knox . . . This is indeed

delightful . . . And so punctual . . . You still keep English time and not Japanese time, I see . . .' He had scuttled out from one of the buildings and his hands pressed to his sides (the fingers almost entirely concealed by his overlong sleeves) were jerking up and down with the unreal enthusiasm of a puppet at the *bunraku*, his long face an overripe gourd cracking open to reveal orange, pip-like teeth. 'Come in, come in. This is our common-loom.' I was glad when the bows—to each of which I felt obliged to respond with an embarrassed nod of the head, like a Protestant caught at a Catholic service—at last clicked to a halt and the clockwork, which seemed to regulate all his motions, then changed gear to carry him up the steps and into the house. The common-room was empty; not, as I then assumed, because my colleagues had already gone to their classes, but because they had not yet arrived.

'A gleat honour . . . A distinguished lectuler . . . Scholar of lepute . . . This far flom worthy post . . .' (All right, all right: now that's enough! Get down, sir! Down!) '. . . Indeed lucky . . . Humble University . . .' (*Down!*)

At last, like the bowing, this slavering also came to an end. From one of those brief-cases, as inseparable from a Japanese as from a Swedish or German university-teacher, he drew out a sheet of typed paper, looked at it as though to read it for the first time, and then handed it to me. (A profound bow: a hissing intake of the breath. 'His Majesty is pleased to accept his subject's humble petition . . .' I felt I should pronounce.) 'Your plo-glamme. As we agleed, two periods of one-and-a-half hours each. . . . Loom Four, the new building. . . . And now I must reave you.' Suddenly the clockwork whirred forward with an amazing rapidity. Click-click . . . Honoured, delighted . . . Click-click . . . Welcome, distinguished . . . Click-click . . . Hope, happy . . . Crrr . . . Bow . . . Crrr . . . Bow . . . And he had gone.

Alone in the vast, dusty common-room, I looked at the programme:

Mr. W. Knox		Room 4, New Building
1.0 -2.30	Techniques & Forms in English Poetry	Postgraduate Students
2.40-4.10	Conversation	Beginners

Then I wandered out to find Room Four.

Two women students were seated on a bench watching a game of tennis, and having worked out my question in Japanese in my head it was they that I approached: 'Excuse me. Could you please tell me which is Room Four, the New Building?' They looked at me, they looked at each other; then they began to titter, raising tiny hands to their cat-mouths. 'Room Four, the New Building. The New Building,' I repeated. They still tittered uncontrollably; but I sensed their mounting alarm. At any moment they would summon help from the two brawny youths wearing green eye-shields on the tennis-court, who would mash me to pulp with their rackets.

'*Wakarimasen*,' said one, choking on her giggles. ('I do not understand.')

'*Wakarimasen*,' echoed the other.

'*Wakarimasen*,' they both got out simultaneously, shaking with hysteria.

In most countries the natives tend to assume that they will not be able to understand any foreigner who addresses them; and my Japanese is, after all, still rudimentary. But Mrs. Crawley told me that, even after a lifetime in Japan, there are still times when people refuse to believe that she is speaking their language. Well, I should have to try someone else. On this second occasion I picked on a wizened youth, in horn-rimmed glasses so vast that they covered most of his cheeks, who was making his way, with a curious sideways gait, up the path ahead of me, a pile of books under his arm. Two of the books, I noticed with relief as I approached, were parts one and two of the *Shorter Oxford English Dictionary*. I was in luck.

He did not giggle when I addressed him in English; instead— more alarming—he shied, tossing his head frantically back and forth in the air and rolling his eyes until he at last managed to choke out as though I had a hand on his windpipe: 'No understand . . . Please, no understand . . .' ('But you've got *Daniel Deronda* under your arm, and, yes, *Seven Types of Ambiguity*— you must understand.') 'Excuse, please.' And he scuttled off, crab-like, under his load of useless erudition.

Similar experiences followed; until, at the end of a corridor, I succeeded in wedging a mild, elderly man—the President of the University?—into a corner, with my knee barring his escape. 'The New Building, Room Four.' I repeated the phrases, first in English and then in Japanese, over and over again until the hypnotic rhythm of my voice seemed to soothe his alarm into comprehension.

'Follow me, please.' Up a flight of stairs; down a flight of stairs; through a class-room where a middle-aged woman, presumably a colleague of mine, was seated alone reciting into a tape-recorder ('. . . a banner with a stlange device . . .'); then up some more stairs.

'Thank you' (breathless).

'Thank you.'

Simultaneously 'Thank you, thank you, thank you, thank you'; followed by that ever-present anxiety that my bows are neither low enough nor frequent enough.

'Good morning.' Silence. 'Or should it be good afternoon? One is never sure at one o'clock. . . . Well, as you know, this course is concerned with Techniques and Forms in English Poetry. . . . Techniques and Forms in English Poetry. . . . That is the subject of this course.' (I have learned to say everything at least twice, preferably in different words, when lecturing abroad.) I then began to speak my little piece—which is every other foreign teacher's little piece—about Japanese poetry being directed chiefly to the eye and English poetry to the ear. They all stared at me. No one moved. No one scribbled a note. Indeed, no one had a notebook.

'. . . Our first period will be concerned with Blank Verse. BLANK VERSE. B-L-A-N-K V-E-R-S-E.' (Write it on the blackboard.) 'Now what do we mean by Blank Verse? Hm? Yes? Blank Verse—What do we mean by it?' (Quick: a handkerchief to catch the sweat running off the tip of the chin.) 'Well, let's put it another way. What famous dramatist—the most famous of all English dramatists, perhaps the most famous of all dramatists in the world—wrote in Blank Verse?' The sweat was now running down my spine; a disagreeable sensation, as though it were a spider slowly crawling from between my shoulder-blades to the small of my back. I looked from one face to another to catch some gleam of a response. Nothing.

'. . . Well, that then is what we mean by "Blank Verse".' (Fifty-five minutes to go!) 'Now we come to the Heroic Couplet. You know, of course, what I mean by Rhyme. RHYME. R-H-Y-M-E.' (No more chalk.) 'Chalk, talk. . . . That is an example of rhyme. Schools, fools . . . Numb, dumb . . . Now do you understand what Rhyme is? Do you understand?' Silence.

Faster and faster I spoke, pacing up and down the dais, gesticulating, attempting now a fortissimo and now a whisper in the hope of surprising those steamed puddings before me into some reaction, however unfavourable. I had the sensation, as the sweat streamed off my body, that I was tied up in a polythene bag. Recklessly I used up my notes for the following week (the Quatrain), the week after that (the Shakespearean Sonnet) and for yet another week (the Petrarcan Sonnet). At last the period ended. All right, dear post-graduates, you may go—if indeed you are not wax dummies and are capable of movement. . . . Yes, go, go, go. . . . And let me never see you (I am unlikely to hear you) again. With a peculiar reluctance they rose, glanced nervously at me (yes, indeed, I might sink my teeth into the jugular vein of one of you just to see if there is any blood) and then filed out. . . . I strode over to the window in the hope of a breath of air. But from the stone courtyard below the heat rose up in nauseating wave upon wave. My mouth was dry with chalk-dust; it was the only thing dry about me.

In twos and threes the next class began to appear: the beginners. ' Good morning. Or should one say good afternoon? ' They tittered. ' Good afternoon, or should one say good morning? ' I was beginning to feel the lightheadedness that accompanies a fever. One by one they had begun to freeze into the same immobile, glassy-eyed postures as their predecessors. Well, I'd better begin. ' This—is a—Conversation—Class. A—Conversation—Class.' Very loud, very slow. ' During—this—period—I shall—talk—to—you. You—I—hope—will—talk—to—me.' Repeat. And again. And now to business. I pointed a finger at a man with a sad, crumpled little face and thinning hair over a tumescent dome. ' Where—do—you—live? '

At first he ignored my pointing finger; then, as though I were accusing him of some crime, pointed his own finger at his nose and squeaked: ' Me? '

' Yes, you.'

' Well, sir, before the war we lived with my grandfather in Koshien-Guchi, in a pretty little house overlooking the Hankyu Railway Line—you know the Hankyu Railway Line?—but when the fire-bombs began to drop, we think we go to Hokkaido, but Hokkaido too far from my aunt, she works in the Prefectural Office, see, so we think that maybe we go to Ise, Ise Peninsula—you know Ise?—but my grandfather, he says . . . ' (There was no stopping him; it was like one of those terrible party-games when one sees who can talk longest without a pause.)

'Yes, I see. . . . I see. . . . Thank you. . . . Yes, thank you. . . .' (Whoa there! Whoa!)

Some ten minutes later, I again pointed my finger: a puffy girl, the skin of whose elbows was a deep shade of mauve. 'What —are—your—hobbies?' Bang! It was as if I had fired a starting-pistol. Down the track she streaked (how suitable the white socks, the blue-and-white canvas shoes, and the cotton vest): 'Hobbies, sir? Hobbies? Well, sir, I guess I have many hobbies. I like music —Beethoven, Gershwin, Chopin, Lehar, Brahms, Louis Armstrong and the March of the Bridge on the River Kwai. And Mozzat. Yes, I like Mozzat, sir. I like painting, European painting and Japanese painting. Sometimes I paint myself, flowers maybe, bamboos maybe, birds maybe. But I no paint people. Then I play sports—basketball, softball—you know softball, sir?—tennis, ping-pong. . . .'

Slowly, like the nauseating waves of heat which had risen up from the courtyard, a realisation was coming to me. (No, it can't be! It can't be!) I looked at my programme. (No, it can't! . . .)

'Just one moment, please. One moment please!' She slithered to a stop. 'Tell me, is this a class of beginners or of post-graduate students?' But already I *saw*: the thinning or greying hair; the pouches beneath eyes dulled by too prolonged a study of *Sir Gawain and the Green Knight* or Meredith's *Modern Love*; the paunches and bunions and false-teeth. 'Well?'

All those eyes which had held me in their unwinking gaze had now swivelled downwards and were covered by citron lids. No one stirred. No one seemed to hear me.

I repeated the question in a loud, cracking voice: 'Tell me, is this a class of beginners or of post-graduate students?' with memories settling on me, like flies, of occasions when at prep-school I had been sent to Coventry. I pointed to the girl—but, of course, she was not really a *girl* but a woman dressed up to resemble an American college-kid: 'Are you a beginner?' A nerve twitched on the side of her throat, jumping like a frog: her only answer. 'Are you a post-graduate student?' Two jumps. One for no, two for yes? I pointed at the man next to her. 'Are you a post-graduate student?' Silence. 'But I must know!' I cried out. (In Japan to lose one's temper or one's nerve is to lose face. Control yourself.) I swallowed on the chalk-dust in my mouth and began patiently: 'Don't you see, if you are beginners, we have one kind of class. If you are post-graduates, on the other hand . . .'

Well, in the end I assumed that they were post-graduates and started again where I had started at one o'clock. 'The chief difference between Japanese poetry and English poetry is that, whereas Japanese poetry is directed primarily to the . . .' The spider was once more scampering down my back-bone.

Later when I told the story to my colleagues in the common-room ('But, Mr. Knox, you have gone on so long! It is customaly here to begin quarter of an hour rate and to finish quarter of an hour early') I asked them: 'But why didn't they tell me? Why? Why? Why let me go on for an hour-and-a-half saying things no beginner could understand?' There was silence: as terrible and as tense as the silence in the class-room. Then a young man who had been at the University of Stanford for a year spoke up:

'But they *couldn't* tell you that you had made a mistake.'

'But I hadn't made a mistake.'

'Well, that the Secretary had made a mistake—that a mistake had been made.'

'Why not?'

'Face, Mr. Knox.'

'Face?'

'Well, yes, I guess so. Face.' He tittered; and though he had acquired an excellent American accent, I noticed that he raised his hand to cover his mouth when he did so.

It is these two incidents—first the Dean's elaborate welcome followed by his hurried abandonment of me to find my own way to the class-room; then the idiotic 'good manners' of the students —that first prompted my aphorism. (Let us, after all, imagine the same situation in England. 'Ah, Knox—there you are! I was expecting you rather earlier. I'm afraid I'm in a hurry getting off to a class of my own. I'll just take you up to your class-room. . . . Oh, this is your programme—mustn't forget that. I expect that as usual the Secretary has made a balls-up of it. . . .' And then: 'But, sir—excuse me, sir—there *must* be some mistake. . . .')

A third—and related—incident took place on my journey home. Foreigners have written at some length on the subject of the Japanese railways: both about the punctuality of the trains themselves and the ill-manners of those who use them. I have suffered from both. When I first travelled from Tokyo to Kyoto, I placed two of my suitcases in the carriage, stepped out on to the platform to fetch the remaining two, and turned to discover the train had gone. On other occasions I have either been prevented from getting off the train by the mob pressing to get on, or have been catapulted out, to land on hands and knees. Inevitably, since the train I was now to catch had come from Kobe, there would be no seats on board and I was resigned to that fact. Nonetheless I joined a queue, since every rail-traveller joins a queue, standing between the parallel white lines notched at regular intervals along the platform. When the train comes in, the lines are forgotten; but perhaps like myself, everyone cherishes the pathetic belief that, just as one day there will be a world without war, so one day there will be a journey without a battle. In front of me there stood one of those ancient peasant-women whose appearance of itself fills one with simultaneous pity and awe. Her skin was as brown and wrinkled as a toad's and her scab-like mouth had fallen in over two or three teeth which were revealed, like burned matches, when from time to time she gave a susurrating cough. Her head stuck out tortoise-fashion from between her shoulder-blades and her eyes were dull and rheumy. In either claw she gripped innumerable bundles tied up in rags or paper. What a commentary on human existence—and the endurance required to get through it !

Behind me a young man was alternately whistling and chewing gum : a student, in the conventional shiny black student's uniform, his bare feet balanced on a pair of *geta* and his luxuriant hair redolent of mimosa. From time to time he wandered away from the queue and then returned to it, or executed a few clattering paces forwards or back. On one occasion his *geta* struck my heel, but I heard no apology.

The train came in at exactly the expected hour; and exactly in the accepted fashion the queue broke up. The old woman had been first and, showing more spirit than myself, she was determined to remain so. She and the young student managed to wedge each other into the door, her parcels about his neck and his elbow in her stomach. Then, with a concerted shove, they launched themselves into the carriage. There was one vacant seat, and the old woman was leading. But the boy scrambled past her, knocking her sideways against two passengers, and with the triumph of an Olympic winner, hurled himself on his prize. Then he did what to me was the unforgivable thing : he looked at the old woman, threw back his head and laughed.

I expected that at this action there would be protests from their fellow-travellers and that someone might even set on him. *But everyone else was laughing too.*

I pushed towards him: 'Your behaviour is disgusting.' He looked down at his feet, raised one and picked at a bit of loose skin on the bare heel. I tried to say the same sentence in Japanese. He still took no notice. And then I realised that not only he but everyone else, including the old woman, was deliberately pretending that I did not exist.

Suddenly someone touched my arm. I thought I should hear some comment on the behaviour either of the youth or myself, but instead a voice lisped: 'May I prease spik Engrish with you?'

How I have come to loathe that question! An American colleague of mine always replies to it with the disconcerting monosyllable 'Why?' but from a mixture of cowardice and residual good manners I usually come out with a mumbled 'Oh, all right' or 'Yes, if you wish.'

'What did you say?' I temporised on this occasion, swinging round at the same time to view the pigmy-figure whose face was uptilted to mine to reveal teeth worn with all the chunky effrontery of cheap costume-jewellery. ('Dearest, you are growing older, silver teeth among the gold . . .')

'And you have leal Oxford accent!' Wisps of hair stuck out from under the check cap pulled down to ears the size of his hands, and there was a yellow encrustation along the lids of each of the enormous eyes which yearned up at me in a craving for knowledge. The first impression was one of shabbiness, which is common enough in Japan: the second of dirt, which is not. 'I see that you are not Amelican man.'

'No, I am not American man.'

'Engrish?'

I nodded.

'I do not like Amelican Engrish. But what am I to do? I do not know Engrish man. But now'—the grimy hand again closed on my arm—'I have you. Now I can practise King's Engrish. Prease —do I say King's Engrish or Queen's Engrish?'

We were too closely packed for me to attempt to move away; and my growing coldness was as vain as an attempt to freeze the Niagara Falls. It was so lucky that he had met me because next year he would visit Europe and English had become the international language, hadn't it? One could not learn to swim without going into the water and one could not learn to speak English without speaking it. (He liked that analogy and, having tittered at it—the barbaric necklace of gold-capped and silver-capped teeth emerging as though fished from a stagnant pond—proceeded to repeat it.) I nodded; I grunted; and from time to time I mumbled, 'Yes, yes, of course.'

Then the surprise came: he was going to Europe, because he had written a script for a film which, it was hoped, would be shown at the next Venice Festival.

'But has the film been made?' I queried sceptically.

'Almost it is completed.' He raised a knee, balanced his brief-case upon it, and thrust in a paw. The script—in Japanese, and therefore meaningless to me; some stills; some newspaper-cuttings, two with his photograph. . . . The story, he went on to explain, was 'the rife of a plostitute-woman . . . very tlue, very shocking'.

'You know plostitute-woman?'

'Yes, I know prostitute-woman.'

'This girl works Shinjuku-ku. First she makes money. Then she makes baby, but she has baby taken out. Then she makes more money and has lich, lich man. Then she has disease, beneleal disease. You know beneleal disease?'

'Yes, I know venereal disease.'

He lisped on about the film until, either from politeness or because he had no more to say on the subject, he began to question me instead:

'How old are you?'

'Forty-four.'

'Forty-four! I think you much older. Fifty-one or fifty-two, maybe. How old you think me?'

'Forty-eight,' I hazarded maliciously.

'Forty-eight! Oh, no, sir, no, no, no! You are joking. This is your Engrish sense of humour.' (Yes, strands of pond-slime were actually festooning the necklace, I could see it clearly. Had he been eating sea-weed?) 'I am only thirty-four. That is why I am called one of Japan's most plomised younger writers in your *Times Riterary Supplement*. Plomised, plomiseful?'

'Promising.'

He tee-heed again. 'Forty-eight! You joke! You joke! . . . And have you wife, sir?'

I shook my head.

'But you are forty-four.' At first he was bewildered; then comprehension came to him. 'Ah, I understand. I understand! You are a gay.'

'A what?'

'A gay. Excuse—this is Amelican explession. A gay, a sodomist. You like sister-boy?'

'Certainly not.'

'Many foreigners in Japan are sodomists. I think thlee years ago that may be I am a gay. I go with foreigners I meet at bar in Osaka, but they say I am not leally intelested. One Amelican sailor hit me, hit me very much, afterwards. Maybe he not preased because I not leally intelested.'

It was a relief when the train began to draw into Osaka Station and my companion prepared to fight his way out. 'My card, prease. . . . Here Japanese, here Engrish. Mamoru Taiichi. Taiichi means Fat-Big but I Thin-Small!' His tee-heeing was like a sneezing attack. 'Your card, prease?'

'I'm afraid I haven't got one with me,' I evaded.

'Your name?' he then asked, as he began to pummel and jab a way for himself.

'Knox.'

'Your addless?' he shouted over his shoulder, his cap knocked askew by the violence of his passage.

Purposely I mumbled it.

'Again!' he squealed. 'No hear! Again!'

But thank God it was, by then, too late; he was out on the platform.

When I returned home, I was so upset by the incident of the old woman and the youth in the train that I called in to tell Setsuko about it. She laughed: 'Oh, you were lucky, very lucky! The boy might have seemed to disregard you, but to criticise him like that in front of all those people. . . . It was madness. You cannot conceive how he felt—the loss of face.'

'Face! Oh, how I hate face!'

'Hate it by all means. But don't pretend that it doesn't exist.' She then went on to tell me a story which had been in the papers the previous day. Smoking is forbidden on public-transport; and a conductor on a bus in Kyoto, seeing a young man smoke, had politely asked him not to do so. The young man continued to puff at his cigarette and no more was said. The next morning the same bus conductor was stabbed in the stomach while collecting his fares. His assailant was the young man whom he had asked not to smoke.

'So perhaps next morning I too shall be stabbed!'

'Perhaps.'

I heard sounds of the front door being slid across and movements in the hall. But instead of Mrs. Furomoto, as I had expected, it was Colethorpe and her Japanese friend who entered. I was even more surprised when, without getting to her feet off the floor, Setsuko merely gave them a casual 'Hello'. Colethorpe shook hands with me, the Japanese girl executed a number of bows, and they then crossed the room and went through into the room next to it, pulling the door across behind them.

'You didn't know that they had come to stay here?'

'Come to stay here?'

'And yet you live a stone's throw away. You're not very observant.'

'But when did they move in?'

'Yesterday evening.'

'Oh, Endo-San, who knows everything, told me you had some guests. But I didn't realise that he meant guests to *stay*.'

'The poor things had nowhere to go.'

'But I thought that your uncle——'

'Aileen has quarrelled with him.'

'Aileen? Oh, Colethorpe, you mean.'

'The crisis came on the evening after the exhibition when he called round, late and uninvited, and more or less ordered her to give up painting in the way she wanted.'

'What business is it of his?'

'Oh, she's one of the group. And dependent on him. That's always excuse enough for Furomoto to make a show of power. She came to me for advice—you remember I had invited them both to tea—and I told her to assert her independence. So she wrote a letter, a silly thing to do. And the letter itself was a silly one. Poor Aileen! Anyway the upshot was that he suddenly decided that he would need the shack for some purpose or other by the end of the month—he would never do anything so crude as tell her to clear out, in so many words—and so——'

'And so you came to the rescue.'

'Well, I felt I had to. Since I was, in one sense, the cause of the break-up.'

All this information vaguely annoyed me; though I find it

difficult, even now, to explain exactly why. I suppose it is that I am enough in love with Setsuko to resent both that she should do things of which I am left in ignorance and that she should concern herself with lives other than mine. You really are a busybody, Setsuko, was my first thought; followed by: And to land yourself with such a couple for God knows how long!

At that moment the two guests returned. The Japanese girl knelt decorously at the table; while, in contrast, Colethorpe threw herself full length in a corner, lying in such a way, on her side, that her enormous right hip was pushed up and out as though it were a deformity.

'Sanae used once to attend Bible Class at the mission down the road,' she announced, chewing on a hank of her blonde hair.

'Is Sanae a Christian? I'd no idea.'

'Was one.'

'Maybe I am still. But I have not been to church for more than a year.' I was surprised by the girl's decisiveness; perhaps this is how Japanese women speak among themselves, when their menfolk are not present to demand a child-like naïveté of them. 'I think that one day I shall go back.'

'Oh, no, Sanae, don't!' Setsuko hates religion, whether Buddhist, Shinto or Christian; and Christianity most of all.

'I think that I shall go back,' the Japanese girl repeated.

'Well, dear, if you find it helps you . . .' Colethorpe said.

Now that I was seeing the two girls for the first time since Setsuko had told me that she thought that Colethorpe was 'one of those', I was alert for any signs; and both the protective tone with which these words were spoken and the use of the 'dear' struck me as symptomatic.

'Does one judge a religion by whether it is helpful or not?' Setsuko demanded. 'I should have thought that truth was a better criterion.'

Colethorpe considered this, gnawing at her hair while her right hand scratched her left armpit. 'Well, I see what you mean . . .' she said at last. 'Yes, I see what you mean.' I wondered if she really did. 'The opium of the people and all that.'

'Are your family Christians?' Setsuko asked.

'I have no family.'

'Oh, I'm sorry . . .'

'I was brought up by American missionaries. In Hiroshima.'

'My God!' Setsuko exclaimed. 'You mean . . . ?'

'I went through it.' The girl nodded. 'Or must I say, I came through it?' All these replies were produced with a chilling impassivity.

'I never realised.'

'But you must have met others?'

'Yes, I suppose so.'

Mrs. Furomoto entered at that moment and I think that each of us was glad that she did so. She greeted me with the usual ritual of bowing and murmuring the same phrases of greeting over and over again and then crossed the room to pick up a lacquer work-box and some embroidery.

'Won't you sit with us?' Setsuko suggested.

Her aunt did not reply to the invitation, but instead turned to ask me how I had got on at the University. 'I won't bore Setsuko by telling you the story all over again,' I replied to her question. 'It's enough to say that I hated every moment of it.'

'Poor Mr. Knox! I sometimes think that you hate every moment of your stay in Japan.'

She repeated the bowings and murmurings and slowly disappeared into the next-door room; and it is only now, as I recollect the whole passage, that I realise that she never once either addressed Colethorpe or Sanae or even glanced at them.

The Japanese girl looked at her watch and rose to her feet. 'I must start out to work.'

'Already?' Colethorpe slowly raised herself off the floor to a kneeling position.

'You know it takes at least an hour-and-a-half to get to Osaka.'

'I do wish you'd chuck it.' Colethorpe was scowling down into her capacious lap.

'I wish I could.'

'You know jolly well that——'

'You've little enough for yourself without having me to support,' the Japanese girl replied coolly.

'There *must* be some other job you could do instead of——'

'Well, find one for me, then. And please make sure that it is equally well paid.'

When Sanae left the room, Colethorpe exploded: 'It's horrible to think of her having to parade naked in front of all those disgusting drooling old men.'

'More than half of them are women, so I'm told.' (Was Setsuko trying to bait her?)

113

'She's so plucky, and she's had such a raw deal from life. If only I had some money!'

'Perhaps she likes her job.'

'Likes it!'

'I think I should prefer to do that than make other people's beds in a hotel or clear up other people's messes in a hospital. And you heard her say that it was well-paid. There are all kinds of prostitution and hers seems to me one of the least disagreeable.'

'Prostitution! Are you suggesting that poor Sanae——'

'Of course I'm not. You're missing the point.'

'Well, then, what do you *mean*? I don't understand.'

'Wasn't yours a kind of prostitution to Furomoto? You called it that yourself, I seem to remember.'

'Oh, that!' Colethorpe was mollified.

Sanae and I left simultaneously and Setsuko, after the Japanese fashion, accompanied us down the path. When we reached the point at which I cross the garden to my house, I asked: 'Are you going to come over now or later?' Setsuko had promised to help me with my Japanese.

'Oh, later, I think. I'll walk with Sanae down to the tram-stop.'

'What time shall I expect you?'

'Any time,' she laughed. 'Must we be so precise? Expect me when you see me.'

'Very well.'

I was furious; but I hardly expected that she would not come at all. Yet now it is past ten o'clock and Colethorpe has just been over, ostensibly to borrow a dictionary, but in fact to tell me that Setsuko eventually accompanied Sanae into Osaka.

'I can't think what possessed her. She said she was going to walk with her to the bus-stop—or is it the tram-stop?—and the next thing was that she telephoned from Kyoto Station to say she was taking the train. I asked her if she was going to go to the performance and she laughed in that maddening way of hers and said, "Perhaps." She can be awfully odd, can't she? . . . Oh, I don't mean anything bad by that,' she added hastily. 'She's been most terrifically kind to us and I do admire her and like her most enormously. But it's annoying of her to go off like that because, you see, a friend of mine—a friend from the mission down the road, actually—asked me to go to the cinema with him tonight and I'd have gone like a shot if I hadn't thought it might seem rude on my second night at Setsuko's.'

114

I wonder if 'the friend from the mission' is a fiction created for my benefit; or if Setsuko has perhaps been wrong. 'We women always feel these things about each other—just as you men do.' But do we? I myself am perpetually surprised at discovering the sexual peculiarities of my most intimate friends.

EIGHT

THERE were always some 'foreign' numbers: half-naked negro slaves picking cotton in the Deep South under the supervision of a white-yellow girl-supervisor armed with a whip, twice as long as herself, which she made efforts, usually ineffectual, to crack in the air over their heads; an Apache dance during which the 'male' slowly ripped the clothes off the female until, when she was naked, there was a black-out as he gripped her by the throat and plunged a dagger between her breasts; the gipsy revel, to a pot-pourri of tunes from *Carmen*, with a maniacal clacking of castanets and stamping of feet and an incessant twirling of skirts to reveal the nudity beneath them; and the London scene. Tonight it was the London scene—the Changing of the Guard outside the Houses of Parliament—which concluded the show. Beneath a cardboard replica of Big Ben (twelve chimes sounding from the wings) four girls stood at attention in jack-boots and towering bearskins, each clutching a wooden rifle horizontally across her stocky, sweat-flecked body. To the strains of 'Colonel Bogey', mewed and clattered out on two violins, an accordion, a piano and the drums, four other girls goose-stepped on to the stage led by a 'sergeant-major' accoutred with a crimson-and-gold bandolier and a golden stave which she tossed into the air. The nine girls proceeded to execute a series of perfunctory manœuvres: the newcomers now interweaving with those already on the stage; here a high-kick, there a somersault or cartwheel; ten paces back, ten paces forward; link arms; rotate; reverse. . . . Meanwhile the 'spectators' were crowding around them: two girls dressed as a couple of typical English toffs; a nursemaid with a pram; a Pearly King and Queen, all pearls and nothing else; a child with a hoop. . . .

Sanae, like the rest of the girl-guardsmen, had gone through the motions of this scene often enough to be able to concentrate all her attention on the audience: even though, on this evening, she had mislaid her own pair of jack-boots and had had to borrow a pair which were too small for her and pinched.

Most of the seats were filled with the usual riff-raff: peasants in Osaka for the day; students who found admission to the theatre cheaper than to a brothel; women, usually in pairs, in kimonos or Western dress, with opera-glasses which they carried in leather-pouches. But, yes, there was the Korean's banker. So he had come back for a second time, though none of them, not even the Korean herself, had expected him to do so. Last time he had given her a brooch of cultured pearls; perhaps this time he would take her away from the theatre for good. She was in luck: obviously no one had told him about her thieving and lying, and he had been too much blinded by his passion for her to notice her filth.

Behind him Sanae could see the 'Professor'—he called himself that, but the girls had soon learned that he was a teacher at a middle-school—who had recently come out of a sanatorium, with a ghastly scar which curved all the way from below his breast-bone to his back-bone (she had never seen it herself), and who always started to show the blurred snapshots of his wife and five—or was it six?—brats as though they were dirty postcards. Ikuko (the lumpy girl from Shikoku with the swollen ankles, now on her right) sometimes took pity on him, and no doubt he would show his gratitude by infecting her with tuberculosis. . . . That one over there was the wife of a real Professor and herself well-known, so they said, for her work among the down-and-out. One of the girls had seen her on television. Ito-San, yes, that was her name; and she was a Christian and her photograph with the English Archbishop at a dinner at the Miyako Hotel had appeared in the paper. You would not expect a woman of her age and position to be seen in this kind of theatre; though no doubt she was clever enough to pretend that it was all part of her social work and that she was helping these poor girls to return to the right road. Ugh, the hypocrisy! But the little bitch she fancied seemed to have got attached to her; said that she was more considerate and less exacting than a man. Yes, but where did that get you? Women seldom had the money to be really generous. The Saito woman was an exception—owner of one of the largest newspapers in Japan, so that her wretched little husband had to take her name—but she was stingy and, rare among women, a 'butterfly' into the bargain.

Ma, this thing on her head! If that's what English soldiers had to wear, it must have been hot work retreating in the jungles in the war. The Korean was out of time; she always was, even though her neighbours on either side were counting for her ' *one,* two, three, four, *one,* two, three, four. . . .' Now she had all but dropped her rifle.

Suddenly, Sanae had all but dropped her rifle herself. In the third row, but at the side of the theatre furthest at that moment from herself, she had glimpsed a grotesque figure, tipped out like a half-set jelly from some preternatural shape to slop over the seats on either side of it. Nakatani! The jelly seemed to be throbbing, either in time to the music or at the gusts of excitation which buffeted the auditorium in occasional whistles and high-pitched squeals. The light from the orchestra-pit glistened on the grey-green mucilage of his upturned face, in which the eyes seemed to be no more than two holes poked there with a forefinger. Why was he in the theatre? Had he come there by chance? Had he wished to meet her again? Or had Furomoto sent him? She had been too often disappointed to feel any thrill at the last of these possibilities; but those previous disappointments had given her an iron-like inflexibility of purpose. If it had to be a man, it would not be a Nakatani or a consumptive self-styled ' Professor' or even a small-style banker like the Korean's most recent conquest, but a Furomoto. Many of the girls mistook her ambition for prudery or virtue (according as to how they viewed their own sexual laxity, with pleasure or shame) and told her that she was a fool to let her opportunities slip, as they flaunted their necklaces of cultured pearls, their real leather handbags or their furs. But the opportunities she let slip were those which she did not consider to be worth the trouble of taking.

Yet the other girls were not wholly lacking in discernment. The steel strands of cynicism, calculation and ruthlessness were plaited with softer fibres; and there were moments when she not only loathed her companions and the men whose appetites they served, but loathed herself also for taking part in what she often described as ' a filthy racket'. In giving her a Christian education, the well-intentioned missionaries, scurrying in after the Bomb with their indiscriminate loads of blood-plasma, cookies, Bibles, vitamin-tablets and recorded hymns, had also given her a sense of guilt to add to her Japanese sense of shame. ' Oh, you naughty girl! You're going to feel badly about this!' they would chide her for some misdemeanour; and now she would go on feeling badly about this, that or the other for the rest of her days.

In the changing-rooms, one to half-a-dozen girls, everyone

became oddly modest and hastened into a wrap. Two girls in Sanae's room began to wrangle—one accused the other of taking her lipstick—and then suddenly they were clawing at each other and tugging each other's hair until the remaining girls intervened and dragged them apart. They all knew that it was not a lipstick but a man (and what a man! a retired municipal official already in his dotage) for whom they were now spitting and swearing at each other. Sanae shuddered, although her whole beautiful body was gleaming with sweat. They were like animals, disgusting; with the same determination to battle to the last mouthful of flayed fur rather than give up something which neither of them really craved and which could never even begin to assuage their appetites.

This contretemps was followed by another: when Ikuko, the girl with the swollen ankles, suddenly let out a yelp and jumped on to a box containing the scanty costumes and props used in the scene just ended. She continued to yelp at five-second intervals. 'What's the matter?' asked the Korean, who had already seen what was the matter and was continuing to rub her body down with a cloth doused in cheap eau-de-Cologne. 'Labour pains?'

A large dun rat was hanging, half in and half out, over the edge of the bucket into which the girls chucked their refuse. There were so many rats in the theatre that all the girls, except Ikuko, had long since grown inured to them and there was an archetypal story, told by the patrons, which went more or less as follows: 'There I was, watching them prancing back and forth and suddenly I saw this girl—a beauty, a real beauty. So I turned to the fellow who'd been getting a bit restless in the seat next to mine and said: "Take a look at that one, back row, third from the left." But there was no fellow there at all—just a huge rat, sitting up in the chair and watching, as excited as I.'

'She's had worse than that up her,' another of the girls laughed, kicking out at the bucket with her slippered foot. The rat slithered away under the partition between their room and the next.

Sanae removed her stage make-up and then worked over her face with extreme care. She had heard about Furomoto's proclivities: that he liked girls to be young, innocent and, if possible, virgin. Well, it was too late to do much about that last requirement. But the youth and the innocence she could still put on as facilely as she was now stripping off the layers of grease-paint.

Probably Nakatani's visit had nothing to do with Furomoto at all; but she could not take that chance.

At last she and the Korean, who was taking equally elaborate pains, were alone in the room together.

' Going out with anyone? '

' I don't know.'

' *Arama!* ' The girl had laddered her stocking. (That would teach her to cut her toe-nails more often.) ' Now what am I to do? '

' Don't wear any.'

' But he's sure to take me somewhere grand. Last time it was the Manhattan and I can't dance without stockings. Lend me yours! Please! You can wear mine; it won't matter if you're not going out with anyone.'

' Did I say that I was not going out with anyone? I said I didn't know.'

' Well, you never have a date. Do you? You know you don't.' She tossed her head and her breasts, hanging loose under her wrap (it was they, unusually large for Japan, which attracted her customers), swayed from side to side. ' I think it's mean of you.'

Sanae did not reply, but continued to apply lipstick to her mouth and then to rub it off, over and over again.

' Why don't you make up your mind once and for all how you want your lips? '

Again Sanae was silent; for she knew, from experience, that this was the most effective way of goading the Korean into one of her furies.

' Stuck-up . . .' the Korean began to mutter. ' Wouldn't hand one a glass of water if one were dying. . . . Stupid . . .' Worse abuse followed; but the other girl still refrained from any response.

Eventually the two of them left the darkened theatre at the same time; the Korean trailing in the rear, still muttering to herself as, near to tears, she tugged at a garter and glanced backwards and down at that ladder of hers.

Would Nakatani be there? And would he be in the Jaguar? Perhaps Furomoto himself would be reclining in the back, his feet in their hideous stub-toed shoes crossed, as usual, the one over the other.

' I thought that you were never coming out! Either that, or that you had used another exit.'

'Setsuko! I—I imagined . . . You told me that you were going back to Kyoto.'

'Well, that's what I planned. But then I said to myself, "Why not see one of these nude-shows which everyone is always talking about?" So I bought myself a ticket.'

'Sanae! Sanae!' It was the Korean calling, in a voice of saccharine falsity, as she stood, her banker beside her, before a Cadillac. (*Hired*, Sanae thought with contempt, glancing down at the number-plate.) 'Sanae dear! Just one word! Sanae!'

Quickly Sanae decided that if she were now to utter the crude phrases that came to her lips, she would lose face irretrievably; before Setsuko, before the banker, and worst of all, before that Korean *ama* herself. But, on the other hand, she could not ignore this insistent calling of her name. So at last she began to walk slowly towards it.

'You don't want that sort of thing,' the Korean came across to meet her and whisper; loud enough (as she intended) for the banker and probably for Setsuko herself to hear. 'It's not for you at all. And even if you begin doing it just for a good time, you soon get a taste for it. Look at Iori with the Ito woman. He'— she indicated the banker with a toss of her hennaed hair—'says he has a friend who wants to join us, make up a party. What d'you say?'

Sanae bowed with that superb Japanese irony so often mistaken by foreigners for courtesy. 'You are very kind. And so is your—your friend. But you have not—forgive my saying this—you have not understood the situation at all. This lady is not another Ito-San; neither in position nor—nor in any other respect. We are just friends'—again she bowed deeply—'as you and I are friends. But thank you, thank you.'

As she walked away, she knew that she had triumphed, over the girl and, even more important, over herself. Yet mingled with the pleasure of that triumph was a rage against Setsuko which she would now also have to conquer. To put her in such a position! And worse, she had now glimpsed, far, far off down the street, minuscule as a child's toy left abandoned in a gutter, the Jaguar from which Nakatani and perhaps even Furomoto himself must have been watching the whole scene. They, too, like the Korean, would make the obvious but false assumption; for it was notorious in all Japan that women of abnormal discrimination frequented such shows quite as much as men of a normal promiscuity.

Setsuko had already hailed a taxi. 'You must be tired, you poor thing.'

'Oh no.' But the tonelessness appeared as a confirmation; as did the sinking back deep into one corner of the limousine.

'You seemed to be one of the few girls who put something into it. The job must soon become as boring as scrubbing a lavatory floor; but at least you were determined to have that floor really clean by the time you had finished with it! What struck me was the complete *sexlessness* of the whole business. You might have been a troupe of performing dogs.'

'Thanks.'

Setsuko laughed at the monosyllable, not suspecting the savagery behind both it and the impassive profile revealed intermittently in lurid bursts of neon from the streets on either side. 'But extremely attractive dogs! Or should I say bitches?' She laughed again. 'That one who spoke to you just now—she's a real beauty. I bet that she's a favourite with the customers. *Ne?*'

'Oh, yes.'

'She's certainly got a magnificent pair of legs. That's where Japanese women so often fail. You don't,' she added. 'Yours are long too. But so many of them look so stocky when they're not perched up on *geta* in kimono. It's the distance between knee and ankle that is nearly always too small. Have you noticed?'

Sanae on this occasion did not even incline her head.

'There's something I'd very much like to know—please don't be offended! It's this. Of course one knows why people go to such places—and the old jokes about the tired business-men who arrive carrying plastic raincoats even on sunny days. But how many of the audience actually link up with the girls afterwards? And how many of the girls are, *sate*, in fact——'

'Prostitutes?'

'Oh, that's too harsh a word. I was going to say 'promiscuous'. . . . Do tell me, Sanae. You're not cross with me for asking? It's your work and that's why I'm interested—because I'm interested in you.'

'I don't know.'

'But you must have formed some kind of opinion. After all you've been there—how long is it? Four months? Five?'

'Yes, but I don't know. I've never thought about it.'

'Haven't you friends among the other girls? Don't you tell each other things?'

'I try to have as little as possible to do with them.'

'Very wise of you, I'm sure.' Setsuko's right hand, beautiful in its strength, covered the girl's, no less beautiful in its childlike fragility. 'I should think that they're a grisly crowd—looks apart. And the men must be even worse. Not to mention the women!' She gave her laugh, so different from the usual Japanese titter. 'I saw three faces I knew—people about whom I'd had my suspicions for some time.'

'And they saw you.'

Setsuko failed not merely to see the implications of this quietly vicious remark but even to see its viciousness. 'Of course, I'd known for ages about the Ito woman. She's completely brazen. Once I was at the cinema and she and a friend were carrying on a conversation in French about the maid of someone they'd just visited. I suppose that they thought that English might be risky but French would be perfectly safe.'

They had arrived at the station.

'I must go to the "o-toilé".' The word, derived from the West, had recently come into vogue. 'I have my "mens".' Few Japanese women would make such an admission even to their closest friends, and though Sanae had heard the girls at the theatre use the same faulty Latinism, now part of current slang, it shocked her that Setsuko should do so.

'Coming? Or will you wait for me here?'

'I'll wait for you here. I'll buy the tickets.'

As she picked up her change, jostled on all sides by impatient travellers, a voice said: 'Good evening' and she saw, on one of the two parallel bars which ran up to the guichet, a massive hairless hand with the nails gnawed down to the quick.

She raised her eyes to the blubber-face, but made no other response.

'She coming back?'

'Who?'

'The niece. He sent me for you. He's waiting at the Midori.'

'Well, he'll have to go on waiting.'

'You're not going to pass up a chance like that?'

She shrugged. Setsuko, had she witnessed the scene, would have been astonished by the laconic assurance with which Sanae handled Furomoto's emissary. 'What can I do? I've got another date.'

'Slip away before she gets back.'

'That's a clever suggestion. I'm staying with her.'

'So I discovered, for him, yesterday. . . . If you please Furomoto, you won't have to bother about places to stay for the rest of your life.'

'Like you? . . . Thanks.' It was as if she had stuck a nail-file into the mass of grub-grey jelly; it shivered and all but subsided in a heap. 'I don't know that I want to run a bar or even a house for the remainder of my days.'

'Better than working in either.'

'I don't want her to see you talking to me.'

'What'll I tell him? He's not going to be pleased——'

'I can't help that. That's your look-out. Oh, tell him that I was busy and'—she gave an ironic bow, similar to those she had given to the Korean—'express my regret and, of course, my gratitude for singling me out for this attention. And say that there are always other evenings, and that his niece is not my usual companion, and that—that I should be honoured to meet again someone of his pre-eminence. Is that enough?'

Nakatani was bemused; not merely by her coolness, in so great a contrast to the twittering trepidation of most of those girls whom he used to approach on behalf of his master, but by her use of a number of words at whose meaning he could only guess with difficulty. Still he understood enough to realise that she was not averse to meeting Furomoto again; and so eventually he gave his baby-grin, said 'O.K.', using the Americanism, bowed, one podgy hand on either deliquescent knee, and then melted into the throng.

A moment later Setsuko appeared. 'That's better. There are times when I hate being a woman. Don't you? No, of course you don't! I think that you're the most feminine person I've ever met.'

Once in the train, Setsuko at last fell silent, for lack of any response from her companion. That was the trouble with Japanese women, she decided; few of them had been trained to converse. Sanae was a dear little thing and it would be unfair to say that she was bad company; but there were times when she was just no company at all. What went on in her head during her long, impassive silences? What went on in the heads of most Japanese women? Probably nothing. How lucky they were!

As Setsuko thought this, watching the large drops of rain gather like blisters on the window, burst and begin to weep, Sanae bent forward and picked up the paper, the *Mainichi Daily News*, which some traveller had abandoned on the seat in front of them. 'No, dear, never pick up things you find lying about in railway-carriages. You never know who touched them last, or where they've been.' The twang of dear, dead, silly Miss Pilot's voice came back to her with the tooth-paste smell of chlorophyll tablets and the abrasive texture of her well-scrubbed palm. She had gone back to America, already an old woman—to where was it? Boston?—and had then returned to Japan only to die. In a Japanese inn, some-where among the foothills of Fujiyama, alone. Alone. She had sent Sanae a letter asking her to join her and—had she even answered? She *must* have answered, surely. Anyway she had not gone. No fun in accompanying a tedious old woman about Japan, forever obliged to translate her complaints, listen to her reminiscences and attend to her wants. Besides, she had not known that this was Miss Pilot's valedictory journey. How could she know? It was only later that she had learned, from one of the other Hiroshima girls. But now the thought both of the Ameri-can's death and of her own failure (but it *wasn't* failure!) blunted the edge of her vindictiveness against Setsuko and made her feel depressed instead.

What rubbish they printed! Even she, a Japanese, could see that without Colethorpe telling her. The English girl was always most scornful about the letters to the Editor which were signed 'Disgusted American', 'A Visitor from Adelaide', 'Irish Mother', etc., etc., but were so phrased that their writers could only be Japanese. Here was one, for example: '. . . to protest the in-commodity caused to innocent tourists by the harassment of pandas who infest the doorsteps and even the lobbies of Japanese hotels, howking their illicit prospects . . .' Even Sanae could see that there was something wrong with that, in spite of the re-assuring signature 'Major, U.S. Marine Corps'.

But the next letter, though equally blatant in its factitiousness, she read with a mounting unease. '. . . Seeing in your estimable publication the announcement of the decease of yet another Hiroshima maiden of a leucaeme attributed by many highly-regarded doctors to the delayed effects of atomic radiation, I write, as an American lady who has for long lived in your beautiful country, to ask: " SHOULD SUCH NEWS BE PRINTED? " I pray you to think of the mental TORTURE which every such news must afflict those who survived the Bomb, now reading and fearing for themselves. . . .' So there it was; what she had often thought

125

herself when she had happened to glance at the curt announcement of the death of this or that survivor of the disaster. In the case of her mother, the wait had been brief: the mysterious bleeding, the lassitude and nausea had set in only a few weeks after they had congratulated themselves on their miraculous escape. Her cousin, several years later, had developed what had seemed to be tonsilitis; but within a month had died. No connection, no connection at all, the American mission-doctor had told them over and over again in a kind of angry, agonised panic. But of course he *wanted* to believe that; he was too kindly a man to face the hideous truth of cause and effect, responsibility and guilt.

. . . So He waited for one: death. One day one would feel tired without a reason and decide that it was a change in the weather; or something would seem to have disagreed with one; or one would buy vitamin-pills because one's gums seeped blood. That would be the enemy, showing his hand at last: his patience exceeding one's own impatience as one stifled the coward's scream of 'All right, all right! But let's get it over! Let's get it over as soon as possible!' But He did not care to hurry. Why should He? Like some somnolent beast of prey He lay curled up, ravaging snout to tail, and one could not prod Him into action.

'What's the matter, Sanae?'

'Nothing. Why?'

'For a moment you looked so *odd*. Perhaps it was because I was seeing you in reflection—here, in the window. You looked quite —quite frightening.' Sanae laughed.

'Did I?'

'Perhaps you were reading about one of those murders they report in such disgusting detail.'

'As a matter of fact, I was looking at the letters.'

'*Sate*, they're even more terrifying!'

Later, in bed that evening, Sanae tried, by thinking of Furomoto, to obliterate the desolation in which she had lost herself. After the death of her cousin, when such panics were almost nightly occurrences, she found that she could overcome them if she dwelled, with an intensity of concentration, on every physical particularity of the youth, also a mission-boy, with whom she was in love and who was later to become her first and, in one sense, her only lover. But the charm of Furomoto's immense wealth had not the same power as the charm of newly-awakened sexuality.

She went over in her mind the car, the restaurant where he had been waiting for her, journeys to Hokkaido, Hong Kong, Manila, New York, jewellery (no cultured pearls!), clothes, a house of her own. The terrible dazzle still flickered around her. Yet once she had been able to say 'His . . . his . . . his . . . his . . .' and she had been free, miraculously free at once. One could not say such things of Furomoto; what disgusting images would be conjured up for one!

Colethorpe stirred in her sleep and grunted on the *futon* beside her. She lay in a foetus-in-womb position, knees to chin. Nothing would ever wake her; probably not even a man, Sanae thought vindictively. Yet, when at last she began to pray, she half-lay and half-knelt in her *futon* for fear that if she got out of it she might be seen by her companion. Why should that matter? Oh, she would certainly either tell Setsuko next morning or start exclaiming: 'Good Lord, Sanae, what *are* you doing? Is something the matter?' Did one pray only when something was the matter? Well, in her case, usually yes: she had to admit it.

Like a roll of contact-prints, shoved into the back of a drawer to gather dust in oblivion, the prayers now uncurled, one after the other: potent, not merely for themselves, but for their long-forgotten and now remembered associations—Miss Pilot's voice; the visiting minister who had taken it on himself to tell her at the conclusion of service that she had scurf in her hair; the time, at Christmas, when she had influenza and shivered in a dry, feather-light ecstasy until at the blessing she had been blown clean off into unconsciousness; the giggling, whispering, boredom, contrition, flashes of belief and near-belief. . . . Oh, God, save me, save me, save me! . . . I do not mind what you do with me, but do it now, do it quickly, do it now. It is the disuse, not the use, that is excruciating.

Early next morning, Colethorpe once again stirred and grunted, milking dry this sleep which was like some invisible maternal presence into which she had been enfolded; then opened one gorged eye, followed by the other, to see Sanae already clothed. 'Lordy! Are you up already? What time is it?' She hiccoughed, like a puking baby, and repeated: 'What time is it?'

'Oh, very early. Go back to sleep.'

'What are you doing?'

'I'm going out for an hour.'

'Going out? Why?' But she was already nuzzling back, the

invisible dug between her puffy lips, with no interest in the answer which in fact never came. Sanae had decided to attend the Bible Class at the mission.

It was many months since she had last made her way up the path which flanked the tennis-court (on one occasion that friend of Colethorpe's had been swinging between parallel-bars erected at one end) and entered the class-room with its smells of chalk, stale sweat and, less explicable, vinegar. (Perhaps one of the students had wrapped up in his *furoshiki* the *sushi* he would eat for his lunch.) It had been raining all through the night and the bench on to which she slid was damp, almost slimy. The peculiar green light under the low, livid sky seemed to emanate from the rash of mould which covered the tennis-court like scum over a pond. She looked about her. After all these months—nine, ten?—she had either forgotten all the faces or they had changed. Japanese enthusiasms, whether for religion or English, tended to be brief in their intensity; so no doubt this crowd was new. But, yes, there was the tiny, crumpled woman, in the folds of whose dress and skin the dust and grime lodged themselves impartially, with her large, vacant eyes in contrast to the tiny mouth which actually seemed to masticate the prayers in which she always insisted on joining aloud.

Welling entered, as always, exactly on the hour. He had grown thinner, she noticed at once, and—were that not impossible—taller. One bony hand grasped the Bible and register while the other smoothed his wavy red hair. Momentarily his close-set, blue eyes fixed themselves on her, with the unfocused gaze of someone who has forgotten to put on spectacles. Then the eyes shied away and the small mouth became smaller as he drew it in, opened the register and began to call the names. Hers was no longer there and when he had come to the end of the list, he stepped down off the dais and walked across to where she was seated below the window.

'I'm afraid I've forgotten your name.' She told him. 'What?' He leant forward, one hand cupping his freckled ear, and she repeated it. 'Yes, of course, of course.'

He looked round, vaguely scowling from under his bushy eyebrows, as the door opened and a young man entered, his arm in a sling. Sanae remembered his face, though he too was thinner and his expression of dissatisfied arrogance had become more pronounced. Still the same old blue suit and still the black tie knotted into a hard, frayed ball! But she had never seen him in *geta* before, his feet bare and far from clean. He did not apologise for his lateness; and when Welling began the introductory prayer, Sanae noticed, glancing sideways, that instead of sitting with head bowed, he was, to all appearances, perusing a newspaper he had laid out on his desk. She had always disliked him, even though she was prepared to admit what appeared to her to be his sickly good-looks and the sharpness of a mind he had more than once used like a razor to hack at Welling's convictions.

Instead of getting lighter, the class-room was darkening. The green thickened; there was a vague stench of sulphur to mingle with those other usual class-room smells. She felt the sweat breaking out under her armpits and wondered if her white blouse (the one in which Welling had actually first noticed her) was already showing the marks. Thunder boomed; and Welling's voice seemed to have a forced cracked note to it as he raised it in competition: '. . . Men's hearts failing them for fear, and for looking after those things which are coming on the earth. . . .' His nose, with its fine marbling of blue and purple veins, looked pinched and over-sharp; altogether there was about him a pathos which Sanae had never felt before. Sweat was running down the cheek which was turned to her and, following the firm line of the jawbone, now swelled in a large drop in the cleft of his chin.

Suddenly a tremendous blast of wind scattered rain, as though it were hail, across the desks, floor and students. The young man's newspaper rose into the air and then wrapped itself round the bony legs of the noisy eater of prayers, who gave an attenuated squawk. Some of the class jumped to their feet; others mopped themselves with the strips of towel which so often serve as hand-kerchiefs in Japan or giggled with suppressed hysteria. Only Sanae thought of going to close the window; and then, as she struggled with it, pressing it as though against some invisible animal which was fighting to get in at them, all at once there was Welling beside her. A memory flicked its tail and was still: 'I've been here before.' Momentarily his hand brushed hers and then, the catch secured, he was grinning and saying breathlessly: 'That's got it, I think. Thanks.'

She bowed.

The lesson continued. Outside, the rain, in drops the size of marbles, bounced on to the tennis-court to shatter itself in splinters. Inside, the room nuzzled deeper and deeper, like a foundered ship, into suboceanic slime and gloom. Welling's voice rattled about, a stone in a tin; a stone in her head. What was it about?—thunder, feet shuffling, the swish and slap of rain, and words, words, words ('Heaven and earth shall pass away: but my words shall not pass away,' that she understood). As he stood there, mouthing out this nothing, she thought of the illustrations in the Bible from which Miss Pilot used to read to them. 'David summoned before Samuel'? No, that was not it; the David like one of those brisk American girls in uniforms who drove high-ranking officers about in cars with fluttering pennants. Christ? No, Christ was also too emasculate, with his blond beard and ringlets and the large blue eyes which seemed always to be turned either upwards or down. St. John the Baptist? Yes, that was the one! There was the same starved fanaticism in the bony face; and the same straining of the whole lean body as though to carry some burden too heavy for it. Detail by detail the picture came back to her: the Nordic figure in the tattered Semitic robes, bestriding a rock, a stave gripped in one hand while the other was raised histrionically above his head, to harangue a crowd of grey-beards, centurions, and women whose arms were loaded with bracelets. When, like a transfer, the whole scene had unpeeled itself off in her mind, she once more looked back at Welling; to find that he was staring at her.

After the brief cannonade of rain, the sun had begun to flood, molten, over the sill of the window and Welling was asking: 'Does that sunlight bother you?'

She started and shook her head at the same moment as Asai, his face the same grey as the sling which supported his arm, said grumpily: 'Yes, it gets across my eyes.' Welling's question had not, of course, been intended for him.

Simultaneously Sanae rose and Welling stepped down from the dais; so that once again they were both at the window at the same embarrassing instant. What followed was even more embarrassing. The old woman, Sarah, who both looked after Welling and cleaned the mission class-rooms, had fastened the cord of the blind, not around the hook intended for it, but lower down, on to the handle of the window itself. However, another cord, which drew the black-out curtains on those occasions when slides or film-strips were shown, was twisted around the hook. Sanae began unwinding this higher cord at the same moment that Welling released the cord below it. The slats of the blind clattered

130

downwards in a shower of dust, with as much noise as if each were a sheet of corrugated iron, and the loop, shooting out of Welling's hand, caught itself under Sanae's chin. 'Good Lord! Oh, I am sorry! I say!' The whole class was convulsed with laughter: not because of anything inherently comic to them in this scene of knockabout farce, but because the unexpected and the sudden in Japan often serve to release, like a sharp knock on the handle of a tap, a gush of long-withheld hysteria. Sanae herself covered her face in her hands, while her whole body shook with giggles. Welling, who had already removed the cord, was still apologising. 'Did I hurt you? I thought I was going to strangle you. It would have been terrible if you'd been yanked up as high as the curtain-rail, out of our reach!' This humorously-intended picture seemed to him to elicit the right kind of response, in a renewal of laughter. (And yet people said that the Japanese were lacking in a sense of humour!) But in fact each of those present was laughing because each, in imagination, was seeing this pretty little student in her over-tight white blouse, dangling, with swollen, purple face and protruding tongue, high up among the curtain-folds.

'Sure I haven't hurt you at all?'

Incapacitated from answering by shame, embarrassment and the giggles she still could not control, Sanae scurried back to her place where she buried her face in her arms for several seconds on end.

Now Welling himself, as he resumed his lesson, began to sense something peculiar. The response which had seemed to him a moment ago to be wholly right now seemed to him to be wholly wrong. It was the prayer-eater who had first given him the clue: her tiny mouth chattering, as though in extreme cold, while the laughter fell out of it like ice-cubes and her vast eyes were frozen in a strange panic-despair. Asai, too: his grin more a grimace, expressing, not amusement, but derision and even a kind of sadistic enjoyment. (Really! I'm letting my imagination run away with me!) And the girl: if her giggling continued, he would be tempted to give her the classic slap recommended in cases of uncontrollable hysteria. It was all a little unnerving.

. . . Slowly order, or a semblance of order, returned. The gnome-woman began to masticate, under her breath, on the text which he himself was reading; Asai's grin-grimace subsided into his expression of usual sulkiness; and Sanae was now sitting up straight, with only a faint pinkness about the throat to betray her previous fury of embarrassment.

When the lesson was over, Welling watched her as she walked out of the class-room last of all the students. He felt an idiotic impulse to talk to her—why? what about?—and was glad when he noticed that Frank, who had been limbering up on the parallel bars beyond the tennis-court, had waved to her in greeting. 'Hi, there! Sanae, hi!' Now he was even calling out, in that high-pitched, nasal voice which was so oddly belied by the deep-chested magnificence of his physique. Sanae hesitated, and then at last halted. She bowed to him as he approached. 'Tell Aileen that she made a mistake in not coming to the movies with me last night. It was a fine show. Wasn't it, Mike?' Welling had just emerged from the class-room. 'I had to take him along, since Aileen failed me. A poor substitute!'

'So you know one of my pupils?' Welling said.

'Sure. Sanae here is the room-mate of Aileen Colethorpe. You know Aileen.'

'It's a long, long time since you last came to class.'

'Yes, I was—busy. I am sorry.'

'Well, you know the story of the prodigal son!' Frank squeaked.

Sanae bit on her lip, frowning. Welling was always vaguely irritated by his colleague's jocularity, suspecting, rightly, that the Japanese tended to be either bewildered or offended by it.

'The prodigal son?'

'Yes. Mike here ought to be rejoicing over your return to the fold far more than over the constancy of those who have stuck his class out for weeks and even months on end.'

Sanae gave first a nervous smile and then a jerky bow. 'Well, excuse me please. Goodbye, Mr. Ryan. Goodbye, Mr. Welling.'

The two men watched her as she picked her way along the path, careful not to wet her shoes, and then disappeared from sight. 'Some girl!' exclaimed Frank.

'Yes, she's a pretty girl,' Welling modified.

'But it's an odd thing—you know, somehow I don't go for these Japanese girls.'

'Perhaps that's just as well.'

'Take Sanae and Aileen, for example. Well, I'm not going to pretend that Aileen is the more beautiful of the two. Of course she isn't. But she's the one I go for. The other—well, maybe it frightens me.'

'Frightens you?'

'Guess so. Don't know where I am. Those Japanese women—they might do anything to you. No, sir, I wouldn't marry one of them, not in a thousand years. . . . Still, she's a lovely girl. A lovely girl.' He swung himself between the parallel bars and then flicked his body over once, twice, thrice. 'I don't deny that. A lovely girl. Lovely.' Again the three flicks of the body. 'But she's yours, all yours. All yours, Mike.'

NINE

SETSUKO often tells me that I am never happy or even moderately contented in Japan: an exaggeration, of course, just as I unconsciously exaggerate, in order to entertain her, my dissatisfaction with this or that aspect of Japanese life. But it is certainly true that I tend to wake up each morning with a groan of despair and a tugging of the bedclothes over my head rather than an exclamation of delight and a throwing-back of the bedclothes; and that perhaps is as good a test of happiness as any other. How different are my wakings here from my wakings in Athens! I remember how I used to lie in bed watching the early sunlight pulse more and more strongly over the Acropolis, Phaleron and Aegina, and the dry, hot air was like some drug, with none of a drug's cruel aftermath. Ahead of me lay a day bristling with difficulties: the need to get the Aliens Police to renew my residence-permit; classes of students grown refractory and even openly hostile because of the Cyprus situation; and always the ever-present anxiety of how to earn enough to feed myself. Yet that air seemed to float me out over this dismal prospect and I could look down and view it with a complete equanimity. 'I can't understand why you hang on. Life must be a misery'. It was often said to me; and yet I have never been so happy in my life and shall probably never be so happy again.

But the nastiness of waking here! One grows conscious of a dampness of the cheek, hair and neck, and of the dampness of the sweat-saturated pillow beneath them. One raises one's head and has the sensation that an elastic band has been slipped around one's temples, congesting the blood-vessels. Nine hours! And yet one feels as if only three or four had passed. Endo-San will have already heard one move and will be preparing the breakfast; next, he will run one's bath and set out one's clothes. At the University the students will be attentive and respectful; and later in the day one will go to a reception given by the Mayor or the Governor or the Chief of Police. All smooth, all easy; and yet as savourless and indigestible as a Japanese bean-cake.

Sometimes I ask myself if, in making this contrast between then and now, Athens and Kyoto, I am not merely trying to externalise what is, in fact, not a change of circumstances but a change in myself. (The old problem, is it one's own train which is moving or the trains on either side of it?) This combination of disgust, horror and pity with which I increasingly view the spectacle of life in Japan; might I not now feel it for life *anywhere*, even in England, even in Greece? Is it the Japanese who are different from others; or is it I who am now different from my former self? I do not know; I cannot know until I get away from here.

Yet this morning I awoke as I used to awake; not, admittedly, to that marvellous panorama of bald, humped hills, with houses scattered like shoe-boxes around them, of infinite sea beyond and of infinite sky above, but with the same light-headed euphoria, which on this one occasion survived my usual sensation of having spent the whole night curled up like a caterpillar in an empty jam-jar. Was my pillow tacky with sweat? The top sheet twisted, a monstrous wet-compress, around my left leg? Lukewarm rain spattering into the garden as though into a slime-covered tank? None of this mattered. I lay back contented: listening, with a dreamy pleasure, to all the sounds—hissing of water into kettle; tinkling of crockery; clatter of milk-boy—which usually get on my nerves merely because they are so many invisible filaments jerking me, a fish gasping, not for water, but for sleep, out of my bed.

It is all, of course, connected with Setsuko. Last night we returned from a trip to the Ise Peninsula.

We had often talked about this expedition; but as in the case of many other plans which she has broached to me, I never expected anything to come of it. Setsuko is one of those people for whom an exhaustive discussion of some project—the production of one of Yeats's Noh-influenced plays; an anthology of poems written in English by Japanese writers; Easter in Hong Kong— becomes a substitute for the project itself. Yet, she has too much practical shrewdness to be typical of those who prefer fantasy to reality. How does one explain it? . . . The Grand Shinto Shrine of Ise, the pearl-fishing of Toba: although I told myself over and over again that the former would be pretty-pretty and clamped, the latter simply another tourist-attraction like the cormorant-fishing of Gifu, yet for some reason I could not rid myself of the idea that these two would be different; the shrine awe-inspiring, numinous; the pearl-fishing beautiful in its primitive simplicity, with naked women plunging off rocks into the sea to return with their treasures. Well, about the shrine I was not wrong.

At the last moment Setsuko nearly did not come. The Japanese girl had developed a sore-throat and since Colethorpe had to go into Osaka to see the owner of a gallery where she hoped to have an exhibition, Setsuko at first declared that she would have to stay with her guest. It was (as I pointed out, not without annoyance) absurd: the girl had not even got a temperature, Colethorpe was unlikely to be away more than two or three hours, and Mrs. Furomoto would, in any case, be at home. 'Yes, but she and my aunt don't get on. Don't you understand?' 'Whether they get on or not, your aunt is unlikely to refuse to help her when she is ill. Not that she is *really* ill.' 'You're so unsympathetic.' Eventually it was Sanae herself who, with unusual firmness, insisted that Setsuko should on no account cancel the trip. What was Setsuko about? Did she, at the next to last moment, decide that two days in my company would be tedious or even embarrassing? Or did some motive of coquetry, whether conscious or unconscious, impel her to dangle me over that cliff before twitching me back to safety? I cannot really believe that she was anxious about Sanae, because ill-health, whether in herself or in others, fills her with impatience.

She had borrowed a car—a Chevrolet which had obviously been driven beyond endurance for the eight or nine years of its existence and was now on the verge of a total collapse—from one of her friends in the laboratory and it was into this that we piled our luggage and ourselves and lurched off into the rain. Every conceivable disaster followed: a puncture; a total failure of the brakes; a second puncture; a leak of the radiator; a puncture again. But with her, in her mood of that morning, none of this mattered. She flagged lorries and cajoled their drivers into stepping down and giving us their help; and when, on a stretch of road oddly deserted for over-crowded Japan, no lorry appeared, she herself insisted on changing the tyre. 'No, no, I'm much better at this kind of thing than you are! When I worked for the Americans, I was always doing it.' She had brought a delicious lunch prepared, she told me, by herself: a Vichysoisse which we took it in turns to drink out of the cup of the thermos; liver pâté, spread thick on hunks of flaky new bread from the German bakery; cold chicken and salad; and those mammoth Japanese strawberries each wrapped, like liqueur-chocolates, in paper and arranged in a wooden box. 'I forgot to wash them. Are you nervous?' Setsuko teases me about what she calls my hypochondria. 'Yes. But they look too good to miss.'

She was sitting cross-legged on the ground-sheet, the uptilted breasts never more beautiful than in that man's check-shirt and the face never more expressive of health and serenity. How tired one grows of the Japanese mask which conceals everything—or nothing; and what a relief (almost like the cessation of some physical pain) to look into a countenance where everything is set out as well-lit and ordered as the exhibits in a museum show-case for one's loving observation. I suddenly felt an impulse to slide forward—that was all that was needed—to place my head in her lap, my arm round her waist; but as I shifted my weight on my haunches, she had suddenly risen, brushing away crumbs and then yawning, her arms stretched above her. 'That wine has made me sleepy. I think I shall doze for half-an-hour in the car before we drive on. That way we'll get to Ise at about three. Don't forget to wake me.' She went over to the Chevrolet and curled up on the back seat, leaving both doors open; and I remained where I was, to watch her. The rain had stopped about an hour ago, but with each gust of wind raindrops spattered down on to me, the remains of our meal, and the roof of the motor. Lazily I began to tidy up: taking my time about it, with an occasional glance at her motionless, slumped form. Ten minutes to go now; I wanted a cigarette. Then I remembered that my case was in the breast-pocket of my jacket and that I had taken off my jacket in the clammy heat which had followed the rain. I went close to the car. The jacket rested along the top of the back seat, one sleeve dangling down so that her head actually reposed on it. Yes, I could reach the pocket without disturbing her. Like this. I leant over her, careful to make no contact, and inserted my right hand in the pocket. She made a curious sound, half gasp and half groan, and shifted over on to her back, drawing up one knee which struck against my shoulder. Until that moment I had had no intention of touching her; but now, helped no doubt by the wine, I stooped and kissed her on the side of the throat. Again that curious sound, the gasp-groan which seemed to well up from within her and force its way between her slightly-parted lips. No more, however. Emboldened, I kissed her throat again, then her cheek, her forehead, her lips. At the last, she stirred and seemed to whimper like an animal in sleep. Then, all at once, awoke.

'Oh, heavens! Is my time up? I had such a wonderful, wonderful sleep.' She tossed her hair away from her flushed face, on to the side of which the sleeve of my jacket had imprinted a crimson rectangle.

'I wish I knew what I had been dreaming about, I can never remember my dreams.'

'Something nice.'

'H'm. I think so.' Did I imagine that for a moment a shadow of unease passed over her radiance? 'Oh, it's maddening not to know! . . . Well, let's get started. But give me a cigarette first, please. It'll help to wake me up.'

At Ise she found some distant relative of hers who was a priest at the shrine. There are a few places—Delphi and Stonehenge are among them—which give even a materialist like myself a shudder of the supernatural; and it was that same shudder which I now experienced as we walked under the huge, ancient cedars dripping water, from hundreds of feet above, on to the lush, steaming vegetation below. By the river, our guide pointed out to us the pilgrims who washed their hands and rinsed their mouths there before worshipping at the shrine; and at once Setsuko sprang down the bank to join them—an odd action for one who had so often scoffed at Shintoism, and indeed at all religion, in my presence. Perhaps she too had felt the touch of that invisible wing which time and again that afternoon I sensed beating above us. Yet what mumbo-jumbo she herself had said it all was: the sacred mirror handed down by Amaterasu-Ohmikami to Prince Ninigi; the reporting of all news of national importance to the shrine; and the frequent visits of the Emperors!

Later, as we drove away, she was strangely silent and thoughtful; until at last she said: 'You know, there was something in that place. It did something to me.'

'To me too.'

'I've always hated Shintoism. In Buddhism there is a great deal one can respect, and in Christianity too. But Shintoism represents all that is most nationalistic and stupid and narrow in Japanese life. Yet . . .' She shrugged her shoulders. 'It got me.'

'Yes, I understood at last what was meant by a Sacred Grove. It was really "awful"—in the original sense of the word.'

'Perhaps all the millions of pilgrims have made it so—just as I think that all the millions of pilgrims have made Lourdes what it is. If the same people, with the same belief and fears, trekked out to pay the same homage to the Statue of Liberty or to Big Ben, then perhaps they, too, would give one the same shiver down the spine. All that emotion must in the end accumulate a deposit, even when it itself is spent; as when water has evaporated.'

In Toba we found, what we had not expected, that all the hotels appeared to be full; nor did we have to look for a reason. Along the narrow main street were parked at least a dozen tourist-buses, each bearing, back and front, a placard which read:

Kansas is a City in which Everything is New
But we also Love the Old
Greetings to the Lions of the World from the Lions of Kansas

Eventually we found an inn of the third-class where, we were told, there was one room vacant. We looked at each other.

'Well, I don't mind,' Setsuko said. 'Do you?'

'Not in the least. It always seems to me so silly to imagine that two doors and a few feet of corridor will prevent people from doing anything that they want to do.'

'Or that the absence of two doors and a few feet of corridor will oblige them to do it! . . . I expect that, in any case, the room will have one of those glassed-in porches—so we can observe the proprieties of having a wall of some kind between us when we sleep.'

Not so good: and she was right about the porch, a common feature in Japanese inns.

We were advised by the maid that if we wished to have the bathroom to ourselves, we should go down at once. Setsuko went first, making it clear that she expected me to wait my turn; and while she was away, I tried to read the guide-book she had brought with her. But I could not concentrate on it. What was going to happen? And what ought I to do to ensure that what I wanted happened? The Japanese bath, when my own turn came, loosened these knots of anxiety and tension as effectively as it loosens muscular aches and fatigues, and I soon ceased to trouble myself. One way or another, it would all work out, I decided.

The meal was brought to our room, in the Japanese fashion, by the maid assigned to us and we sat facing each other, each in a yukata or summer-kimono provided by the hotel, while we ate.

139

The meal, like most Japanese meals, was wonderfully pretty; but to devour a picture by Dufy would be equally palatable. Our maid was suffering from a cold; but since, in Japan, to blow one's nose in public is considered impolite and even immodest, she preferred to sniff over us, with a nauseating rattle of catarrh, as she fed us this or that tit-bit or poured out the saké. Eventually I could stand it no longer and, going over to my suitcase, I pulled out a handkerchief which I presented to her. '*Arigato gozaimasu . . . Arigato . . .*' The thank-yous, smiles and sniffs succeeded one another for seconds on end; long after the handkerchief had been slipped, unused, into the bosom of her kimono. Again I went to my suitcase, pulled out another handkerchief, and blew my own nose into it with a violent snorting; then I pointed at her. At last she understood and scuttled from the room.

'You are naughty!' Setsuko reproved me.

'I wish she'd leave us alone for good. I hate all the fussing that accompanies a Japanese meal. And the more expensive the meal, the worse it becomes.'

After dinner we wandered out along the beach. The intermittent rain of the day had ended in an evening of an extraordinary clearness and stillness. The waves lolled inwards and crumbled, as though composed of something more solid than water, their crests extending in grey, unbroken lines, one behind the other, under the low moon. Suddenly from one of the houses overlooking the beach we heard the sound of Chopin's famous Polonaise strummed out on a piano that was not quite in tune. 'This is Japan!' I exclaimed. 'Here are we two in our *yukatas*, walking this deserted beach; and over there is the *torii* of a temple——'

'A shrine,' Setsuko corrected.

'Well, then, a shrine. And there, in front of us, is the kind of moon and the kind of sea which we've seen in innumerable Ukiyoe prints——'

'And which innumerable poets have described——'

'And now, from that house, we hear that abominable imitation of Rubenstein playing that abominable Polonaise. Probably some schoolgirl is seated in her kimono—not at the *shamisen* or the *koto* which would be appropriate—but at a cottage-piano——'

'Yes, it's a pretty picture! But I'm sure you're wrong. The pianist is an American.'

'An American?'

'Of course. A Lion. What do you bet me?'

140

But I could already see that she was right. The house was a Japanese inn: and we had by now moved far enough around it to be able to see into a Western-style 'lounge', all bamboo furniture, chintzes and mirrors, where two men and a woman sat slouched (asleep? ruminating? listening to the music?) while a third man, his back to us (three rolls of pink flesh under thinning, grey hair) pounded at the piano.

'Oh, Setsuko, that spoils it all!'

'Docs it? Why? That's also modern Japan.'

We stared into the hideous interior; and as we did so I moved a step sideways and slipped an arm through hers.

'It's too awful to contemplate,' she said; disengaging herself and walking on.

Back in the hotel, she played an elaborate game of patience on the floor, using three miniature packs of cards she had brought along with her, while I again tried unavailingly to concentrate on her guide-book. As she stooped over to move the cards, the fold of her *yukata* would fall away to reveal the pink of her brassière and an expanse of skin that was luminous in the sidelong glance of the lamp on the floor next to her. At last she began to sort out the cards. 'Silly game. One spends endless time on it and at the end one is no better and no wiser. Just a way of pushing round the hands of the clock.'

'Is that necessary?'

She laughed. 'Did that sound rude? . . . Well, I suppose we'd better turn in. I'll get the maid to bring in the *futons*. Do you want the porch or this room?'

'Oh, you have the room. The porch may be draughty.'

'Sure?'

'Sure.'

'Then I'll go and sit downstairs while you undress—the porch is far too narrow for that—and you can call me when you're ready.'

'Oh, really! Is all that nonsense necessary?' I wanted to exclaim. With many other women—my dead wife, for one—I could have said those words. But Setsuko has a kind of chilling authority which halts one; as though she herself were saying aloud: 'No further. Get back. Enough.'

I lay in bed, having substituted a pullover rolled into a ball for the small, tough, Japanese pillow, and, my hands behind my head, watched her shadow on the paper-screen. The lamp distorted it crudely; it might have been that of the catarrhal maid, the American woman whom we had seen slumped sluggishly in a bamboo chair in the next-door hotel, or indeed anyone else. But it was Setsuko; and it filled me with an intolerable excitement.

'Well, goodnight,' she called at last. 'Goodnight.' Click; darkness. And at once I began to shiver; at first intermittently and then with a violence that shook my whole body and made my teeth rattle in my head. We had been right about the porch being draughty; but to shiver like this on a summer night could only mean either a fever or an excessive nervous tension. Was I really so wrought up? It was odd to have to ask myself that question; but I just did not know. I had not felt a similar malaise since my days as an undergraduate.

Outside the porch I could see the long line of the waves sweep gently inwards, with an audible swish and thud; and I could still hear the piano. Dvorak's 'Humoresque'! Would I ever be able to sleep? From below there now came a nearing clop-clop—horses or high-heels?—and suddenly an American voice, a woman's: 'No, I don't think Japan is expensive, Ida. Think how little you can buy for seven dollars in Hawaii, or even Manila. . . .' Seven dollars? Why seven dollars? Why not one—or ten? The magic number? The piano had stopped; and Setsuko, what was she doing? Asleep? I tried with a conscious effort to control the shuddering of my body; and then became aware that I should soon have to empty my bladder, yes, now, now. But how could I get to the lavatory without passing through the room? Well, pass through it! And at the same time I could fetch a sleeping-tablet from my suitcase. Setsuko could hardly upbraid me for having to perform an unavoidable function of that nature. Only now do I see that, of course, there must all along have been an unconscious determination to return to the room; and that I provided myself, again unconsciously, with the best of all possible pretexts. As I tiptoed past her, no more than a humped shadow in the moonlight filtered, like milk, through the paper-screens, she stirred, mumbled something and at last got out my name: 'Bill?'

'Yes, it's only me.'

'Oh.' A gasp.

The lavatory seemed to be even icier than the porch; and the water (it was nothing else) poured out of me in a never-ending stream. Above the wash-basins was a long, blotched rectangle of a mirror and I stared at myself in it. God! Even in an hour and a half I had the appearance of having produced a whole night's growth of beard. My consternation was, I now realise, also part of that subconscious decision somehow to sleep with her which had brought me to the lavatory in the first instance and would now carry me back, to God knows what folly. I rubbed a hand down the bristles of my right cheek: yes, she would hate that—I all-but thought, thought and did not think.

When I re-entered the room, she was lying as she had lain when I had kissed her in the car: on her back with one knee raised and a hand flung out behind her. She was breathing deeply in apparent sleep. I went over to my suitcase and took out the glass cylinder of tablets; and then once again my body performed the seemingly involuntary action which, in fact, I willed it to perform. The cylinder fell from my fingers, scattering tablets here, there and everywhere. I knelt to pick them up, my hands groping over the *tatami*. One gleamed in the crook of her arm, from which the sleeve of her pyjama-jacket had rucked up to expose the flesh. I stretched and at the same moment, as if in sleep—perhaps really in sleep, I cannot even now be sure—the arm rose and encircled my neck. 'Setsuko!' The eyes remained shut; the breathing continued with the same regularity. I threw myself out on the floor beside her, turning my head so that my lips now rested on the palm of her hand. Slowly, with the same trepidation (but infinitely magnified) which I had experienced in the taxi on the way to the art-gallery, I let my own hand crawl towards her *futon*. I slipped it inside; felt her big-boned shoulder, the smoothness of her neck, her breast and then at last the nipple, gorged with an astonishing desire. At that last contact, she tossed from side to side, as though in a nightmare and finally, as I increased my pressure, arched her whole torso and began to moan like some victim tied to the rack. 'Setsuko!' But nothing would rouse her from her condition of trance.

No longer caring what I did or what might be the consequences, I slipped into the *futon* beside her. Fingers clutched at my hair and jerked it in a frenzy; then her teeth snapped on my lower lip. As supple and as steel-like in its coiled strength as a tiger's, her body thrashed and writhed beneath me, while strange groans, whimpers and inarticulate cries burst from her. Soon we were both streaming with sweat. But her eyes never opened; she gave no overt indication of consciousness.

When I left her at long last, the salt taste of blood in my mouth and my whole body aching, she was lying exactly as she had been lying when I had first entered the room : on her side, knees drawn up, with her breathing coming in a slow, steady rhythm which seemed now, as I stretched out again in the porch, to be only an echo of the rhythm of the waves crumbling endlessly on to the empty, moonlit sands.

'Well, how did you sleep?' She had drawn back the screens and, already dressed, was smiling down at me. I rubbed my eyes and then propped myself on an elbow. 'It's a lovely morning. I've just had a swim.'

'A swim!'

She nodded. 'My first of this year. Wasn't it brave of me? No Japanese ever swims until August. I felt that everyone in the town was watching me as though I were an escaped lunatic. . . . Breakfast will be up any minute now. How was it here? Not too uncomfortable, I hope.'

'No. . . . No. . . .'

'I slept wonderfully. I suppose I must have been far more tired than I realised. I tend to wind myself up and then, when I finally relax . . .' I had extricated myself from the *futon* and was beginning to slip into the *yukata* provided by the hotel. 'Did you pass through the room at some time during the night? I seem to remember that I was half-awake and I *think* I even called your name. At first I thought that it was a rat. These old wooden buildings are infested with them, of course.'

It was incredible; it is still incredible to me. Was it a consummate piece of acting? Or could she really have been in some state of hysterical trance? Or am I the one who is a victim of self-delusion? I know, of course, that the Japanese have an astonishing gift for not letting the right hand know what the left hand is doing : a form of hypocrisy so subtle and so all-pervading that it makes what is commonly regarded as British hypocrisy seem mere pantomime in comparison. But can any woman deceive herself, or be brazen enough to expect to deceive someone else, on such a scale?

'Yes . . . Yes, I did get up once. I went along to the lavatory. And then, because I couldn't sleep, I took my pills out of my suitcase.'

'Oh, that explains the two pills I found on the floor! Did you drop them?'

'Yes.'

144

'Here, I'll give them to you.'

There was no trace of shame or even embarrassment; no hint of complicity in that frenzied scene. And so it continued throughout that whole day.

The pearl-island—to which one has to travel in a motor-boat even though the short distance between it and the mainland could easily be bridged—proved to be even worse than I had feared. But Setsuko would have none of my complaints. She was in a mood when everything was interesting, amusing or beautiful; and she herself was all these three things to a degree I had never known before. The real culture of pearls takes place elsewhere and it is virtually impossible to see it; no doubt because it is both more laborious and more squalid than this show put on for tourists. From shed to shed we were herded: now to the Museum of Pearl-culture; now to the Laboratory where girls in kimonos, obviously selected for their pert good-looks, were introducing into the oysters the nuclei about which pearls would form themselves; and now to the shop where the products were on sale. In the shop a blue-haired woman with a long, red nose was telling her friends: 'Well, my advice to all you people is: Wait until we get back to Tokyo and I can take you to this man of mine in the Imperial Arcade. He's so honest, you can be sure of him. First time we went in, he gave me this cute little brooch—just like that; said he'd taken a fancy to me—me, can you imagine!' She pointed with an index-finger to a minute opalescent drop which looked as if it had just slipped off the tip of her nose on to her freshly-laundered blouse. 'Pretty, isn't it? He told me it's a special kind of pearl—from where was it, honey?' The man who had been playing the piano the previous night poked his head about on its three rolls of pink flesh and eventually got out, 'Can't remember.' 'Why, he remembers nothing! Not even the way that Polonaise thing of his should end. . . . Well, after that, we knew we could trust him—that he wasn't the kind to gyp us. So we went back and back and back and took a lot of our good friends along . . .'

The final attraction was an exhibition of actual pearl-diving by four girls dressed in long white shifts, with circular masks over the faces. By then it had again begun to drizzle and we, the spectators, stood huddled in raincoats or under umbrellas while the divers took it in turns to bob beneath the greasy waters. 'My, but they must get cold!' The woman with the pearl-drop was at my elbow, a ciné-camera in one hand and a Leica in the other.

'Let's go,' I said to Setsuko. 'We've seen enough, haven't we?' 'Oh, no!' She turned to me, astonished. 'This is the most interesting part of all. I don't want to miss any of this.' 'But it's all exactly the same. First one goes under, and then the next, and the next, and the next. And it's not as if they ever bring anything up.' 'But they might. That's the thrill of it.' Exasperated, I wandered off to a rain-speckled pond in the depths of which somnolent red-carp brooded. But 'Please', a voice soon roused me from my vaguely erotic meditations on the events of the previous night. 'Please.' It was one of the girls who acted as guides, each of them dressed like an air-hostess, with a whistle dangling on a string around her neck. She pointed to the others. 'Thank you, I am quite happy here.' 'Please?' 'I—am—quite—happy—here.' 'Pearl-diving—you see pearl-diving?' 'I have seen it.' 'Please?' 'I—have—seen—it.' 'Pearl-diving not finished.' At that I turned away and walked off resolutely towards the ludicrous museum, deciding that the Japanese are as much upset by the odd man out as a hostess by the appearance of a kitchen-spoon among the cutlery on her dinner-table.

When I returned, the diving was over; but Setsuko, the American woman still beside her, was now in conversation with two of the shivering, grinning divers, the skins of their hands and feet like crêpe-rubber and their shifts clinging to their squat bodies. They, too, had obviously been selected for their looks rather than skill and were accustomed to being photographed, as they now demonstrated by posing, arms around each other's necks, for the American woman. 'Do ask them for their address and I'll mail them a copy just as soon as they're ready.' 'And I'd be very grateful if you'd send me a copy too.' 'Why, yes, I'd be delighted. . . . Now let me photograph you as well. With your——' she eyed me, hesitating, and at last finished—'Both of you together. Yes, that'll make a lovely picture. Now smile, people—smile!'

When we at last got away, Setsuko was full of the charm of the divers; the kindness of the American woman; and the interest of all that we had seen. I myself felt wet and disgruntled. The inevitable consequence was that we soon began to bicker.

'You spoil things for yourself. And not only for yourself, but for others too. Why should you call that poor woman a horror?'

'Well, she is a horror.'

'I thought her extremely nice and friendly. You British are all so stuck-up and standoffish. And the way you were looking at those girls—as though they were two jelly-fish which had been washed on to the beach.'

'The comparison is not a bad one.'

'Oh, I know that they're not educated, not sophisticated. But have you no interest in how people different from yourself think and feel and live? Sometimes I find you so——'

And so on and on and on, until lunch and a bottle of saké brought an end to it. Then we began the journey home. Setsuko had not allowed me to drive on our way out, but now she said that she was sleepy and asked me to take the wheel from her.

'I wonder how Sanae is getting on?'

'Why?'

'Why! Have you forgotten that the poor thing has a bad throat?'

'Ah, yes.'

'Aileen is fond of her, of course, but she's such an impractical sort of girl and she doesn't look after her as she should.'

'But does Sanae need to be looked after?'

'Of course she does! She's still terribly young—and terribly vulnerable.'

'I wonder.'

'You don't know her.'

'Yes. That's true enough.'

'I feel so sorry for that girl. What a life! She hasn't a single relative left in the world, not a single one. And one can imagine the sort of things she has to put up with in that theatre. Aileen tells me—and I'm sure she's right—that though all the other girls have their lovers, Sanae has always refused to play that game. Of course if she did, things would be much easier for her. In one sense. Japanese men are generous with their women—though the women, God knows, have a lot to put up with. Did you know that kissing was almost unknown among the Japanese until after the war and that it's still confined only to the educated? The idea that a woman ought also to achieve an orgasm would amaze most Japanese males . . .' Eventually she drowsed off; no doubt because I was so intent on avoiding the lorries that bounded up out of the swirling rain at us that I made little attempt to answer. It was then that the third extraordinary event happened.

Deeper and deeper into the seat she settled herself, breathing with a slow regularity, until her head suddenly slid on to my shoulder.

A moment later it was her whole body that tipped against my own. And then her hand gave a brief, convulsive flutter and rested —was it merely an accident? Or behind that mask of apparent sleep was her will orchestrating each of her movements until this final cadence was achieved? I put my own hand over the hand resting on me (all but colliding into the back of a braking lorry, as I did so); caressed the finger-tips and the smooth palm, then briefly kissed her forehead. But no vestige of response came to match my own increasing insistence.

. . . Her eyes did not open until we had reached her house. Having helped her in with her suitcase, I was about to take my leave when Mrs. Furomoto appeared. I have always thought that she likes me; but it is difficult to tell, and now for the first time, I started to wonder. After all, I never even suspected that she did not care for Sanae until Setsuko told me. 'How was the journey?' she asked.

'Oh, wonderful,' Setsuko replied.

'I am glad to hear that.' For a moment she looked closely into her niece's face and then spoke some words in Japanese of which I only caught—or thought I caught—'. . . red . . . Sanae . . . cold . . .'

Setsuko laughed and replied in English: 'But I've never felt better in my life! I didn't realise how tired I was: the trip was just what I needed. And don't you think Bill looks better too?'

Mrs. Furomoto merely inclined her head, with a faint smile.

'How is Sanae?'

'Oh, she left for her work a few minutes ago. Miss Colethorpe went with her.'

'For work! Is she crazy?'

'She said that she was better. She spent all day in bed.'

A Japanese-style visiting-card lay on the table and Setsuko now stooped and picked it up. She gave her aunt a look of enquiry.

'Yes, he called round about half-an-hour ago.'

'What did he want?' Now it was Setsuko who spoke Japanese. Mrs. Furomoto's answer was incomprehensible to me.

As Setsuko put down the card again, with a brief look of impatience, I tried, by glancing down at it, to make out the name: impossible, both because of the distance and because it was written in kanji.

'Who is it?' I suddenly asked. Even Mrs. Furomoto displayed a momentary surprise at my inquisitiveness; but I was in that condition when the lover must know even the most trivial things about the loved one and I could not restrain myself.

'Oh, that boy.'

'Which boy?'

'I think you met him here once before. The one that works—or used to work—in one of my uncle's factories. Remember?'

'Oh, that one.'

'Yes, that one.' She smiled: 'Satisfied?'

The odd thing was that somehow I had known all along that it could only be he and no one else. And yet how was that possible? Of all their innumerable Japanese friends why should I pick on him? I had met him only once; Setsuko had shown no special interest in him; I had no cause for jealousy.

'I did so enjoy it, Bill.' She came down into the garden with me. 'Thank you again.'

'Thank *you*.'

'We must do it again. Soon. Very soon.'

What was I to make of those last words? They could mean everything; or nothing.

TEN

ASAI'S friend, Kanizawa, came of a family of *eta* or outcasts and he still lived in the outcasts' quarter. The *eta* have no more official existence in modern Japan than anti-Semitism has in modern Germany; but as tanners, slaughterers, petty criminals, sellers of human manure and pedlars of old clothes, they still congregate in the same narrow, rat-infested alleys of weatherboard, corrugated-iron and bamboo, and still inbreed among themselves for want of partners from classes superior to them.

Asai stepped fastidiously over or around the puddles in his way, and kept covering his mouth and nose with a handkerchief as some stench of a particularly nauseating pungency slithered out and pounced on him. Momentarily he stopped to watch a man, wearing only a loin-cloth, grappling with a hag who was flailing her skinny arms about his head and shoulders and shrieking abuse. Asai never considered, for an instant, the possibility of intervening. What would be the use? The man would certainly get the better of him, even if his arm were not in a sling; and, as often happened, the harridan would probably join in on the side of her assailant. Only a few days ago the paper had been full of the story of a well-intentioned German tourist who had been found, lying unconscious with one kidney ruptured, after attempting to rescue a woman who had at once joined her lover in kicking him almost to death.

Further on two children, with the precocious, etiolated beauty of the slums, sat playing a game with pebbles and bits of wood in the dust under a wall. Asai, without realising it, stepped on to one of the lines which marked out their domain, making them at first cringe away from him, as though in fear that he would assault them, and then, when he was at a safe distance, shrill out abuse of a terrifying obscenity. It was all too hideous; wipe them out, wipe them out, wipe them out, as one wiped out their diagram from the dust in which they had scratched it!

Yet if he had cared to look, there were patches—here a bruised flower, there a charred branch putting out leaves in the general devastation—of order and grace. Sometimes it was only an old woman crouched in a doorway, shelling peas or weaving a basket; sometimes, glimpsed through the parting of paper-screens, a mother suckling her baby at her breast, in somnolent absorption; sometimes two students, perched like birds on the parapet of a well to discuss their classes of the morrow. Were all these too to be wiped out? If asked, Asai would have said 'of course not'; but each throb of his hand in the sling and each fainter throb of his head was saying 'Yes, yes, yes.'

The Kanizawa family lived like well-to-do farmers in a house which was itself like a well-to-do farmhouse, untidy and permeated with the smells of animals but well-built and spacious, in the heart of the ghetto which they and a few compeers could with accuracy be said to rule. Like farmers they were provident, even stingy, and had a dislike of any interference from the state. It was rare for a child from the *eta* class to enter a university and they were proud of their son's feat; even though they blamed on this 'education' a dissatisfaction which they could neither share nor understand. Did he wish to be like that Asai boy who was never even properly fed and whose mother was known to sell herself for what little food did in fact come his way? And what, on the death of old Kanizawa, was to become of all the innumerable small businesses which pullulated, as hidden yet persistent as roots of couch-grass, through the teeming soil of the quarter? Jiro had no interest in them; and how could his two sisters, for all their spirit, manage in his stead?

Asai had visited the house only once before, and now, having lost his way, he had to ask a scabby youth on a bicycle to direct him. The boy, who was wearing close-fitting black trousers and a locket on a heavy gold chain around his attenuated neck, omitted all the usual courtesies as he simultaneously tinkled on his bell and drawled out his answer. Asai could have struck him. Yet he was always railing against the meaningless politeness, conventionality and hypocrisy of Japanese life and demanding why people could not show outright what they thought and felt.

To approach the entrance to the house he had to make his way through an ample courtyard which was soggy with rain and manure. He could hear some pigs thudding about, squealing and grunting; it appeared, from within the house itself. Piled one on top of each other, as in the Asai's own backyard, but far more numerous, were rusty wire cages containing poultry with rheumy eyes and beaks, or rabbits with twitching noses alert for food. In the dimming light of evening he could make out, in a shed, the white form of a girl bent low to milk a goat which was crunching on something green and leafy.

'Oya, Asai!' Kanizawa had been lying on the floor of the room, in the semi-darkness, listening to the baseball scores on the wireless; now he jumped up and plunged at the light-switch. 'Come in, come in.'

Asai remained poised for a moment on the doorstep as though hesitant to enter, his eyes fixed with a gaze at once wary and sardonic on the baby-face revealed, smooth, greenish and beatific in welcome, beneath the naked light-bulb.

'How is your hand?'

Asai shrugged. 'They lanced it yesterday and gave me another injection. But it seems to be coming up again. I think I have a fever.'

'But it's weeks since it started!'

'They say that my general condition is poor. I need a holiday.' Now at last he came into the room and threw himself down on a cushion. 'I feel as if the whole of me were poisoned, not just this finger. If you pricked me, I expect that pus, not blood, would ooze out.'

Kanizawa's face crumpled squeamishly. 'Don't!' he protested. 'What a stench you live in! How can you stand it?'

The other was not offended by a remark which had been intended to be offensive. 'Iya, habit. Habit makes everything tolerable.'

'I've been living twenty-six years. Oughtn't that to have become a habit by now?' Kanizawa had turned the wireless down, not off, and was still half-listening to the scores. 'How someone of your intelligence can waste hours not even playing that idiotic game—that would be better—but just listening to news about it!'

The other clicked the wireless off. 'Yes, I know. But it's a relaxation like any other. When I come back from the laboratory, my mind is too tired for reading—or even for intelligent conversation.'

'As if you got any of that here!'

Again Kanizawa refused to take offence. 'You misjudge my father. He's not educated, but he's shrewd. I'd far rather listen to him than to'—the baby-face split in a grin—'than to myself. He has much more to say.'

At this moment old Kanizawa could be heard coughing out-side, each cough followed by an obscenity; then he entered, his feet bare and grimed, the toe-nails like talons, and his whole diminutive person giving forth the same sourish odour which, far fainter, exuded also from his son. He was almost entirely bald, with four or five strands of greasy hair brushed forward from the back of his head on to the forehead which bulged out over a face that was at once foxy and womanish. He dressed like a peasant and behaved like one; but few peasants ate as well or drank so much. He disliked Asai, who, more than his son's other friends, seemed to him to have infected the boy with both discontent and a craving for change, and for that reason he now dispensed with any elaborate formalities and merely grunted his greetings. (Like one of his own pigs, thought Asai; but they were probably cleaner.)

'Hayashi is bringing an American to look at the two dogs,' he informed his son. 'You'll have to translate.'

'All right.'

'And just translate what I say. Don't add anything, don't leave anything out. And don't change anything.' The boy grinned as his father turned to their guest: 'He's no use as an interpreter. I know what I want to say, I know exactly, but he always has to say something different.'

'Sometimes you're rude.'

'When I *want* to be rude.' The old man again began to cough and then pulled back one of the paper-screens to void the phlegm in his mouth into the yard. 'We don't often see you.'

'No.'

'Is your work going well?'

'H'm. . . . Yes.'

The old fox had probably heard of his dismissal and was now either nosing for further information or was trying, obliquely, to get at him. But it was better not to rise to the provocation. What would one gain?

'I hope they pay you more than this fool here gets. I could put him on to a hundred-and-one ways of making ten times what he brings back from that laboratory of his each week. What's the good of all his education when he has to come to me when he needs a new shirt? Yes, that one he's wearing now. My money paid for that. Even his shirt I have to pay for.' He slunk away, muttering and coughing to himself, into the dark, noisome recess of the house, as though it were some subterranean lair.

'He's right, of course. It's a disgrace what they pay. If I'd learned to be a carpenter or a paperer . . .'

'But you're useless with your hands. I remember at school.'

Once more Kanizawa merely grinned good-naturedly. 'Yes, I'd not make much of a carpenter or a paperer, I admit.'

'What are these dogs?'

'Oh, two Akita dogs that he found.'

'Akitas! Then they must be valuable.'

'I suppose so.'

'Of course they are. How did he find them?'

'They were strays, I think.'

'But who would allow dogs like that to stray?'

'I imagine that they must have got loose. I think that my father said that the bitch was on heat. She must have broken her chain and the dog must have followed her.'

'And how did they come into your father's possession?'

'*Sate*, you know that he deals in dogs. He's a kind of—well—unofficial dog-catcher.'

Kanizawa was becoming increasingly uncomfortable; and Asai, alert to this, was encouraged to persist in his interrogation.

"*Unofficial* dog-catcher? What do you mean?'

'You know that there are city dog-catchers, don't you?'

'Yes, *city* dog-catchers.'

'But, apart from them, there are other people who are allowed to pick up stray dogs. They're not paid, like the official catchers; their money comes from—from eventually selling what they find.'

'And how do people reclaim their lost dogs? From these *unofficial catchers*, I mean.' Purposely he surrounded the two words with an aura of suspicion and sarcasm. 'I know of course that there's a pound for dogs caught by the catchers employed by the city. But in the case of these . . .'

'I don't know.'

'Haven't you ever asked your father?'

Kanizawa shrugged and reached over to turn on the wireless. 'I've never thought about it.'

'And these two dogs? I suppose the American is going to buy them.' He had to shout against the announcer's voice. 'Oh, turn that radio off!'

Kanizawa merely lowered the volume. 'I think that that's the plan.'

'And the dogs that aren't bought—what happens to them?'
Kanizawa was silent. 'Well? What happens to them?'
'Some go to the hospitals. But they pay little. It's hardly worth the trouble.'
'And the others?'
Kanizawa giggled. 'They're eaten.'
'By you?'
'Of course not, *baka*!' The giggle had acted as a release and at once he was relaxed again; even switching off the wireless as he explained: 'The Koreans and Chinese and some even of our own people in this quarter pay high prices for dog-meat. Didn't you know that? Especially if the dog is red.'
'Red?'
Kanizawa nodded and again giggled. 'Don't ask me why. They think that if a dog is red, the meat will be better. Like brown eggs—equally unscientific.'
'And they'll pay for such—such offal?'
'Oh, yes, yes. Otherwise my father wouldn't be interested. *Ne?*'
'It's astonishing the things he undertakes! I'd no idea that this—this *catching* of dogs was one of his occupations.' Asai used the Japanese verb *toru*, which could mean either 'catching' or 'stealing'.
'You'd be surprised.'
It was annoying that Kanizawa persisted in not being riled: such good nature was in itself a provocation.
'And to think that only a few days ago I threw out four puppies. Imagine. I suppose that I could have got a good price for them. Are puppies more expensive than grown dogs?'
'I haven't any idea.'
'After all, veal is more expensive than beef, *ne*? But what a sensible solution! And I never knew it existed. There's no doubt about it, Chinese and Korean civilisation is far superior to ours. There are too many dogs in Japan, so let's eat them. Especially as there is also too little meat.' He jumped up and began to stride up and down the room, watched by his friend. 'And human beings, too—why not? What an excellent plan! *Ne?* Instead of having all these Buddhist scruples about the taking of life so that dogs and people alike are dumped out on the rubbish-heaps to die of their own accord—painfully—disgustingly—without any assistance. Suggest it to your father. It should appeal to him.

Man-catching instead of dog-catching. I can tell him all sorts of places to go for his prey. There's a sewer which comes out into the Kamogawa river, large enough to drive a train through, and you'll see hundreds of people sleeping in it every night, wrapped up like parcels of meat in newspaper—he can take his pick! Or the railway-station. There's a bar opposite—did you know?—to which old men go to pick up other men. You just stroll along the entrance at midnight, examining those louse-ridden wretches. You shake a shoulder, "Want a meal?" you say. It's as easy as that, I'm told. Of course they want a meal and they'll do anything you wish to get it. Your father could drive a van up and bundle them all in—no one would care, no one would even notice.' Sweat was streaming down his contorted face, and as these words poured from him, he kept rocking his bandaged fist back and forth in his other hand. Kanizawa began to regard him, not with amusement but with a mounting alarm.

'Sit down, sit down,' he cried out at last. 'I'm sure you've got a fever.'

'Yes, I'm sick. You're right. I'm sick.' Like all those who habitually conceal their emotions, the Japanese luxuriate in them histrionically on those rare occasions when they have started to put them on display. Asai now clutched at his head with his sound hand, tears bursting from his eyes to mingle with the sweat already streaming down his face. 'If you knew how sick I felt. And not only sick with this'—he extended his bandaged hand—'but sick with life, sick of life. I want to end it, end it all.' He flung himself down on the floor again, on his stomach, and buried his face in the crook of his arm, as he reiterated: 'To end it, end it, end it.'

Kanizawa moved on his knees towards him, his baby-face doleful and yet for once attractive in the readiness of his sympathy. 'But it's not as bad as all that,' he coaxed. 'You have a bad finger which will get better. You've lost a job, but you'll soon find another one. If it's money you need—sa—I can probably get my father to——'

'Oh, you don't understand, you don't understand! You're so stupid.' Kanizawa recoiled, his lashless eyes blinking, as though his friend had punched him in the face. 'It's not me, not myself. It's this whole—whole stinking world.' Asai let out a brief, hysterical laugh. 'And I don't just mean this quarter of yours—though few places could be worse, I agree.' Then all at once, he

156

sobered up, raised his body, and faced his friend, his legs crossed beneath him. 'Kanizawa—you've got to help me.'

'Of course, of course.' In his eagerness Kanizawa even put his hand inside his jacket to draw out his wallet.

'No, not like that, *noroma*! Not a job. Not money. This is something different. Something—more difficult. But you've got to do it for me, do you understand? You've got to do it, because it's the last thing I'm ever going to ask of you.'

Kanizawa's small eyes rounded; even though he reminded himself that Asai, in the way of many Japanese students, had often enough talked of suicide in the past without ever attempting it.

'What is it?' he quavered.

'You must get me a bomb.'

'A bomb?' Kanizawa now squeaked.

'Yes, a bomb, a bomb. Must you repeat everything I say?'

'But where should I——?' He stared at his friend with the horrified suspicion that he must have gone out of his mind.

'Don't they make bombs in that laboratory of yours? Couldn't you make one?'

'But . . . but the kind of bomb on which we are working . . .' He giggled: from a combination of pent-up hysteria and the thought of attempting to purloin for Asai the still imperfect nuclear device on which the director of his institute, a Nobel prize-winner, was working in semi-secret.

'What's the joke?'

'Nothing. But you don't understand. The sort of bomb you want—we—we just don't have that——'

'Then make one for me!'

'Make one?'

'Didn't I tell you not to repeat everything I say in that imbecile fashion? Your laboratory must have everything needed to construct a simple bomb.'

'But I've no idea how one——'

'You're a scientist, aren't you?'

'A theoretical one. You said yourself that I'm useless with my hands.' Again he gave his dreadful giggle. 'If I made you a bomb, it would either never go off or go off too soon! You know that, Asai.'

'Oh, what am I to do, what am I to do? And I thought that I could count on you.' Again he buried his face in the crook of his

157

arm and tossed and writhed, as though in some physical agony, on the floor.

'But why—why do you need this bomb? What are you planning? What is it? '

Asai stared up: not at his friend but, over his friend's shoulder, at nothing.

'I have to kill someone.'

'Kill someone? '

'Someone. Or many people. I'm not sure.'

He must be joking! Kanizawa told himself; and then again the thought slithered, cold and venomous as a snake, into his mind: He must be mad!

'But—but why, Asai, why? '

'To say No. To say Stop. To say I've had enough and you've all had enough.'

The smooth forehead crumpled as the baby-mouth pouted in bewilderment. 'I—I don't understand you——'

'Of course you don't. *Baka!* ' Asai leapt to his feet; and then, becoming his normal self with an abruptness which should have put Kanizawa on his guard, but did not do so, smiled down: 'Never mind. I shouldn't have mentioned the scheme to you at all. There are other ways of getting what I want, others who can help me. . . . Never mind, never mind! And don't go on goggling at me like that! '

Kanizawa beamed his relief, his puffy white cheeks all but touching his pencil-thin eyebrows. 'For a moment you frightened me.'

'That's nothing to the state you're going to be in.'

This cryptic remark was lost in a shout from the older Kanizawa. 'Oi, Jiro! *Oi!* The American is here! '

'I must go and translate. Coming? '

Asai shook his head. 'No. I'll start for home.'

'Why not stay and eat with us? '

'Dog-meat? No thanks! '

'Of course not, *noroma!* '

'Only human meat will do for me now.'

Asai was smiling; and Kanizawa therefore again tittered at what he presumed to be a joke.

In the yard, old Kanizawa was standing beside a vast, silver-haired man in a shaggy tweed-suit of the same improbable purple as his face and swollen hands. This was Ed Schneider, the alcoholic

American correspondent. Towards them, a third man, ancient, and as insubstantial as a wisp of smoke, was attempting to drag two huge black dogs with triangular faces at least twice the size of his own. 'Come on, Jiro, come on,' old Kanizawa snapped at him; while the American walked towards the dogs. 'Take care.' Asai paused to watch.

The dogs were snarling, their teeth gleaming against the red of their drawn-back jowls. 'That's all right. That's all right. Good boy. That's right. Yes, yes, yes. That's right. Yes. . . .' The slurred, nasal voice (Schneider was drunk, though no one present as yet suspected it) was as hypnotic as the movement of the purple hand alternately down the spine of each of the crouched dogs, lulling them into docility. 'That's it. Easy now. Easy. . . .'

The Kanizawa son bowed. 'I am Kanizawa. I speak a little English. This is my friend Asai. I translate for my father.'

'Well, these are handsome beasts, very handsome, Mr.—Mr. Kawakami.'

'Kanizawa.'

'Yes, very handsome. Where did your father steal them?'

The boy stared at the foreigner, with open mouth, as the colour flooded up into his cheeks and then spread to his forehead. Schneider took the two leashes from the old attendant: 'Not that it really matters. I don't mind. But of course it makes a difference to their price.' Suddenly he turned to the father and astonished them all by addressing him in perfect Japanese: 'Yes, they'll do. They're what I want. I'll give you ten thousand for the two.'

At this last sentence they were even more stupefied. 'Ten thousand!' old Kanizawa exclaimed. 'Ten thousand! But such dogs are worth at least fifty thousand each.'

'Yes, on the open market, *sempai*. But do you really want to sell them on the open market? Would that be wise? Eh?' He rocked back and forth on his heels, at the same time rubbing his swollen hands down the sides of his purple jacket.

'I can easily find someone to offer me more than that.'

'Can you? How many Japanese can afford to feed such brutes? Can you, for example?' Suddenly he fixed his bloodshot eyes on Asai, putting the question to him. 'Of course you can't! You probably feed at less cost than one of these. No, *sempai*'—he turned back to old Kanizawa—'sell them now, sell them at once. While you have the chance. Before anyone knows that you have them. And before they eat you out of this dung-heap which you regard as house and home.'

Kanizawa began to mutter furiously under his breath to his son: foreigners, and especially Americans, were known for their rudeness, but this one exceeded all bounds. Asai and the attendant were, on the other hand, both of them delighted to witness the old rogue's discomfiture.

'Well, that's my offer,' the American continued. 'I can't wait. Here's my card. If you're interested, call me before nine o'clock this evening. Not after nine o'clock because I shall be in bed. . . . Goodbye. . . . Goodbye. . . . Goodbye.' He handed the two leashes back to the attendant and then turned to give each of them in turn a parody of a Japanese ceremonial bow.

ELEVEN

TODAY the students of my University have been having what they call a Field Day and we should call a Sports Day. Ignoring an invitation to attend, as well as compositions to be corrected and the lecture, still unwritten, which I must deliver at the American Cultural Center on Monday next ('American Expatriate Writers'), I decided to spend the afternoon in the garden, reading through a stack of back-numbers of the New Yorker which Mrs. Ambleside lent to me when I recently attended a bazaar at the mission. The rainy season is over; but I feel that with so much else that it has washed away, it has soaked out all my initiative and energy. Even Setsuko, the most desirable object which Japan has to offer to me, sometimes now seems to be not worth the trouble of attainment.

I had barely stretched myself out on a deck-chair and begun to read when Endo-San emerged from the house and walked noiselessly down the gravel-path towards me. 'Gentleman, two ladies to see you, sir.'

'I'm out!'

'Yiss, sir.' He bowed, but remained where he was.

'Tell them that I'm out!'

'Yiss, sir. But gentleman, two ladies see you flom load.'

'Who are they?'

'Yiss, sir. Mission gentleman, two Japanese ladies.'

Hell! I chucked the New Yorker petulantly back on to the heap. 'Bring them out here.'

'Yiss, sir.'

'And bring some more chairs.'

'Yiss, sir.'

It was Welling, followed by a diminutive, vaguely grubby, middle-aged woman in a mottled blue skirt and a straw hat with artificial rosebuds around the brim, and a girl of seventeen or eighteen, all protruding bones and teeth.

'Sorry to disturb you like this. This is Okada-San who attends one of my classes. And this is her daughter, Chiyoko. Chiyoko wants to study in England and so they came to me for advice. Some hope! As if a backwoodsman like myself from the wilds of Austraïlia '—he seems to be incapable of saying that word without deliberately distorting the vowel—'knew anything about Domestic Science colleges in the old country.'

'Do sit down.' Endo-San had already carried out two deck-chairs and deftly erected them. 'Please.' At this invitation, the mother gathered up her voluminous skirt in both hands, as though it were a bundle of dirty linen, and with a coquettishly artificial simper, sank into the chair I indicated. Her daughter merely glanced at Welling, who cried out: 'No, no, sit. Chiyoko, sit! I'm not a Japanese man, you know. Ladies first for us! I can wait.'

'Sit,' her mother translated.

The girl sat; but hunched forward, on the horizontal wooden slat, her bony elbow resting on one equally bony knee, as with her other hand she scratched at a ring of mosquito bites about her ankle. I was afraid that at any moment her chair would tip over.

The enquiry was of a kind to which I have long since grown accustomed. The girl had no degree, no qualifications of any kind; she could not even speak more than a few words of English. On television she and her mother had seen a film about a Domestic Science college in England and they had both there and then decided that she should go to it. 'But I am a widow,' the mother explained. She gave her artificial simper: 'Excuse me, I am poor.' I explained that the journey to England alone would be dear; apart from all the expenses once the girl had got there. 'Yes, I know, Mr. Knox. I cannot pay the ticket.' Why then, I wondered, discuss the project at all? 'In that case . . .' I said; I smiled, I shrugged. Welling bit on his unlit pipe, and then took it out of his mouth and pointed at the mother: 'Okada-San thought that perhaps Chiyoko might win a scholarship.' A scholarship! Was she crazy? And was Welling crazy enough to encourage her in such a notion? Mastering my exasperation, I began to explain that the competition for scholarships to travel abroad was probably stronger in Japan than in any other country of the world. 'But she is such a clever girl!' the mother interrupted. 'And she is Chlistian girl, too. I have her glades here, all her glades.' She opened a bag so vast in comparison with her own diminutive size that I expected her head to disappear entirely inside it. 'One year she has diphthelia, she velly ill. Next year her glades not so

162

good. But now velly good, velly, velly good.' The pathos of it was awful; but Welling, reclining beside her and biting on that unlit pipe of his, seemed totally unaware of any pathos at all.

At last the two women decided to go : the mother ruffled and resentful that I had been of so little help. She wanted, I knew, to be coldly dignified as she thanked me and said goodbye; but her height would have made that difficult even if she had not contrived to clip her bag shut on a fold of her skirt—a fact which her daughter was trying to convey to her by gestures so agitated that she might have been suffering from chorea. Welling stayed, explaining that he would like to have 'a little pow-wow' with me —'if you're not too busy, that is.'

'Nice little woman,' he murmured as he once again settled himself in his chair.

'But, God, how dreary!' There were people—admittedly few in Japan—to whom I might have said that; but not to him. I decided to keep silent.

'She never misses a class. Once she had flu—in the big epidemic last year—but did she stay away? Not on your life.'

'How very inconsiderate of her!' But again I could not say it.

'I thought that you might know of some sort of scholarship or grant for which she could apply. You must have a lot of contacts with the academic world.'

'Very few.'

He took that for modesty and merely smiled benevolently at me as he knocked out his pipe on a strut of his chair. There was a silence, broken at last by Endo-San who appeared with a tray on which, unbidden, he had set out tea.

'Oh, you shouldn't have bothered,' Welling said, not realizing that I had not bothered at all. 'This is very hospitable of you.' He sipped from the cup I handed to him and the marbling of purple veins on his long, thin nose became more pronounced. 'Excellent. A real English cup of tea, nothing like it.' The tea had, in fact, been given to me by an American friend who had got it from the PX. 'Well, how has life been treating you?'

'Not too badly. But I can't stand this climate.'

'Or the people, from all accounts!' he grinned. Someone— Mrs. Ambleside? Mrs. Crawley?—must have been gossiping to him.

'Well, they're like the climate. They take getting used to. And there's something humid and muggy about them too, I find.' The tea, I realised, was in fact disgusting; chiefly because of the chlorine which has impregnated the water ever since the rainy season began. 'I have no energy here. And I'm normally an energetic person.'

'I feel rather *down* too. I don't know what it is. Not ill, not worried about anything in particular. Just vaguely depressed. Know that sensation?'

'Who doesn't?'

He frowned into his cup. 'Wonder what's the cause of it?'

'Oh, something physiological, I'm sure of that.'

'Physiological?'

'Something trivial which is wrong with one's liver or one's gastric juices or one's blood-pressure or one's bowels.'

'But I haven't had a day's illness in years!'

'I don't mean an *illness*. Just some kind of temporary imbalance.'

'Imbalance?' Clearly he neither understood nor liked that word. 'You mean——?'

'I don't know what I mean. I'm just theorising. Let me give you some more tea.'

'Thanks. I haven't had a cup of tea like this for—well, since I was with your boys for a spell at the end of the war.' Again he sipped; and again the nose darkened and grew shinier. 'Perhaps it's the news from my wife,' he at last got out tentatively, as though he were nibbling at something he suspected of being poisonous. 'It may be that.'

'Nothing bad, I hope?'

'Oh, no. But she's had to delay her return. She hasn't picked up as quickly as the doctors hoped and they want her to have some further treatment before allowing her back. Nothing serious, nothing serious at all. But they don't want her to take any risks.'

'I expect you miss her.'

'I'll say! Being unmarried yourself, you probably find it hard to understand how a man can——'

'I was married once.'

'Were you? I'd no idea! Then I've really put my foot in it. That's it, Welling—always the tactless clot. Honestly, I'm sorry if I've said anything that might have——'

'Of course not! How were you to know?' It was like brushing aside the apologies of someone who has inadvertently bumped into one's recently vaccinated arm or trod on one's foot. 'All I wanted to say was that I can understand how you feel. Very well.' And you're lucky, I continued; but in silence. You know that she'll come back; or, at least, you expect that she'll come back or hope that she'll come back. It's the lack of all expectation and hope that is the worst part of all. Like having to undergo an operation for a condition which you know to be inoperable.

'You know, I'm only realising now, for the first time, how much I depend on her. You must meet her when she gets back. You'll still be here, won't you? . . . You have certain things in common,' he added, as though he had only just thought of this.

'Have we?'

'Oh, of course she's not as brainy as you. She's just another crude Australïan, like yours truly. But you've both got a kind of—kind of toughness."

'Toughness!'

He laughed. 'That doesn't sound too complimentary, does it? But I mean it as a compliment. I bet people turn to you for advice and support, as they do to her.'

'And to you too, I'm sure.'

'Only because of this.' He gripped his clerical collar, as though to wrench it off. Then he sighed: 'Without her, I'm only half what I am when she's along. You'll see. At present I'm like a car that's running on only two of its cylinders. It's an effort, I can tell you. Of course I've got friends—Americans, English, Japanese —masses of 'em. But if you knew how lonely I sometimes feel——'

I was growing increasingly embarrassed; and it was therefore with relief that at this moment I heard a voice shrilling 'Hi, there! Hi there! Mr. Knox! Hi!', even though my relief was soon to change to consternation. A pair of false teeth seemed to be opening and closing of their own accord between two of the privet-bushes which made up my hedge. Then a chubby child's hand appeared, waving up and down. Then the peak of a tweed cap. Oh, God, God, God! It was the scenario-writer who had asked me in the train if I were 'a gay'.

'You are supplised to see me?' The pigmy-figure toppled out of the hedge, crushing a clump of asters. (Endo-San was furious when he saw the damage later.)

'Well, yes. My guests usually come through the front-door.'

'You are velly difficult man to find. Velly difficult.' He saw Welling. '. . . Please, I am Mamoru Taiichi. Taiichi means Fat-Big, but I am Thin-Small.' He tee-heed, as he had tee-heed on the train when making the same witticism, and at the same time clutched Welling's hand in both of his. 'But I am clever. I have not your addless but I am clever. Today I visit German fliend who is much intelested in Zen—you know Zen?—and I think, maybe German fliend knows Engrish fliend. German fliend says that you teach University, so I go University, and from University I come here. And you are having Engrish tea-party? I have always wished to partake of Engrish tea-party.'

I shouted to Endo-San to bring another cup and refill the teapot and we all sat down.

'You are clergy man?'

'Yes, that's right.'

'I velly intelested in clergy man. Ploblem of sex and religion. Velly intelesting.'

Welling merely bit on his pipe and scowled.

'This is big ploblem, I think. Clergy man no mally, but clergy man have sexual desire like other man. How to do?'

'But in my church the clergy *do* marry.'

'You mallied?'

Welling nodded.

The little man clapped his hands together in delight. 'You mallied! That is good, velly good! You mallied man!' He seemed to think that, in getting married, Welling had performed some act of exceptional bravado. 'Then for you ploblem is non-existent. But this ploblem intelests me. I want to write scenalio about pliest who loves girl. At first I think boy, but girl better, I think. Geisha girl maybe? Plostitute maybe?' He dragged his brief-case, as battered and worn as his shoes, up on to his knees and released the right-hand strap from its buckle (the left-hand buckle was missing). 'I have blought short-story in English for you to collect please. Storly of poor young man from countly who has nowhere to sleep, lain falling, velly cold, so he goes into mortualy, has intercourse with dead woman. Maybe he catches disease from her, maybe not. I not decided yet. Prease.' A sheaf of tattered typescript was thrust into my hands. He swung his legs back and forth, like a child on a swing: 'Storly good, Engrish maybe not so good. You collect, prease, and then we send *Atlantic Monthly*.'

All at once Setsuko, Sanae and Colethorpe had appeared in the part of the garden that belongs to Mrs. Furomoto.

'These ladies live with you? One is Engrish lady, I think? I am intelested to meet Engrish lady. Engrish ladies too cold, Ameli- can ladies too hot. Is that tlue?'

'I wonder if we might join your party for a moment? Furomoto has just called on my aunt and none of us wants to meet him,' Setsuko said.

'Please. I am Mamoru Taiichi. Mamoru Taiichi, Mamoru Taiichi.' He had thrust himself in front of me and began to shake hands in turn with each of the women. 'Taiichi means Fat-Big but, as you see, I am Thin-Small.'

'You know Mr. Welling from the mission?' I asked.

'No, I don't think I've met either of these two ladies yet.' He shook hands with Setsuko and Colethorpe. 'Kato-San is a member of my Bible Class.' Welling laughed: 'An *occasional* member, perhaps I should say. But a very welcome one, none the less.'

I went indoors to tell Endo-San to bring three more chairs. When I returned, it was Welling, and not Mamoru as I had expected, who was talking. '. . . I can't understand how we've never met. Of course I've heard about you both. Mrs. Ambleside sometimes visits your aunt, doesn't she?' Setsuko nodded. 'And you're a friend of Frank Ryan. He's often talked about you to me. He's a nice boy, a very nice boy. And what a physique!' These last remarks, though generous in intention, had about them a clumsiness which obviously caused embarrassment to Colethorpe.

The comment which followed from Setsuko struck me as even more likely to cause discomfort; but, in her case, I suspect that she knew exactly how and where she was treading. 'I often wonder that Aileen and Frank Ryan get on so well. After all, as a missionary, he must take his religion very seriously. Whereas Aileen is almost as anti-clerical as myself. Aren't you, Aileen?' Colethorpe turned her head away from Setsuko and stared at the bed of asters which Mamoru had crushed, in a pretence of not hearing what was said to her. 'It says a lot for their friendship that it can bridge a gap of that kind.'

'Excuse, prease. Is this lady in love with clergy man?'

We all, even Colethorpe, laughed; there seemed to be no other answer possible. Mamoru glanced from one to the other of us in hurt bewilderment, wrinkling his little nose. 'There is joke?' he asked at last.

'Of a kind,' I answered. Then I hurried to change the subject: 'I didn't know that Furomoto and your aunt still saw something of each other.'

'Of course you knew. I told you myself. But you've forgotten.' She was right; but there seemed to be no reason for the note of

167

acidity on which she spoke. 'He comes to her for advice, odd though that may seem. When he's specially worried about something. I don't think she's ever very pleased to see him. She'd never say so, even to me, but I'm sure that she dislikes him, even hates him by now. Not surprising, really, after the way that he's treated her.'

'Excuse, is this Furomoto of Furomoto Industries?' I had thought it indiscreet of Setsuko to talk in this vein: Mamoru now sat agog, clutching at his knees on which his brief-case rested, so that the flap touched his chin.

Whether intentionally or by accident Colethorpe provided a diversion. 'Oh, look at your flower-bed! What has been happening to it?'

'Mr. Mamoru made a somewhat unconventional entrance; that's all.' The comment was an unusual one to come from Welling and its dry acerbity made me realise how much Mamoru's blundering remarks must have annoyed him.

'He's going,' Setsuko said.

We could hear Furomoto's voice from the other side of the hedge and then his driver's; but Mrs. Furomoto's was too soft to carry to us. Mamoru jumped up and, again trampling on the asters he had flattened, peered through the hedge.

'Big car,' he said. 'Big man, big car.'

The engine of the Jaguar could be heard, followed by a crunch of tyres on gravel. Then there was a high-pitched, tinny rattle and the squeal of brakes. We all went over to the hedge. On the other side of it, in the gutter, gleamed up a hub-cap towards which the driver was waddling. Furomoto was watching with cold menace; then, as the driver turned, the retrieved hub-cap under his arm, the abuse came at him. I could understand little of it, but later Welling told me that Furomoto had called the man a fool not to put back the hub-caps firmly; an imbecile; a moron. What was the use, he had continued, of buying one of the most expensive cars on the market if the driver was going to wreck it? And so on, and so on: a show of temper both childish and repellent.

When it was all over, and the car had driven off, we returned to our seats in silence. On the Japanese the effect of a scene like that is similar to the effect of a typhoon; it paralyses them, often to such an extent that they are incapable even of saving their own skins. Inevitably it was one of us Westerners, Colethorpe,

168

who spoke first: 'What a pretty display! And very much in character. The only thing that makes it tolerable is that Nakatani really enjoys being shouted at in that fashion.'

'Nakatani?'

'The driver.'

It was only then that I looked at Setsuko. She lay back in her chair, her head tilted sideways and her eyes closed; her face grey and clammy. I thought that she had fainted; but as I rose to go across to her, she looked up at me with a glance so unnerving in its seeming hostility that I halted and did not even ask her if she were all right.

I am still puzzling about that look; I cannot get it out of my mind.

TWELVE

IT was a week now since she had heard the news of the death of her business-man and the Korean's face was still blotched and puffy from the tears which flowed out of her like some never-ending discharge. Even Sanae, who had at first declared that she was weeping merely over the loss of a source of pocket-money ('She knows that men as trusting as that aren't easy to find') and then that the girl was out to attract attention, had now begun to feel sorry for her.

He had been discovered, lying on his face, in a gas-filled room of his house, and no one had been certain whether he had died by accident or design. The gas had come from a ring in his study, on which he used often to heat up a pot of coffee when he was working late. Since the pot was on the ring when he was found (or so his wife declared) the police tended to believe that he had dropped off to sleep, and then, by one of those fluctuations of pressure so common in Japan, the gas had been extinguished, to flow back unlit. The Korean herself refused to accept this theory, declaring that any widow as rich as her former lover's could persuade the police to talk any nonsense the family wanted. 'I'm to blame,' she would go on. 'I and that wife of his. He just couldn't stand it any longer from the two of us. First I'd nag at him and then she'd nag at him. We both wanted him for ourselves and we couldn't understand that he wanted us both. I knew that she found out about me, he told me so, and what most upset her was that he was spending so much money on me. And just before it happened I was a fool myself—made a scene with him because he failed to keep one of our appointments on account of some family anniversary.' At that point the blubbing would usually become so convulsive that she could not go on.

Sanae was lavishing the same care on her face and dress as on that previous occasion when she had seen Nakatani in the audience. But now the other girls, instead of hurrying out before her, were hanging about in the dressing-room to be joined by girls from the adjoining dressing-rooms, some already dressed and some still in kimonos or, more sophisticated, in Western-style wraps and high-heeled slippers. Sanae paid no attention to them except when she had to squeeze past a group first to get to the wash-basin and then to a cupboard. The Korean sat alone at the table in the centre, holding herself with a peculiar rigidity so that her generous breasts stuck out above the clutter of used tea-cups, cheap magazines and empty cigarette packets before her.

'Where's Rumi?' one of the girls asked. 'Let's begin.'

'Yes, let's begin. I've got to catch a train home.'

'Home! It's a long time since you spent a night at home.'

The first girl giggled. '*Sate*, I've got to catch a train somewhere. And I mustn't be late.'

'Hasn't anyone seen her?'

'She said she had to telephone to that doctor friend of hers——'

'Not again!'

'Her boy friend, *anta baka, ne*? He's so jealous that she was going to tell him to come along, if he wanted. She's afraid he won't believe her.'

At that moment Rumi slipped into the room. Half-negro and half-Chinese, she was the tallest of the girls, with a bony elegance at which they mocked, calling her 'Skeleton-Woman' or 'Galloping Consumption', because secretly they envied it. She always wore Western style clothes, glittering with sequins and trimmed with feathers or fur, and seemed to possess an inexhaustible collection of boots and shoes of all shapes and colours: another source of mockery to the girls, who sometimes also called her 'The Shoehorn'. For a reason no one could understand, it was only this nickname, and not the others, which would send her into a rage if she was addressed by it. She had recently joined the troupe.

'Rumi—at last!'

She raised one of the pencilled arcs which did service for eyebrows and fluttered her immensely long, obviously artificial lashes up and down as she drawled out, in her weird accent, half-Harlem and half-Shanghai: '*Darlings*, he didn't believe a word of it. So I told him to come along. If he does, remember, I want no nonsense under the table while I'm "out".'

Rumi was a medium; and the girls had decided to hold a séance to discover how the Korean's friend had really met his death. Once before she had consented to perform for them; and the extraordinary shivering which had preceded her trance, no less than the epileptiform seizure which had followed, had convinced all

the girls, who were in any case disposed to believe in the supernatural, that she was possessed of extraordinary powers.

'Ready?' Rumi put one of her hands on the Korean's shoulder.

'Rumi—I don't know. . . . I don't know if we ought to . . .'
The Korean gave the hiccough which she produced when her
supply of sobs was exhausted.

'What's the matter?'

'Well—is it—is it right?'

'Right?'

'I mean, ought we to—to meddle in such things.'

'You want to know, don't you?'

'In a way . . . yes.'

'Well, then?'

'It's just that . . . that . . .' Again she hiccoughed, raising
her hand to her nose.

'The truth, however bad, is better than uncertainty,' another
girl put in. 'That's what I always feel. Isn't it?'

'Aren't you staying, Sanae?' the girl from Hokkaido asked.

'I can't, I'm afraid. I have to get home. My room-mate had
some bad news from England'—she lied impromptu—'and as she
was so upset, I said I'd be back immediately.'

'Someone of hers died?'

Sanae nodded; she could not be bothered to think of an
alternative.

'It's the stars. Bad for unmarried girls at present. My sister
broke her leg two days ago. And one of the two dressmakers who
live opposite us, the younger one, has had to go into hospital for
her parasites.'

'Come on, girls!'

In the telephone-booth outside the stage-door, Sanae lied to
Colethorpe with the same facility. '. . . You remember I told you
about my Korean friend, don't you? Yes, that's right. Suicide—if
it *was* suicide. She's in a very bad way this evening; can't stop
crying. We're all afraid that she may go home'—she lowered her
voice, to add verisimilitude to what she was saying, not because
anyone might hear—'and do something foolish. You know what I
mean? So I really think that I ought to go back with her for the
night. Yes, it *is* a nuisance, but what am I to do? I should feel
so responsible if anything were to happen to her. She has no
family, you know. No friends. Nonsense—anyone would do the
same for a friend in trouble. You would, I know. . . . As she

172

hung up the receiver, she could hear, in imagination, Colethorpe passing on the news to Setsuko: '. . . Sanae really is an angel. . . . And that girl has been rude to her on more than one occasion, I know for a fact. . . . But Sanae would forgive anything to anyone. . . . Some beastly little hovel, I expect . . . rats . . . bugs. . . . And Sanae hates filth. . . .' For the first time since she had decided to embark on this truancy, she felt a pang of remorse.

'Where are we going?'

Furomoto and Nakatani had been waiting in the Jaguar exactly where they had agreed.

As Furomoto slipped his hand on to her knee, she noticed with distaste the stains of nicotine on his forefinger and middle finger; there was a similar stain on the right hand corner of his upper lip. 'To my house,' he replied.

'Oh, no! Not there! We can't go there!'

He kissed the lobe of her ear and then gave his brief, falsetto laugh. 'Why not?'

'Let's go to the Midori. Anywhere. To a hotel.'

'But what's wrong with my house, *nuketeru*? Are you afraid it won't be luxurious enough for you? Is that it?'

'Of course not. I was—I'm thinking of you. Of your wife—the servants. . . .'

'My wife is in Switzerland. You don't have to think about her. Ever.' She had heard him use the same tone, peremptory and chilling, to Nakatani and Colethorpe; never, until now, to herself. 'Or to talk about her. She has nothing to do with you, or you with her. As for the servants, you must leave me to judge whether I can trust them or not. Nakatani here has been with me for many years and he knows all my secrets. He would never repeat them to anyone. One of our maids is away and the other maid used once to be my nurse. She dislikes my wife,' he added. 'Mothers and nurses tend to dislike the people one marries.' The last remark came like the uncoiling of a dangerously overwound spring; he even smiled.

When they arrived at the house, he himself conducted her to Lisa's quarters. 'Good enough for you?' he asked. 'There's a bathroom and so on through there. I should change out of that'— she was wearing a Western-style print-dress—'into a kimono. Far more comfortable. There's one hanging over there. I'll be back in twenty minutes and we can have a drink and some sandwiches.

173

Or would you prefer some noodles or *domburi* or something of that kind?' This last question was, on the face of it, an expression of a desire to see that she had everything she wanted; but the implication (as he intended) was not so flattering: she was unused to Western-style living and would prefer some native dish, probably one of the two he mentioned, favourites of the working-classes in Japan.

The moment he left her she made a hurried inspection of the room, and at once decided, from the cupboards and drawers crammed with clothes, that these were the quarters of his wife. The realisation disgusted her. Why couldn't he do as other men did, and take her to a hotel? That was the decent way to go about it. Probably he got some nasty thrill from having another woman here. One of the girls at the theatre had met a man like that. That one even went as far as to turn his already sleeping wife out of bed in order to prepare some tea; and the wife (if one could believe the girl) actually seemed to enjoy the humiliation, for all her snivelling and abuse.

It was the first time she had ever drunk champagne; but when Furomoto asked her: 'Ever tasted this stuff before?' she at once answered, 'Of course, Furomoto-San.' As he sipped from his glass, he glanced around the room, and at once noticed from a door she had failed properly to close that she had been exploring the cupboards. He had expected it; it even added to the perverse pleasure of sitting with her in this room and looking at her in the kimono which he himself had given to Lisa last New Year—or was it the New Year before that? Probably she was honest; but he was wise to have locked up in the guest-room next door all the small objects which might tempt a girl to steal, in the assurance that a dread of scandal would keep a man of his position from going to the police. At least she could probably be relied on not to play the trick of that drab, found by Nakatani wandering homeless outside the Osaka Grand Hotel, who had left wearing two of Lisa's evening-dresses hitched up under her rags. It had been an anxious few hours while Nakatani set off to retrieve them before Lisa got back from Tokyo.

Suddenly Sanae began to feel queasy: perhaps from the champagne; perhaps from the sandwiches; perhaps because Furomoto's caresses, which grew more and more intimate as the colour of his face deepened from the effects of the alcohol, were filling her with a mounting disgust. 'What's the matter, *Kimi*?' She had

174

pushed away the nicotine-stained hand and clenched her teeth against the rubbery contact of his half-open mouth. 'What is it?'

'Nothing. But I like to do things in order. Let's finish with this first.' She took another sandwich and bit into a corner, telling herself: 'Don't be a fool, don't ruin this chance. You'll never get another like it. It's no worse than a hundred other humiliations. What about that audition for the theatre, when you had to strip, on a winter's day, before the stage-hands and electricians on an unheated stage, and all the time you were doing that dreadful number, you could hear their comments and titters? Give him what he wants, he'll soon get tired. He always does, they say. And then he'll pay you off. If you're clever, you can see that you get something better than a bar or a house. It's only a matter of making enough of a nuisance of yourself for long enough. That's all. . . .'

'Drink up.'

'Don't hurry me. You're terribly impatient for your age. You might be a boy.'

'Yes, I might be.'

She braced herself, put her emptied glass on the tray, and slipped a hand beneath the fold of his *yukata* to discover, with surprise, that the flesh of his torso was not flabby but muscular and hard. Again the rubbery lips nuzzled at hers. She closed her eyes and murmured mechanically: 'M-m-m! I see what you mean. Yes, you might be a boy—a young university student, doing it for the first time in weeks.' A boy, a young university student: she tried to think of him as he would have been thirty years ago, playing baseball, or in a running vest and shorts, or diving into a pool. Thirty years ago! But she was thinking of him as if he were a student now. . . . Once she and another of the girls had gone into the Compa, the bar where the students congregated in Kyoto, and there had been a youth there, a high-school kid really, who had got into conversation with them and told them that he was a school Judo champion or a boxing champion or something like that. The other girl had tried to flirt with him, but he had not understood, imagining that they were really interested in the newspaper cuttings of himself defeating this or that opponent. . . . Furomoto could never have had a physique like that, he must always have had those over-small hands and feet, and the legs too short from knee to ankle; and the lips oddly savourless. . . . Again she was seized with a revulsion that whirled her down and down and down from disgust to despair to loathing to horror. What was she doing? Why had she ever started on this adventure? Even the pillow on to which he was now pressing her head exuded faintly that same odour which had inhabited the drawers and cupboards; probably the kimono which he was now stripping off her, with frantic gestures as though it were on fire and he were trying to save her from being burned, was also his wife's.

Oh, God save me, save me, save me. Save me by some miracle. But what miracle? Send a typhoon to blow down the house; let an urgent message come for him; make him drop dead of heart-failure. Yes, make him DIE, DIE, DIE. I'll do anything for You; I'll never forget to say my prayers; I'll leave the theatre; I'll go to the mission every Sunday. . . . Only let him die. But the miracle, when it came, was an unexpected one. As she thought of the mission, she thought of Welling, standing beside her and laughing as he fumbled to extricate her from the blind-cord which he had jerked around her throat (Furomoto caressed her throat with a growing savagery); the sunlight gleaming on the reddish hairs of his naked forearm and on his bony cheek (lamplight on Furomoto's shoulder, the shoulder flecked with sweat); then his arms around her and his lips at her temple and no longer the dust-defiled and defiling class-room but a river, grass, night, coolness, silence, trees, alone (the dream of what had never happened but was happening now, more real than Furomoto's threshing body and his grunts and stifled cries). 'Oh!' she cried out. 'Oh! Thank you! Thank you!' (Thank you for the miracle: to God or to Welling? She had cried out in English.) Then she began to weep, still murmuring: 'Thank you, thank you.'

After he had left her, she lay awake, dreading his return in the morning; but once again, at dawn, the miracle was repeated, and once again he was overjoyed by the wildness of her response, never guessing that the response was not to him but another. Momentarily she had vanquished his ever-present fear of increasing impotence and in gratitude he left behind for her (as he went out whispering, 'I must go early to work; sleep on as long as you wish; I'll send the car back for you') an exquisite spray of diamonds and rubies.

Even the early mornings in Japan in the summer have the atmosphere of a pressing-shop, with the same smells of scorched cloth and long-exuded sweat and the same febrile dampness, like so many invisible cobwebs, trailing over one's body and getting into one's mouth. Yet Asai was shivering. Down the road from Furomoto's house there was a curve from which one had a superb view of the whole bay of Osaka and since many cars and tourist-buses stopped there, a refreshment kiosk had been constructed of bamboo, with low *tatami*-covered platforms, on which the customers would squat, dotted out-of-doors around it. Asai did not squat, but sat perched on a corner, his feet in the dust and his elbow resting on one knee so that his hand, now unbandaged, the finger still shiny and purple and swollen, supported his head. He had a half-finished glass of orangeade before him and, though it was many minutes since he had sipped from it, the metallic taste was still on his tongue. He suddenly stooped, pulled his brief-case from under the platform, and clicked it open to stare into its interior. Then he closed the brief-case again and looked at his watch. Quarter-past eight. He must have a fever, he decided; why else should he be shaken with these tremors, so violent that when he ordered his orangeade the hag in charge of the kiosk had stared at him in astonishment? Even his teeth were chattering and the desire to micturate was becoming stronger and stronger. But he must not leave his post: not now, not so soon before Furomoto usually appeared.

A figure was striding up the road, at an astonishing pace considering both the heat and the gradient: a foreigner, in grey flannels and a blue shirt, with a rucksack on his back from which dangled a white coat, presumably of linen. Asai watched him through lids narrowed against the newly-risen sun; and then, suddenly, it was as if someone had struck a blow upwards, within him, from the pit of the stomach to his throat. It was Max whatever-it-was; his sister's German friend. Asai jumped up and retreated under the awning, turning his back to the road and facing the startled hag, who asked if she could fetch him anything.

He made a peculiar croaking noise at the back of his throat, as the realisation smote him, another blow upwards through his entrails: he had forgotten the brief-case. Not that it mattered; who would find it under the platform and, having found it, would succeed in purloining it under the eyes of the crone and himself? 'Have you . . . have you . . . ?' What? He could think of nothing. And then, perhaps prompted by his most urgent need of that moment, 'Have you any water?'

The woman, who brought her water by cart from a neighbouring house, sniffed, took a glass from under her counter, and held it to the tap of a cylindrical metal cistern which rested on two wooden blocks, all without a word. Asai was watching the road as it was reflected, like a lividly swollen vein, in the side of the drum at which she stooped. Had Max already seen him? Would he see him now?

'Hello, there! Hey! Asai!' he shouted in English.

Asai had an impulse to turn round and say: 'I'm afraid you've made a mistake. My name is not Asai. I don't think we've met.' But, instead, he glanced over his shoulder—the woman was holding out the glass, lukewarm, for him to take—and said faintly, 'Hello.'

'What are you doing here?'

'Oh, I am waiting—waiting for a friend.'

'Certainly you have chosen a beautiful spot to wait. What a view!'

The German stood with his legs, in their stained flannel trousers, wide apart and his large grimy hands on his hips. It seemed as if he were going to gaze down at the bay of Osaka for ever. 'Yes, what a view! Fantastic! I am obliged to leave my motor-bicycle down at Ashiya. I get off it for a moment to buy a newspaper and when I return, the back-tyre is flat.' His joviality had all at once vanished and his small blue eyes were now squinting with a paranoic intensity out of the blond fuzz which obscured most of his face. 'I think someone does this for me. I leave the tyre full and when I return, it has a hole. Someone wishes to be my enemy. Do you agree?'

Asai sipped at the lukewarm liquid which tasted as if it had been fetched from a stagnant pond. 'What?'

The monosyllable obviously exasperated the German and even intensified his suspicions. 'You come from Ashiya?'

'No. From Nishinomiya.'

'And you wait here long?'

'About . . . about half-an-hour.' To his horror he saw that one of the high twin-gates of Furomoto's villa was being pushed open; and that Nakatani was now waddling out, to make his way round to the garage. This German imbecile was going to spoil it all, he thought in panic. He must get rid of him. Get rid of him. At once.

'It is difficult to be a German in the world.'

Now the nose of the car had emerged and, a moment later, the

178

whole beautiful body swung out and round to crunch, in an aura of ochre dust, up to the entrance. Asai went rigid, like a cornered animal, then his upper lip drew back as he hissed with a venomous desperation: 'That ought not to surprise you.'

'What do you mean?'

'After the manner you Germans have behaved! *Schwein!*'

The German swung round; it seemed, for a moment, as if he were going to pummel the other with his large, waxen fists. Then he shrilled: 'And the Japanese? The Japanese? I think you puncture my motor-bicycle. I think you lie. You lie! ' He shouted over his shoulder as he hurried on up the hill: 'I tell police. I find police. You puncture my tyre.' He began to trot, his long blond hair shaking up and down on his bony skull, with occasional backward glances as though he feared pursuit.

It was all right; all right. Asai's hand was shaking so much that he could barely put the glass back on the counter. But it was all right. The Jaguar was still there and that hairless monster was still leaning against it, his eyes half-closed in the sunlight as he scratched at his crotch with one of his swollen paws. The important thing now was to sit in such a way that the imbecile could see only the back of his head; otherwise it was just possible that he would recognise him, even though they had met only once. Asai darted across to the platform: yes, here, on this corner, like this. (But what a close shave!) Hugging the brief-case to him, he could see the car, distorted and tiny as a child's toy which has been crushed under foot, in the metal of the cistern. Now he must keep calm; it was easy, if only he kept calm. He turned his head slightly; his eyes were beginning to smart from his concentration on that glittering band of metal. Ah, there Furomoto was! Somehow he had never imagined when he had gone over the whole scene so many times in his head, that, at this distance, he would actually hear his voice. It must be some trick of the hillside curving about the house to act as a vast, natural megaphone. 'Have you got the brief-case?' Brief-case! Asai clutched at it. '*Noroma!* Go in and get it. And hurry—hurry—hurry!'

Nakatani stumbled and almost fell flat in his zeal to put right his omission. Meanwhile Furomoto strolled up and down in front of the car, whistling to himself. 'Oh, what a beautiful morning, oh, what a beautiful day. . . .' One heard the tune everywhere those days; even Asai, who loathed most things American, knew what it was.

179

'All right. . . . No, give it to me, *noroma*. Yes, that's right. Now, get going.'

The door slammed on either side, each like a buffet to Asai's head. Then the car began to slide gently forward as though it were merely the slope that sucked it along, and not its engine that propelled it. Asai inserted his hand into the case; but with so much clumsiness and haste that he stubbed his poisoned finger, from which he had stripped off the bandage before setting out, against the buckle of the strap. He almost screamed from mingled pain and shock. . . . How cold the object was! Like some stone which had been lying at the bottom of a well. And how heavy it felt now!

Suddenly, as he was tensing his muscles to swing round and hurl it, there broke into his consciousness, as though cutting through the actual bone and membrane of his skull, an extraordinary tinny clanging, which grew louder and louder and nearer and nearer. He swung around in terror to face it; forgetful that he had decided that on no account must either of them in the car see his face until the moment came for the act. It was a disc-like object, bouncing over the stones and glittering, a wheel of fire, until it landed in the dust at his feet. The car had stopped, some fifteen yards from him, and Nakatani had jumped out and was running at the kiosk, his long arms swinging loosely from the massive shoulders and his slack mouth agape. Furomoto was shouting—what was it? Dolt . . . idiot . . . fool . . .

Asai pulled out the nugget and jumped to his feet; and at the same moment Nakatani, stooping to retrieve the hub-cap, glanced up and flashed his recognition. The boy tugged at the pin; but he could feel nothing but the agony shooting up his arm from the poisoned finger pressed to the icy, sweating metal. Then the giant came at him with a great noise and darkness.

'Nakatani! Nakatani! Nakatani!'

Furomoto's voice wailed out on a single note of horror as he lurched through the smoke and dust. 'Nakatani! Where are you? Are you all right?' He heard a whimpering from the ground the other side of the kiosk; but when he rushed there the bundle of charred rags was not the sumo-wrestler but a woman who raised herself up on all fours, like a wounded animal, and turned to him a face from which the jaw-bone dangled. . . . Curse her!

'Nakatani! Nakatani!'

Then, as the atmosphere cleared, he saw the cistern tumbled on

180

its side with the shreds of flesh and clothing stuck to it and the vast, fluttering, crimson stain that was all that was left of the awning. Nakatani and Asai had been perfectly fused together in an oblivion where Furomoto's voice could no longer reach them as he sobbed out over and over again: 'Nakatani! Nakatani!' and then, in a fury of despair, '*Kono yaro! Kono yaro!*' Who would want to do such a thing? *Kono yaro!*

THIRTEEN

EVERYWHERE one goes, one hears of the attempt to murder Furomoto. I use the word 'murder', though most people prefer to say 'assassinate', as though he were an emperor or prime minister. When I was walking back from the University this morning, with the dragging lethargy which this heat and humidity induce, I was overtaken by Mrs. Ambleside, who, to judge from her flushed face under an enormous, floppy hat of straw and the way that she gasped at me, must have been hurrying to catch me up. 'Good morning, Mr. Knox, good morning. Returning from the University? Well, here I am on my way back from a visit to Mrs. Crawley. She's been taken bad again with what she *says* is chronic gastritis. I really don't know. I wonder if she isn't perhaps a little unwise not so much in *what* she eats as in *how much* she eats. Poor dear, working as hard as she does, she needs all the nourishment she can get. But when one reaches a certain age, the body doesn't require what it requires when one is young—as I keep telling her. Still, she has so few pleasures and deserves those she has. . . .' All this was panted out at speed, before she got on to the subject which was really uppermost in her mind. 'Now I wonder if I oughtn't perhaps to call on poor, dear Mrs. Furomoto. What do you think?' She jerked a small handkerchief out of her bag and held it, first against her upper lip and then against the right side of her long, yellow nose which, at the pressure, seemed to seep even more moisture, like a sponge. 'In condolence, as it were?'

'Condolence?'

She tugged at the brim of her hat. 'Well, perhaps that is not quite the word. But the shock . . . poor woman . . . and such a nice woman, isn't she? You like her, don't you, Mr. Knox? There are people, I know, who mistake that—that slight *remoteness* of hers for unfriendliness. Mrs. Crawley actually said that she thought her stuck-up. . . . Of course she and her husband have been divorced for years, but even so—some kind of link must remain, mustn't it? They say he even visits her from time

182

to time. Is that so? I think that Mr. Welling told me that the other day, when he was calling at your house . . . ? '

' Yes, that's right.'

' Well, it's much nicer when divorced—or is it separated?—couples remain on good terms. Especially when there are children as well. Though in their case . . . Oh, these cab drivers ! ' She had been so busy talking at me, the vast brim of her hat bouncing up and down each time that she gave any special emphasis to a word, that she would have waded into the stream of mid-morning traffic, had my arm not restrained her. ' Of course, you know that he was one of our Bible Class students, don't you ? '

' Furomoto ? ' I was astonished.

' No. The—the assassin—murderer—whatever one should call him. Yes, a boy called Asai—Mr. Welling taught him. And what's so odd is that apparently they first identified him by his mission-card—all our students register and we give them a card, you know. Can you imagine? The boy was quite unrecognisable but that little card was found a long, long way up the road, just a wee bit bent at the corners, that was all. One could almost call it a miracle.'

' Asai, did you say ? '

' Yes, Asai—or was it Arai? His photograph was in the *Mainichi* of this morning. Didn't you see it ? '

' But I—I think I met the boy, Asai? Of course I did ! '

' It's wrong of me to say it now—seeing that he is dead—but none of us really cared for him. I remember one morning when poor Mr. Welling came to breakfast more upset than I'd seen him since the news that his wife would have to have her big operation. The boy had said outright to him that he only attended class to improve his English. Can you imagine the gall of it? . . . Still, as I said to Mr. Welling, in a way it makes it less bad to know that he wasn't ever really a Christian. Though, of course, in another way '—again the handkerchief was pressed to the side of her nose—' it makes it—makes it kind of worse? ' The note of vague interrogation seemed to hint at some conflict either within the whole mission or merely within herself.

She puffed on in the same vein until we reached the turning where we must separate; and even there would have detained me on the corner or even perhaps accompanied me to my house, had I given her any encouragement. But by then I was not listening, so engrossed was I in my own recollection of Asai. Who would have thought that he would commit such an action? was my first amazed reaction, followed by: But I did half think it! (Just as, at night, I used to wake to mysterious thuddings and scratchings overhead and would murmur to myself 'Rats'; but never actually believed in their existence in the house until one scuttled across my bedroom in the light of day.)

Colethorpe was weeding in the front-garden, squatting on her haunches, with a bucket in front of her. I greeted her and she looked up and smiled through the blonde hair trailing across her face. 'I have to do this when Mrs. Furomoto and Setsuko are out.'

'Why?'

'They always get cross and say that the weeding-woman will come tomorrow. No need to pay her, I answer, I can do the job myself. But they don't like that. I suppose I lose face, and make them lose face.'

'Is Setsuko really silly enough to think that?'

'Not silly. Just more Japanese than perhaps you realise.'

'I've just heard about Asai—the attempt to kill Furomoto. . . .'

'Yes, isn't it extraordinary?' She got stiffly to her feet, and dusted her hands off on the sides of her tattered pair of jeans. 'He came here sometimes. I never cared for him. I used to wonder what Setsuko and Mrs. Furomoto saw in him.'

'Did they see anything at all? I thought that he just wanted their help in his row over his job——'

'Well, yes. That was how it started, of course.' She arched her torso backwards, pressing one hand to the small of her back. 'Ouch! I must be getting old.' She giggled: 'Too bad he didn't succeed.'

'Who?'

'Asai. Furomoto is really a horror. I'd forgive him everything else if he was as good a painter as he's persuaded everyone in Japan to think him. But he isn't. He's a fraud. . . . And instead of him, the one to get it had to be that pathetic eunuch-slave of his.'

For the first time I felt vaguely interested in Colethorpe, instead of merely regarding her as an irritating appendage to Setsuko.

'Sanae at home?'

'She's lying down. The night before last she had a bad time with one of the girls in the theatre; seems the girl's boy friend went and killed himself and the girl was threatening to follow suit. Sanae stayed with her and returned here last evening looking an absolute wreck. She's far too sensitive for that cut-throat sort of world. I dare say the fact that she had met Asai and Furomoto here also added to her general depression. She went straight to bed and has been there ever since. Japanese don't *talk*, do they? I can get nothing out of her. It would be better if they did.'

While I ate my lunch, I read the *Mainichi Daily News*, at which I had only glanced this morning in the hurry of getting to the University on time. The photograph, though it must have been four or five years old, was unmistakably of Asai. In the paper too the words 'assassin' and 'assassination', as in the conversation of all those who had discussed the affair with me, did service for 'murderer' and 'murder'. 'Political Implications?' I read at the top of a paragraph. But what possible 'political implications' could there be in the effort of a half-crazed unemployed youth to murder his former employer in revenge for an engineered dismissal? The writer described Furomoto's controversial position as an *éminence grise* of the government; the part he was accused by the opposition of having played to ensure that recognition was withheld from Communist China; and his present efforts to engineer a revision of the Security Pact with the motive (it was merely hinted) of increasing his sales of every type of equipment to what was now the diminutive Japanese Defence Force, but would, if he succeeded, become the Japanese Army, Navy and Air Force. Rubbish! I decided. But in the *Japan Times*, which I next began to read, the same facts were set out with even less ambiguity and with the additional information that Furomoto was shortly to set off on a journey to America, ostensibly on business but (so it was generally thought) in fact as a government emissary.

At that point in my reading Setsuko appeared. Her aunt had sent her over to ask if I wished her to arrange for the weeding-woman to weed my half of the garden when she came the next day to weed their half. Presumably they had caught Colethorpe at it.

'Oh, no, it's not worth the expense. Endo-San and I can manage between us.'

'You?'

'I enjoy the relaxation.'

'But the woman charges only three hundred yen for a whole day. That's nothing.'

'It's something to me, Setsuko.' So Colethorpe had been right!

The idea of my grubbing about after weeds obviously upset her. 'Sit down. I never have the opportunity to talk to you these days. You're always so busy.'

'And I'm busy now.'

'Doing what?'

'Oh, a hundred and one things.' She was behaving oddly, I realised; glancing, not at me, but rapidly about the room as though it were a cell from which she was planning to make her escape, while her voice progressively bogged down deeper and deeper into the tonelessness of extreme exhaustion or grief.

'Nonsense! Sit down. . . . You look tired.'

'I am tired.'

'The Consul gave me a bottle of Martell brandy when he had lunch here yesterday. Let's open it. It'll cheer us up.'

'Do you need cheering up?' There was the faintest emphasis on the 'you'.

'Very much so. Come on!'

She slumped into a chair beneath the window; and I then noticed, for the first time since her entry, how shiny and flushed her cheeks and forehead were, and how peculiarly brilliant her eyes. She might almost have had a fever.

'That's better.' I rummaged in the cupboard for two glasses and the bottle. 'I've just been reading about the attempted "assassination"—as they will insist on calling it.'

'Oh, that.'

'It seems to me so obvious that the boy had no political motives at all. Why do these wretched journalists always want to make things even more sensational than they are already?'

'Thanks.' She took the glass from me and sipped at it.

'Did you ever imagine that Asai would do such a thing?' She sipped again and shook her head. 'It's been a shock for you. Of course it has. After all, he *was* your uncle.'

'I wonder why the Japanese can make such good "Scotch", but can't produce a brandy.'

'Let me give you some more.' At a gulp she had drained all that was left in the glass.

'I'll get drunk. I haven't eaten yet.'

'But I thought you ate at twelve.'

'We do, usually. But today I wasn't feeling hungry. . . . Oh, very well.' She extended the glass, with a slight tremor of her wrist, for me to pour the brandy into it. 'Thanks.'

186

'I can't understand the mentality of anyone who does a thing like that.'

'Like what?'

'Well, throwing a bomb.'

She drank greedily. Yes, she would be drunk very soon, if she went on like that; on an empty stomach, too. But so far from now wishing to check the process, I was eager to hurry it on. Somehow if she were drunk and I were drunk, it would become so much easier to tell her all the things I had wanted to say for so many weeks, but had never dared to say. I gulped at my own glass, and gulped again and yet again.

I began to explain: 'Just now I tried to imagine myself doing the same kind of thing. But couldn't. Oh, I can see myself losing my temper with someone—you know how quick my temper is!— and stabbing him or shooting off the top of his head or pushing him under a train. But to plan something in cold blood like that . . . and a bomb, too. . . . You know, I think it's the bomb that started all this business in the Press about a political assassination. Bombs always mean anarchists, communists, subversion of some kind. That's how one has come to think of them—except in a war. Don't you agree?'

She ran her forefinger round the rim of her glass and then licked its tip.

'More?' I asked.

She held the glass out.

'In any case, political assassinations are so *démodé* now.' (The brandy was already beginning to make me garrulous.) 'People have begun to realize that they achieve nothing at all.'

She started and looked up, as though I had aroused her from a nap. 'What's that?' With the movement some brandy had splashed on to her skirt; but she made no attempt to mop it up. 'What did you say?' Her voice bumped and slid over the consonants, as though dragged along with an effort. 'What?'

'I said—people have begun to realise that political assassinations are absolutely useless.'

'Have they?'

'Surely! What does one gain by them? We all realise now that one man doesn't create all the evil and misery about him; rather, the other way about. You get rid of your tyrant, but there are always a hundred tyrants waiting to take his place. Quite as ruthless, efficient and cruel. Do you suppose that, if

Furomoto had died, there would not have been other Furomotos? '

'Then kill them too! '

I looked at her in amazement. 'Kill them? '

'Kill them. Why not? And go on killing them—until not a single one is left.'

'Do you honestly think that? '

She had been staring down into her half-empty glass; but now she turned her flushed face up to me, biting on her lower lip and gazing at me with an odd, predatory kind of intensity before she replied: 'Yes, I do think that. If something has disagreed with a man's stomach, he has every right to put a finger down his throat. And if a creature like Furomoto poisons the lives, not of single individuals, but of millions of individuals at a time, then those individuals have every right to vomit him out too.' On other occasions she had harangued me with the same violence and I had always hated it. Now there was my additional recoil from the actual views she was expressing. 'And it's nonsense, anyway, to say that nothing is achieved by an assassination. That's true sometimes, but not always. At the most there's a change, and there are times when a change, any change, is better than lying still. If you're in agony in one position, you don't bother to think whether another position will be equally agonising. You move; and the act of moving is in itself a temporary relief.' She got up and slouched over to the window, pulling the screen back and forth so that it screeched along its groove with a noise that set my teeth on edge. 'Besides, the act of killing has an effect not merely on the person killed, but on the people in whose name the killing is done. Don't forget that.'

I frowned at her, muzzily uncomprehending.

'You assassinate your Furomoto and you may or may not put a stop to all the bestialities which he initiated. But that's only half of the point of the assassination.'

'The other half? '

'You have made an assertion of will. On behalf of all the people who thought they were without one. That's important; quite as important as blowing Furomoto into pieces and stopping his exploitation of the country.'

'Then you approve of Asai's action? '

'Certainly. Of the action. But not of the way in which he bungled it.'

'Bungled it? '

188

'Of course. When Nakatani started to run towards him to pick up the hub-cap, he should have decided, there and then, that he would have to wait for another occasion. But, instead, he panicked.'

'I suppose he'd wound himself up and up and had got into a state. . . .'

'Yes. Typically Japanese.' She spoke with contempt. 'We had the same experience with the *Kamikaze* pilots in the war. The difficulty was not to make them commit suicide, but to make them wait to commit suicide until they had a target of sufficient importance. The death-wish with us is like an orgasm; when we've worked ourselves up to it, there's no going back.'

'But, Setsuko, you horrify me. You can't approve of murder, surely?'

'Let's not use the word "murder" which has all kinds of moral associations. Let's say killing. Certainly I approve of killing in certain circumstances. Don't you?'

'Of course not.'

'You fought in the war.'

'But this—this is entirely——'

'Different? In what way? Do you suppose that this isn't a war too—and a war of far more importance to the majority of the Japanese that one carried on for the glory of the Emperor and the expansion of Japan? Of course it is! You must be logical, my dear Bill. If you accept wars as instruments of policy, then you must accept assassinations as instruments of survival. Because that's what they are.'

'But you yourself could never——'

'Why not? I might. Did you ever kill anyone in the war?' I nodded. 'Well, then? Given all the right pressures, I think that I could do exactly as Asai did.' She held out her glass, her hand and wrist both relaxed in such a way that the stem was almost horizontal with the floor. As I poured, she slowly tipped the bowl upwards to prevent the brandy spilling. 'Yes, it wouldn't need much to drive me to kill Furomoto. The old brute!' She spoke with a sudden intensity of drunken hatred.

'But he's your uncle——"

'Really, Bill! You're so naïve. Almost all the most brutal crimes take place within families, you know that.' She giggled, staring down into the glass which she was turning round and round in her powerful fingers. 'Oh, yes. I should enjoy flinging a bomb

189

into *his* face. It would be very *satisfactory*.' The adjective seemed peculiarly repulsive; quite as much so as the relish with which she brought it out and the second giggle which followed. 'Perhaps one day I'll have the courage to do it. . . . Yes, I'm being very serious, Bill. I'm not joking, as you hope.' Suddenly she had turned on me savagely.

'But why choose Furomoto? He's not the worst, is he? '

'For me he is.' She gulped at the brandy and when she took the glass away from her lips, some was trickling down her chin. 'Do you know why my aunt left him? '

I shook my head.

'Because of me . . . I was just fifteen. Yes, my dear Bill, the thing that at this moment you're hoping that I'm not trying to say is exactly what I am saying. He seduced me. I'd been very fond of him—children always like the grown-ups who spoil them and are generous to them. It's a fallacy that children are good judges of character, they're hopeless at it. My aunt was in hospital at the time—she tried many times to have children but the result was inevitably a miscarriage—and he seized his opportunity. The awful thing was—is—that I actually enjoyed it. Oh yes.' She again gave her tipsy giggle, at once revolting and intolerably saddening to me. 'I was shocked, frightened, hurt—all the conventional things—but I also enjoyed it. He told me it was our secret, and I also enjoyed that. The next day he bought me the bicycle I wanted. . . .'

I was listening appalled: imagining Setsuko as a child and then imagining Furomoto, all those years ago, and then imagining . . . That final picture made me want to retch, like a kick in the genitals; and yet, like that kind of kick, it brought, as its aftermath, a peculiar sensation of all but unbearable sexual excitement.

'It was many weeks before she found out. And it was only when she found out, that I woke from what had all along appeared to be a thrilling and enjoyable day-dream and realised that, in fact, it had been a nightmare. Oddly enough the operation—yes, I was pregnant by then—came not as a culmination of the horror but as an escape from it. They were cutting it all out, they were taking it away from me: not merely the wretched little foetus, but the pleasure and guilt and feverish excitement and remorse. He was still generous, he always has been generous to me. The best room in the best nursing-home, the best surgeon. . . .' She put down her glass. 'Well, it's all in the past now.'

'Is it?'

'Is what?'

'Is it really all in the past? If that were so, why should you now wish to kill——?'

'Oh, let's leave the subject of Furomoto! I've drunk too much. Far too much.' She raised a hand, which was trembling slightly, to her flushed forehead. 'You asked for it.'

I went up behind her chair. 'Poor Setsuko. What a hideous experience for anyone. But I think that the good thing is that you look back on it all with such horror and disgust.'

'The *good* thing?'

'Yes, I mean that. . . . One of my best friends at Oxford was a—a queer and I remember that he once told me that he had been seduced as a boy of eleven or twelve by the headmaster of his prep school. My first reaction was: My God, what a brute! But my friend wouldn't have that at all. Oh, no, he was a nice old chap, a dear old thing—though naughty, yes, rather naughty. My friend still sometimes visits him in retirement. Can you imagine?'

She was hardly listening to what I was saying, her eyes once again looking hither and thither about the room as though seeking for a face in a crowd invisible to me but not to her. Suddenly she pressed a palm down on to each arm of her chair and levered herself up.

'Oh, don't go, Setsuko, don't go.' I placed one arm about her waist to restrain her, and then with my other hand gripped her shoulder. 'Stay. Stay a little.'

'I'm not quite as drunk as all that. You don't have to support me.' The words were uttered with no apparent sarcasm, as though she did in fact believe that I had touched her merely to prevent her falling. At that she began to walk towards the door; and after her first two or three tottering steps, I was astonished by her steadiness. It appeared that her drunkenness had been conquered by some astonishing exercise of the will. Or had the drunkenness been a pretence?

'So you don't want the woman?'

'The woman?'

'The weeding-woman. Tomorrow. You don't want her.'

'No. I don't want her.'

It was as if all our talk about the attempted assassination, assassination in general and her seduction by Furomoto had been

191

no more than an immense parenthesis in our discussion of a topic of far greater importance: the weeding of my garden.

'But it's only three hundred yen.'

'Yes, I know.' I smiled. 'You see, I actually enjoy weeding, Setsuko.'

'You're very odd.'

'Not nearly as odd as you.'

'Well, goodbye.' She sprang down into the garden. 'And thank you for my drink. It was just what I needed.'

I wanted to call out after her: 'The drink, my dear, was almost a third of a bottle of brandy'; for I was angered out of all proportion to its gravity by this additional act of falsification. But I was too late; she had already disappeared behind the hedge. I returned to the room and, sipping at yet another glass of brandy, began to muse once again on that long-ago drama: Furomoto and the frightened yet excited child with her secret and her bicycle. . . .

FOURTEEN

SANAE willed him to see her at the bus-stop and he did. Everyone in that district knew the low-slung green M.G., since it was a car of a type which the Japanese have yet to imitate. She herself had glimpsed it, far away, at the top of the road, parked outside a shop, and had wondered which would reach her first, it or her bus. *Oh God, God, make the car come first . . . the car . . . the car . . .* Then, realising the absurdity of that little prayer, she had begun instead to focus her whole being on the object she desired; and as so often happened to her, at once achieved it. The bus was late.

'Hello, there!' That he should actually stop, with a ripping noise of tyres on gravel, astonished her. 'What are you doing?'

'Waiting for the bus. But, as usual, it's not running on time. I've been here for at least ten minutes.'

'Can I give you a lift?'

Welling had dreamed about her the previous night, he remembered as soon as he glimpsed her in her white crêpe-de-chine dress; perhaps had even dreamed about that dress—the low-cut, circular neck, revealing the smooth skin of her throat and even the beginning of the cleft between her breasts, the skirt extravagantly pleated. Yes, he was sure of it; it would come back to him in a moment. He fumbled for the recollection with a growing excitement, but still it evaded him. He could smell it, he could see a white flash of it out of the corner of his eye. . . .

'Where are you going?' Sanae asked.

'Oh, into the town. I have to do some shopping and see about one or two other little chores. And you?'

'I'm on my way to work.'

'In Osaka, isn't it?'

She nodded. 'How did you know?'

'Oh, Frank happened to mention it. By train?'

'Yes.'

'Then I'll take you to the station.' She hesitated, holding her bag in front of her, at attention, while her eyes moved over the

car. 'What's the matter? Get in! Afraid the car looks too racy?'
He leant across to prop the door open. 'Come on!'

She frowned thoughtfully as she slipped in beside him. By
tomorrow morning the whole district would know that he had
given her a lift. Surely he must realise that. As a married man and,
more important, as a missionary, he ought to be more prudent;
and she herself ought to have been more prudent.

'Well, what is it? I'm a very careful driver.'

'Are you? I heard that you knocked down a woman a few
weeks ago.'

'Gosh! How on earth did you hear that?'

'One hears everything about everybody in Kyoto.' She took
courage to go on. 'You probably don't realise that, foreigners
seldom do. You ought to be careful.'

'As a driver, you mean?' He took it as a joke.

'No. In general. . . . For instance, everyone will talk about
my travelling in your car at this moment.'

'Everyone will *what*?'

She nodded gravely; and then had to laugh at his expression of
mingled surprise and indignation. 'It does not matter so much
to me. They talk about me enough already. But for you—it is
stupid. I ought not to have accepted.'

'But, heavens, a lift in the car—in broad daylight—to one of
my students . . . !'

'Yes, I know. But such people look at things in a different way.'

'To the impure all things are impure,' he muttered. But he was
honest enough with himself to know that there was some faint
smudge of guilt over the face of the innocence which he was now
so vehemently protesting to be immaculate. The gossips would be
wrong to say that there was 'something' between him and the
girl; but was he right to assert that there was nothing between
them?

'It is bad for a married man to be seen with an unmarried girl
in our country. Perhaps not in your country. In Japan it is
bad.'

'If one knows that one is doing nothing wrong, one shouldn't
bother too much about what others say.' He spoke this sentence
slowly, as though the opinion were an original one which he had
just hammered out after an intense deliberation. 'Don't you
agree?'

'In Japan we must bother. Japan is different.' Something now

194

impelled her to speak about herself with a total frankness. Probably she would shock him; perhaps he would regret that he had offered her a lift. But her self-revelation would, whether he wished it or not, transform their whole relationship. An intimacy, even if only an intimacy of shame on the one hand and disgust on the other, would be established between them. 'And besides, I am not just an ordinary unmarried woman.'

'No, you're not at all ordinary.' Was he purposely misunderstanding her? she wondered. But Welling was not so subtle.

'To most of the people in this district,' she went on doggedly, 'I am a bad woman.'

'A bad woman?' He laughed. 'Now why should they think that? What have you done to annoy them?'

'Did Frank not speak to you about my job?'

'No, I don't think so. Why?'

'Perhaps Aileen has never told him. I thought that she would.' She felt grateful to the English girl.

'And what do you do?'

'I work in a theatre.'

'And is that so very sinful?' he demanded flippantly.

'Not an ordinary theatre.'

'What kind of theatre then?'

'A strip-show. You know strip-show?'

The revelation, when it came, caused him no surprise. My dream, he thought; my dream. He was sure now that he had dreamed it. In the dark cupboard his groping hand had at last touched the object he sought. 'Yes, I know what a strip-show is. There are better jobs for a girl. But the fact that you work in such a show doesn't automatically mean——'

'To *them* it does!'

'Them?'

'These people here.' She waved to either side of the crowded street through which they were passing.

'Oh, don't worry about them! But you ought to try to find some other job,' he added. 'Don't you think?'

'What kind of a job?' she asked bitterly. 'As a maid?'

'There must be things better than that.'

'In Japan? I haven't ever been to University.'

'Does that matter?' But he had lived long enough in the country to know that it did.

'Of course it does.'

'Would you like me to make some enquiries for you among my friends? There may be something. You never know.'

'If it will not be too much trouble. Please!'

Her first reaction to the suggestion had been: 'Yes, I can guess the kind of job any friends of yours would offer. No thanks!' To be followed, immediately, by a feeling of gratitude, like a hand at her throat. How kind he was; and how unlike other men with their sexual greed and emotional pusillanimity. How unlike Furomoto. . . . And at that, as though she were dropping down and down into some icy well, she remembered that after the show Furomoto would be waiting for her . . .

'Perhaps Mrs. Crawley will know of something,' he said more to himself than to her. 'I must stop here for a moment, to pick up some snaps. I want to post them to Mrs. Welling. She's back home in Austraïlia at present.'

'Yes, Frank told me.'

He hurried into the shop and was out again in a moment, slipping the yellow folder into the car-pocket beside him, as he told her: 'I'm a hopeless photographer. The only ones that are any good are those that were taken for me by one of my students. Still, as those are the ones I'm going to send Mrs. Welling, it doesn't really matter.'

'Your wife—Mrs. Welling—has been away a long time?'

The unattractively thin mouth tightened for a moment before he replied: 'Yes. Several months. She's been sick. But she's on the mend now. . . . Now, if you don't mind, I'll just slip into the chemist's here and then I'll take you straight down to the station. What time is your train?'

'Oh, not for another quarter of an hour. Your car is much faster than the bus.'

'I'm afraid the shops may be closed if I don't do my shopping now.'

'Please. That's quite all right.'

As soon as he had disappeared, she jerked the folder out of the pocket and hurriedly leafed through its contents. Most of the snapshots appeared to be of some mission outing to the sea. Mrs. Ambleside, seated under a vast straw hat, the shadow of which obscured the whole of her face with the exception of the chin; Frank, in swimming-trunks, leaping for a ball at the same time as a diminutive, hairy Japanese, both of them fuzzily indistinct; a huddle of half-naked, grinning girls who looked as if the sea had just washed them up against the rock to which, lank-haired and sand-covered, they were clinging; Miss Rosenthal with an open thermos in one hand and its bakelite cup in the other, staring ferociously into the camera; and then—one, two, three, four, five —snapshots of Welling. He had been right; only these last showed any photographic skill. In two of them he was seated in slacks and an open-necked shirt, surrounded by Japanese who looked like midgets in comparison; in the third he was cooking *sukiyaki* over an open fire, with a handkerchief tied, pirate-wise, over his head; in the fourth, he was wrestling with Frank who had him pinned on the sand, both of them laughing; in the fifth he lay outstretched, in his swimming-trunks, one hand behind his head and the other resting on his thigh. . . . It was at this last photograph that she stared longest. It was one of an extraordinary clarity, so that even the beads of moisture—sweat? water?—on the hair of his legs and forearms and chest were each as distinct as fragments of crystal in the sunlight. The long, sinewy body appeared to be wholly relaxed; perhaps—it was impossible to tell because of the dark glasses he was wearing—he was even asleep. What amazed her was that this was exactly how she had imagined him when she had clutched at him, a ghost, and had silently entreated him to save her from Furomoto: the reddish hair, in a thick triangle over the lean but muscular chest; the tufts of hair under the armpits; the stomach falling away beneath the rib-cage; the faint freckling over the bony shoulders and the shins. . . . He was coming back. In the door of the shop he was exchanging a word with one of the assistants, his back half-turned to the car. On an impulse she slipped the fifth photograph into her bag, hurriedly replaced the others in the folder, and then leant over to thrust the folder back into the car-pocket.

'Sorry to have kept you waiting. You must have got bored.'

'Not at all.'

'That assistant I was talking to is one of our flock. When we have more time, I must show you the photographs. He appears in one or two of them. A mission picnic. He's our best swimmer'—he grinned—'myself excepted.'

'All Australians swim well.'

'Well, not all. But many do. I love the water myself. Do you?' She nodded. 'Then you must join us on our next expedition. How about it?'

'Thank you. I'd like that.' The Japanese seldom use superlatives

197

and she used none now; but, though she spoke without any evident trace of enthusiasm, Welling was suddenly aware, with a mingling of panic and joy, of a kind of inaudible vibration that this last exchange had set up between them, thrown back and forth, back and forth in the silence that lasted until the car swooped to a stop outside the station.

'It's a damned sight too hot for games of this kind.' The Korean mopped at her sweat-flecked body with a towel the gamy odour of which seemed to permeate the whole dressing-room. 'Or any kind of games.'

'How was your American?' Rumi, the medium, asked the stocky, thick-ankled girl from Hokkaido, as she drew the end of a stick of white grease-paint slowly down her nose. Most of the girls adopted this bizarre form of make-up in a futile attempt to achieve the Caucasian features so admired by Japanese men.

'Ma, this isn't the time of year for Westerners. They smell too much.'

'I read in the Asahi Shimbun that that's because they eat so much meat,' another girl put in. 'Some doctor said it.'

'And he's stingy. He gave me dinner and five dollars—and that was all. When I looked at the five dollars, he said, "It was a short time, honey!"' She gave a passable imitation of the American phrase. '"Short time"!' She snorted. 'You should have seen how I had to work.' At this moment Sanae returned, in wrap and slippers, from the lavatory. 'Oh, Sanae-chan. You're the best of the girls at English. I want you to help me.'

'What with?'

'A letter.'

'A letter! Are you writing to him? Did he give you his address? What are you going to say?' The girls all paused in their changing and making up and some even crowded around her.

'Mind your own business! No! This is just between Sanae and me. No! Now, please go away!'

Eventually she and Sanae were able to whisper alone in private in one corner.

'. . . This is the letter I've written to him—to my American. Do you think it's all right? It took me hours to get it down on paper. But remember, Sanae, this is just between us two. Promise?' She knew that, in fact, Sanae was the only one of the girls whom she could trust never to gossip and it was precisely because of that

198

knowledge that she had selected her instead of Rumi, whose English was as good and whom all the girls liked better because she was all the things that Sanae was not: a good sort, a real pal, fallible as themselves, equally promiscuous, and equally prone to depressions and calamities. 'Here!' She slipped a crumpled envelope into Sanae's hand. 'I'll copy it out again if you think it should be different. But don't let anyone see it.'

Sanae opened and smoothed out the sheet of ruled paper and began to read:

My dear Tom,
            I enjoyed my evening with you very much and I never minded those things you wanted to do. But, Tom, you hurted me in my body and now I cannot even dance at the theatre. I must see doctor, but I am afraid to speak to father or mother. This is our secret. So please send me 20 dollars as soon as possible so that I can see doctor. One day I'll do something for you too. Your friend,
            Michiko.

'Is it all right, do you think?'
'Perfect. It couldn't be better.'
'Do you honestly think so?'
'Of course.'

The little vixen! Sanae thought as she slipped into the grass-skirt (always disagreeably prickly even in cooler weather) which she had to wear for the Hawaiian number that followed the interval. The phrasing of the letter was masterly: first, the assurance that the evening had been enjoyable (American men, unlike Japanese men, were as anxious to give, as receive, pleasure); then the reminder that Tom's tastes were unconventional; then the news that he had injured her and so jeopardised her livelihood; then the discreet reference to 'our secret'—the poor fool was a married university teacher with grown-up children and a wife who, he declared, never gave him a moment of solitude or peace except when he visited Kyoto from Tokyo to lecture; and finally the setting down of the modest sum (not large enough to goad him to refusal) which would buy, no doubt only temporarily, both her silence and his own peace of mind. But it was low, Sanae thought; lower than she herself would ever descend. Or wasn't it? She began to wonder whether circumstances would ever drive her to try

199

out a similar trick on Furomoto. He, too, after all, had a wife from whom he was determined to hide all his squalid affairs; though it was said that she knew all about them and cared not a damn.

'I'll post it as soon as the show is over.' Michiko was beside her, whispering. 'I'm glad you think it'll do. He's nice really,' she added dubiously. 'And with all those children and grandchildren perhaps he can't afford to be more generous. But after all he did hurt me—though I exaggerated that bit a little in my letter—and he did want to do something that I don't really like doing at all. In fact, it was the first time. And to give one only five dollars for that!' Suddenly she grew vindictive. 'Nasty, smelly brute! Just think, he was wearing woollen socks—in this weather, can you imagine—and I tell you, Sanae, they were *soggy* . . .'

The room in the hotel, which was one of Furomoto's properties, had an air-conditioner but, in spite of that, his whole body was drenched in a rancid sweat as he lay gasping beside her. She had no idea of the time: it might be midnight, it might be nearly dawn. All the images which had streamed through her mind, as though she were a patient under gas, were already beginning to fade at the edge, thin and disintegrate; only Welling, the central one, lying out as he had in the photograph, retained any clarity. She closed her eyes: yes, he was still there, his was the panting mouth at her temple and his the sticky hand on her thigh . . .

'That was wonderful,' Furomoto sighed.

'Good. But this isn't exactly the weather for love-making. One of the girls said the same thing at the theatre tonight.'

'One has to get on with one's job whatever the weather.' It was the kind of brutal remark which it gave him pleasure to make; and it was typical that he followed it with a prolonged caress.

'Tell me, Furomoto-San—excuse me—there is something I want to ask you. . . .' She lay on her back and spoke up to the shadowy ceiling, through full, barely parted lips. 'Why—why did Asai try to kill you?'

'I've no idea. You've read the papers. I didn't even know of his existence. He was sacked from one of my factories for some petty dishonesty—stealing some parts, I think, something like that— and I suppose that he worked himself into a state of hysteria and thought that I was the one responsible. As if I had time to concern myself with such a triviality. The egotism of people!'

'It was bad luck'—she smiled, her lips dividing over the perfectly formed teeth which gleamed in the semi-darkness—'for him, I mean—it was bad luck to lose his own life all for nothing.'

His stubby nicotine-stained fingers fumbled at her breast. 'Inefficient,' he said. 'He's not the first,' he added.

'You mean——?'

'Oh, yes, others have tried to destroy me. I forget how many. Sometimes they think they'll wipe me out with a bomb or gun or a knife; sometimes with a combine, or a new anti-cartel law, or—after the war—with a spell in prison. But the odd thing is—' his lips travelled up the line of her jaw to her temple—'the odd thing is that they succeed only in destroying themselves, like that stupid youth.'

'He got Nakatani.'

As soon as she had spoken, she realised her error. The body beside her, relaxed in a voluptuous exhaustion, all at once seemed to knot itself as he repeated her words out of a contorted face: 'He got Nakatani. Yes, he got him.' Nakatani! He saw the awning, hanging in shreds which themselves looked like shattered viscera, and smelled again that nauseating stench of smoke, hot metal and newly-spilled blood. With arms outstretched, he was running towards that carnage, shrieking the name. . . . He flung his legs off the bed. 'Must have a shower and get home. You can stay here all night or I can drop you off at the station.'

'What time is it?'

'Half-past eleven.'

'Only?' She was astonished: barely an hour.

He grunted. 'My wife's none too fit. I want to get back to her.'

'I thought that—in Switzerland—she was to have an operation . . .'

He swung round, furious. 'Who told you that?'

'You did.'

'Did I?'

'Don't you remember—the last time we met.'

'Well, I can't think why I said that to you.'

In the bathroom his good humour evidently returned to him; she could even hear him sing in a light, surprisingly musical baritone as he dried himself. When he came back, naked but for the towel around his loins, she thought: Well, he's not really as repellent as all that. For a moment she even saw the attraction which other women found in him: the body that of a man in his thirties, with the barrel-chest and the short, muscular arms and legs; the neck powerful; the waist slim. . . . He grinned at her from under a tangle of jet-black hair (did he dye it, like so many middle-aged Japanese men?). 'Yes, they all go,' he said. 'They go. Not Furomoto.' He saw her look of incomprehension and went on: 'They think they're going to be clever and make an end of me. But they make an end of themselves.' He began to tie about himself the *haramaki* or Japanese stomacher, which he wore, like many Japanese men, beneath his Western clothes. Adjusting it, he glanced up at her, as she lay still naked beneath the sheet, and once again he grinned: 'So, don't you try any tricks!' he warned her in joke. 'It's just not worth it. No one ever gets the better of Furomoto. No one. Ever. . . . Remember that.'

FIFTEEN

THIS morning I decided that, now that the University term is crawling to an end, I ought to begin to make my arrangements to leave Japan: either for the vacation, or for ever. Preferably for ever. But this evening I decided that I never wanted to leave.

It was a bad night, full of dreams in which my identity seemed to blur with the identities of others, as though we were all a pile of jelly-fish melting into one deliquescent mass: Setsuko (of course), Welling, Sanae, Colethorpe, Furomoto—all of us who have been cast up and together on this hot, desolate beach. When I dragged myself out of bed, my naked shoulders felt stiff and raw: the result, no doubt, of having the fan play on them, without the protection of either sheet or pyjama-jacket, for hours on end. I remembered the picnic ahead, and it was like remembering a pending examination at school. Why had I agreed to it? After breakfast, I looked for my map of the Kii Peninsula and the screw of my bad temper tightened and tightened as though it were something tangible inside my throbbing head. Not there, not there. . . . I dragged out suitcases or drawers, ransacked them and left them, gutted, where they lay. Then I thought of the cupboard in the hall where my winter clothes hung. . . . My God! 'Endo-San! Endo-San!' I began to bawl; until he materialised, soundless and white as ectoplasm, out of the kitchen where he had no doubt been gobbling the innumerable bowls of glutinous rice which make up his breakfast. 'Look at this! Look at these suits of mine! And these shoes! Ruined! Absolutely ruined!' I knew that the mould would dust off, once the sun had dried it; and a servant in any other country would have reminded me that I knew it. But he merely watched me impassively as I jerked and heaved one suit after another out of the wardrobe and flung it to the floor. 'Go on, pick them up, pick them up! How often have I told you to keep an eye on my clothes? What's the use of my spending money on a servant. . . .' I ranted on and on, conscious, not merely that I had made him lose face by drawing attention to his omission, but that I was losing face myself. Then, still trembling with rage, I picked up the map from a pile of old magazines stacked in one corner of the wardrobe, carried it into the sitting-room and tried to focus my attention on it.

'A letter for you, sir.'

The letter was from the solicitors of one of my aunts and told me the exact sum which I had inherited from her. It seemed to come so pat: as if to say 'Well, you fool, why do you continue to stick it out? No need. This will take you to places where you can sleep without a fan playing on you to give you rheumatism and where mould grows only on cheeses and bread.' The sum was exactly the kind of sum I had often wished for, neither large enough to make me lazy nor small enough to oblige me to do any job I did not wish to do. How often had I told myself, and even told my friends, that if I had just that much money, I should settle down and write the book I was always planning: in my 'twenties, a novel; in my 'thirties a work to which I had even given a title, *The Brownings in Italy*; and now, in my 'forties, something I vaguely called: 'Oh, just another book about Japan. . . .' But with the money at last provided, I realised—and how saddening the realisation!—that its absence had merely been an excuse. If I now threw up my job, it would not be to settle to the vocation of a writer, but to fritter away my remaining years in Corfu, Las Palmas or Siena (places in which I had always wished to live) or to eke out an income from part-time work in London. . . . At that, I felt an astonishing resentment against my poor dead aunt: like a baby from whose mouth a dummy has been plucked.

We set off in two cars: Colethorpe, and two female teachers from the mission with Frank in what he calls his 'jalopy'; Setsuko, Sanae and myself with Welling in his M.G. I was still in a bad temper and wished, not merely to sit with Setsuko, but to avoid sitting with the two American women, whose voices at that hour seemed uncomfortably piercing and persistent. My, yes! they knew all about me; and they were determined to tell me all they knew. When we had at last silenced them and coaxed them into Frank's car and Setsuko and I were ourselves bundled into the back of the M.G. with our knees touching our chins, she whispered to me: 'What's the matter? Got out of the wrong side of your bed?'

'At the moment I feel as if I hadn't got out of bed at all.'

After that we both fell silent; but Sanae, unusually talkative for her, kept up an incessant chatter—sometimes with us but more often with Welling. He himself seldom did more than grunt, chuckle or exclaim 'Gosh!' or 'Gee whizz!' I noticed that some shaving-soap was caked on one of his large, freckled ears, and that he had nicked himself with his razor at the temple and the point of his chin.

Since this is the season for bathing in Japan, every beach is crowded. Fortunately either Welling or Frank had telephoned in advance to reserve two rooms for us in a Japanese-style inn over-looking the sea: one for the men and one for the women. 'My, but isn't this *pretty*! Have you ever seen anything quite so cute as this building?' Miss Rosenthal, her small hands clutching at the straps of a camera, bag and binoculars, as well as the brim of a sun-hat, began to exclaim in delight even before her stumpy body had followed her close-cropped head out of the car. 'Norah, isn't it just the loveliest place? Frank, look at those pines—and that cute little girl playing with the ducks on the pond.' The cute little girl was, in fact, throwing pebbles at the ducks. 'Mike, you can feel the ozone in your lungs, can't you? Just breathe it in, Miss Colethorpe—like—like champagne. Not that we mission-aries know much about champagne!'

It was certainly a beautiful place, in spite of the people con-fetti-thick wherever one looked between the sea before us and the jagged mountains behind. Our two rooms were side by side, with a small garden, cramped but exquisite, through which a narrow, stone-paved path led down to the shore.

'I wonder if it's wise for Norah to swim.'

'Why, of course it is, Ruthie!' The large sleepy girl wriggled irritably and scowled.

'She's had Jap-tummy for the last three days, Mr. Knox. Do you think she ought to swim?'

'The water's very warm.'

'But the germs! . . . She's so obstinate, if she sets her mind on something. . . . Aren't you, dear?'

The girl now grinned sheepishly as though her friend had paid her a compliment. 'Well, I like to have a good time,' she said.

Frank was the first to undress in our room, stripping off his clothes as though he were about to rush out and plunge into the sea to rescue someone. I had guessed that his physique would be good; but not so good. He caught me eyeing him and at once, with a kind of strutting coquettishness, took three or four paces up and down the room, drawing in his breath deeply and then expelling it, cheeks inflated, before he all at once hurled himself into three hand-springs, followed by a cart-wheel. Welling, wandering about the room and examining the few objects in it, paid no attention to him. Probably he was used to these antics.

'Then just a quick dip, dear. In and out.' We could hear Miss Rosenthal's voice from far down the beach as the three of us men picked our way along the path. She sat fully dressed, with dark glasses on the end of her short nose and a parasol, of a hideous shade of mauve, held open above her. Around her, on a plastic sheet, were littered her belongings. 'Please, Mr. Knox, make sure that Norah doesn't stay in too long. I entrust her to you. I don't want her to have another night like the one she went through on Friday. She looks strong but she isn't really, you know. She gets sick so easily.' I began to suspect that Miss Rosenthal had plans to get the two of us ' off ' (as she would no doubt have put it) and for that reason merely gave a vague smile and turned away to Setsuko: ' New costume? '

' Yes. Do you like it? '

' Very much. But surely your aunt doesn't approve of it? '

' I haven't shown it to her.'

Welling, Frank and Sanae soon began to play ' pig-in-the-middle' with Sanae as the pig. The American girl lumbered over to the edge of the sea, gazed down morosely at the frill of foam, fruit-peel and drift-wood, placed a shapeless foot firmly down in it as though she were stamping on something, and then returned. Meanwhile Colethorpe had pulled on a rubber bathing-cap and with vigorous if ungainly strokes was making for the diving platform.

' Come,' Setsuko said to me: this one monosyllable filling me with an extraordinary excitement.

She is a wonderful swimmer and I had difficulty in keeping her in sight, let alone in keeping up with her. Out and out she went, her strong arms churning a path through the other bathers, and out and out I followed, until we had broken through to a complete solitude and quiet. She turned, her teeth flashing: ' All right? '

' Pretty winded.' I was treading water as I gasped for breath. ' If I drown, you'll be responsible.'

'Oh, I won't let you drown. Don't worry. . . . Let's float for a little. Float ! '

'I can't.'

'Of course you can.'

'No, I can't. I've tried and tried, but I can't.'

'But everyone can float. Just imagine that you're a log of wood.'

'I've done that, often. But the result always is that I become a lump of lead. Truly.'

'Well, try ! Try again ! '

I tried; and at once I slowly tipped backwards, as though on an invisible see-saw, until my legs were in the air and my head was under water. I emerged, spitting and gulping, to find her laughing beside me.

'There ! You see ! '

'I'll help you. You've got to learn. Here.' One hand touched the base of my neck; and then I felt the pressure of her other hand in the small of my back. 'Now. . . . Easy. . . . Yes. . . . That's right. . . . That's right. . . .' Each contact between us might have been accidental and wholly innocent; and each might have been planned by her with the most perverse ingenuity. I could not tell. For a long time—how long? It seemed an infinity, and yet when it was over it all seemed to have passed in a flash—she grappled with me and we would grapple with each other, laughing, kicking, splashing water into each other's mouths and eyes, clawing, shouting. Then, at last, she lay back, perfectly still on the perfectly still water, with her eyes shut. 'You'll learn,' she murmured. 'You're almost there now.'

'Almost.' Her words could have equally well referred to something else.

'But you must learn to relax more. That's the secret.'

'Yes.'

'It's the secret of almost everything in life. . . . Oh, I'm feeling hungry ! Shall we go back? '

'Yes.'

This time we swam slowly, side by side, she with a powerful side-stroke and I a breast-stroke.

'Well, dear, if you insist, just in and out. But don't dawdle ! ' It was the same conversation which we had left who knew how long ago. 'Now, there's a lovely piece of prose.' She was showing a book to Colethorpe, who sat knees clasped beside her. 'I do it with some of my tots. I suppose you think it's too difficult '—she was puffing greedily at a cigarette between phrases—' but you'd be surprised what these eight- and nine-year-olds will take. . . . *Travels with a Donkey*, Mr. Knox,' she explained as we squatted beside her. ' I know I'm old-fashioned to be so crazy about Stevenson. But I find him hard to beat.' Her hand had been fumbling in her bag and now emerged holding a cigarette which she at once lit from the one in her mouth. ' This bad girl '—she meant Colethorpe—' coaxed me into having a cigarette and now I just can't stop. And I haven't got my holder with me and my fingers will be ruined.' I noticed, for the first time, the orange stains on forefinger and middle-finger. ' I've been telling her that she's too young to smoke. She'll ruin her health.'

' Oh, I never smoke more than ten a day.' Colethorpe's attention was really focused on Frank who was doing press-ups a few feet away from us.

' Ten a day ! ' Miss Rosenthal screeched. ' Mercy ! I doubt if I smoke that many in a week.'

' I'm sure you must,' Setsuko said in a quiet voice, and at once asked : ' Where are the others ? '

' Mr. Welling, you mean—and that pretty little Japanese girl? They just swam away and away and away, like you two people, and disappeared from sight. You missed a fine exhibition of diving from Aileen. I may call you Aileen, mayn't I, dear? I'm Ruth—Ruthie to my friends. . . . Now, Norah, dear, do what I said and come out of that sun. First it'll make blisters, just as it did after that afternoon on Mount Hiei. And second it's the worst thing for your tummy——'

' Oh, all right, all right ! ' Norah dragged her towel over the sand towards us and threw herself down on it, in the shade of a tree.

' My, you do fuss ! ' she said.

' If nobody fussed over you, where would you be? In the hospital, I guess.'

' Oh, there they are ! At last. I'm getting hungry.' Colethorpe pointed towards the bamboo-plantation to our left, all the lower branches of which seemed to be totally denuded of foliage as they stuck out, matchstick thin and white, over a clogged litter of people, bottles, tin cans, used wrapping-paper and empty *sushi* boxes. For a while I could distinguish no one : until suddenly, between one patch of shadow and the next, Welling and Sanae emerged, bare-foot and in their bathing-costumes, he seeming preternaturally tall and she preternaturally tiny beside him. The light under the trees, in contrast to the dazzle in which we ourselves were basking, was green and soupy, like the water at the bottom of a stagnant pond, and it gave to the flesh of the two advancing figures a curious metallic sheen as they were wafted, on somnolent wave after wave of it, towards the beach and us. At one point they had apparently forsaken the path to take a short-cut which brought them to a steep slope. Welling jumped down; Sanae hesitated: no doubt with that assumed helplessness which Japanese women imagine to be attractive to their men. He held out his arms but, instead of jumping into them, she grasped only one and slithered down with its aid, in a shower of dust and pebbles.

'Silly of them to go off like that,' Setsuko said.

'Oh, it's impossible to get lost in a place of this kind,' Miss Rosenthal said, plugging her half-smoked cigarette into the sand beside her.

'I didn't mean getting lost.'

'Then——?' Already the furtive hand was groping about inside the bag: an old-fashioned, capacious affair of crocheted brown silk with an amber frame and cracked amber clasp.

'Mr. Welling is married, isn't he? And a missionary, too.'

'Oh, my dear!' Miss Rosenthal extended her hand, rough little palm upwards, with the cigarette in it, as though she were offering it to Setsuko. 'But he's old enough to be her father. I don't think we need have any fears—any fears at all.' She gave a falsetto tinkle of laughter and inserted the cigarette between her lips.

'She's one of Mike's Bible Class, you know,' Frank said, picking at a piece of loose skin between his toes.

'Mr. Welling is no wolf. Oh my, no!' Norah put in.

All three of them had obviously been annoyed by Setsuko's remark; and yet I fancied that each of them had secretly thought the thing which they were now so anxious to repudiate.

'I'm not suggesting that he's a wolf!' Setsuko laughed. 'It's the last thing that I'd suggest about Mr. Welling. I'd be much more likely to suggest that little Sanae was a wolverine. That's the feminine of wolf, isn't it? If not, it ought to be.' Colethorpe looked sharply at her and might even have said something in Sanae's defence if Setsuko had not gone on: 'I'm sure that their little walk was entirely innocent. All I'm wondering is if it was also *wise*.'

'Why, what do you mean, Miss Furomoto? . . . Oh, this wind! I'll never get this cigarette lit.'

'You've lived in Japan long enough to know how people gossip. And being a missionary, I expect you know how much all you missionaries are under scrutiny. People love to catch you out. It's natural—human.'

'Well, yes, I guess we are in a kind of—kind of prominent position . . .' Miss Rosenthal conceded uneasily.

'And so you must be careful not merely about what you do, but about what you appear to do.' I felt that Setsuko was taking a cruel pleasure in reminding them of their vulnerability. 'Half Kyoto is here today, and there must be all sorts of people who know Mr. Welling, if only by sight. It's a little unusual, you know, in this country for a man to wander off alone with a girl— with a Japanese girl. If Frank here wandered off with Aileen, that would cause less comment. They are both Westerners and so no Japanese rules could really be applied to them.' Frank's watery eyes seemed to become smaller and his receding chin to recede yet more, as he reddened at this last remark.

'Well, you two people, where have you been? We're all starving. We thought that maybe you were lost.' The note of forced joviality in Miss Rosenthal's voice betrayed the unease which Setsuko had succeeded in creating in her.

Sanae had stopped to extract a thorn from her bare foot. She looked up and smiled: 'We were playing ping-pong,' she said.

'Ping-pong!' Norah exclaimed.

'Yes. The other side of the wood they have a kind of fun-fair. You should see it.' Welling squatted beside me, relaxed, cheerful and totally unaware of the comment his absence had aroused. 'We found three ping-pong tables out of doors, so I challenged Sanae here to a match.' 'Sanae!' It was the first time I had heard him use her Christian name.

'He beat me,' Sanae said. 'He's too strong for me. He ought to play with Setsuko. She plays like a man.'

'Nonsense,' Setsuko put in crossly. 'I'm a very average player.'

'Well, people, how about some food? I'm the only one of you who hasn't done any exercise and I seem to be the hungriest.' I had noticed that, at Welling's approach, Miss Rosenthal had at once thrown away her recently lit cigarette. 'Pass me that bag, dear.' She pointed to an object which looked as if it had been made out of a discarded macintosh and Norah dutifully brought it to her. 'Now, Norah, this package of sandwiches is specially for you. Yes, dear, I had Mukai-San make them specially. There's nothing in them that can possibly upset you. . . . Why, Mr. Knox, what's that you have there? A bottle of wine! And at mid-day and in this sun! You'll have us all tipsy in no time at all.' Her giggle of shocked delight would have been more appropriate if I had produced a phallus from the picnic basket.

Only Colethorpe, Setsuko and I drank the wine in the end and it made us so sleepy that, as soon as the meal was over, the three of us dragged ourselves up to the hotel to lie down for an hour. Colethorpe and Setsuko went, inevitably, into the one room and I into the other, and I found myself cursing the English girl for her impeding presence. There was a bed of a kind with a mattress stuffed with straw and on to this I threw myself. For a time, half-asleep and half-awake, I went over Setsuko's attempt to teach me how to float; then I lost consciousness.

. . . 'Bill! Hey, Bill!' I was roused by her hand shaking my leg above the knee. She was seated on the bed beside me. 'You're missing all the best part of the afternoon. Come on! Get up!' I raised myself on an elbow and at once she moved her hand to my shoulder and again shook me: 'Come and have a swim!'

'What time is it?' I yawned. My mouth felt as if it were stuffed with cobwebs.

'Half-past three.'

'And the others?'

'Oh, Aileen and Frank have gone off on one of those pedal-boats. They're rather fun, like a bicycle. We might try one. Norah has at last been allowed to go into the sea and the two of them are now reading women's magazines—the kind that tell you how to turn an old raincoat into an attractive picnic bag!'

'So you noticed that bag, too. And Welling and Sanae?'

She frowned. 'The silly little rabbit! She must realise how unfair it is to him.'

'And shouldn't he realise how unfair it is to her?'

'Much less so. Sanae has little to lose, you know.'

'How so?'

'Oh, everyone has a pretty shrewd idea about her.'

'But you don't mean——'

'She's a nice little thing and a pretty little thing. But let's face

211

it, she's a tart. And people in Kyoto are clever enough to know it already—without her trotting off into the bushes with Welling.' There was a quality, both vindictive and brutal, in not merely her words but her tone and her expression, which vaguely shocked me.

'But what reason have you for saying that, Setsuko?' I asked.

'In the first place, her job.'

'She's been doing that job ever since you've known her. And yet there was a time—I remember it well—when you regarded her as a poor little innocent whom it was your duty to protect from a cruel and corrupting world.'

She did not care for that reminder. 'Yes, I was hoodwinked by her, as Welling is now. And in my case there was less excuse. After all, I *know* Japanese women—I'm partly one myself. All that simpering and giggling and bowing and pretence of knowing nothing and having experienced nothing—it's nauseating really, when one is aware of what's behind it and beneath it.'

'But in the case of Sanae, have you any proof that——'

'Not in black and white. But she's got a boy friend all right. Perhaps a whole series of boy friends.'

I had got off the bed and we had now begun to take the path through the garden to the shore.

'I can't believe it!'

'Of course you can't.' She laughed. 'No Western man can. Oh, yes, the little minx has someone, I'm sure of that. She often doesn't come home for the night—has some excuse about having to look after a Korean friend whose lover recently killed himself. I don't believe it for a moment, even if Aileen does. No, she's up to something and up to something pretty lucrative to judge by the clothes she's bought herself recently. That swimming-costume, for example. . . . It's Italian, not Japanese, and she paid a fortune for it. What was particularly suspicious was that she at once took out the Italian tag and sewed in a Japanese one. She didn't know that I'd seen the costume before she had time to make that little change!'

How she had seen the costume she did not explain; and I thought it more tactful not to ask her.

'One can't really blame her,' Setsuko was going on. 'She has no University qualifications, no family, no money. And she's not all that bright. She's a beautiful girl—that's her only asset.

So her one chance is to find herself a lover before she gets too old and to ensure that, before he abandons her, he sets her up in style. If rich enough, Japanese men usually do their discarded mistresses proud.'

'I thought you liked her.'

'Well, of course I do. Of course I like her. But I can speak about her dispassionately.'

'But that's precisely what you can't do,' I wanted to protest; but did not.

'Are you interested in cooking, Mr. Knox?' Miss Rosenthal looked up to ask as we approached.

'No. Only in food.'

'Well, that's a pity. There's a fascinating little article here on the 'Bachelor in the Kitchen'. It's written by an English author who's also a lord—I'll find it for you—and he explains how he prepares all those delicious meals for his guests in his lovely little house somewhere overlooking a park in London. You may know him, perhaps.'

Eventually, to escape from the two women, who were themselves pathetically eager to detain us, Setsuko and I decided to take a pedal-boat, Miss Rosenthal calling after us in warning: 'Oh, do be careful now, Miss Furomoto, Mr. Knox. Those boats have a habit of suddenly deflating. A very dear friend of mine was almost drowned one summer at Biarritz and if it hadn't been for this lifeguard . . .' The rest of it was inaudible.

We pedalled out and out in silence; the two seats, built for Japanese not Western bodies, so narrow that our thighs rubbed against each other with each rotation and our arms touched. Clefts in the mountains behind us were already brimming with shadows as the sunlight glanced diagonally across the water, ripping a path through the waves. 'Oh, it's so beautiful,' Setsuko sighed. Then she laughed: 'If only we could pedal in time! You're rubbing my knees raw.'

'Let's try.'

We tried. But 'No, no!' she cried out after a few seconds. 'Our rhythms are quite different. And your legs are much longer than mine.'

'Does it really matter? At least the boat is moving.'

'But it's so uncomfortable.'

When we had gone far, far out from land, she stopped pedalling, stood up, braced herself and then, without a word, executed a

213

perfect dive into the water. 'Come on!' she shouted, lying on her back and churning the water into spray.

'And the boat?'

'It won't travel far. The tide is going in.'

My own scramble to join her was far less graceful; and, as Setsuko at once reminded me, I had forgotten to take off my dark glasses.

'Blast!... Never mind. I can see. After a fashion. And I never put my head under the water when swimming—if I can help it.'

'But you look quite ridiculous. Give them to me and I'll take them to the boat.'

'No. It's not necessary.'

'Give them to me.'

'No.'

It was a childish contest. 'Give them to me, I say, or I'll fetch them.'

'Fetch them, then.'

With three swift strokes she was upon me and we began to wrestle. 'Take care! We'll lose them altogether!'

'Serve you right!' One arm encircled both my arms, while she raised the other in an attempt to jerk off the glasses. I slithered away, churned round behind her and, placing both hands on her shoulders, attempted to duck her.

God knows how long it would have gone on if an immense white motor-boat had not suddenly borne down on us, goring for itself a jagged arc exactly concentric with the wider arc of the bay. Its roar became a buzz as we found ourselves buffeted hither and thither by the diminishing shocks of its passage.

'That's bloody dangerous,' Setsuko said. The boat pursued its course, distant now, like a stone whirled at the end of an invisible piece of string, regardless of bathers. 'Someone might get killed. And it's just to show off, just to say: "Look, we've got a beautiful new boat, while you have to swim!" Some "parvenu" family from Osaka, I expect.'

Again the boat ripped through the sea towards us, and this time Setsuko began to wave her arms and shout in Japanese: 'Go away! Leave us alone! Can't you go somewhere else!' I had to laugh; it was like running at a tank with a kitchen-knife. No one on the boat could possibly hear her. Then suddenly she stopped, once more we were deafened and flung hither and thither.

Choking on water and thrusting her hair away from her face with both of her hands, she asked: 'Do you realise who that was?'

'No.'

'Guess.'

'The Emperor.'

'Don't be silly. . . . Furomoto.'

'Furomoto!'

'With his wife. It's not often she goes out. In an absurd white yachting-cap and dark glasses even larger than yours. Just like the old brute. It must give him a kick—oh, a tremendous kick—to send people flying to right and left of him, and if he drowns one or two—well, what the hell?'

'Who else was with them?'

'No one, except that muscle-bound youth who has taken the place of Nakatani. He was last year's University boxing champion or wrestling champion or something like that.'

'Do you think Furomoto recognised us?'

'I doubt it. We were just another two victims beneath the wheels of his triumphal car.'

At that she began to swim towards the pedal-boat and I followed her.

'Did you see your uncle's boat?' Norah asked as soon as we reached the shore.

'My, what a beauty!' Miss Rosenthal exclaimed. 'You know, I've always wanted to meet your uncle. He must be such an interesting man.'

'Oh, yes, he's interesting. Psychopaths usually are.'

Miss Rosenthal gave an unreal laugh. 'You know him, Miss Colethorpe, don't you? I'm sure you wouldn't describe him as a psychopath.'

'Oh, yes, I would! If I felt in a charitable mood.'

Miss Rosenthal's cigarette hung from her lower lip in mingled perplexity and dejection. 'You two girls are having your joke,' she said at last.

During this conversation Sanae had got up and wandered off alone. I watched her, thinking how curious was the whole process of sexual attraction. She was young; physically she was perfect in every way; Setsuko could not compare with her. Perhaps even her character was better than Setsuko's. And yet, as I gazed at her, admiring now the incredibly graceful walk, now the polish of the

215

skin, and now that neck and the head poised above it, I felt not even the feeblest stirring of desire for her.

Suddenly she let out a squawk and all her movements—of panic, turning, retreat—became jerky and ungainly. What was the matter? Then I saw that two vast, wolf-like dogs were advancing along the beach at a loping pace. She began to run; and seeing her run, they quickened in pursuit. An American voice rang out: 'Ben! Bertha! Here! Come here! Come here, I say!'

'Mercy me!' Miss Rosenthal wailed.

'Oh, do something, do something, do something,' Norah gulped.

In the end it was not I, Frank or Welling who did something but, surprisingly, Colethorpe. She grabbed Miss Rosenthal's macintosh-bag and rushed towards the dogs, shouting and waving it at them. They halted; they looked at each other, their tongues hanging from their slavering jaws; one snarled; and then they trotted off.

'Oh, good for you, Miss Colethorpe! Good for you!' Miss Rosenthal applauded her as though she had scored a decisive point at tennis. 'That was just wonderful.'

It was only then that I noticed that Sanae had scuttled to shelter behind Welling, where she now crouched, doubled up, in a state of hysterical giggling. 'Thank you, Aileen,' she controlled herself enough to say. 'Thanks.'

'Sorry about that,' a voice grated behind us. 'They're disobedient brutes. But you ought never to run away from dogs. That's asking for trouble.'

I turned; and discovered that it was Ed Schneider, the American journalist whom I had met at the 'Art Insaissible' exhibition, his vast, protruding belly concealed beneath a check shirt worn outside his khaki trousers like a maternity-jacket, and a grey linen sun-hat perched at the back of his head, with the silver hair sticking out in prongs from under it in front. Two plastic leashes were wound tightly round and round one swollen, purple hand and even up the dropsical wrist.

'Hello, Mr. Schneider,' Colethorpe said. She had presumably met him at the exhibition.

'Why, hello, m'dear.' He drew a crumpled handkerchief out of his trouser-pocket and rubbed it over his face with what was more a groan than a sigh. 'This heat!' He looked down at Sanae: 'Yes, little girl, never run away from a dog. That's the way to invite it to kill you. . . . Hello, there,' he smiled and nodded

216

at me and then, glancing down, noticed the bottle of wine in the shade of the tree against which Miss Rosenthal was propped. 'Do you like this Japanese ink?' He extended a small foot in a grubby tennis-shoe.

'Better than nothing.'

He picked up the bottle. 'What is it?' He examined the label, and then drew out the cork and sniffed at what was left of the contents. Suddenly he raised the bottle and gulped. 'P-o-o-o-h!' The purple face contorted itself, the loose lips curving outwards until the upper one almost touched the bulbous, heavily-veined nose and the lower one the chin. 'Disgusting!' But he gulped again and yet again. 'Poison. Sheer poison. Gut-rot. . . . Down, you monster, down!' One of the dogs had scampered up and was jumping around him, as though eager to share the liquor. 'Down, I say!'

Frank approached the dog warily. 'That's a nice dog,' he said. 'What is it?'

'Akita.'

'Nice dog.' Frank put out a hand.

'No, don't touch him, don't touch him!'

'Why? Does he bite?' Frank hurriedly retreated.

'Sometimes. But only Japanese. You don't have to worry. . . . No, it's the smell. Get that on your hands and you'll have a time getting it off.'

'Why, don't you wash him?' Miss Rosenthal enquired.

'Wash him! We're always washing him. But as soon as we've finished, he runs out and finds some muck or other and rolls in it. Usually something dead—and something that's been dead a long time. A real necrophiliac, you might say. Seems to have no other interest. . . . No, old boy'—it was with a parody of a British accent that he now turned to address me—'you shouldn't drink this stuff.' Wheezing and grunting, he stooped to replace the bottle by the tree. 'It's not even made from the grape, you know. Just neat alcohol and some chemical flavouring. Bad, very bad. Take my advice. . . . Come *here*, Bertha! Come here! . . . Well, so long, folks. It's been nice seeing you. Real nice.' The mimicry seemed all at once to have been switched from me to Miss Rosenthal. 'Bye there!'

'So that's Ed Schneider,' said Frank.

'My, but it's sad!' exclaimed Miss Rosenthal. 'People say he was one of the best foreign journalists they ever had in Japan.

And so handsome. It's a kind of—kind of warning to us all, I guess.'

'He ought to keep those dogs on a lead.' Sanae got up from where she was still crouched behind Welling and, taking a comb from her bag, began to tug it through her hair. 'They're dangerous.'

'And imagine keeping a dog that likes to roll in things that are *dead*!' Norah exclaimed. 'It *did* smell, too. I could smell it.'

'Oh, that child's so sensitive! She's always smelling something or other. . . . Now, people, how about a little spelling game? Yes, Sanae, Miss Furomoto—you can play too. It's very simple. It's like this. I begin with a letter, and then Mr. Welling here. . . . My, I do believe Mr. Knox has fallen off to sleep. Nudge him, Norah dear. Nudge him.'

SIXTEEN

PROBABLY it was Colethorpe's growing dissatisfaction with Frank which impelled her that day to quarrel with Sanae. Soon—but not yet—she would be quarrelling with Frank himself. He was always considerate, kind, admiring, affectionate, generous: what more could she want? Nothing, she had thought at first. But he bored her. Occasionally she even found herself comparing him with the Englishman next door, until she had to check herself, appalled by her disloyalty. Knox was middle-aged; his figure was beginning to sag; his hair was thinning and turning grey; he tended to be disagreeable, off-hand and sharp: and yet she found herself actually envying Setsuko because he was in love with her. An affair with him would be seldom enjoyable; but at least it would be interesting.

That morning Frank had inspected some of her pictures. 'Why, they're gorgeous, honey, just gorgeous.' He held one to the light. 'You've got something there. I like this coffee-colour you've started to use. Yes, I like it.'

'Do you really?'

'Sure. . . . You know, when I look round at all this work of yours, I feel so small. I wish I had this creative thing. A wonderful thing to have.'

The terrible part was that he meant every word of what he said: he admired her and he admired her work, and even if he understood neither, he believed them to be, as he now put it, 'unbeatable'. ('Yes, it's unbeatable, this new technique you've started. Furomoto can't touch it.')

Soon he began to talk about the holiday which he, Colethorpe and the two Amblesides were planning to take in his car. He pulled out maps from his brief-case and some brochures which he had just collected from the Japan Tourist Bureau. 'This is how I'd planned it. . . . Now, wait a minute, wait a minute. . . . Yes. . . . We drive first day to Nagoya, that's it. . . . We drive first to Nagoya. . . .' She followed his pencil over the map, but took in nothing of what he was saying. Two weeks, two weeks in his company ! And yet a month ago she would have been delighted by the prospect.

'. . . It's a pity we can't camp out, as we planned. But Mrs. Ambleside—well, she's getting to be an old lady, I guess—and she'd rather we put up in hotels.'

'Yes, hotels would be better.'

He took her tonelessness for an indication that she was displeased by the inclusion of the Amblesides in the party. 'I know it would be lots more fun if we were just us two together, but you do see——'

'Well, of course, Frank. Of course I do.' In fact—though she would not admit this to him—she was now actually relieved by the presence of the Amblesides.

'It's like Setsuko said. We may not do anything wrong, but we mustn't even let anyone *think* we're doing anything wrong. You remember she said that? Well, she's right. Setsuko's a pretty clever girl and she knows Japan, as we don't. We missionaries—well, like she said—we're vulnerable people. We've got to be careful.'

'I've never complained about the Amblesides coming with us.'

'No. But I know how you feel about it. And I know how I feel about it.' He put an arm round her shoulders and gave her a couple of perfunctory kisses, first on the line of her jaw and then on her cheek, looking, with his receding chin and long nose, as if he were taking two half-hearted pecks out of her. Embarrassed, he soon released her to ask: 'Sanae in?'

'No. She's gone to do some shopping.'

'Good. . . . You know, dear, I want you to have a word with her. You can do it best. You and she are such close friends, she'll take it from you.'

'A word with her?'

'About Welling. We're all a bit worried at the mission. It's like Setsuko said—we're vulnerable, we missionaries, pretty vulnerable, and we've got to be careful.' Frank tended to repeat phrases; and they were usually not his own phrases, but the phrases of others. 'Now Welling's a good fellow, but he's obstinate. There's been gossip about him and Sanae—seen together here, seen together there; sometimes he waits for her in his car to take her to the station—all innocent, nothing wrong in it, nothing wrong in it at all. But people *talk*, in a town like this they talk. Seems Mrs. Crawley heard something from a Japanese girl-friend of hers—quite an important woman in the Christian community, a Mrs. Ito, maybe you know her?' Colethorpe shook her head. 'Then one of the girls in Norah's drama group hinted something—just hinted it, there was nothing much to go on. Norah couldn't even take her up on it because maybe there was nothing there at all in the first place.'

'Oh, who cares! If people have nothing better to do than to talk about things that are no business of theirs, well let them talk.' This world of missionaries, constantly preoccupied with what others would think of them, was not her world, and she was regretting more and more that she had ever allowed Frank to draw her into it. She had finished once and for all with that kind of nonsense (as she phrased it to herself) when, five years ago, she had marched out of her Bolton home and set off for Spain in the company of a man, a fellow art-student, who wished neither to marry her nor sleep with her. 'Really, I can't be bothered. I've no use for convention. I'm sorry.'

'Well, that's all right for you, Aileen. You're an artist. An artist enjoys a kind of freedom. But for Welling—or for me—it's different. We've got to think of the work of the mission—we mustn't do anything that might damage the work of the mission. You see that, don't you?'

'In that case it's Mr. Ambleside's job to speak to Mr. Welling. He's the head of the mission, isn't he?'

'Sure, he's the head of the mission. And he did try to speak to him.' Frank cupped what there was of his chin in one of his muscular hands, while his watery blue eyes focused themselves on the *collage* he had set down on the table.

'Well? And what was the result?'

'Welling got mad at him, real mad. He's a good man, Welling, one of the best. But obstinate. And he's got a temper. . . . Then Ambleside asked me to talk to him. Well, I didn't like the assignment, but what was I to do? We're pretty close friends, and maybe Ambleside thought he'd take it from me. But no indeed!'

'And so you want me to poke my nose into the whole business as well?'

'It's for the sake of Sanae quite as much as for Welling's sake. She's your girl friend, isn't she? And for the sake of the mission,' he added.

'To hell with the mission!' Colethorpe almost burst out. But she restrained herself. 'Sanae's quite as stubborn as Welling. You don't know her. I've never been able to persuade her to do any-

221

thing she didn't want to do. Besides there's no harm in this friendship, and if she gets something out of it, what right have I to come along and tell her to put an end to it? '

'Sure, there's no harm in it. As I see it—and I told the others the same thing this morning—it's a kind of father-daughter business. The poor kid's an orphan, isn't she? And Welling's wife is away and his son is away. He's got this protective thing, he's got to have someone to protect, someone to look after. You should have seen him when his wife fell sick. . . . But if they go on like this, he's going to harm himself—and harm our work too. And, of course, harm the girl.'

'Well, I can't help. I'm sorry.'

The firmness of her refusal made him jerk his head up at her, hurt and astonished. She felt a pang of remorse. 'It's just not my line,' she went on, trying to conciliate him. 'You know that as well as I do. There's nothing I loathe more than poking my nose into the private affairs of others—unless it's others poking their noses into mine! Sorry, Frank dear. You mustn't be angry with me.' She went over to him, put an arm round him, and then slipped a hand inside his shirt. 'Frank! Don't be angry.'

'Aileen, I'm not angry! Why should I be angry? ' He was, in fact, acutely embarrassed, as always, by any show, other than verbal, of the affection between them. Again he pecked at her, and then moved away. 'I respect your attitude. It's a fine attitude, very fine. But it leaves me worried. We're all worried, at the mission. Gosh, I wish that Mrs. Welling would get better soon! '

After a short while he hurried off to take part in a baseball match between members of the American community and a team from one of the Universities.

'Coming to the ball-game? ' he asked.

'I don't know yet. Perhaps.' From time to time she had to watch him playing in some game of this kind and invariably it bored her. If they got married, she would have to do it for the rest of her life, she now told herself.

'Try to make it, dear. If I know that you're out there, cheering for me, somehow I feel better.' She had never once cheered for him; and that made his plea even more difficult to resist and her guilt even sharper.

'I'll try.'

'That's the girl! '

He left her, as he usually left her these days, with a feeling of

222

combined tenderness, remorse and irritation; but it was the irritation that now predominated. Physically he was the type which always attracted her and she had fallen in love with others like him: a rugger-playing medical student; a swimming-instructor at Sitges; a German in Rome with more talent as an amateur boxer than as the artist he imagined himself to be. All these men had had in common an ox-like physique; a coquettish vanity; great kindness; great stupidity; and a total inadequacy as lovers. For a time these last two defects had even exerted on her an additional charm; until, as in the case of Frank, they had begun to exasperate her, and eventually had annulled all other attractions.

When she returned from the hall, the realisation smote her: 'I shall never marry him.' But having got in so far, how was she to get out again? With a guilty panic, she thought of all the humiliation and pain she had had to inflict in the past on men who had never ceased to protest that they could not see what they had done wrong or what had gone wrong. Probably it would be easiest for her, as on those previous occasions, to pack her bags and fly. But Japan was so far from anywhere and she had so little money. What an idiot she had been! And as she thought that, she also thought resentfully of Frank for having made such an idiot of her.

At Sanae's return, Colethorpe's anxiety and annoyance drove her to do the exact thing which she had told Frank, less than an hour before, that she would on no account do: speak about Welling. Sanae was singing as she entered the house, in one hand a shopping-basket and in the other a fan; and her obvious happiness was an added goad.

'Frank was here.'

'Oh, was he?' Colethorpe had long ago guessed that both Setsuko and Sanae found Frank as tedious as she herself did now. 'I thought he had a game.'

'He has.'

'Aren't you going?'

'No.'

Sanae undid a parcel and pulled out a silk dress-length—a pattern of autumn maple-leaves—which she held up against herself. 'Like it?'

'Very pretty. Who gave it to you?'

'Nobody, of course. Who gives me presents? Apart from you.' She answered with apparent naturalness. 'I bought it. At Takashimaya. It was marked down. Look.' She showed the price-ticket. 'They have a sale. You ought to go.'

'I haven't any money. . . . It's ten days, you know, since we gave Setsuko anything towards the housekeeping.' Sanae, smoothing out the silk, took no notice. 'You'd better not let her see that you've been shopping. She might think that any money you had to spare ought to go to her.'

'Oh, they have plenty,' Sanae said, off-hand.

'I don't know that they have. But, anyway, that's hardly the point. Is it? '

'Any letters? '

'I don't think so.' From whom, Colethorpe wondered, was she expecting to hear? This was the second time that day that she had asked the question.

'Perhaps Setsuko hasn't finished opening them.'

'What do you mean? '

'Oh, she's so inquisitive ! '

'I'm quite sure she wouldn't dream of——'

'Sometimes I think that I want to leave here.'

'Leave here? '

Sanae shrugged and said in a composed voice: 'Why not? '

'But where would we go? Or'—she added as an afterthought —'do you mean that you want to leave alone? '

'I don't know.' Seeing the look of shock on her friend's face, Sanae added, in the same calm, measured voice: 'I like being with you, Aileen. We are good friends. You leave me alone, and I leave you alone. That's good. But Setsuko——! '

'Why on earth have you got your knife into poor Setsuko? She's very fond of you, I know.'

'Yes, I know. That is why.'

'I don't understand.'

'I feel that she is everywhere. Everything I do, every place I go— she gets mixed up in it. I don't want her. . . . You're different. You have your own business, I have mine.'

'But now I'm going to have to interfere in your business, Sanae. Probably you'll think that I'm as bad as Setsuko. But I feel I must.'

Sanae paused in the doorway; clicked open her fan and waved it back and forth, three or four times, before her face. 'Oh, it's so hot! ' she exclaimed. Then she smiled: 'Well, what is it? '

'They're worried over at the mission. Frank's just been telling me.'

'At the mission? Has the mission something to do with me?'

'You know it has. There's been talk about you and Mr. Welling. The whole town is buzzing with it. Don't you think you're being a little indiscreet?' She spoke of the journeys together in the car—and such a conspicuous car—and of their walk alone in the woods on the Sunday they went to the beach; while Sanae leant against the wall and listened, with an irritating smile of benign amusement. 'I'm not at all conventional, you know that, Sanae. But to do these things with a missionary——'

'Frank is a missionary.'

'But not married. That's the difference.'

Suddenly it was as if the two of them had grappled with each other. 'Mr. Welling is my teacher. We have done nothing wrong. He is a friend, the best friend I have.'

It was impossible for Colethorpe not to feel a pang of jealousy at that declaration; and it was precisely because she knew this that Sanae had made it.

'Of course.' An ironic inflection hinted disbelief.

'You cannot understand this, but for the last few weeks I have felt closer and closer to my religion. And for that I thank Mr. Welling. He has made it real to me again.'

Colethorpe gave a smile of malicious amusement. 'Yes, I see.' She crossed her arms under her capacious breasts, pressing them upwards so that they bulged against her grubby white cotton blouse. 'Well, I've said my little piece. For what it's worth. If you like him and respect him, then you don't want to hurt him, do you? . . . Do you?' she repeated, sensing that this argument had gone to its mark. 'You don't want to make his work here impossible.'

Sanae hung her head, pulling at her lower lip between her small, glittering teeth. When she looked up, Colethorpe was astonished to see that there were tears on her eyelashes: 'No, I do not wish to do anything to—to make his life in Kyoto difficult. But . . . but . . .' Suddenly she hardened again, having come so close to softening. She laughed, on a note of restrained hysteria: 'Yes, you are as bad as Setsuko, after all! You unmarried women cannot bear to have others happy!'

Colethorpe flushed: 'I may be unmarried, but I'm hardly the frustrated spinster you seem to imagine.'

'I must go and put these things away and tidy my room before I start for work.' Her beautiful mouth became momentarily ugly as the corners turned down in what was half a smile and half a grimace. 'The room must be tidy for Setsuko.'

'For Setsuko?' Colethorpe did not understand.

'Oh, when she comes to make her little inspection. . . . At least, I think it is her and not you.'

'Her inspection?'

'Yes. Perhaps she also inspects your room, when you're out. Have you noticed?'

'Setsuko would never dream of doing such a thing!'

Sanae shrugged faintly and once again smiled.

'What reason have you for making such a nasty suggestion?'

'I know where I leave things. And I know how I leave things. I fold something *so*, and, when I come home, it is folded *so*. I put a letter *this* way into its envelope and I find it *that* way.' She mimed these differences, the fan now dangling from her wrist and her parcels on the floor about her.

'You're imagining all this.'

Sanae shook her head.

'Of course you are. Apart from anything else, Setsuko is far too busy to snoop about your room. Besides, what would be the point? What interest could your things have for her?'

'She is interested in me.'

'I'm interested in you. But I don't ransack your belongings.'

'No. But that is—different.' The two women faced each other: Sanae's face serene and smiling; Colethorpe's flushed and contorted with bewilderment and indignation. 'Don't you understand?'

'I see no difference.'

'There is a difference.' Sanae went out and then returned to say: 'This evening I have promised to stay at the Korean's. Please do not expect me home.'

'Again!' Her voice and her expression both expressed the same disbelief which she had so indignantly repudiated that morning when Setsuko had voiced it to her. ('You know, Aileen, there's something more than a little fishy about these evenings that Sanae spends in Osaka. . . .') 'Surely she must have got over it by now. It's weeks and weeks.'

Sanae shrugged: to all appearances not in the least embarrassed by her friend's incredulity, and perhaps even unaware of it. 'I guess she loved him more than we thought. And these Koreans are all

226

funny. She thinks that maybe his ghost visit her if she is alone.'

'Sanae. . . .' Colethorpe checked the other girl as she was about to leave the room again. 'You are—you are telling the truth, aren't you? About staying with the Korean, I mean.'

Sanae swung round, her face twisted in fury. Colethorpe, in all the months they had been together, had never once seen her like that before. 'What do you wish to say?' she demanded savagely. 'Do you think I lie to you?'

'It just struck me . . . I just thought . . .' Colethorpe faltered; suddenly an inexplicable sensation of terror had come over her.

'Do you imagine that I go to someone else?' Sanae challenged again. 'Do you?'

'Well . . . it . . . all seems so—so odd . . . This Korean— not really a friend of yours—and so many nights, two and three each week. . . . Sanae, you're—you're not—it's not—it's not Welling, is it?'

'Mr. Welling! Are you crazy?' Her fury seemed to rise up before Colethorpe like some vast wave, to batter down and suffo- cate her. 'Are you crazy? You—you are worse than Setsuko. No, not worse. Setsuko has said this to you. This is Setsuko. But you too. You are both—both disgusting. You cannot understand the friendship between Mr. Welling and myself. You think that it must be the same as your kind of friendship with Frank or hers with that Englishman. . . . Mr. Welling and I have never even kissed. Do you understand? We have never even kissed. But you will not believe that! You will only believe the dirt Setsuko makes you believe!' Suddenly her flushed face crumpled up and she began to gulp with horrible, tearing sobs, biting on the knuckles of her right hand. 'He is a good man. He does not think of sex, sex, sex. I tell you, he has never even kissed me! Never, never, never!'

She rushed up the stairs, her sobs becoming louder and louder and more and more uncontrolled. Colethorpe was appalled. Mrs. Furomoto, no doubt having heard the noise, appeared from the back of the house where she had her quarters. But she made no reference to the scene.

'Sanae has left some parcels here.'

'Yes. I expect she'll come back for them.' Colethorpe could barely speak; her lower jaw was trembling and she felt icy. It was some seconds before she was aware that the old woman had begun to pick them up off the floor and went across to help her.

'Perhaps you would like a cup of tea?'

'Thank you. Yes. That would be nice.'

'And shall I take a cup to Sanae?'

'I expect she'd like one.'

The old face was beautiful—just how beautiful, Colethorpe only now realised for the first time—in its habitual expression of serene resignation. How little one knew about her—even though one knew so many of the facts: the translations of Thoreau and Richard Jefferies made when she was young; the prolonged cruelty of the marriage to Furomoto and its sudden explosion; her present absorption in brush-work, flower-arrangement and the tea-ceremony. . . . Perhaps with a Japanese woman of her generation it was impossible for any foreign woman of Colethorpe's generation to establish an intimacy. It was now nearly three months that they had seen each other daily under the same roof and the period might have been three hours.

Mrs. Furomoto had picked up the *collage* and was holding it out before her in those small, heavily ringed hands of hers which were always trembling slightly. 'Yes, I like this,' she said.

'Do you really?'

'Better than the ping-pong balls.'

'Then perhaps Furomoto was right.'

'Oh, never listen to him! You are a better painter than he is.'

She said the words without malice or ill-will towards her former husband or flattery to the English girl. They were, in consequence, strangely impressive. Colethorpe was touched. She even began to think that perhaps she was not as feeble an artist as she had increasingly supposed in recent weeks.

At that, Mrs. Furomoto slipped away, with a bow.

Not long after, Setsuko came in.

'This heat gets worse and worse. Why haven't you put on the fan?'

'I didn't think about it.'

'Didn't think about it! Then you must have something very important to think about! I can think of nothing else. . . . This morning Professor Miyawaki gave me some quite simple calculations to do for him and they took me most of the rest of the day. I must have a bath. It's ridiculous that in that laboratory of ours we should be working on everything from electronic brains to journeys to Mars and yet have no air-conditioners. . . . What's the matter?'

228

'The matter?'

'You look so odd.'

'Do I?'

'Perhaps it's the newspaper that's made you go so green. That wouldn't surprise me.' Colethorpe had been gazing down at a copy of the *Mainichi Daily News* when Setsuko entered.

At that moment, Mrs. Furomoto appeared with a cup of tea and a bean-cake on a diminutive saucer. She set both down on the table, and only then greeted her niece in Japanese and offered to bring some tea for her as well.

Setsuko refused; and Mrs. Furomoto glided out.

'Why on earth does she still bring you a bean-cake? I don't believe you've ever eaten one since you got here. Have you?'

Colethorpe shook her head.

'Perhaps she thinks that one day she'll break your resistance if she keeps up the pressure. That's just like her. Endless, quiet, steady pressure: so quiet and so steady that you forget all about it. But she doesn't. And she gets what she wants. She'll get you to eat bean-cakes—you'll see! . . . What is it, Aileen? Something has upset you?'

'No. Nothing.'

'Sanae?'

The clairvoyance of this astonished Colethorpe to such an extent that she nodded before she was aware of what she was doing.

'Did you have a row?'

'Not really a row. No. She got a bit excited, that was all.' Colethorpe's first loyalty being to the Japanese girl, she did not now wish to side with Setsuko against her.

'I suppose you challenged her about these evenings out?' Colethorpe stared bleakly into the other's face as it approached nearer and nearer to hers. Setsuko flopped down on a cushion on the other side of the table. 'Quite right, too. Do you suppose it's Welling? Or someone else? Or Welling *and* someone else?' Colethorpe continued to stare, without replying, her mouth parted to reveal her irregular teeth, while one hand fiddled with the zip-fastener of her skirt. 'She's a sly one, all right.'

Mrs. Furomoto again entered. 'I can't get any reply from Sanae.'

'I'll take it.' The two women had risen simultaneously; but it was Setsuko who first reached the cup of tea.

Mrs. Furomoto glanced at Colethorpe. 'Perhaps, Miss . . .' But Setsuko had already left the room.

Setsuko tried the door; and then she called: 'Sanae! I have some tea here for you! It's Setsuko. Sanae!'

'Go away.' The words were spoken distinctly and calmly, without any apparent rancour or ill-temper. But they were odd words, none the less; especially since Sanae was a guest in the house and she and Setsuko had had no overt quarrel.

'Is something the matter?' No answer. 'Sanae, is something the matter?'

'Please leave me alone.'

'But tell me what's happened? Sanae . . .'

Suddenly Setsuko could hear the screw-fastening being undone, and then, a moment later, the door slid across. Sanae was standing there, dressed to go to work and smelling of one of those Japanese scents, over-sweet and over-clinging, which she tended, like so many Japanese women, to use too liberally in spite of Colethorpe's protests.

'I don't want to talk to you.' She spoke with complete composure. 'Or to Aileen. In a moment I shall go to work.'

'But, Sanae, I think that you forget . . .' Setsuko's voice acquired a sharp edge. 'As a guest in this house—you can hardly refuse to have anything to do with one of your two hostesses.'

'I shall leave tomorrow. It's too late to leave tonight.'

'Leave! But, Sanae, why? Why? What's happened. What's all this about? You must explain. I don't understand.'

'You understand very well.'

Suddenly Colethorpe called from below in a strange, constricted voice, as though through a gag: 'I'm going out. I have to go to the post.' She hated 'scenes' and all her life had done everything possible to avoid them. When she was a child and her mother and father started one of their endless, nagging quarrels, like two dogs impelled to scratch themselves raw, she would do exactly as she was doing now: leave the house on any pretext, no matter how unconvincing, and walk, walk anywhere, until she was sure that it would be over.

'Wait a moment,' Setsuko shouted back; and then: 'Can't Sanae post your letters at the station?' But Colethorpe pretended not to hear her as she rushed out into the roadway.

Setsuko turned back to Sanae. 'Sanae, I have absolutely no idea what you're talking about.'

'I don't like to be spied on.'

'Spied on?'

230

'Yes, spied on. You know what that means, don't you?' Sanae spoke with the strident vulgarity of the girls at the theatre when they had their quarrels; to Setsuko she seemed wholly transformed. 'Do you think that I'm so unobservant that I don't know when someone has been through my belongings? Do you? I'm not such a fool.'

'I am afraid that you must be hysterical.' Setsuko spoke with a contemptuous detachment; but she kept making a curious gesture with her right hand, raising it to her mouth and then plucking at her lower lip with her forefinger and thumb. 'Completely hysterical. What interest would there be for me in going through——?'

'Why do you ask a question to which you already know the answer? But remember—"it is not only the owl that can see at night",' she quoted.

'What does that mean?'

Sanae came closer to her. 'Let me give you a little hint. You're not very clever, you ought to be more careful. You never remember to replace things as you found them, when you've finished your prying. That's bad. For example, that suitcase.' She pointed to a corner of the bedroom. 'It's upside down—notice? It was upside down when I left here yesterday, but when I came back it was right side up.' Suddenly the colour flooded into Setsuko's face, beginning at the neck and rising to the forehead. 'Not very clever, Setsuko. I'm surprised.'

'Really, Sanae . . . I can—I can assure you . . . This is some kind of persecution mania of yours . . .' But the words carried none of the incisiveness with which she had spoken until this moment. 'I can't pretend to understand——'

'When you found the photograph, what did you think? Do tell me. The photograph must have fully satisfied this—this curiosity of yours. No, don't pretend, don't pretend.' Setsuko was shaking her head, as if in agonised denial. 'You found it, of course you did. And it must have confirmed all the suspicions with which you have been filling Aileen's mind as well. Yes, the photograph of Welling. In the drawer over there. I locked the drawer, but of course you had another key. You didn't notice, though, that I had put some face-powder *here*.' She went across and showed Setsuko, running a finger along the ledge. 'It's an easy trick. I'm surprised you weren't on your guard against it. . . . Well, do tell me. What did you think when you found Mr. Welling's photograph? "So *he* is her lover. This proves it. A photograph of Welling!" Yes, I can imagine it exactly. Well, you're wrong, do you hear, you're wrong!' In sudden hysteria she turned on Setsuko, almost as though she were about to throw herself upon her and claw at her face.

'Sanae. . . . Please . . .' Setsuko was now completely cowed and abject. 'I don't care what you and Welling do together. It's no business of mine. I don't care, I just don't care! What's come over you? Why are you speaking to me like this? We've always been such friends.'

'Friends!'

'You seem to think of me as someone—someone hostile to you. Why? Why? I've always liked you—I like you—so much. It's been—we've so much enjoyed having you here. I'd never want to do anything to hurt you—harm you in any way. I'd do anything for you. Anything in the world.'

'No, no! Don't touch me! Don't come near me!'

'But, Sanae . . . Please . . .'

'No! No! Leave me! Leave me alone!' She gave Setsuko a gentle push and then a second push of far greater violence. 'Don't you see? Don't you understand? You . . . You make me feel uncomfortable.' She gave a little shudder. 'Sick. You—you nauseate me.'

Setsuko drew back, rounding her shoulders with her arms clutched in front of her, as though in a spasm of abdominal pain. Her chin sank low on to her breast. Then, suddenly, her whole body flicked open with the appearance of an animal pouncing on its victim. 'Thank you. Thank you for that pleasant little speech. Your gratitude impresses me. And now, Sanae, I suggest that you set about finding somewhere else to live. With Welling perhaps? No, that would hardly be possible at the mission. Well, I've no doubt you have other contacts as well. But get out!' Suddenly she shouted. 'Get out! And get out soon!'

At that moment the two women, confronting each other white-faced and trembling in the doorway of the bedroom, became aware that Mrs. Furomoto was standing motionless at the bottom of the stair-case, gazing up at them. They did not know how long she had been there or how much she had heard.

'Setsuko,' she said softly, when her niece's eyes focused on hers. 'There's someone here . . . Someone . . . Could you come down?'

Setsuko looked from her aunt to Sanae and then back to her aunt.

'He's come about the gramophone records—those records you ordered.'

'Just one moment!' Setsuko's voice was husky. 'Yes . . . the records . . . yes. . . .' She was putting out an effort to control herself and to make the return from the shelf of rock on which the two of them had been grappling so dizzily, far above the preoccupations of day-to-day. 'Yes, I'm coming.'

As she began to hurry down the stairs, Sanae went across to the banisters: 'Do you wish me to go now? I can go now, if you wish. But I shall be late for the theatre.'

'No, of course not. Not now. No. I didn't mean that.' She turned to mumble her answer in an embarrassment which seemed to have its source in the continued presence of her aunt in the shadows beneath them.

Sanae closed her door and began to follow Setsuko downstairs. She was entirely composed. Mrs. Furomoto had drawn back the screen-door into the sitting-room and, as Setsuko passed through ahead of her aunt, Sanae was able to look from the landing down on to the squat tousled figure which seemed to have been left, like a badly-wrapped and ill-addressed parcel, on a cushion on the floor. The man scrambled up to his feet. An unusually Mongolian face with liver-coloured blotches spattered here and there upon it; a gold tooth glinting in one corner of the mouth as it was eased into a somnolent smile; a short-sleeved shirt, open at the massive, loose-skinned neck, with a damp patch beneath the arm held out in greeting . . . Then the shutter slid back. Sanae frowned. It was odd, that extended hand; the absence of a bow. She tiptoed down to the bottom of the stairs and stood close to the screen. It was only just possible to hear their voices; they must have moved into the inner recess. But what language were they talking? Not Japanese certainly; not even English.

She glanced at her watch. Well, she could not wait here any longer. She was already five minutes late; and Welling was invariably punctual.

At the corner where the road joined the main thoroughfare, she and Colethorpe came face to face. Colethorpe shied, ducked and was about to scurry on as though they had never met. But Sanae spoke at once; totally ignoring their recent disagreement. 'Oh, Aileen! There you are! I am in a terrible hurry. I can't explain it all to you now. But Setsuko and I—we had a terrible quarrel, terrible. And now she wants me to leave. And I do not know where to go and I have so little money.'

Colethorpe experienced a momentary despairing shock; followed by relief. Only now she realised that actually she also had been wanting to quit the house. 'If you go, then, of course, I'll go with you.'

'Oh, Aileen, no! No! What will you do?'

'I'll manage. Somehow.'

'But you're as broke as I am.'

'We won't starve. Don't worry. I'll think of something—find something.'

'If only we had some money!' Money! Money was freedom and dignity and self-reliance and the ability to say 'Go to hell!' to the theatre, or to Furomoto or to Setsuko. She must make money. Without it, she would never be really happy. Money. Money.

'Oh, money is never really important.'

'It is, it is!'

'One can manage. Somehow one can always manage.'

'I must go. I'm awfully, awfully late.'

'Well, don't worry. There's nothing to worry about. Probably Setsuko didn't really mean what she said. I expect she lost her temper.'

'But whether she meant it or not, we must leave, Aileen. We must leave.'

'Yes. Eventually. But don't let's hurry ourselves.'

At that the two girls parted, still as if nothing had recently churned up the serene surface of their friendship.

Welling was already at the bus-stop. 'I'll have to drive pretty fast if you expect to make that train,' he said.

'Yes, I'm sorry, I was ready and then '—she hesitated; should she tell him or not?—'and then '—no, she could not keep the scene to herself—'Setsuko and I started to quarrel and I thought that I should never get here at all.'

'And what was the quarrel about?' He was not really interested; after all, if four women lived together under the same roof, it was inevitable that they should get on each other's nerves.

'Oh, many things. But I suppose—chiefly—you.'

'Me?'

She nodded.

'And why did you quarrel about me?'

'Oh, she's jealous, I suppose.'

'Jealous!'

'Yes. It is difficult for you to understand. I cannot explain. She does not wish me to do anything in which she cannot also share. Everything of mine must also belong to her—everything I think, everything I feel, every action of mine. I cannot explain,' she repeated.

'Possessive.' He grunted. 'But she has so many interests of her own. So many things to keep her busy. Not to mention Knox.'

'Oh, the Englishman! She is not really interested in him. Someone ought to tell him. It is useless for him.'

'Anyway, what had she to say about me?'

'She did not say it. But she made Aileen say it for her.' She stopped, wondering if she were wise to relay to him Colethorpe's plea.

'Well?'

'She thinks I am harming you by being seen with you. Harming you and the mission.'

'Yes.' The long, thin mouth became even less generous. 'Yes.' He repeated the monosyllable; then he sighed. 'Well, they've been getting at me too.'

'Who?'

'Oh, Ambleside. Frank. All of them at the mission. I think they half believe what everyone else in this town believes entirely!' The words came out on a brief spurt of anger. '"Judge not that ye be not judged . . ."' He laughed contemptuously. 'But there it is. They have judged; everyone here has judged. Maybe—maybe we ought not to see each other like this.'

She sat in stunned despair, her hands folded in her lap and her face turned away from him to look out at the sweltering street through which the car was racing. 'Well, if you think that . . .' she at last got out tonelessly.

'I don't know. I just don't know. It's not only myself I'm considering. There's you. And there's the mission.'

'For me it does not matter.'

'But of course it does.'

She shook her head. 'No. It does not matter.' Then, taking courage, she went on in a strange, tremulous voice: 'Only this matters. Here. Being here. With you.'

That disconcerted him. It was hot; but not hot enough to cause

235

the sweat to trickle down the razor-sharp line of his jaw and splash on to the front of his aertex-shirt. 'Well, I like being with you. Enormously. But if your reputation—and the reputation of the mission and myself . . .'

'I tell you, my reputation does not have importance. We need not think of that. But if for your—for your good . . .' She broke off and then resumed on that same strange, tremulous note which filled him with mingled panic and joy: 'For you I can do anything.'

'I don't know. I just don't know,' he repeated. 'Anyway, these car-rides . . . Frank was right about them. The car is too conspicuous. Everyone knows about them. I think we ought to stop them, Sanae.'

'But we've never done anything wrong!'

'I know. But still—I think we ought to stop them.'

'I have so few other chances to see you.'

'We can still see each other. But less often. Less obviously.'

'Secretly?'

'Not publicly.' He shied away from her word, with its connotations of guilt and intrigue.

'Oh, why do these others have to spoil this thing for us!'

'It doesn't have to be spoiled. It won't affect our friendship.' He was now careering down the street dangerously fast, as though to escape from the gathering implications of each of her sentences.

'But it will, it will. All this suspicion—imagining that we are doing something bad—talking about it . . .' Suddenly he noticed that she was crying: noiselessly, her small face wrinkled up and the tears trickling down her cheeks.

'Sanae! What's the matter?'

'Oh, it is so difficult, so difficult. . . .' At that moment he drew up at the station; and to his horror she all at once slipped over and placed one damp cheek on his hand as it rested on the wheel.

'Sanae.' He touched her shoulder, whether as a caress or to get her to sit up he could not himself have said; and then he became conscious of her lips on his fingers.

'No . . . no . . . you mustn't . . . you mustn't . . . people will see.' But he no longer cared if people saw: the protest was no more than a reflex conditioned by his calling. She slipped an arm up and around his neck, hanging on to him as if she were drowning. 'Your train,' he said feebly. Then he could hold out no longer and took her in his arms.

He had never seen her look more beautiful; and she had never been more vivacious. But Furomoto realised that he was getting bored with her. Now would begin the process of prising her off, like a limpet from a rock; one which, he had learned, was in the long run less painful to the limpet if performed with a single, brutal jerk. This pregnancy was lucky; if indeed she was pregnant and it was not a ruse to get money out of him. The abortion would interrupt her visits and it would be easier not to resume them after that period. He would have to think of paying her off: though she would, no doubt, be pained to discover that he was less generous these days with his discarded mistresses than when he was young. Lisa's illness and her visit to Switzerland; the collapse of a scheme of his to produce cultured pearls in Australia; outstanding and probably irrecoverable loans to three ministers; the museum of modern art he was planning to build, stock and endow . . . He had decided that he must be less extravagant in his pleasures.

Probably he could pass her on to one of his friends; old Washizu, the former finance minister who had failed to survive the last National Railways scandal, or the younger Sawada, semi-imbecile son of a man almost as rich as Furomoto himself. To Washizu he had already mentioned the girl, making the wrinkled, bleary-eyed old rogue slaver at his description of her charms: not that he could see these days whether a girl was beautiful or not, or do much about it since his last operation. The thought of the operation reminded Furomoto.

'It's your own fault, you know. I asked you whether you wanted me to do anything about it or whether you'd see to it yourself.'

'Yes, I know.'

'What happened?'

'I was lazy—careless.' She herself could not understand what had happened. 'I don't know.'

'Have you a doctor?'

'One of the girls has recommended someone to me.' Since abortion is legal in Japan, there was no difficulty. 'She's been to him—twice.' The 'she' was Rumi. 'He lives in Kobe and has his own clinic.'

237

'You'd better go to a surgeon I know. No use taking any risk. These things are as simple as a tooth-extraction if the right man tackles them. Otherwise. . . .'

He made this suggestion, not out of kindness, as she supposed, but to safeguard himself. Many years ago an innocent-seeming girl from a village in Kyushu had told him, with noisy lamentations, that she was pregnant. He had given her a considerable sum for an operation. She had then sent round a friend, a grim woman with warts all over her face (Furomoto could see her now) who had announced that the poor child was dangerously ill with septicaemia. Furomoto had paid again; and again. Later, he learned, by a coincidence, that during her supposed spell in a clinic, she had in fact pleasured one of his friends in an expensive brothel in Ginza. Another girl had taken the money for the operation and had told him that it had passed off satisfactorily; but eventually she gave birth to a child, sued him for paternity and won her case, so that he had had to pay out money to her until only last year. . . . No, he was not going to be that kind of fool again if he could help it.

'Oh, I don't think there's any danger with the man in Kobe. He's very well known.'

'Still . . .' He put an arm round her and slipped a hand inside her wrap. 'You're too precious for anything but the best. I'll telephone to my man tomorrow morning and you can visit him in the afternoon. Here, I'll write down the address for you.' He got off the bed, struggling into his *yukata* as he did so, and went, barefoot, across to the chair over which he had draped his jacket and trousers. From his diary he carefully tore out a sheet, and wrote on it. 'He's a nice fellow. You'll like him.'

Sanae took the strip of paper, gazed down at it with a frown of seeming incomprehension ('What's the matter? Can't you read?' he felt like snapping at her in exasperation) and then placed it under the ash-tray, piled with ash and half-smoked stubs, on the bedside table.

Furomoto wanted to be off, but the car would not return for him for another half-hour. The car! His suspicions, chill and clammy, slithered back to coil around his heart. He had been a fool to employ a mere youth, and one so handsome and—beddable (Lisa's epithet crawled back to him, leaving a trail of slime). Nakatani she had always treated with contempt. But with this boy she was always joking or pleading or pretending to fly into a rage because of some omission or error on his part. Of course, she had changed since her visit to Switzerland; she had changed, there was no doubt of that. When he had hinted this to her, she had given her brief, harsh laugh: 'Well, of course I've changed! I realise that I'm no longer dying.' But was it merely the success of the operation, or some other success, achieved while he was pouring out a small fortune to keep her at the clinic? It was the first time he had ever had cause to feel jealous of her; he did not like it.

Yes, the boy had been a mistake. But after the scare of Naka-tani's death, he had wanted someone to replace him who was not merely physically strong but mentally quick. Besides, there was Furomoto's debt to the boy's father, the head of police in a small provincial town, who had been of priceless service to him in breaking a recent strike.

'What are you thinking about?' Sanae was lying on the bed, propped on one elbow, gazing dispassionately up at his face.

'Oh, nothing of any possible interest to you. Business.' He roused himself from his abstraction and stretched out beside her; soon beginning once again to fondle her.

'But I'm interested in business! Very interested. Are things not going well?'

'As usual. No better, no worse.'

'Colethorpe-San and I have to leave your niece's.'

'Oh? Why?' He barely pretended any interest.

'We—I—quarrelled with her.'

'You women always quarrel. If there's a man in the house you quarrel over him. And if there isn't—well, you find something else to quarrel about.'

'I don't know where we shall go. Colethorpe-San has sold only one picture in the last two months. She gives English lessons, but students never expect to pay more than they would for a cinema.'

Suddenly he got the drift of these remarks. If he had not been thinking of Lisa and the driver, he would have been quicker. She was asking him to be generous; putting an oblique pressure on him. 'She ought to get a proper job—as a nurse, governess, secretary. Something like that. There must be American families . . . She can't expect others to support her for ever. That painting of hers is never going to be much good.'

'But I thought you said. . . . You wrote that piece about her —she showed it to me.'

239

It was Furomoto's practice to denigrate artists whom he had extravagantly praised before, should they be rash enough to attempt to emancipate themselves from his influence. But he did not care to be reminded of these caprices. 'Yes, I wanted to help her and I'm afraid I exaggerated. And I really did think for a while that perhaps there was something to her work. But the more I saw of it, the less I saw in it. Just the repetition, over and over again, of a few banal tricks. . . .' Though he did not realise it, this last verdict might as aptly have been applied to his own painting.

'Well, I know nothing about art,' Sanae said. She wished to defend Colethorpe, but was at a loss how to do so. 'Many people say that she's good. People who really know, I mean.'

'Such as?'

She could think of no one but Knox. 'Well, the Englishman who lives next door,' she answered doubtfully.

'Englishman? Oh, yes, I met him once. I don't suppose he's much of a judge. The English are twenty years behind both America and Europe in painting anyway.' Furomoto had once financed an exhibition of his own work in London at a small, recently-opened gallery; and the fact that it had been almost totally ignored by the Press and unvisited by the public had been far more wounding to his self-esteem than the hostility he had sometimes aroused in Japan.

'It was my fault that Setsuko turned us out. Well, not turned us out, but asked us to leave.' She sighed; and at the same moment became conscious that he was appraising her with a glance at once cool and penetrating. She had herself been barely conscious what she had been up to; but now they both knew and they faced each other, like two hard-headed and hard-hearted business-men across a table. 'If only I didn't have this awful job. One gets paid so little and it's so—so humiliating.' She gave a little shudder of disgust.

'But you must make a number of useful—contacts.' He gave the last word the same almost insulting emphasis which Setsuko had once given to it. 'Which it would be harder for you to make in some other profession,' he added.

'Contacts of that kind don't greatly interest me.' Her face hardened.

'I regard that as the most charming of compliments to myself ! . . . But a beautiful woman like you—I am sure that you will

240

never be in want. Whatever profession you may decide to adopt.'

She pretended to ignore these counters slid forward with a deceptive casualness in a game they both knew now that they would have to play out together to its bitter last trick.

'And now, if I'm sick . . . When we're sick, they put us on half-pay, if we're lucky. Sometimes they even refuse to pay us at all.'

'They've no right to do that.'

She found a sardonic amusement in his indignation against this act of a bad employer. She believed, as everyone in Japan believed, not entirely with justice, that he was himself utterly ruthless with his workers.

'Well, they do it none the less.' Her mouth sagged in a genuine dejection: 'Oh, it's no fun being a woman and on one's own in Japan, I can tell you! In the West it's different.'

'What do you know about the West?' he asked, amused.

'Colethorpe-San has told me.'

He glanced at the watch on his small, hairy wrist. By now the driver would have fetched Lisa from her bridge-party and returned her to the house: if, indeed, she had gone to a bridge-party—he must check on that tomorrow. He got slowly off the bed, looking, for once, all of his fifty-six years, yawned, and stretched his sinewy arms above him so that his rib-cage rose away from his slender waist, each rib distinct to her gaze. He tugged his vest off the chair: 'Must dress,' he grunted. 'The car will be here in ten minutes. I'll give you a lift to the station.'

'It's too late. The last train has gone. I'll spend the night here.'

He was not sorry. Already he had been wondering if he could trust that boy with his secrets, as he had always trusted Nakatani. Nakatani! The fluttering awning, the smell, the shoe—yes, only now he remembered the soggy, upturned shoe on top of the splintered ice-chest. . . . He continued to dress in silence.

When he had finished, his last act being to run a comb through his hair, he drew out his wallet and counted out the notes: three more than usual. 'There you are, Sanae-chan.' He clicked open her bag and stuffed them in, knowing full well that though she now ignored the whole transaction she would at once jump off the bed when the door closed behind him and count them. 'Now, go to the doctor tomorrow afternoon and arrange things with him. No need to pay him anything, understand? I'll have telephoned and the bill will come to me direct. And don't worry. It's nothing,

241

nothing at all. He gives you an injection—the latest thing. No worse than having a bad go of dysentery or a tooth pulled out. All right? ' He smiled at her, and then went across to kiss her first on the forehead and then on the cheek she turned passively up to him.

' When shall I see you again? '

' Sa . . .' He thought, staring at his own reflection in the mirror on the dressing-table behind her. ' Sa . . .' Obviously it would be folly to reveal his intention to break with her until the operation was over. Then it would be he, not she, who would hold the advantage. ' Let's see. Yes. The same time, the same day, next week? I'm terribly busy until then, I may even have to go to Tokyo for a couple of days. All right? '

She nodded and then repeated ' All right' in a flat, despondent voice. What more did she want? Could it be that she was falling in love with him? It would not be the first time; one girl, only the previous year, had been found half-dead in her own vomit on the floor of a bedroom in this same hotel, because she had sensed his growing apathy and had swallowed a disinfectant. She had had no real intention of putting an end to her squalid existence: oh no. It was the usual Japanese form of blackmail.

' What's the matter, Sanae-chan? '

' Oh, I don't know. I'm so tired of life. Nothing goes right for me. And now we've got to leave the house, and how am I to——? '

He must stop all that, quickly. ' Then, here's a little extra something to cheer you up.' He extracted another two notes from his wallet and stuffed them into the bag with the others. Cheap at the price, he thought, if they spared him a repetition of all that business about Colethorpe and the lack of money and the misery of her job. ' And now I must hurry.' He took her briefly in his arms and kissed her on the lips. ' Thank you, Sanae-chan. . . . And, don't forget, see that doctor tomorrow.' He tapped on the slip of paper, the corner of which rested under the ash-tray.

She nodded morosely. But as soon as he had closed the door behind him, she picked up the paper and, having glanced once at it, tore it into shreds which she buried, with a used matchstick, under a mound of ash.

SEVENTEEN

As we plunged down the hillside into the gorge below, Colethorpe, jumping from rock to rock and from tree to tree, soon vanished from sight. Sanae we could still glimpse occasionally, Colethorpe's camera slung over her shoulder and a string-bag in her hand. But she too was rapidly outdistancing us.

'How old they make me feel! And I keep thinking that the further we go down, the worse will be the climb up again.'

Setsuko had been silent, even morose, all that morning: something was on her mind and I now began to wonder if, without thinking, I had done or said something to annoy her.

'Trousers suit Sanae. As they suit you,' I added in insincere flattery. 'They suit most Japanese women. Whereas poor Colethorpe——! Whenever she bends over, I'm afraid that a seam is going to split.' I held out a hand to help Setsuko over a ledge of shale, but she ignored it. 'But I'd no idea that she'd be so athletic. She's carrying far more than any of us.'

'Oh, your English women are the toughest in the world. With the exception of the Russians.' Setsuko stopped and raised a hand to shield her eyes from the dazzle of the midday sun as she gazed down at the rapids, boiling up in a yellowish-white frill, like a trickle of milk at the bottom of a heated saucepan, still hundreds of feet below us; her slumped posture and the tonelessness of her voice both prompting my next question:

'Tired?'

'Of course not!' The emphasis with which people repudiate that suggestion is, in itself, often an affirmative; and I felt it to be so then. 'We've hardly walked any distance at all. Are *you* tired?'

'No. But I'm still thinking of our return.'

'Perhaps we can walk down the gorge.'

We resumed our descent in silence.

'I suppose this will be my last expedition into the Japanese countryside. For several months at least.' I was getting breathless. 'Perhaps for ever.'

'For ever?'

'You know that I may decide not to return.'

'Oh, I never took that seriously. I thought you just said that when you were more than usually disgruntled with life. Do you really think that you may not come back?'

'Would you mind if I didn't?'

'Of course. My aunt and I are unlikely to find a tenant we like quite so much.'

It was a neat reply; but not, of course, the reply for which I had been angling.

'I don't feel that Japan has a great deal more to offer me. And now that my little legacy has provided me with a certain independence, I think that the time has come to return to the part of the world where I feel most at home.'

'England?'

'Good God, no! The Mediterranean. I want to go back to people who charge one's own dying battery, instead of draining it of what little energy it still contains. And I want to be able to make scenes again.'

'Oh, but we Japanese make scenes. You'd be surprised.'

'Well, to make scenes and to know that the following day they will be both forgiven and forgotten. Temperamentally I'm too impatient and irritable and energetic and quick for Japan. It was never the right country for me. It's not really the right country for you, Setsuko,' I added.

'I wonder which country is. That's the worst of being a mongrel—one belongs nowhere.'

I was ahead of her and I now halted in the narrow path so that I blocked her way. Gazing, not at her, but downwards, where I could make out the shadow of an immense, lead-coloured rock, I mumbled: 'You're the only thing that could bring me back here.'

She paid no attention to the remark. 'They've not chosen a very good place. The sun will move round. The other side would be better.'

'Setsuko, you're not listening to me.'

'Of course I am.'

'I've got to say this to you. In less than a week I shall be on my aeroplane. We may never meet again. Never. Do you understand?'

'Yes, of course I understand. And it makes me awfully sad.

244

But talking about it only makes it worse—for both of us. Let's pretend that you're going to live next door to us for the rest of your days. Let's pretend that aeroplane does not exist.'

'Pretend!' The word seemed to focus, in a single burning ray, all her inconsistencies and emotional dishonesties. 'But I don't want to pretend. I know that's the Japanese way, but I hate it. Please, Setsuko, just for once—if it's the last thing I ask of you —forget about pretence. Please!'

She broke a twig off a bush, and as she scrambled down the hillside ahead of me, she began to peel it as though she were going to eat it, with an abrupt, voracious tearing. I sensed that my plea had unnerved her; but still she did not respond.

'Setsuko, I've got to get this off my chest. I know you don't want to hear. But I've got to. You must have guessed long, long ago that I'm in love with you. I'm not going to say "madly" in love with you, because at my age madness has little to do with it. I don't think of you every minute of the day as I should do if I were twenty years younger, and I can walk with you alone like this without feeling that life has nothing better to offer me. I'm quite unromantic about you; quite unromantic and yet . . . Setsuko, listen to me, listen to me!'

'I am listening. But please, Bill—don't, don't! Don't go on! You only make a mess of it all.' Suddenly she turned, her face at a level with my waist and uplifted to beseech me, while with the peeled twig she lashed at her bare leg. 'Don't you see?'

'A mess of it? What do you mean? I want to marry you, Setsuko. I'm in dead earnest about this. To marry you and to settle down with you here in Japan—yes, I'd do even that for you—or to take you to England, to America, to Greece, to anywhere you wished.'

'Please!' she cried out in a kind of agony of protest. 'It was all so nice before. We were friends and I loved being with you. That's how I want it. Not—not all this marriage business. Just friends.'

'But I don't want to be friends!' I shouted in exasperation. 'That's not what I want at all.' I was maddened, beyond endurance, by this continuing lie. Friends, just friends! Had she forgotten those occasions when, with a perverse dissimulation, she had given herself to me when supposedly asleep or engaged in some innocent act of play? Did she imagine that I would continue

245

to support her in this deception not only of myself but probably of her own self as well? Would the logical conclusion to all this be that eventually she would marry me under the pretence of doing something wholly different: paying a visit to the Mayor's office to argue about her municipal taxes, for example, or to the Consulate to request a visa?

'Bill, you make it all so difficult. Please, please stop!'

'But tell me, Setsuko. . . . For once be truthful with me. For once be frank. Is it no good? Is it really no good? Won't you —won't you even think about it?'

'Think about what?'

'Oh, for God's sake!'

'Bill . . . I'll—I'll—I'll tell you what I'll do.' Again she stopped to face me. 'I'll write to you. I'll write you a letter and, when you get to London, there it will be. Waiting for you. I don't like talking about these things. Emotions—I'm no good at them, I can't manage them. I'm sorry, Bill. Let me write you a letter. In a letter I can explain. But not, not like this. . . .'

'A lot of good a letter will be! What's the matter with you? I don't understand you. We're two adults, aren't we? Aren't we? Can't we discuss something quietly and sensibly together? If only you'd cease to pretend—if only you'd be yourself for a moment. That's all. Tell me, calmly, what you feel: what you feel about me—about this marriage business. . . .'

Twice she looked round at me, while I said those words, jerking her head back to show me her face contorted with misery, fear and perhaps even rage. Then suddenly I heard a cry and in a clatter and whirr of loose stones and soil, she was tumbling and slithering down the slope ahead of me. I leapt after her.

'Setsuko! Are you all right? Setsuko!' I found her lying out on a ledge of rock, her skirt torn and one leg twisted under her. Without thinking, I put an arm around her to lever her up; and simultaneously she gave a little moan and struggled to free herself. But a moment later she was clutching at me, shaken with sobs.

'Have you hurt yourself? Have you hurt yourself, my darling?'

She continued to gulp and hiccough, her face pressed to my chest. I tried to examine her. One knee was badly grazed and so, to a lesser degree, were the palm of her left hand and her left cheek. She had also bruised her forehead. Compassion, with the force of love, seemed to pour over me like the blazing sunlight in which we were sitting, shrivelling up every other emotion of the previous half-hour.

'Setsuko! Answer me. Answer me, please. . . . Are you all right?'

'Yes. . . . Yes. . . . I'm all right. . . .' She got out at last between her diminishing sobs. 'All right. . . . Just—just the shock. . . . Silly of me. . . .' She gave a small, hysterical laugh. 'Thought I'd never stop. . . . Thought I'd just go on and on until I landed on top of Sanae and Aileen. . . . No, I'm not hurt.' She controlled herself, relinquished her hold on me, and at last sat up.

'Just these—these few cuts. . . .'

At that moment Colethorpe and then Sanae rose up from under the ledge: both of them pallid, sweat-drenched and gasping for breath.

'Is she all right? Is she all right, Bill?'

'I think so.' I knew that, without them, it would have been difficult to help Setsuko either down or up the slope; and yet their appearance at that moment filled me with a rage, at once impotent and illogical, which I had to exert myself to control. Then, if ever—when Setsuko was unnerved first by the insistence of my pleas and then by the nearness of her escape from death—then, if ever, I might have forced her to look into the mirror untarnished by lying or self-deception. But they, in their clumsy anxiety and desire to be of help, had dashed the mirror out of my hands. As I stared down over Setsuko's head into the gorge below, it seemed to be its fragments, and not the rapids, that glittered up at me.

From then on I was never alone with her; and she herself seemed to be determined that we should never be alone. If Sanae and Colethorpe showed any tendency to stray off together, she would always find some excuse, however implausible, to detain one or the other. It was Sanae who bathed her cuts and Sanae who improvised some bandages out of a handkerchief of mine and a napkin in which we had wrapped a lettuce. 'What a wonderful nurse you'd make, Sanae!' It was the conventional expression of gratitude which I had heard spoken in the past, and had spoken myself, to people with the clumsiest of hands; but in Sanae's case it was deserved.

'Perhaps that is the right profession for me: nursing.'

'But all your male patients would fall in love with you!' Colethorpe exclaimed.

247

'And would that matter? It would hasten their recoveries—or make dying easier.' Setsuko patted the bandage on her knee. 'Yes, very professional. Very professional indeed, Sanae.'

Sanae seemed to become increasingly embarrassed by her praise; one might even imagine that she was annoyed by it, as she went off to unpack the rest of the picnic. Setsuko's eyes followed her with a curious, unfocused kind of gaze; until, becoming aware that I, in turn, was looking into her face, she jerked her head away. 'One doesn't think of someone as exquisite as Sanae being practical.' She was all but sarcastic now. '. . . Now let's have a drink. It's lucky Bill, and not I, was carrying the sherry. Otherwise the bottle would certainly have been smashed.'

When I gave her half a tumbler of it, she gulped at it with a greediness which reminded me of the time when she had come over to my house and got drunk on the Consul's present of a bottle of brandy. I knew now that that was the time—not at the hotel at Ise, not during our swimming lesson—when we had drawn closest to each other; and I sensed, with a chill of foreboding, that we should never draw so close again. As I sipped at my own glass, I went over once again in my mind that sad, terrible confession of hers, gazing at her the while. How I hated Furomoto, how easily I could kill him! And yet, when she had said the same thing to me, I had been shocked into a vehement protest. Obscurely I now felt that it was he, seducing her so many years ago, who had brought me to my present predicament.

'Why are you staring at me?' Her voice sounded hostile and panic-stricken.

'Was I?'

'At me or through me.'

'Through you, then. My thoughts were miles away. Years away, rather.'

That evening we had arranged to go to the *Kabuki* Theatre. I thought that Setsuko would probably not now wish to attend, but she dismissed my suggestion that I should try to return our tickets. 'Oh, nonsense! I feel perfectly all right. What are a few scratches and bruises? I wouldn't miss it for anything. Besides, Sanae will be disappointed. She only gets one evening off in ten.'

'I can go with Colethorpe-San,' Sanae put in.

Again Setsuko fixed on her that strange, unfocused gaze I had

248

noticed at the picnic. 'Yes, that's true,' she at last agreed; her mouth and eyes hardened.

'But it would be far more fun if you and Bill were also with us.' Poor Colethorpe's pathetic attempt at diplomacy only served to underline the ungraciousness of Sanae's original remark. 'Do come. If you feel equal to it, that is.'

Colethorpe showed the same clumsy diplomacy when it came to seating ourselves in the theatre. Setsuko placed herself between the other two women; I imagine, in a deliberate attempt to avoid being next to me. But Colethorpe at once intervened: 'Now we three girls are all huddled together and Mr. Knox is isolated. Sanae, you'd better change places with him. In any case, Setsuko is more of an expert on *kabuki* than you and can explain to him better.' As I changed my seat, she turned her shiny face up at me, through its lank blonde hair, with a grin of conspiratorial triumph.

After our long walk in the blaze of the midday sun, I was already feeling sleepy; and *kabuki* in any case tends to stupefy me. The gorgeousness of the costumes, the grandeur of the sets and the measured exaggeration of the playing in a language which I can seldom follow, all combine first to overwhelm me and then to daze me into somnolence, like some protracted banquet. Soon my mind becomes unfocused and a hundred irrelevant images start to intrude around its edges: until, briefly, some pose of an exceptional beauty or some gesture of an exceptional force tightens the lens and concentrates it. Such was the case now. The story was *Suetsumuhana* or 'The Long-nosed Woman' from the Genji Monogatari. Genji has once spent a night with the long-nosed woman who subsequently never forgets him, but waits in sorrowful patience for his return to her. A message, intended for another of his loves, is brought to her by mistake: he has come back to Kyoto and that night he will visit her. She restrains the wildness of her exultation when she hears this news and commands her servants to wash, scent and robe her and dress her hair. Then she sits and waits. At first she is joyful as she practises on the *shamisen* the songs with which she will entertain him; then she grows restless and asks the time or sends her servants hurrying down the road to look for his coming; finally she is seized by the most terrible of forebodings—he will never come. . . . It was at this point, as her attendants try to console her, that the lens began to blur. I started to think of the events of the picnic, culminating in Setsuko's fall down the hillside; then of my flight in five days time; then of innumerable trivial tasks I should have to perform before then—the return to a student of a thesis I had corrected for him; a visit to my bank; the checking of the inventory. . . . Suddenly all these intrusive images whisked out of my consciousness, which found itself once again focused, with a diamond-sharp clarity, on to the play. Genji had entered along the *hanamichi* or extended ramp which led down the auditorium on to the stage and was now talking to one of his attendants outside the house of the long-nosed woman. Beside them and in front of a wayside shrine was a high pile of stones and, magnificent in his youth and aristocratic beauty, he was asking what it signified. The attendant hesitated, and then replied: and suddenly I remembered the incident as I had read it, who knows how many years ago, in Waley's translation. Each morning and each evening the long-nosed woman had come to this shrine to pray for Genji's return to her; and each time she had marked her prayer by adding one stone to another stone until this whole mound had grown from her devotion. Genji listened; and that listening alone was a flawless exhibition of the art of the *kabuki* actor. Interest, surprise, bewilderment, incredulity, shock, and then that mingling of pity, exasperation and guilty pleasure which we experience when we are the objects of a love we cannot return, succeeded each other on his face. ' So she loved me so much—and loved me so long. . . ! ' He did not need to say the words; he had already conveyed them to each of us and they were the words we were saying to ourselves.

It was then that the flutter of something white at the extreme corner of my vision made me turn my head; and I saw that Setsuko was crying. It was not unusual that a Japanese woman or even man should be doing so; there were people sobbing audibly around us, with the hysteria of emotion long repressed. But that Setsuko should cry ! I had always thought her too much in control of herself; too hard; too detached; too Westernised; too selfconscious. Unaware that I was scrutinising her, she sat hunched forward in her seat, her contorted face tilted upwards to the stage so that the tears glittered on her cheeks and eye-lashes, while her hands passed back and forth, back and forth, between them the sodden handkerchief which had first attracted my gaze. Her absorption in the scene was as complete as it had once been in the act of making love; and probably she would obliterate all memory of her grief now as completely as she had obliterated all memory of her joy then. These were rooms into which her spirit might, from time to time, stray involuntarily; but for the major part of her existence they must not merely be kept locked, but must also be assumed not to exist.

After that consummate *coup de théâtre* the drama ebbed; its pulse growing more and more sluggish as Genji and the long-nosed woman finally confront each other for the last time. When the lights went up, there was no indication, as on Sanae's tear-blotched face, that Setsuko had been moved at all. 'So that's that,' she said. 'Some good moments. But, as always, too slow. And too protracted.'

'I thought it marvellous,' Colethorpe declared. 'I couldn't understand a word, but I thought it marvellous.'

'Well, it's certainly a beautiful spectacle.'

'Oh, not only as a spectacle.'

'Do you want to see the next play?' Setsuko turned to me. 'Personally, I think I've had enough. One play seems to me just right. Shall we go and eat?'

As so often she had asked what we wanted to do; and then, without waiting for an answer, had told us what she wanted to do. And, of course, we did it.

When the time came for us to say goodbye, she left Colethorpe and Sanae on the steps of the house and walked a few paces across the garden with me. I intended to slip an arm through hers but, as I neared her, she seemed to sense what I was about to do and at once left the path to examine a flower. 'I didn't know that there were any tobacco-plants in this garden.'

'Didn't you? I could have told you that. But then I do the weeding.'

'It's been a lovely day, Bill. It's sad that these times together will so soon be over. . . . Come back to us. Won't you? Japan's not so bad.' She spoke the words as though they were no more than the conventionally 'gracious' ones any neighbour might speak to someone who planned to go away for ever. I hated their emptiness and artificiality and, at that moment, I also hated her. 'Here! Take this flower. It's from our part of the garden, so I'll give it to you. It smells heavenly.' She handed the flower to me.

'But tobacco-flowers die almost at once. Didn't you know that?'

'Oh dear, do they? How awful! Then I've murdered it.'

I raised the already crumpled petals to my nose; I think that I

251

shall always now associate their scent with her. 'Never mind.'
'Well, good night, Bill. . . . If you need any help—with your
packing arrangements—just let us know. . . .' She was dis-
appearing into the shadows; already she was no more than a
glimmering blur. Her voice grew faint: 'Anything . . . anything
we can do. . . . And that letter . . . I won't forget it . . . I'll
write it, Bill. . . . Promise . . . letter . . . promise. . . .' The
words faded as she herself faded from sight.

EIGHTEEN

S ETSUKO had said nothing further about Sanae and Colethorpe
leaving; and when Colethorpe herself had at last ventured on
the subject, she was immediately silenced. This was when
Colethorpe offered Setsuko a contribution towards the housekeeping expenses, having at last succeeded in selling one of her
collages for a negligible sum to a gallery in Osaka.

'Oh, no, Aileen,' Setsuko had protested. 'It's quite unnecessary. I know that you're short of cash. Go and buy yourself
something nice with the money and then, when you sell another
picture, you can make the offer again. Please.'

'But I'd like you to take it. If you do, it'll make me feel—feel
less—bad. About hanging on here, I mean.'

'Why should you feel that?'

'Well, I know you'd like us—or Sanae, anyway—to leave. But
it's so difficult. This, as you know, is the first picture I've managed to sell in weeks and those two students who were here
yesterday for a lesson have still not paid me. Sometimes I think
I ought to send them packing. But then I'd never get the money,
would I? Yesterday I went to see Mrs. Crawley and the Amblesides to ask if they knew of anything—a job, I mean, any job.
Mrs. Crawley thought she might be able to do something. She
has a friend; a Mrs. Ito. Apparently rich and influential——'

'Oh, that old Lesbian! I'd be careful of her if I were you. You—
and Sanae—would let yourself in for something, I can tell you, if
you accepted her favours.'

Colethorpe was disconcerted by the venom with which this
emerged. 'Well, anyway, something will soon turn up. And just
as soon as it does, I promise you that we'll get out. I know
how maddening all this must seem to you. And it worries me
sick——'

Setsuko laughed. 'But, my dear Aileen, there's no need for you
both to go at all. Unless you want to. Don't be silly! I'm delighted
to have you here.'

Colethorpe's face became blotchy as she tugged in embarrassment at a hank of her hair and gazed rapidly about the room. 'But—but Sanae said—she said that you said——'

'Oh, don't tell me that the little fool took all that seriously! Well, really!'

'Then you don't—you don't really want us to——'

'Of course not! She lost her temper and I lost my temper. We both said some silly things which I see no point in remembering now. I'm astonished that she should still remember them. How idiotic of her!'

'She's more sensitive than one realises.'

'Evidently. I'm glad, anyway, that our little scene had one good result.' In answer to Colethorpe's look of incomprehension she went on: 'She's stopped seeing Welling. I'm told that for several days now the M.G. has not been at the bus-stop.'

'Oh, I think——' Some instinct made Colethorpe check herself before she revealed what Frank had told her: that Sanae and Welling had twice been for walks together since their supposed break. 'Yes, I think she's decided to be sensible about him.'

'And a good thing too.'

Later, when Colethorpe told Sanae that Setsuko did not really intend them to leave, she encountered, not the relief she had expected, but cantankerous obstinacy. 'I do not care whether she wishes us to go or stay!' Sanae had exclaimed with such vehemence that Colethorpe feared that Setsuko would hear her from downstairs. 'I wish to go. As soon as possible.'

'But, Sanae, she was terribly nice about it all. And terribly nice about you.'

This only annoyed Sanae more. 'She is not nice! She is never nice! I—I hate her,' she murmured on a sudden quiet note which chilled Colethorpe with its icy ring of truth.

'Sanae!'

'Yes. She—she disgusts me. I hate her.'

'But why, why?'

'There is no "why".'

'She has been so good to us——'

'Good to us! Only for her own disgusting purposes.'

'What do you mean?'

'Oh, Aileen, you are innocent! You cannot believe bad of anyone, can you? Never mind.' She saw the expression of pain and bewilderment on the English girl's shiny face, and contrition smote her. 'Never mind. Forget what I have said. . . . But'—

again her voice resumed that same harsh, ringing note, as of metal striking ice—'when we have enough money, we leave. Do you understand? We leave. Or I leave. You do what you wish to do.'

'But of course—if you want to go—then I—I go with you.'

Sanae nodded; then she put a hand on Colethorpe's shoulder: 'You are my only friend, Aileen. Do you realise that? You have many, many friends. I have only you.'

'What about Welling?' The thought came and was dismissed, before it could be put into words. Colethorpe was profoundly touched, even though, at the same time, she was aware of a smudge of sentimentality and even perhaps emotional dishonesty over a corner of that otherwise shining declaration. Her lower lip trembled and pouted: tears came as easily to her as they came with difficulty to Sanae. She brushed the back of one hand over her eyes.

Sanae was continuing: 'For the present we must be nice to her, because there is no other way. When she falls and cuts herself, we must bandage her cuts.' She smiled, revealing to Colethorpe now, for the first time, the insincerity of all her attentions to Setsuko after her accident. 'We must laugh at her jokes and thank her for her kindnesses. We must even let her go through our drawers and read our letters. But when we have some money, then we can tell her what we think of her. Tell her what we think of her—and go.'

Colethorpe sighed. 'I wonder when that will be.'

'When what will be?' Sanae demanded sharply.

'When we have enough money to go our own way.'

'Don't worry. We'll find it. I'll find it. Don't worry, Aileen. Soon, soon we'll have it. You'll see! I'm cleverer than you think. Far, far cleverer. . . .'

Every Thursday in recent weeks, Mrs. Furomoto had attended pottery-classes as the pupil of an old friend of hers, himself once a pupil of Bernard Leach and now regarded as one of the three greatest living potters in Japan. This interest had come to her too late: tragically too late, thought the potter, who found in her a natural aptitude far greater than in any of his younger pupils. She herself refused to take her work with any seriousness and when asked to exhibit it, or even to show it to her friends, invariably declined. 'I'm an old woman. This is just my way of helping the time to pass until my end comes,' she said more than

255

once; and on each occasion the wizened little potter, who was terrified of death, made a clicking noise with his tongue on the roof of his toothless palate (he wore his false teeth only to eat or receive guests) and accentuated the perpetual tremor of his head from side to side to make a vehement shaking.

The link between the two old people was closer than any of their mutual friends suspected: even those who knew that they had once wished to marry and been prevented by her parents who wished for her a better match than a poverty-stricken and tubercular artist from a village in the mountains. After each lesson, when the other pupils had tidied up, scraping smooth the wheels and stacking the pots on the shelves ranged about his workshop, she and he would go deep into the recesses of the house, to a small, cool room, lit only from a skylight, and there, lying out on the *tatami*, would smoke a pipe or two of opium together. They had done it for years, long before she had started to study with him; and it was seldom that they did it more than once each week. The potter had learned the habit when, as a youth, he had gone to China to study his art; and she, in the first desolation of leaving Furomoto, had learned it from her friend. Their supplies they got from a pedlar in the outcasts' quarter: the father of Asai's confidant, Kanizawa. Of this tenuous thread still joining her to the dead youth Mrs. Furomoto was unaware.

This time, when she arrived at the potter's house, she found some of his pupils standing in the street while others were already drifting away, singly or in groups. She rarely spoke to them; and though she already had a presentiment of disaster, she did not speak to them now, but walked instead to the door, her head bowed, with her usual small, tottering steps, and rang the bell. The potter's son appeared: himself a potter, talented, but with none of his father's genius. He bowed low and she bowed low, each several times, before she asked: 'Is your father not at home?'

He shook his head. 'They've taken him to hospital. Less than an hour ago. I'm going there now, myself. I waited to tell his pupils that the lesson was cancelled. Next week, perhaps I can take it.'

'Then he's—he's seriously ill. . . .'

Again he nodded. 'A stroke. He's an old man; far older than people realise.' (As if she didn't realise!) 'The doctors are very worried. It's not his first, you know.'

'Yes, I know.'

'Won't you come in? There's no one in the house but the two assistants in the workroom and the maid. You won't be disturbed if you'd—you'd like to rest a moment. The—the usual room is ready.' He knew all about the smoking and saw nothing wrong in it, even though he felt that it was something 'Eastern' and therefore demeaning to the dignity of a Westernised graduate of one of the Methodist Universities, like himself. 'Please. . . .'

She hesitated and then shook her head. 'Thank you. No. I'll telephone this evening, to ask how he is doing. Give him my—my best wishes, will you?'

'At present he is unconscious. But I'll do that later, of course.'

In the taxi going home she experienced a terrible panic and desolation: the effect (she kept reassuring herself) of not smoking on the accustomed day and hour. He was dying, she was certain of it; one more preceding her up that moving-staircase, which one could neither halt nor leave, to step off into—what? What? So many of them had gone; so many of them were ailing; and those that were still left were those, like Ito-San, for whom her affection had long since shrivelled. Furomoto was nothing to her; her brother, a successful surgeon in California whom she had not seen for years, was nothing to her either; her sister had never been anything to her, anyway. Only Setsuko remained. Only Setsuko. It was terrible to feel glad that Setsuko's father and his Russian wife had both been killed; but she was glad, she had to admit it, like the bankrupt who is glad of the death that brings him a legacy to save him.

She paid off the taxi-driver and made her way, noiseless and distraught, up the two steps and into the house. Colethorpe or that little chit had again been careless and failed to slide the door fully across. That Setsuko might be to blame never occurred to her. Her *tabi* made a faint rustle, no more, on the *tatami*-covered floor as she crossed the hall, drawing a handkerchief from the reticule which dangled from her bony, blue-veined wrist and pressing it first to her upper lip and then to her forehead. This heat!

. . . Ah, so Setsuko had come home early: nearly two hours early. Perhaps the Professor had gone to Tokyo on a visit; or perhaps his wife's baby had arrived sooner than expected. Mrs. Furomoto could hear a drawer being pulled open and then feet crossing and re-crossing her niece's room. 'Setsuko! Setsuko-chan! Such bad news. I feel so upset. . . .'

She and Sanae faced each other.

'What are you doing? What are you doing in my niece's room?'

'What she does in mine!'

'What are those papers?'

'Don't you know?'

'Give them to me! Give them to me at once!'

'Oh no. No. I'm sorry. Not yet. Not until Setsuko and I have had a talk together.'

'You—you thief! Give them to me!'

The old woman tried to snatch at the envelope; but Sanae pushed aside her arm and then, with a high-pitched laugh, pushed her again, this time on the bony shoulders, so that she reeled and fell against the edge of the desk with a sharp pain that brought the tears to her eyes.

'Come back! Come here! I'll . . . I'll have the police. . . .'

She realised that she was alone. Tottering to the window, she saw Sanae hurrying exultantly down the road, the envelope still clutched in one hand while with the other she wrenched from time to time at the leaves of the privet-bushes which flanked the garden.

'*Aie!* I've forgotten my cigarettes.' Furomoto leant forward and touched the driver on his shoulder. 'Got a cigarette, Fukushima?'

'You know I don't smoke.' The insolent drawl infuriated Furomoto, but he said nothing. 'Sanae?' Before she could answer, he had begun to insert his stubby, nicotine-stained fingers into the bag that rested on her lap.

'No! Don't! No!'

'Why? What's the matter?'

'I haven't any cigarettes. I don't smoke.'

'Why all the fuss? Don't tell me that you're carrying around a bomb like that poor fool with his brief-case!' He often shocked his friends by making such joking references to the attempt on his life: none of them perceiving that by doing so he was not displaying callousness, as they assumed, but his continuing obsession with the death of Nakatani. 'Is that it?'

'Of course not! But don't you know that it's rude to look in a lady's bag without asking permission.'

He gave a brief, contemptuous chuckle. 'Thank you for that lesson in manners.' He bowed. 'I'll remember it.' Then again he leant forward to touch the driver's shoulder: 'Fukushima. Stop the car a moment and buy me some cigarettes. No, not here, you fool!' Sometimes he still forgot that this boy was not Nakatani and could not be addressed in the same terms. 'Not here! Can't you see the sign? Do you want me to pick up another ticket?'

Fukushima looked impassively at his watch. 'I shall be late for madam if you wish me to take you to dinner first.' With him, as never with Nakatani, Furomoto attempted to keep up the pretence of merely taking Sanae to the hotel for dinner. But the boy now gave a peculiarly insulting emphasis to the word 'dinner' which announced that he had not been deceived. 'It's twenty minutes from here to the hotel and at least thirty from the hotel to the club. We're near the club here.'

'Do what I say. Get me my cigarettes. But stop in a side-street.'

Fukushima parked the car in silence and then clambered out. Something in his attitude and the faint smile with which he turned and strolled away from them renewed Furomoto's jealousy and forced him to one of those instantaneous decisions for which he was known in the business-world of Japan.

'Look, Sanae-chan . . . I wanted to tell you this alone and not in front of the driver. I can't take you to the hotel tonight.' He saw the stunned look on her face, as though she had just witnessed a street-accident. 'I'm sorry. But I've been working late night after night and I feel exhausted. And then there's my wife. I've been having difficulty with her, of a kind, ever since she got back from Switzerland. You know, she's never cared what I did and I don't think she cares now. But I feel she's—she's slipping away from me and I mustn't do anything—mustn't give her any cause for . . . mustn't . . .' When he had started his explanation, he had had no intention of speaking about Lisa or revealing his inmost anxieties: he was merely going to say 'I'm sorry, I've been busy, I'm tired. We'll meet another evening.' But he needed someone before whom he could spill out the whole bile-bitter secretion of his jealousy; and now that Nakatani was dead she had suddenly appeared as a substitute.

At that moment Fukushima returned, opening the car-door and handing Furomoto, with an ironic bow, the packet of cigarettes and his change.

'We're discussing something. Please wait a moment. Here'— he held out a hundred-yen note—'go and play a game of pachinko and come back in five minutes.'

'Thank you, sir. I don't play pachinko.' Of course, he wouldn't.

Nakatani was content to spend hour after hour in front of one of the machines, which stretched in serried row on row down the ' Parlour ', his small eyes squinting angrily at the whizzing and colliding balls and the tip of his tongue protruding from one corner of his mouth.

'Well, get yourself a cup of coffee. I take it that you drink coffee.'

'Thank you, sir.' Fukushima bowed, bowed again with a faintly insolent smile at Sanae, and then strolled off, massive bruiser's hands in pockets, without taking the note which Furomoto was holding out.

'He'll have to go. My wife's taken a fancy to him. But he'll have to go.'

She looked actually frightened as she asked: 'So you want me to return to Kyoto?'

'I'll give you the money for the hotel, if you prefer to stay here. I'm quite willing to do that.'

'No. I'll go back to Kyoto.' The words came out so slowly that he thought that she was about to burst into tears.

He felt a momentary twinge of remorse. 'You don't look very well. I suppose it was the visit to the doctor. . . . It was silly of you not to go to my man. Why didn't you?' But, while she hesitated, he seemed already to know what answer would come.

'It—it hasn't been done yet.'

'Not yet?'

'No.'

'But, Sanae-chan, you can't go on leaving it. It becomes harder and harder with each month that passes.'

'I know.' She clicked her bag open and then shut, gazing out of the window. He waited: as tense as if that joke had been true and she really had a bomb. 'But I'm—I'm'—suddenly she turned to him and smiled—'I'm not really sure that I want to get rid of it.'

'Oh, you must, you must. There's no question of that.'

She eyed him coolly: all fear and nervousness gone as she told herself with an inner exultation: 'You've got him where you want him.'

'But I think—I think that I'd like to have it, Furomoto. In spite of all the difficulty—disgrace. If you'd help me a little, give me a little money—just a little. . . . Couldn't we? I'd never tell a soul. I promise. It would be our secret.' ('. . . You hurted me in

260

my body. . . . This is our secret . . . ten-thousand yen. . . .'
The long-forgotten phrases came back to her from the letter which
Michiko composed to her American.)

'No, it's quite out of the question. I can't hear of it.'

'But, Furomoto-San, why not, why not? If you get me a little
house—a very little house, in one of the cheaper quarters—then
you can visit me whenever you want. I'll always be there for you.
I and—our child. It's a wonderful idea! Don't you see? You'll
spend far less money that way than by taking me to expensive
hotels and giving me presents.' Behind her simulated eagerness, he
sensed the inflexibility of a will akin to his own: at last he had
ceased to despise her as he despised all the women who yielded
to him. She was different, he saw; very different. How idiotic of
him not to have guessed at that difference until now.

'But, Sanae, you talk as if we were going to spend the rest of
our lives together! You must realise . . .' He shrugged.

She stared at him. 'Then you mean—that all this—that everything that has happened—that it's all meant nothing to you?'

'Not nothing. Of course not! I've enjoyed it very much. You're
a beautiful and charming girl—ne?—and we have passed some
wonderful hours together. But you know that I never once even
hinted that this was to become—a permanency. I have my wife
and that is the one permanency in my life. I don't want another.
The rest—all the rest—is just—sa—just entertainment.'

'Entertainment!' The tears were now actually glittering along
her lower eyelids and beginning to trickle down her cheeks. 'So
that was all it was to you!'

'Now come, Sanae. You can't have had many illusions when
you first——'

'Entertainment!'

'In fact, I wanted to tell you this evening—I planned to break
it to you——'

'Break what to me?'

'That the sun has reached the mountain-tops.' The country
phrase, typically Japanese in its avoidance of any overt brutality,
was one which he often used on such occasions; and her reaction
to it was equally typical, as she let out a little whimper and raised
her hands to her face.

'Oh, no! No, no!'

For a moment the terrible doubt assailed him: Was he wrong?
Were her grief and shock both genuine? Had he made her the

innocent victim of his cynicism and suspicion? He extended a hand:

'Sanae—control yourself! Surely you guessed——'

'No, no, no!' She still wailed. Then, between sobs, she demanded: 'What is to become of me? What am I to do? After all these months——' (Ah, that was more like it; he had heard those same reproaches often enough.) She wrenched a handkerchief from her bag, jerking out with it some crumpled papers which she stuffed back at once. 'How can you do such a thing? Just—just abandoning me like this—for no reason, no reason at all—just on a whim—because you're tired—tired of me. . . .' Sobs racked her. 'And to think that all because of you I lost a chance of getting married.'

'Because of me?' he queried in ironic disbelief.

'Yes. A boy of a good family. Rich. He'd have looked after me —taken me away from that horrible theatre. . . .'

'I'll introduce you to someone else who'll look after you quite as well.'

She turned on him in fury. 'Someone like yourself, I suppose! Someone who will use me and then finish with me! That's the idea, I suppose! Is it?'

He smiled and then chided her gently: 'Sanae! Please! Don't become so hysterical!'

'*Iya*, I don't want any of your introductions. Do you hear? I don't want any of them.' Then, with a sudden dangerous calm, she leant towards him: 'But you've got to take care of me, Furomoto. You can't escape from our problem. You've got me into this state—pregnant—sacrificing a chance of a good match. . . . You're to blame. You've got to help me.'

'Of course, Sanae. . . . When I part from a friend like you, there's always a little present. I expect you know that, already.'

'No, not a little present, Furomoto. You're too big a man to make little presents.'

'The recipient doesn't usually specify the size of a present. You must leave that to the decision of the giver.' He spoke with a chilly politeness.

She looked into his eyes, her own beautiful eyes narrowed and her nostrils white and pinched. 'A big present, Furomoto. You must make it a big present.' She turned away, gazed out of the window, and then turned back: 'Otherwise,' she added quietly.

'"Otherwise?" What does that mean?' He attempted to maintain the same tone of disdainful composure.

'You know what it means. . . . Now you'd better take me to the station. Where's that driver of yours? You mustn't be late for your wife. Must you?' She settled herself deep into the corner of the car; but he remained crouched forward on the seat, peering from time to time to see if Fukushima were coming. The vixen! The dangerous little vixen! But she had a disagreeable shock coming to her if she attempted that kind of blackmail.

'To the station, Fukushima. To the station first. And then to the club.'

'*Shacho-San?*' There was a note not merely of interrogation but, so it seemed to Furomoto, also of surprise and even shock.

'Why don't you listen? To the station first. And then to the club.'

'Yes, *shacho-San.*'

'We must meet again soon,' Sanae leant over to Furomoto to say in a small, tranquil voice. 'For the last time.'

'What are you doing here?'

'Waiting. You're later than usual.'

'But supposing I'd spent the evening in Osaka?'

'I took the risk. Come on, jump in.' Welling was holding open the door of the M.G. 'Jump in. I was at a movie and then, when it was over, I suddenly felt that I wanted to see you and so I came along to the station. All right?'

She climbed slowly into the car without answering and, having placed her bag on her lap, turned her head abruptly to glance out of the rear window.

'What's the matter? Afraid that someone will see us?'

'No. There was a man on the train . . .' Her voice trailed off.

'Who?'

'I don't know. I thought that he was following me.'

'At this hour there are always drunks travelling who won't leave a pretty girl alone.'

She gave a visible shake to herself. 'Maybe. I thought I'd seen him somewhere. . . .'

'What's the matter with you, Sanae?'

'Nothing.'

'Mad at me for something? You're not yourself.'

This mood of hers, taciturn and even sullen, made it even

harder for him to say to her the things he had come to say. But perhaps she had already guessed them, with that intuition which so often revealed to her his inmost thoughts long before he had attempted to express them or even on occasion been aware of them at all. Perhaps there was really no need to say them at all. The supposition unnerved him. Then he began to despise himself, as so often in the past, for his cowardice and lack of resolution. But they were not that! he protested to himself; those were ugly words for what was, in fact something admirable—a horror of giving pain to someone one loved. Loved? As soon as the word flickered across his consciousness, he promptly suppressed it.

'Of course I'm not mad at you. Why should I be? I've just— just had a bad evening at the theatre. That's all. The manager's a pig.' As she spoke this last sentence, she contrived, by thinking of Furomoto, to bring it out with a wholly convincing hatred and disgust. 'I must get away. I can't take it any longer.'

'That's one of the things I want to talk to you about.' He gripped the steering-wheel, the line of his jaw growing even sharper and the freckles standing out more clearly on his forehead as the colour seeped from his face. His brother was screaming out of the heart of that churning horror of blood and foam and he was still bracing himself to leap down from the rock; the car was rushing him away, headlong, from the woman spreadeagled in the road, an anchor for her hysterically bobbing and curvetting dog. . . . 'I have a present for you.' The salt was in his mouth; he was wrenching the car around. Thank God! 'It's not much, Sanae. I can't afford much. But it'll give you a breather—two or three months in which to have a rest and look for something else. I know how much you want to get away from the Furomotos. You do, don't you? Well, with this you can maybe take a little place of your own—you and Aileen. Here.' He leant forward, his eyes still fixed on the darkening river of the highway which was now sweeping them out of the centre of the town into the suburbs; then he pulled an envelope out of the car-pocket before him and thrust it into her handbag. That evening he had been given that same envelope at the bank, with the seventy crisp thousand-yen notes in it: the teller betraying none of the surprise he felt at a drawing unusually large for a customer who tended to live from one fifteen-thousand yen cheque to another.

'What is this?' She sounded panic-stricken.

'No. Don't look at it now. Not now. It's something very small.'

'But is it—is it money you're trying to give me?'

'Yes. As I say, it's much less than I'd like to give you. But I don't have to tell you that we missionaries are far from being millionaires. I have my boy to educate—my wife . . .'

'I don't want it! I don't want your money!' She pulled the envelope from her bag. 'Why did you do that? What did you do that for?'

'Because I want to help you. I want you to get away from that theatre. Don't be silly, Sanae.'

She held the envelope in her small, trembling hands, resting them on her bag; her beautiful eyes looking all at once ugly as they squinted down, with a peculiar intensity, at the crest of the bank.

'Put it away, Sanae. Forget about it.'

Suddenly she turned her head and said in a voice that was little more than a whisper: 'Are you—is this—to pay me—for the last time?'

'Pay you—for the last time?' He repeated the question: stunned both by what seemed to him an astonishing clairvoyance and by her use of these brutal words to express a process so delicate and so fraught with guilt and pain and embarrassment that so far he had not had the courage to define it even to himself. 'Pay you for the last time?'

'Yes, the Japanese way when a man wishes to see no more of a woman. You know that, I think? Probably it is also the Western way.'

'But there is no *paying* involved. This is a gift to you, Sanae, not a payment. Why should I have to pay you?'

'You want to send me away,' she persisted obstinately.

The road was now curving beside the river in a wide, iridescent arc, concentric with the smaller and less brilliant arc of the water. Suddenly, near some trees, he drove the car up an incline, braked abruptly and switched off the engine. Then he faced her, twisting around in his seat.

'Sanae, we must talk this out. And please—no bitterness. Why this bitterness? We must think what's best for both of us— calmly, quietly—like friends.' He tried to say all this in a smooth, composed tone of voice, but a breathlessness, which kept catching up the words, betrayed his tension. 'Soon my wife's going to return. I heard from her today. The doctors say that she's done marvellously well—far better than they expected. As soon as the cooler weather starts . . .'

'I see.'

'Now listen, Sanae, listen! This is how I've figured it all out.' (All that afternoon he had lain out on his bed, a fan playing on to his body, naked but for his pants, and vacillated from one solution to another in a frenzy of exasperation and despair. He did not know which road he wished to take; and both of them frightened him equally. But if he dithered between them, standing in the middle of the cross-roads, he would certainly be hit. But I don't love Sanae, I don't love her! I love her no more than I now love Mary. Then, in that case, why should the prospect of a break with her fill you with so much agony? But we've done nothing together: or, at least, so little. Of course I find her attractive, sexually attractive: that blouse, with the shadows of the nipples beneath it. . . . But that's different; I can soon forget that.) 'Listen! Sanae, listen!' (In the end one chose the road one had already travelled: preferring the tedium of the old to the mysteries of the new.) 'You know that I'm fond of you, Sanae. Very fond of you. But this has—has been getting us nowhere. And now the time has come when it might even get us some-where we don't want to go. You're young, your life's ahead of you—children, marriage. . . .' She was staring at him with an extraordinary intensity; but he could only guess at the meaning of that gaze—hatred? contempt? pity? shock? 'If we go on see-ing each other, I'm afraid, Sanae—afraid of what might happen. . . .'

'Afraid!'

'Yes. Afraid.' He admitted it with a simplicity which suddenly pierced through her hardness and made it first crack and then slowly begin to crumble before his eyes. 'Now I'm fond of you—you know how fond I am of you. But I can still stop. Tomorrow—the next day—perhaps stopping will become impossible. And we've got to stop, Sanae. I'm sure of that.'

'And if I can't stop—now?' She suddenly raised one of her twitching hands and placed it behind his neck. 'What do I do?' The question was piteous.

'You must, Sanae. You must. You're a young and beautiful girl and I'm just——'

'Oh, stop that! Stop that! Not that again!'

They looked at each other in silence. Then, with an effort to resume the tone of judicious moderation with which he had begun, he jerked his body away from hers, stared straight ahead of him at the luminous noose of the river, and once more bent to his task: 'I'm happy in my marriage, Sanae. I've told you that often. I've never tried to hide it from you, I've always been truthful to you. The physical part'—he now began to mumble, because even to her, even at this crisis, to talk of the sexual act filled him with embarrassment—'that's—that's now not—not much good between us. Hasn't been for a long time. But for people of her age and mine, I don't know—I don't know that it's very important. You won't understand that. You're young. Until I met you, I'd stopped thinking about it. Truly. Days and days would pass. . . . No, I no longer love Mary—Mrs. Welling—in that way. But there's so much else between us. We've been through so much together. We were brought up together—known each other ever since we were kids. It would be terribly wrong if I were to leave her now. Especially after her big op. At a time like that a woman feels at her lowest. You can understand that, can't you? She feels that maybe her husband won't want her any longer. Old. Used-up. You should see some of her letters. . . . She's such a brave, uncomplaining person, but when you see those letters—honest, I want to sit down and cry when I get them. It's as if—as if all the will to be happy had gone out of her.' He turned: 'Sanae, help me, help me! Don't just sit there! Make it easier for me! Say something!'

'What do you want me to say?' She spoke out of the open window beside her, her head averted: and the words seemed to fall like stones, slowly, one after the other, into the river.

'I could love you, Sanae! God, I could love you! But it would be so unfair—to her, to you . . . I couldn't leave her, I've told you I couldn't. And what would be the alternative? Meeting secretly; a hole-in-the-corner affair. . . . And everyone would know, they'd soon all find out! Look how they gossip about us already. Oh, Sanae, I could love you, I could!' he cried out in a sudden desperation.

'Then love me! Love me!' Her hand, which had been resting along the back of his shirt-collar, gripped at his neck. With her other hand she forced his head round and then pressed her lips to his. He tried to push away; resisted; and then succumbed.

'No, Sanae. . . . No. . . . No. . . .' At last he freed himself, thrusting her back against the seat with such violence that he bruised her arms. 'No. Stop it.'

'You are just like all the rest.' She flung open the door of the car. 'You—you coward!' The envelope had slipped to the ground as she began to clamber out and, having extricated herself, she stooped and retrieved it. 'Here's your money.' She thrust it at him. 'Take it. Go on, take it.'

'I don't want it. It's for you.'

'Oh, no, no, no. If I take this, then you'll feel good—you'll feel kind and generous and noble. No. Take it. Take it!'

He shook his head, and then lowered it on to his hands which rested on the wheel.

In a sudden frenzy of rage she tried to tear the envelope across; but the coarse paper, with the bulky notes contained inside it, resisted her wrenchings until, in exasperation, she raised its flap and jerked out its contents. The delay served to calm her; or perhaps it was that, having been chronically short of money all her life, she could not now bear to destroy this sum, however tainted. The envelope fluttered downwards; her hands met on the notes. Then she hurled them into the back of the car, shouting: 'Take them! Take them! Take them!' Her arm flew up; the door slammed. She began to run, making her way deeper and deeper into the trees.

Welling struggled with the door, pushed it open and tumbled out to pursue her. 'Sanae! Come back! Sanae! Sanae!' He too started to run.

268

NINETEEN

WHEN I was a child, I used to have one persistent dread. If I put my hand far back inside a drawer; if I stretched my legs down, to their full extent, to the bottom of my bedclothes; if I put my shoes on without first shaking them out or slipped my fingers into a pocket which I had not used for a long time or groped into the recess of a cupboard—what horror might not meet my touch? All my life I have believed in the echoes which surround events, not merely after they have taken place but also before them; so that I now see that what happened last night sent back its muffled reverberations deep into my childhood just as, no doubt with diminishing vibrations, it will equally send them forward into the years ahead.

The evening began with a minor exasperation which, in this temperature, seemed to be a major one. The President of my University, a doctor, telephoned in the morning to say that he had been asked to make an English address to a convention of dermatologists at a dinner to be held at six o'clock. He had jotted down some ideas but since his English was so poor he would be glad of my help. With the reminder that he was after all in a position to do me harm if he wished, I mastered my irritation at being asked yet again to do a service for a man who never acknowledged my presence except when some service was required. (It was only when I put down the receiver, that the realisation came to me— You fool! You don't have to toady to this oaf any longer. In three days you will have spat the dust of Kyoto out of your mouth for ever.)

'Yes. Certainly, sir. When would you like to call on me?'

He began to explain, with frequent interruptions during which I could hear his muffled barkings at his secretary, that he was so busy that he doubted if he could spare the time for a visit. Could I not visit him instead? Since he has four University cars at his disposal and I have none, and it was he who was asking the favour, I too said that unfortunately I was busy and could ill spare the time. Eventually, as a compromise, he suggested that I should meet him for a drink in the bar of the Kyoto Hotel, where the dinner was to be held.

I went down to the hotel, ordered myself a highball, and waited. Ten minutes, twenty minutes, thirty minutes passed. Finally his secretary, an elderly man in a frayed brown suit worn with black boots which curled up at the toes, darted into the bar to stare wildly about him until his bleary old eyes managed to focus on me over bifocals as thick as the bottom of beer-bottles. 'Ah, Mr. Knox! There you are! The President has sent me to find you. He is in the reception-room upstairs with Dr. Hammerstein. Dr. Hammerstein is looking at his speech for him. He wishes me to thank you for your troubles. You understand. . . . Dr. Hammerstein. . . . The President . . . so grateful . . . many thanks. . . .' He gabbled incoherently as he backed away, executing at the same time a series of deep bows, his hands to his knees.

From a bower-like recess, shrouded by ferns in pots, a voice boomed out: 'Well, Knox! How does that make you feel? Like a door-handle or like a football? I can never be sure.'

It was Ed Schneider, his huge bulk slopped out over an imitation Biedermeyer sofa to make it appear as rickety and insubstantial as the bamboo chair in which I myself had been seated. He had a small tumbler containing what I supposed to be neat whisky embedded in one of his vast purple hands, while before him stood a large tumbler of beer. His white tussore shirt was worn outside his trousers, and was open from top to bottom to reveal the sweat-drenched singlet beneath. 'Couldn't help over-hearing,' he explained. 'I saw you waiting over there. But I had some papers to put in order'—his hand flopped down on to the brief-case beside him—'so I didn't speak. Come and have a drink! I've finished now.'

Like the hypochondriacs who always insist that not only they themselves but everyone else is ill, he was one of those drinkers who treat their fellows as though they too suffered from alcoholism; and I therefore found myself being repeatedly exhorted to 'Drink up' or 'Down that one', while my unconsumed 'other halves' accumulated about us. Schneider soon launched himself into one of his anti-Japanese tirades in a voice so resonant that everyone in the bar must have heard what he was saying. Words like 'shit' and 'bastard' and phrases like 'Kiss your ass for you' and 'Kick you in the crotch' squeezed the embarrassed sweat out of me—even in that air-conditioned atmosphere. Yet, if I discounted the violence of the rhetoric, I found that many of his views were merely exaggerated versions of my own. 'But why do you stay here?' I eventually remonstrated.

'Ah, there's a question!' He extended his half-empty tumbler in his purple paw and examined it under the light as though it were a jewel. 'I was asked the same thing only the other day by old Professor Hoshina—— Do you know Hoshina? He's got some guts, one of the few. Well, old Hoshina said to me—he's an old friend of mine, mind you—" Schneider-San," he said—very formal, Hoshina—" Schneider-San, why do you continue to endure us? " Yes, those were his very words! And then he added—and this was the part I liked—" Schneider-San "—very formal, you see—" Schneider-San, you are like a hotel-guest who never ceases to complain of the service and yet will neither leave the hotel nor settle up his bill ".' Highly amused by this remark, even in retrospect, Schneider emitted a peculiar deep-throated, clucking noise, wiped the back of his hands over his watering eyes, and then explained: 'You know, of course, that I owe everyone in Kyoto money, don't you?'

'Do you?'

'Come off it, Knox! Chuck it!' He parodied the accent of a Blimp. 'Of course you know that.'

Two or three times I made efforts to get away; but on each occasion he detained me with the insistence that I have 'one for the road'. Finally he became truculent: 'What's the bloody hurry? What's the matter with you?' To which 'I'm hungry,' I explained. 'Usually I eat at seven.'

'Well, you're going to eat at my place. Yes, yes. . . .' He put out a hand and, grabbing the waist-band of my slacks, jerked me back on to my chair. 'But first I must put through a call to my woman. . . . Waiter! Hey! Boy! Bring the same again. . . . Excuse me. . . . One moment. . . . Boy! . . . The same again. . . . Where's that goddamned telephone?'

The house, to which we travelled much to my relief in a taxi and not Schneider's car, was an old farmhouse on the slopes of Mount Hiei, surrounded by a garden which, though at least five times the size of mine, gave me an impression of choked constriction. Unpruned bushes, between which narrow paths must once have threaded, were now tangled inextricably together. On either side of the drive, and even encroaching on it, grew waist-high grass, out of which stuck up, jagged and silvery in the fading light of evening, thistles of a monstrous size. For an instant, through a vista of trailing leaves, I glimpsed what must once have been a pond; a slime-sealed disc, like an oxidised penny, tossed down on a ledge above the main thoroughfare.

The house was equally huge and equally claustrophobic, spilling out through its maze of outside passages, from which the screens had been drawn back, into the teeming garden which, in turn, spilled into it its insects, floating seeds, burrs and a din of cicadas and bird-song. There must have been many objects of great value scattered among the dusty piles of magazines, the medicine-bottles, the threadbare cushions vomiting their flock, the biscuit-tins, the cases of dead butterflies, the rusty carpentry-tools, the skis, and everywhere the books, books, books. I had always heard that he had a wonderful collection of Chinese and Japanese art; but whenever I stopped to examine any object which caught my eye—a T'ang horseman, a tea-bowl from Korea—he grew impatient, and gave me only the briefest answers to my queries.

The dining-room overlooked the whole of Kyoto, and now that the sun had sunk the garden between us and the city below had taken on the appearance of a sea above which we were floating. There was a long mahogany table down the middle, its surface marked with white blotches where things too hot must have been rested. Schneider waved a hand at one of the two mahogany chairs at the further end, its seat cracked so that the horse-hair stuffing protruded. 'Can't do with this floor-squatting,' he declared. 'My ass isn't made for it. I never know where to put it all.'

His 'woman' appeared; but he did not introduce us, and except for saying a few words to her in Japanese about the meal, he behaved as if she were not there. She was slender, and apart from her greying hair, had the appearance of youth; although I knew that she and he had been together for at least ten years. Silently and swiftly she brought in and set down before us first a tray of drinks; then a tumbler and a pill on another, smaller tray; and finally two charcoal-burners, skillets and plates and bowls piled high with raw food. Schneider swallowed the pill with a grimace and then grumbled: 'I hope you like *Tempura*.'

'Love it.'

He had spent, I knew, much of his life in China; and I began to ask him about those years. At first he brushed aside my questions, as he had brushed them aside when I had examined this or that object on our way through the house; but then, while the Korean busied herself in silent absorption with the preparation of our meal, he suddenly began to talk: lucidly, uninterruptedly, with marvellous flashes of poetry and wit. At last I began to understand how he had acquired his reputation as a scholar and a journalist; and also, from his pungent criticisms of State Department policy and the idiocies of the China lobby, why he was regarded as politically suspect by many of his fellow-countrymen. The sea-food, fish, slivers of chicken-breast and vegetables all fried in balloons of golden batter were brought over to us continually from the skillets; and as Schneider talked, he never ceased to pour out the saké from the earthenware flasks into our thimble-sized cups. The meal must have lasted for the best part of two hours, and at the end I guessed that the next morning I should feel far from well. '. . . So that's part of the answer to your question—and to old Hoshina's question.' An oil-lamp now stood on the table and as Schneider bent forward, crumbs of batter caught in the rubbery folds at either side of his mouth, it threw his shadow, like that of some vast, humped, prehistoric monster, upon the furthest wall and the ceiling. 'I've given my best years to this part of the world. I can't afford to leave it now. I've sunk all my capital—my invisible capital, not money, I've never had much of that—I've sunk it all here. A damned stupid thing to do! But there you are. It's all here, my life. So I have to stay on even if it kills me.' He drained his cup of saké; and as he did so, one of the two dogs with which we had seen him at the beach leapt up, like a bear, out of the darkness on to the narrow outside passage. 'God damn you!' Schneider yelled. 'Out! Out! Get out!'

But the dog, its head lowered so that the hair stood up around its neck like a ruff, loped towards us. Schneider tried to kick out at it; but the only result was that he all but tumbled off his chair. The dog retreated momentarily with a snarl and then again advanced: this time to my chair. 'Don't touch her. If you don't touch her, she's as gentle as a lamb. Come here, Bertha! Here!' He dangled a fried prawn between finger and thumb. 'Here, you brute!'

Silently the Korean woman moved to the dog, put a hand on its collar and led it off.

'She's wonderful with animals. Have you ever seen anything like it? They'll do what she tells them. But I can shout myself purple in the face and damn little they'll do for me.' Since

Schneider's face is habitually purple, the choice of phrase struck me as inapt. 'But it's always like that. If someone arrives to dun me, I send her to speak to him and in five minutes there he is, trotting off down the drive, his tail between his legs.' He belched, raising his hand to cover his mouth. 'Pardon me. My digestion's not what it was. Something to do with the enzymes. They say that alcohol destroys them. Ever heard that? Well'—before I could answer—'you don't have to believe all the rot they tell you. But the Japanese do. If a doctor tells a Japanese that he's dead, well, the man lies down and dies. Idiots! . . . How about a cigar? Or a glass of brandy? Let's make ourselves more comfortable.'

When, eventually, at half-past eleven, I attempted to leave, I encountered the same difficulty as when I had tried to leave the Kyoto Hotel. Was I afraid of missing the last bus? Well, there were always taxis. He would be glad to treat me to one. Or I could walk: beautiful walk, on a summer night like this. It was still early. No self-respecting person dreamed of going to bed before one o'clock. Besides, it was so hot that even if one did go to bed, one could not get to sleep. It was even too hot to fornicate.

At last I managed to prise myself first off my chair; then out of the sitting-room; and then out of the hall into the buzzing, chirping, rustling luminous garden. 'Wait! Wait! I'll walk with you!' Schneider cried. 'I'll take those two brutes. No, no!' He waved his hand in the air when I tried to protest. 'You'll lose your way otherwise. Or walk along the main road where someone will run you over. Just a second. Just let me decant some of that brandy.' He went back into the hall, opened a door and, leaving it open, disappeared inside: he sounded like a horse. 'There! That's better.' He was still doing up his trouser-buttons when he reappeared. 'Now, where are those dogs?' He turned to the two women, one the Korean and the other a servant, who were waiting, after the Japanese manner, to see us off at the entrance, and repeated his question in Japanese. The Korean vanished: soon to emerge from the recesses of the house with the two dogs on leashes. 'Want to take one?' He grabbed the leashes from her, and then offered a leash to me. 'The bitch pulls. So be careful. And don't touch her. Whatever you do, don't touch her.' At that the dog bounded off and I was dragged with her, hearing Schneider yell behind me: 'Hold her, Knox! Hold her!'

When he caught up with me where I was waiting, breathless,

at the bottom of the drive, he was singing, in a surprisingly musical if slightly hoarse voice, Wolf's *Eine kleine dinge.* 'I thought I'd lost you for good,' he broke off to say. 'And that I'd lost the dog for good. That would have been even worse.' He chuckled. 'She's going to litter next month, and I hope to sell the puppies. Though God knows who will buy them. People here have enough difficulty in feeding their brats, let alone a dog—and a dog the size of these!'

We walked on in silence unbroken except by Schneider's gruntings, wheezings and occasional belches and expectorations. 'So you're off in three days time,' he said at last.

'Yes. On Monday. By plane.'

'I envy you. . . . Good thing to clear out before the country has you by the throat—squeezing the life from you. Look at me. I was a fool not to get out when I was offered a Professorship in Oriental Languages back home. Now they'd never offer it to me. . . . Professor Schneider! Not bad, not at all bad. Professor Schneider.' He mumbled the title over to himself three or four times, lashing out, as he did so, with his walking-stick at the dusty bushes on either side of our path. 'Yes, you're lucky. Getting out while the going's good. This country's all right if you want to spend a few weeks gaping at temples and gardens—or even getting yourself a dose of clap or worse in Ginza or Gion. But it's no good for a long stay—and poison for a permanent one. You take my word for it. . . . Here, Bertha—here! Leave that shit alone! Filthy dog. Yes,' he resumed. 'Stands to reason. What was I saying? Yes. You see, if you're brought up to believe in all this "to yourself alone be true" business, every man a castle, that kind of crap, you'll find yourself sticking out here like a twisted pin. Because here spontaneity and individualism are out, right out; or, rather, they've never come in. You don't do things here because your conscience or your heart or even something lower than your heart tells you to do them. You do them because others have done them—and are doing them—and will go on doing them. Customs. Tribal customs.' Again he lashed out with the stick. 'Oh, all this is nothing new. You've heard it all before. Probably thought it yourself. There's no goddam country in the world where people are so much like each other—not good, not bad, just *like*. There are no individuals in Japan; or damned few. Just a race. Termites!'

We had now descended to the river, from which a faint, pearly mist had started to rise, spreading in wisps over the bushes and

275

the lower branches of the trees on the slopes beyond them. Suddenly I felt cold; not because it was really cold, but because of the change in the humidity. Far off something—an animal, a suburban train, the conch of some itinerant vendor of bean-curd or noodles—wailed and wailed again. There was a plop from the water and ripples expanded, in slow, glittering corrugations across its face to expire with a hiss and gulp at our feet. Now I knew where we were: I had walked this way, so many weeks ago, at the beginning of the summer, when Welling had given me a lift in his car from the dinner for the Archbishop. There was the same whine of gnats in my ears; the same mounds and trails of garbage; and everywhere the same nauseating miasma of decay. Suddenly there came back to me a memory of the drunkard I had found vomiting at the foot of a rubbish-heap; and then of the puppy which I had rescued, carried home and then unintentionally killed in my exasperated desire to stop its squealing. Schneider breathed in deeply and then breathed in again, as if to fill his lungs with this atmosphere of dissolution, and then asked: 'Do you know what a French Ambassador once said in his farewell speech before he left Japan? No? "La base de la civilisation Japonaise c'est la merde." La merde! Yes, the rats are underneath the piles and la merde is underneath the lot. . . . He'd got something there. . . . You can let that monster off her leash. No, I'd better do it. She might give you a nip.' The two dogs raced off into the mist as soon as he released them. 'Beautiful creatures,' Schneider said. 'I think it really gives me more pleasure to look at them than at any human being in this place. How old are you? Forty, forty-five? Well, that male dog's about fifty—reckoning in human years. And yet he's still in splendid fettle.'

Again we heard that long-drawn wail, followed by the rattle and panting of a train which passed behind the trees where I had never had any idea that a railway-track existed. Suddenly we heard one of the dogs yelping excitedly; and then the other joined in.

'That means they've found something. What's the betting it's a dead fish, or a dead litter of puppies or kittens, or a putrescent hunk of meat. They'll roll in it, whatever it is, and stink to high heaven. Disgusting brutes! Hey! Bertha! Ben! Come here! Hey!' He began to cough as the mist entered his lungs, putting the back of one of his swollen hands up to his mouth. 'Can you see them?'

I peered: and then, through a break in the drifting scarves of mist, saw the head of one. 'Yes, over there!'

In a small declivity between one clump of maples and another there was a vast cone-shaped pile of garbage, from which tins and bottles glittered in the moonlight. The two dogs were tugging at some object at its base with sudden growls and excited yelpings. Their plume-like tails tossed to and fro and, as they turned round at our approach, their eyes gleamed like agate above their huge bear-muzzles.

TWENTY

WHEN Frank appeared for breakfast that morning, he felt liverish and disgruntled. He had, as usual, begun his work-out at the end of the tennis-court furthest from the room in which Welling's Bible Class was held, when he became aware that, although it was several minutes past half-past seven, people were standing at the windows, looking out at him. He scowled at them and wondered why Welling, who was generally so punctual, should today be late. Some of the students, aware of his annoyance, then began to drift away; but the prayer-eater still remained to gaze with a ferocious intensity, her flat eyes glittering out of the shadow cast by the brim of her straw-hat, while one of her small, knobbly fists tugged at a curtain-cord. Eventually Frank turned his back on her: swinging himself up on the parallel-bars and executing a series of turns the clear-cut brilliance of which had obviously been sharpened by his knowledge of being watched. When he again looked, it was only to discover that everyone had once more crowded back to the window-ledges.

Damn Welling! He must have overslept. Rubbing the back of his hand across the tip of his long nose to catch a drop of sweat, Frank began to walk, with his peculiar rolling, springy gait, as though he were trying out a new pair of shoes, towards the building where the staff's rooms and apartments were situated. But Welling's door was wide open; and the old servant, Sarah, was already cleaning the room out, scratching at the bare floor with a broom, the handle of which her arthritic hands clutched against her ribs. 'Has Welling-San gone out?' Frank asked in Japanese. Useless: she obviously had not understood, as she turned her triangular, bilious face towards him, screwing up her eyes until the lids all but touched the purses of flesh beneath them. 'Welling-San,' he shouted. 'Where is he? Out?' Still she peered at him, the broom now poised off the ground, its handle to her stomach. Then she went across to the window and raised the broom to point—at what? The river? Mount Hiei? Or the mission-chapel, with its hideous, cement belfry, and mauve and emerald stained-glass windows designed and presented by one of their congregation? (Colethorpe had shocked Frank by mocking at both.)

'Is he here?' Now he went close to her and bellowed into her ear.

She shook her head, and her eyes opened in astonishment. What a stupid question! she seemed to imply. Frank gave up, and turned and left her.

When he had walked back with the same artificial athlete's gait to the tennis-court, he found that the students had now wandered out of doors in twos and threes and were standing about as though to wait for him.

'I can't find Mr. Welling. I suppose I'll have to take the class for him.' He spoke to them as if they were to blame. 'I'll take Mr. Welling's class,' he repeated, exasperated as much by their slowness to understand as by the extra duty. 'Come on.'

He was a person who was insensitive to any emotion in others unless that emotion were admiration for his own physique, and he sensed nothing unusual as he opened the Bible, looked around and asked: 'Well, where have you got to?' But he found himself wishing that that middle-aged woman in the straw-hat would master her nervous twitchings and grimacings and cease to stare at him with the pop-eyed, slack-jawed intensity of an inmate in an asylum. 'Well? Someone tell me, please!'

'Has anyone seen Welling?' Frank pushed open the door into the dining-room, so violently that the three occupants huddled at the far end of the table were jolted like passengers in a railway-train when the brakes are unexpectedly applied. Norah even gave a little, stifled scream which she modulated into a giggle as she protested: 'Why, Frank, what a way to enter a room! You startled us.'

Miss Pinter, her large, flat face turned to see who it was, now sighed, crossed her black strap-shoes one over the other, sighed again and then smoothed her black skirt with both of her hands as though she were massaging her thighs to relieve them of some ache. Miss Rosenthal had been smoking: a practice she normally confined to the privacy of her bedroom. And before breakfast, too! Frank disapproved of cigarettes and liquor, especially for women, and had often worried himself with thinking of how his parents would react to Colethorpe's addiction to both.

'He didn't turn up for his Bible Class and so I was the sucker who had to take it for him.'

'Is he—didn't he—you mean——?' Miss Rosenthal prodded at her recently discarded cigarette with a used match.

'I thought he must have overslept. But he wasn't in his room either.'

Miss Pinter raised her face, so oddly luminous under the tight reddish curls which surrounded it like lacquered shavings of wood, and looked first at Frank, briefly, and then at Miss Rosenthal. 'Then he must have heard,' she said at last to the other women in her flat, melancholy, contralto voice.

'I wonder who told him.'

'Sarah, I guess,' said Norah.

'It's a mystery to me how Sarah learns these things.' Miss Rosenthal picked up the coffee-pot, but put it down again without pouring out of it. 'She's supposed to be deaf and half-blind, but when there's any news flying about . . .'

'What is all this? Hey, what is all this?'

Frank pulled out a chair and sat on it, back to front, facing the three of them.

'Haven't you heard, Frank?' Again Miss Rosenthal raised the coffee-pot and this time filled her cup.

'Heard? Heard what?'

'That girl—she's been found dead. Murder, everyone says.'

'They've roped off a whole area by the river.'

'And Mr. Knox and Mr. Schneider found her.'

'Can you imagine! Finding such a thing!'

'But what girl, what girl? What girl's been murdered?'

'Oh, mercy,' Miss Rosenthal gasped. 'I never thought. She's Aileen's room-mate. How terrible for Aileen! Why didn't I think of it?'

'Aileen's room-mate? Do you mean—Setsuko?'

'Why, no—the young girl, the pretty young girl——'

'Welling's fr——' Norah checked herself before she had said the whole word.

At that moment Sarah shuffled in: 'Ambleside-San?' She peered around the room as though she expected him to be hiding somewhere.

'He hasn't come down yet.' Norah walked up close to the old woman and shouted: 'He hasn't come down yet!'

'Gentleman here. To see Ambleside-San. Ikeda-San.'

Ikeda-San was frequently described by the missionaries as 'a pillar of our Church', 'a real Christian' or 'completely one of us': the last two phrases carrying the implication that there were other Japanese Christians whose beliefs were either less orthodox or less sincere than his. He was also a high-ranking police officer.

'Ikeda-San!'

'At this hour!'

'What can he want?'

But all three women already knew what he wanted: obviously he had come to speak about 'that terrible thing up there' (as they were, in future, tacitly to agree to call the murder).

Frank, who had strolled over to the window, now found that the dapper little Japanese was standing in the porch, holding in one hand a brief-case so large when contrasted with his diminutive legs that it seemed to reach down almost to his ankles. 'She's left him to wait outside,' he turned to announce in astonishment. 'Is she crazy?'

'Sarah, take him into Mr. Ambleside's study. Mr. Ambleside's study!' Miss Pinter had extracted a handkerchief from the bosom of her dress and was now pressing it to her cheeks and forehead. 'Sarah!'

'Oh, I'd better go, I guess.' Frank hurried out.

'Where can Mr. Welling have gone?' Miss Pinter asked. 'I hope he isn't doing anything foolish. He's been so odd these last weeks——'

Miss Rosenthal gulped her steaming coffee until the tip of her little beak-nose turned red and the tears came to her eyes: 'My, but I feel sorry for him!' she said. 'If there's one man I feel sorry for!' Again she gulped.

'Why, what do you mean?' Miss Pinter asked. She knew very well what Miss Rosenthal meant, but always kept up a pretence of being unaware of anything derogatory about any of her colleagues.

It was to this monastery, high up among the hills beyond Yase, that Sanae and he had come on their last walk together and their last but one encounter. They had met on the outskirts of the town; had left the car where he had left it this morning, in the court-yard of the village-inn; and had then climbed up, by a rocky path so steep that he had often had to turn and help her. It had been evening then, now it was morning; but the light was the same, pearly close at hand and totally opaque in the distance, and the smells and the sounds were the same. Sometimes he even imagined that, if he looked round, she would be there behind him, her lips parted over her small, even teeth as she smiled at him, gasping for breath. *Gasping for breath.* . . . Everything the same: yet everything different. . . . But how could it have happened? How? How? He saw again the arc of her arm as she flung the money into the back of the car and heard again his own voice shouting out after her 'Sanae! Sanae! Come back!' (His lips moved now, repeating the same words.) Then he was running, tripping over the garbage, stones and exposed roots in his path, here, there, among the bushes and then deep into the trees. . . . But he had never found her. He would never find her again.

Outside the monastery there was an enormous cryptomeria around the trunk of which a circular wooden seat had been built. They had sat there then and he sat there now: jerking a handkerchief from his pocket and wiping first his face and then his neck with it. How could it have happened? How? How? Again he asked himself the anguished question. . . . It was Sarah who had first aroused him with the news, shaking him by the shoulder as she bent above him and reiterated: 'Get up! Get up! Police find girl! Dead girl! Dead!' 'What girl?' he had asked crossly in Japanese; and as he had shifted on the bed, his whole body (that was odd) ached as if after some prolonged and unwonted exercise. 'What girl?' he had sat up and shouted at her.

'Bible Class girl.' She exasperated them all by insisting on speaking English even to those fluent in Japanese. 'Quick!' She was picking up his singlet, shirt and trousers and thrusting them out to him. 'Police find girl!'

Only now, after the turmoil of his walk up here, did the full significance of her behaviour come to him: she was urging him to run, of course! And he had never guessed it. All at once the manner of all those whom he had questioned on his way out to the monastery—the milkman; the man in the paper-shop; Ito-San's servant, getting out early for the market—seemed to him ambiguous. He had been imagining that they had behaved to him oddly merely because they had heard the gossip about his friendship with Sanae; but supposing that they had thought——? Oh, no, no!

Then a strange and terrible thing happened. As he sat there, his elbows on his bony knees, staring down through a cleft in the mountains to the smoking chimneys of the factories in the plains below, he suddenly understood how it would have been possible to kill Sanae. With all the distinctness of memory, he visualised the scene; and its clarity amazed him and even filled him with nausea, since he was not normally an imaginative man. . . . She pulls out the notes and counts them. 'Only seventy thousand?' 'I'm afraid it's all I can manage. Honestly, Sanae. You know that we missionaries——' 'Well, it isn't enough. I need more. At least two hundred. Otherwise.' 'Otherwise?' She shrugs: 'Use your sense. What little you have. You don't want your wife to learn about us, do you? Not after her big operation, especially. And a man in your position can't afford a scandal—a girl from a strip-show, a Jap girl, imagine!' But Sanae would never speak like that; she would never attempt such a vile, squalid trick! How could he imagine such a thing of her?

Then how about this? (A train was passing through the valley; his eyes followed the blue-grey plume of smoke as it wreathed over the landscape and then slowly smudged deeper and deeper into its tranquil lushness.) The caresses, like the caresses on this very bench outside the monastery, reach a climax: she pulls herself free. 'What's the matter, Sanae?' 'No. We must stop.' 'But, Sanae——' 'No, no, no!' He lunges at her; attempts to pin her down, one forearm pressing down on to her mouth; she scratches at him, even manages to kick him on the shin. Then she squirms, tugs at the handle of the door, and manages to tumble out, pulling him after her. She gives a scream and then, staggering to her feet, another scream; then she begins to run. He trips, trips repeatedly —damn the garbage, these stones, these roots—but he gains on her. Near a mound of rubbish, her high heel catches on something and she is wrenched down, full length. He throws himself upon her. . . . And then? In the struggle to possess her, does he strangle her involuntarily? Or is it, afterwards, when, sobbing and bleeding, she reiterates 'I'll go to the police . . . police . . . police. . . .' that he panics and grips her by the throat to choke the threat out of her for ever?

Although the air was still cool up here in the hills and he was in any case sitting in the shade, Welling's face was streaming with sweat, the freckles standing out on it like shrapnel-scars and the nostrils pinched and white. His hands gripped each other as though in an attempt not to cry out in agony.

But worse followed: suddenly he not only saw how he could

have come to kill her but he began to believe, for a few ghastly minutes, that he had actually done so. Why not? 'My mind became a complete blank. . . .' 'The defendant repeated that he had no recollection whatsoever of taking the instrument in his hand or of any of the events which followed. . . .' 'I saw red; I remember no more. . . .' Supposing that the same thing had happened to him? And now, as he tried to visualise once again his fruitless chase after Sanae, his subsequent wait for her at the corner of the road by her house, and then his despairing journey back to the mission, he found that he could not recall a single detail. The garbage, the stones, the exposed roots. . . . Tripping. . . . Tripping again. . . . And calling. . . . But after that —blank. 'My mind became a blank.' He sat appalled.

A novice came out of the monastery, a boy of thirteen or fourteen, the bulbousness of the back of his head accentuated by the shaving of his hair and the lowness of a forehead covered with a rash of pimples. He nodded and bowed and said '*Ohayo gozaimasu.*' He was carrying a rake.

With him, reality seemed also to break through, like a surgical instrument incising and then scraping away the grey, distorting jelly of a cataract. But it hadn't been like that! Of course he hadn't killed her! He—kill Sanae? He laughed to himself: a strange, choking kind of chuckle, which made the boy glance back over his shoulder as he descended the hillside. Until then, Welling had never understood how people came to confess to brutal crimes of which they were wholly innocent. But now he understood.

He stared down at the ground. A dung-beetle, under an immense load, was attempting to hoist itself up over a piece of wood in its path. 'Go round, go round,' he wanted to shout at it. Picking up a twig, he tried to prod it in the right direction. But still it persisted in the futility of its original intention. Idiot! . . . Suddenly, as he watched it repeatedly struggling and repeatedly falling back, Welling's eye was caught by a scrap of paper, the first four letters of which he could make out: MACK. . . . Then he remembered the tin of toffees which Mary had sent him and how they had been in the car and he had offered Sanae one. 'I shall keep it as a reward for climbing to the monastery.' 'Eat that one here and I'll give you another as a reward.' 'No. This is my reward.' He saw her munching contentedly, like a child, as the two of them stared down into the valley in silence. 'Look! A train! A train!' And as, in recollection, he now heard her say that, the train once again trailed its garland of blue-grey smoke across the brightening valley.

'Well, of course. Of course you must question him. Just the moment he gets back. Now how about another cup of coffee, Ikeda-San? Eh? Oh, come along! Just what you need after your gruesome night's work!' Ambleside had adopted the unnaturally jolly, hearty, comradely tone which betrayed to those who knew him well that he was disapproving, embarrassed or rattled. Ikeda-San knew him well.

Ambleside squatted once again on a hideous, chintz-covered pouf, his knobbly knees sticking up from his khaki-shorts and his elbows resting on them. He bit on his pipe, and then ran the fingers of one hand through his thick, wavy hair. 'No, I expect Welling has gone to Otsu. As you know, we have a small mission there, as well. In fact, I remember saying to him only a few days ago that it was time he went over to see how McIver was getting on.' This was not in itself a lie, but since it was now serving the purpose of one, Ambleside mumbled it with a shamefaced air, at the same time knocking out his pipe on a massive chromium ashtray inscribed with the name of the Kyoto firm of builders which had erected the concrete mission tower. 'He'll be back any moment now. . . . But this is a pretty odd business about the car. You're sure there's no mistake about it?'

Ikeda-San raised a hand to tip up the two lenses of his glasses, like skylights on hinges, and then looked across at Ambleside. His eyes all at once seemed smaller, weaker and far less formidable. 'Two independent groups of witnesses saw it—first a courting couple and then two cyclists. There may be others. Those ones called in at the station early this morning because they live in the neighbourhood and so heard the news. When it appears in the newspapers . . .'

Ambleside shifted uneasily on his hams. The newspapers! He had lived long enough in Japan to know what that meant. 'Yes, but people can imagine things. The trouble is'—his teeth ground on the pipe-stem; how was he to put this? 'There's been—well— there's been a lot of talk about Welling and this poor girl. You know what people are like in this town. You've said it yourself, often enough.'

'Yes, I am aware that there has been—gossip.' The skylights clicked down. 'Unfortunate gossip. Unfortunate for the mission,

285

unfortunate for the Church and now—unfortunate for Mr. Welling.'

'Of course, gossip without a grain of truth in it! I know Welling have known him for years. Well, come on, Ikeda-San, you also know him. You know him as well as I do. Almost. You know that he's as steady as a rock. Wouldn't fool around with a girl like that, quite out of character. She was one of his Bible Class and he just felt towards her as any of us feels towards one of our flock who's in a spot of trouble. Not a thing in it!'

Ambleside wondered if he had succeeded in convincing the small, dapper, composed figure opposite to him, one highly-polished pointed shoe crossed over the other and his hands clasped in his lap. It was lucky, he summed up shrewdly, that it should be a Christian in charge of the case; a Christian was likely to try to minimise the scandal, if only for fear of the dirt that would splash up on to any member of the mission or indeed on to the Protestant Church in Japan as a whole.

'Yes, I'm afraid Welling is sometimes the victim of his own kindness of heart. He's a dear fellow, and nothing—certainly not gossip—will ever stop him from doing what he thinks to be his duty. Sometimes he's more generous than wise. As in this case.'

'You know that the girl worked in a strip-show?'

'Oh, dear, yes. Oh, did she?' He had known, as everyone else in the mission had known; but he hastily corrected himself, deciding that it would be more seemly to appear to have been ignorant of anything so squalid.

'Such girls, I do not have to tell you, are generally harlots.' In spite of his three years in America and his work with the American Occupation Forces, Ikeda-San still tended to use such Biblical expressions. Ambleside all but smiled, in spite of his anxiety.

'Ah, but that would make Welling feel all the more under an obligation to do something to help her! Don't you see?'

'Possibly.'

'Oh, I'm sure of it, sure of it! Anyway—who are we—the first stone——?' His enemies always said that, when cornered, Ambleside could be relied upon to produce some Biblical quotation, however inapposite or threadbare, to get himself out.

Ikeda-San rose to his feet. 'Well, until Mr. Welling returns, there is nothing more for me to do here. Mr. Ambleside—' he bowed—'I thank you. And I am sorry for wasting your time.'

'Not at all, my dear fellow, not at all! Any time! Always

delighted ! ' The protestations came out automatically, with no relevance to the gravity of a criminal investigation. 'Any time, any time at all ! You're always welcome ! ' He began to pat and stroke the little Japanese, following his usual custom of seeking some form of physical contact with those whom he felt to be becoming remote from him. 'My wife was saying only yesterday that it was an age since we'd seen you. Except at Services, of course.' He pinched Ikeda-San's left biceps, a hard walnut of muscle, and then threw an arm about his shoulder. 'Be a good fellow and call on us soon. Otherwise my wife is going to be offended. You know how much she likes you. . . . Well, cheerio, old man ! ' He gripped the small, beautifully manicured hand between both of his, noticing, for the first time, that the Japanese was wearing a gold identity-disc around his left wrist. 'As soon as Welling returns, I'll bring him round to the station. Bring him round straight away ! '

'Thank you.'

'Not at all, not at all ! Anything to oblige ! Delighted ! . . . Ah, you have your car. And such a splendid car ! Makes our dear little Hillman look like a baby-carriage, doesn't it ? Well, so long, dear fellow. So long ! Goodbye ! '

He was aware that Frank and two—or was it three?—of the women were watching Ikeda-San's departure from the dining-room window. Why on earth couldn't they mind their own business? But perhaps, he suddenly thought with a mounting distress, this was their business. After all, anything which concerned the mission also concerned them. He sucked on his pipe, dragging his feet along as he made his way down the dusty corridor back to his study. . . . What was Sarah peeping at him for? Her face had suddenly appeared from behind the sliding-screen which marked off the kitchen quarters and then disappeared again. 'Hey, Sarah ! Hey ! ' As if it were any use calling to her ! If she did not wish to hear, she would not hear. Well, if the staff set her such a bad example, one could hardly blame her for her inquisitiveness. Presumably she and the two other servants had already learned the news.

When he was once more seated on the pouf, his eyes fixed unhappily on the empty grate and the pipe in his mouth unlit, Ambleside suddenly realised that he had had no breakfast and was feeling hungry. But he could not face that crowd in there, with their hesitantly clumsy probings. '. . . Do you suppose that . . . ? '

'Early for Ikeda-San to call . . .' 'Mr. Welling hasn't had any breakfast. . . .' 'Terrible news. . . .' 'Nothing serious, I hope, Mr. Ambleside? . . .' He could hear their idiotic feminine voices (somehow he did not imagine Frank or the Japanese house-surgeon joining in) and could see their idiotic feminine faces expressive of shock, fear, curiosity and, yes, pleasure. (Had the three women been aware of dear old Mr. Ambleside's opinion of them at this moment they might have been disconcerted.)

'Here you are, dear. You're much better on your own.' Mrs. Ambleside had entered, carrying a tray on which his breakfast was set out, together with a cup of coffee for herself. 'I suppose the poor things really are disturbed and anxious to be of help— but I wish they wouldn't *talk* about it all so much. It's not as if talk will get us anywhere—or their talk, at any rate.'

Ambleside looked up at her gratefully: it was at such moments that he realised how lucky he had been in his marriage, whatever might be his occasional moods of exasperation at some seeming vagueness of impracticality.

'You've heard?'

'Well, of course I've heard. I'd no sooner set foot in the dining-room, than they began to ask me if I hadn't heard—and to tell me. Poor girl!'

'Poor Welling! But, oh, what an idiot!'

'Yes, it's not been very clever of him. But surely no one imagines that he . . . I mean, whatever the—the relationship with that child, he couldn't possibly have . . .'

'I think that their relationship was perfectly innocent. I've said that to you before, dear, and I'll say it now.'

'Well . . . I wish I could say it too. But—I just don't know. . . . Now look at you! You've spilled egg on to your shorts. Wipe it up.' She handed him a napkin. 'Anyway, I do know that he didn't—didn't strangle her—or whatever it was.'

'There's this business about the car. That worries me.'

'The car?'

Ambleside told her.

'Oh dear! Now why did he have to use a car like that? Mrs. Crawley said to me when he first bought it that she thought it unsuitable for a missionary. And that colour too. Oh dear,' she repeated.

'But after all, as I told Ikeda-San, witnesses in such situations often persuade themselves that they've seen things that never existed at all. Everyone knows *that*—most of all a police-officer.'

'Yes.' Mrs. Ambleside considered. 'But I guess that there must be tyre-marks.'

'Tyre-marks?'

'Yes. Tyre-marks. If he stopped the car where those people saw it—by the river—the ground must have been rather soft. And the marks left by those tyres—new tyres, too—must be fairly recognisable. And shoe-marks too,' she added.

'I never thought of that.'

'I'll bet Ikeda-San has.' She could barely conceal her self-congratulation. 'So, if there are *no* tyre-marks and *no* shoe-marks . . .'

'But if there are?' Ambleside countered.

'Well, if there are . . .' she slowly raised her coffee-cup. 'Then it'll be pretty bad for him, won't it? But even if there are, I still can't believe . . . No.' Suddenly she was definite: 'Welling didn't kill that girl. He's not the type.'

'Is anyone "the type"?'

To that question she made no answer. Unhappily both of them looked at each other, Ambleside mopping with his napkin at a runnel of liquid egg on his chin.

'Ah, there you are, old chap! We've been looking high and low for you.' Welling was seated on the end of his bed, apparently doing nothing, his body hunched forward and his bony hands clasping a handkerchief soggy with sweat, as he gazed up at his visitor. Then, suddenly, he jumped to his feet. 'Where have you been? To Otsu, I suppose? Beautiful morning for a spin, absolutely beautiful. Look at Mount Hiei!' Ambleside strode over to the window. 'Now that the morning haze has cleared, you get one of the best views in Kyoto from here.' He might have been a hotel-manager showing a new arrival his room. 'I wish I could get myself up earlier. I always miss what the Irish—or is it the Welsh?—call "the top of the morning".' Suddenly he went over to Welling and threw an arm around his shoulder. 'What is it, old chap! Feel pretty bad, don't you? It's this news about—about the girl. Stands to reason. One of your Bible Class.' Suddenly he became aware that Welling, his face averted, had raised a hand and was pushing him away; but none the less he went on, in his lifelong faith that words, any words, of reassurance, however fatuous, irrelevant or repetitious, were preferable to the silences in which the spirit becomes aware of its agonised heart-beats failing and dragging to a stop. 'Bad business. We're all upset by it. You should have seen my wife earlier this morning! She hardly knew the girl, but when someone in one's own neighbour-hood . . . Well, there you are! That's how it goes, I suppose! Now, sit down, old chap. Sit down, and let's have a word, eh? Sit down. That's the boy.' He again put his arm over Welling's shoulder and dragged him down to the bed. 'Hot, isn't it?' He had just seen, in a transverse beam of sunlight, the sweat gleam-ing around the other man's eye-sockets and in the hollows at his temples. 'We'll have another corker today, shouldn't be surprised. You mark my words. . . . Now, old boy, let's talk this thing over. I've had Ikeda-San round here this morning—you know Ikeda-San, of course.' Welling had been about to jump up again, but Ambleside restrained him. 'Now, easy, easy, easy! No need to get alarmed. Just a routine call. The girl was one of our Bible Class, we all knew her, she was the room-mate of Frank's friend' —he clicked his fingers—'what's-her-name—English girl. Ikeda-San wanted our help—any help we could give him. Nothing in it. Nothing in it at all.'

'And he wanted to see me?' Welling's bony jaw moved up and down with a peculiar rigidity as though he were suffering from extreme cold.

'Yes, you too, dear fellow. So I—so I said that I'd take you round to the station just as soon as you returned.'

'No.'

'A matter of routine, routine, nothing more.'

'No.' This time Ambleside was unable to restrain Welling from leaping up and going to the window.

'But, my dear chap . . . You really mustn't. . . .' Ambleside went over to him. 'Ikeda-San is a friend. As a convenience to him. He's been out here once already. No harm can possibly come to you. I'll be with you. I'll stay with you all the time. Just a statement, a brief statement. . . . Nothing more.'

'I refuse to go to the station.'

Twice, at the camp, he had been summoned for interrogation: once, soon after his arrival; once in connection with an escape. He remembered the endless choking and gasping; the pressure of the eyeballs; the tongue which seemed to have become an immense wedge of wood; the nausea; the vomiting of water out on to one of the guards who at once kicked him in the groin. . . . And then the talking—the abject words seemed to flow out of him as the water flowed, words, words, any words. . . .

'I refuse to go to the station,' he repeated.

'But don't be silly, my dear fellow. If you refuse to co-operate, you will only make things harder—harder for yourself and for us. Ikeda-San, at the moment, is full of good intentions.' As he said that, Ambleside wondered unhappily if indeed this were true. 'He knows us, he's a friend of ours. Don't antagonise him, please.'

'I won't go. If he wishes to question me, then '—Welling's lower lip trembled—'then let him come here.'

The older man sighed. 'You're being unwise, old chap—very unwise. What have you got to fear?' (The small hands thrusting his head downwards; the simian grins; the half-open door leading into another room from which came one inhuman yelp after another, yelp on yelp. . . .) 'Frankly I don't understand you. I don't understand your attitude. We all know that you are innocent, no doubt of that. Even Ikeda-San knows. And if one is innocent, then one should—should welcome any investigation. Not make it more difficult. Eh? Don't you agree?'

'I won't go!' Welling screamed, turning on the other man like an animal baited beyond endurance. 'Do you hear? I won't go! I refuse!'

Ambleside retreated, emitting, from the back of his throat, a peculiar clucking noise which was intended to calm and console. Then, all at once, he changed. Advancing close to Welling, and dropping all affectations of comradeliness or jolliness, he spoke: spoke with an immense, quiet authority which forced the other man to hear him out in immobility and silence. 'Now listen, Welling. You're in a jam. You've been a fool and you're in a jam. You wouldn't listen to me in the past. I suggest that you listen to me now. If you go along with Ikeda-San, he'll do his best for us and for you. Yes, I say "for us" first. I mean, the mission and the Church. He'll do his best to minimise the filth which the newspapers publish: filth about a girl and you and, probably, filth about the mission. He'll give you a fair deal—and perhaps a bit more. If, on the other hand, you antagonise him, then things will be bad. Your car was seen by the river last night, shortly before that girl met her death——' Welling swung his head around so that for the first time his horrified eyes looked into Ambleside's; Ambleside nodded. 'Yes. Independent witnesses. . . . Did you in fact park your car there?'

'Yes.'

'With the girl in it?'

Welling's lips barely moved. 'Yes.'

Ambleside grunted. 'In that case you must see the danger to yourself. You must see that this kind of attitude of yours . . .'

Welling took three or four tottering steps towards the bed and threw himself across it. Then, to Ambleside's amazement, he caught hold of the end of the sheet and began to jerk it over his head, sobbing out as he did so with a raw, peculiar, hiccoughing sound: 'Go away. Go away. Leave me. Leave me alone. Leave me.'

Ambleside stared down at the shrouded head; then he went out and leant for several seconds against the open passage window, his forehead pressed to the jamb and a shaking hand to his throat.

TWENTY-ONE

'YOU did not come with Mr. Schneider?'
'No.' Since it was already five minutes since I had
been shown into the office, the question seemed super-
fluous. 'I came direct from the University.'

'But your term is over.'

'I had to pick up my salary. I'm leaving Japan the day after
tomorrow.'

Ikeda-San ceased to toy with the gold identity bracelet around
his left wrist and looked up at me sharply. 'You are leaving
Japan?'

I nodded.

'And where are you going?'

'To England.'

'But I am afraid, Mr. Knox . . .' One small hand adjusted the
lenses of his glasses so that they tilted slowly upwards. 'I am very
much afraid—we may need you in Kyoto.'

I had been prepared for this; but now that it came, I felt like a
child from whom a promised Christmas gift has been withheld.
'Need me here!'

'Yes, naturally.'

'But this is—is absurd! I—I can't stay. I have my tickets, my
family are expecting me . . .'

'I understand that a—a change of plan will be extremely in-
convenient for you. I'm sorry. But'—he raised the tiny hands—
'what am I to do? I do not wish to spoil your journey, I assure
you.' He smiled. 'It was foolish of you to find a corpse so soon
before your scheduled departure. You must have known that such
an event was likely to cause trouble.'

Astonished by the discovery that here was at least one Japanese
who had a sense of humour—of a kind—I made no further protest. Instead: 'How long do you think I shall have to stay?' I
queried.

'You know the slowness of the Japanese courts. I remember that
Mrs. Ambleside once said that our legal procrastinations and

293

complexities reminded her of *Bleak House*. I thought the comparison a good one.' ('Procrastinations and complexities!' Evidently Ikeda-San has never learned that it is equally possible to betray that one is a foreigner by speaking English too well as by speaking it not well enough.) He plucked back his sleeve and glanced downwards at his watch. 'Where is Mr. Schneider? What has happened to him?' His show of impatience and even petulance, like so much else about him, was Western, not Japanese. 'He is wasting our time. I know that he himself has unlimited time to waste . . .' He drew from under his blotter two sheets of typed foolscap paper which I recognised as our statements, and then clicked down his glasses at them, forefinger and thumb tweaking simultaneously at his full lower lip.

'I must congratulate you on your English. It really is remarkable,' I said.

'There is no cause for congratulation at this precise moment, Mr. Knox. If it were worse, I might not have been put in charge of a case which is—frankly—distasteful to me.' The light, nasal voice, pattering along, at this point seemed to find an echo outside the window: rain had begun to fall. He got up and closed the window. 'Now it will be even hotter. What a climate!'

'Then you can understand why I'm in such a hurry to get back to England.'

'Oh, I can understand many reasons for that.'

While I silently explored all the possible implications of this last remark, and Ikeda-San continued to read our statements, an altercation suddenly started just outside the door, against which sporadic scratchings and bumpings could be heard. A number of people were involved and among them, all shouting or hissing at each other in Japanese, I eventually recognised Schneider. 'I think that must be Mr. Schneider,' I said to Ikeda-San, who was gazing at the door in astonishment.

'Mr. Schneider?'

'I think so.'

Ikeda-San got up and walked over to the door with the wary nervosity of a cat. When he opened it, he was all but knocked over by Schneider's two rearing, pawing dogs, their tongues fluttering and their topaz eyes rolling as they made frenzied efforts to free themselves from their leashes. 'Be quiet, you brutes! Imbeciles! Down, I say! Grrr! Down! Down, down!'

Behind Schneider's monstrous bulk, diminutive men in uniform were hopping and twittering.

'Good morning, Ikeda-San.' Schneider unwound the leashes from his right hand, leaving yellow weals on the swollen, purple flesh, and held it out. 'Your people don't like my beasts.'

'Good afternoon, Mr. Schneider.' Evidently they knew each other.

'A lot of goddam nonsense! There's nothing wrong with these two. Wouldn't hurt a soul. Besides, they had their rabies shots only two weeks ago.'

'Well . . .' Ikeda-San surveyed the two panting, plunging animals and then gave a faint smile. 'Since they are, in a sense, two of our key witnesses—the first on the scene of the crime as far as we know—perhaps, in this case, we shall make an exception to our rule and allow them to come in.' He turned to speak quickly and quietly, with peremptory authority, to the policemen who were still surrounding Schneider and they at once scuttled off. 'Come in. Please come in'—he glanced down at the dogs—'all of you. Mr. Knox, as you see, is already here. He has been here'— he consulted his watch—'eighteen minutes.'

'Can't think what you want me for.' Schneider groaned and wheezed as he lowered himself into a rattan chair. 'Is this damned thing safe?' He checked Ikeda-San's smile: 'No, I'm not joking. One of these things collapsed under me a few days ago in the house of Professor Yakushizi. He thought it a big laugh. But I hurt a bone in my ass and, hell, did it hurt. The coccyx, that's the bone. Heard of the coccyx, Knox?' I nodded. 'Knox knows everything, Ikeda-San.'

'Yes. I have already been told of Mr. Knox's omniscience.'

'Well, now, what is it you want? We spent more than two hours here last night, making our statements. That other boy—the one who took them down—he's none too bright, you know.'

'Oh, Orito-San. Orito-San is very intelligent. . . . But careful,' Ikeda-San added as though it were a reluctant criticism.

'I'll say!'

'And then the fact that he speaks no English. . . . But I am forgetting. Your Japanese is perfect, Mr. Schneider.' He picked up the statements off the desk and scrutinised them as though for the first time. Taking advantage of his apparent absorption, Schneider immediately pulled a flask from his pocket and gulped at it twice.

'Yes. . . .' Ikeda-San lowered the two documents. 'Oh, before

I forget, would either of you like any refreshment? We can send out quite easily. A soft drink—a vin-cola, an orangeade?' He smiled. 'Mr. Schneider? No?' As we both shook our heads, I was amused to see that the colour of Schneider's face was deepening.

'Good. . . . Now I should like to run over these statements with you—purely as a formality, you understand, nothing more.'

'Nothing more! I should hope not!'

Ikeda-San gave Schneider an appraising glance devoid now of any of the tolerant good humour with which he had first received him. Then he turned to me: 'You had dinner with Mr. Schneider last night?' I nodded. 'And you decided to leave at——'

'Eleven-forty. I know, because I looked at my watch and was surprised at the time.'

'The earliness?'

'No. The lateness.'

'You can confirm that, Mr. Schneider?'

'Yes, I guess so.'

Ikeda-San hesitated over this reply with an obvious distaste either for its ambiguity or the idiom employed. Then he decided to go on: 'What made you decide to walk, Mr. Knox?'

It was a wearisome business; made even more wearisome by Schneider's difficulty in remembering any events clearly other than the actual finding of Sanae's body. Ikeda-San at first seemed to suspect that the American was being deliberately evasive; but then he must have realised that when one is dealing with an alcoholic one cannot demand any accuracy of memory, and at that his manner became less impatient but even more disdainful.

At last, after nearly an hour, we were finished. Ikeda-San got up, stretched himself, and crossed to the window. 'It's still raining. You came in your car, Mr. Schneider?'

'No. I had to walk these two brutes.' The dogs were now sleeping, nose to tail, one under Schneider's chair and the other at his feet.

'May I send you home in one of our cars?'

'No, thank you. Unnecessary—quite unnecessary. I like a little rain. I have here what I call my outsize rubber. Mr. Knox, being English, would, I guess, call it my outsize French letter.' He pulled a plastic raincoat out from his brief-case. 'Neat little thing. These two brutes love a downpour.' He prodded one of the sleeping dogs with his shoe.

I suspected that the reference to the 'outsize rubber' had given an even sharper edge to Ikeda-San's contempt. Making no attempt to coax Schneider to change his mind, he merely shrugged and then turned to me: 'You, at any rate, Mr. Knox, will travel in my car. . . . No, please.' He raised one delicate hand, with a clink of his identity bracelet, to check any objection. 'I have to call at the mission and that is near where you live. I have also to call at the—the victim's house,' he added.

Schneider plunged off before the car had time to pick up Ikeda-San and myself from the porch. As the slanting rain propelled him from behind and the dogs dragged him from in front, he seemed to move without any effort of his own, his raincoat billowing out to give him the appearance of a fugitive balloon.

'Is Mr. Schneider drunk?' Ikeda-San suddenly asked.

'Oh, I don't think so.'

'But he drinks very much—and very often?'

'He drinks. Yes.'

'Is he an alcoholic?'

'I don't know.' I knew very well that he was; but this questioning had begun to annoy me.

'It is sad that so many Americans become alcoholics.'

'People become alcoholics in every country of the world, surely.'

'It is a sign, I think, of a lack of spiritual values.'

'Perhaps it is sometimes the sign of an excess of them.'

Ikeda-San looked at me with the same cat-like wariness with which he had approached the door when Schneider and the dogs were outside it; but this time he left the door closed and my remark was ignored.

We got into the car, a Chevrolet painted white and black, with a man wearing ear-phones seated in front beside the driver, and rode for a while in silence, until Ikeda-San turned:

'This—this girl—she was a neighbour of yours, I think?'

'That's right.'

'You knew her?'

'A little.'

'What did you think of her?'

'Beautiful, I suppose. Though not the type that I myself find sexually attractive.' As soon as I said that, I realised that the phrase 'sexually attractive' had had the same effect as Schneider's reference to his raincoat. But I was not displeased to notice the hardening of the eyes and mouth and the jerking of the small, elegant head to gaze out of the window. 'I think that underneath all that apparent softness and pliancy, she was as tough as the best of them.'

'Such girls have to be tough. The profession of harlot is a tough one.'

If he had said 'tart' or even 'prostitute', my astonishment would have been less; but even those terms seemed to be inapplicable to Sanae.

'Oh, I don't think you've got the right idea about the poor girl at all. She was really quite respectable.'

'Respectable—in a strip-show? In a Japanese strip-show? '

'Yes. Why not? '

He smiled to himself, as he once again gazed out of the window at the rain-battered avenue of maples down which we were swishing. Then he bit on his lower lip, pulling it between his small, perfect teeth. Finally, he turned to me, to speak with a contemptuous irony: 'You are more innocent than I had supposed, Mr. Knox—or more charitable. Surely you know about the lives of such girls? For nearly two years I worked in the Gion Precinct and each week I had to pick up at least a dozen of them—for stealing, for brawling, for blackmail, for fraud. Every so often one of them would be found with her throat slit—stabbed—strangled like this poor wretch. Once or twice horribly mutilated. Yes—did you know that last year Kyoto had a whole series of Jack the Ripper murders? ' Seeing my mounting distaste, he seemed deliberately to wish to intensify it. 'I daresay, Mr. Knox, that when you go to Gion, it seems to you—as to so many foreigners— very charming. Very pretty. Quite different from your own Piccadilly; quite "old world"—is that how you would put it? ' It was the last way in which I should put it; but I knew what he meant. 'Geisha, maiko, bar-girls, girls in Arbeit Salons—don't they seem to you to be no more than dolls, beautiful dolls? I am using a phrase which an American business-man used to me the other day; his wallet had just been stolen. But you must look behind and beneath the elegant surface, as that American was forced to look. Four hundred and something dollars! Can you imagine carrying such a sum? No, Mr. Knox, the lives of such girls are not pretty at all, however pretty the girls may look. And though the girls may be scented, the things they do—the things they do stink! '

I had listened to all this, delivered in his light, pattering voice,

with a mingling of curiosity and repugnance. Now I interrupted:
'Oh, I'm sure you're right. And I'd never supposed that it was
otherwise. But to return to Sanae——'

'Sanae?'

'The murdered girl.'

'Ah, Ogura-San.'

'Yes. About her you're quite wrong.'

Ikeda-San again gave his small disdainful smile. 'And why do
you suppose that?'

'She was living in the house of some friends of mine. And if
she had, in fact, been what you say, they certainly would not have
had her there.' This was not strictly true; after all, Setsuko's view
of Sanae had not been so different from Ikeda-San's. But my
annoyance at his prim distaste impelled me to the falsehood.
'Besides, her closest friend was an Englishwoman——'

'Miss Colethorpe?'

'Yes.'

'And you think that any friend of an Englishwoman must be
respectable?'

'Any friend of that particular Englishwoman. Yes.'

'Mr. Welling is also one of your friends?' The question followed immediately on the one before, but seemed to have no
connection with it.

'Yes, I know Welling.'

'A close friend?'

'No. I should hardly call him that.'

'And he was also a friend of Ogura-San.'

I said nothing: not sure whether this was a question or a
statement.

'A close friend,' he went on.

'You have probably heard some of the gossip that has been
going around about them.'

'It would be difficult not to: especially when one is a police-
officer.' He sighed. 'It is tragic.' One hand, the fingers pink-topped
and the nails exquisitely manicured, played with the identity-
bracelet dangling over the other. Suddenly his face looked peaky
and abstracted.

'What is tragic?'

'A man like that—of Welling's age, education, standing in the
community—becoming involved with such a—such a slut.' The
last three words were venomous. 'Don't you think that tragic?

299

To lose one's head, to forget oneself. To forget all decency and dignity.'

'I think that Welling's relationship with the girl was entirely innocent.'

'Do you really think that, Mr. Knox?'

'If I didn't think it, why should I say it?'

'Oh, out of loyalty, I suppose.'

I was nettled: 'He was a little sentimental about her—as middle-aged, married men tend to be sentimental about beautiful young girls. But I am sure that they were not lovers. It's out of the question.'

He sighed again, even more deeply. 'I hope that you are right.'

After that we sat in silence until the car entered my street. Ikeda-San pointed: 'I think that that is your house?'

'Yes.'

He spoke quickly in Japanese to the driver.

'And that is the house of the Furomotos?'

I nodded.

'I shall have to call there again. But later.' I wondered why he had had to confirm that was the Furomotos' house if he had already visited it. 'Your house looks charming.' We had drawn up at the gate.

'Thank you. It's small and extremely cold in winter. But I like it.' Something had been troubling me vaguely; and now I said: 'Excuse me, Ikeda-San, but I have the feeling that we've met somewhere before. I can't think where. Perhaps I'm just imagining it.'

'No. You are not imagining it.' He smiled, obviously pleased at being able to demonstrate the superiority of his memory. 'April. The dinner for the Archbishop. In the Miyako Hotel. It was, in fact, Mr. Welling who introduced us. And I fancy that that was also the first time that you and Mr. Welling had met.'

'Oh, yes, of course! Then you are a——?' I hesitated.

'A Christian. Yes.' He nodded. 'So you will understand why this case is so—so disagreeable to me. And why I called Mr. Welling's involvement in it tragic.'

Of course I understood! All Ikeda-San's behaviour that afternoon, so bewildering and contradictory, now became clear to me. It had been stupid of me not to have remembered our previous meeting; and even more stupid, not to have guessed Ikeda-San to be a Christian. That un-Japanese censuring of Sanae's and even

300

Welling's 'immorality' ought in itself to have been my clue.

'Thank you for the lift.'

'Not at all. . . . Then you will postpone your departure, won't you, Mr. Knox? If you have any trouble—with your travel-agent or the air-line—please let me know.'

'It's an awful nuisance,' I grumbled. 'This postponement.'

'Yes. A murder tends to be a nuisance.' His lips tightened. 'We won't keep you a moment longer than is absolutely necessary.'

'That's kind of you.'

Although he himself so often uses irony, my own seemed to be lost on him. 'Not at all. . . . We shall, I am afraid, probably have to meet again soon. So I shall say, not goodbye, but *au revoir*, Mr. Knox. And thank you—thank you for your assistance.'

When I went into the house, my first action was to look at the English-language *Asahi Evening News* which was lying in the entrance. 'Murdered Strip-Girl,' I read, low on the front-page; and then, in smaller type: 'Connection with Missionary.' Poor Welling! So it had come out; and come out even more quickly than I had feared. '. . . Handsome Australian missionary Welling, who was once a Japanese P.O.W., was often to be seen in his green M.G. sports-car, joy-riding with the glamorous strip-girl. Their friendship became a frequent topic of conversation among inhabitants of exclusive Kitashirakawa district. Anonymous letters of complaint were even sent to head of mission, Reverend Ambleside, who, however, appears to have ignored them. This case, following so soon on that of Catholic Father Marini, recently expelled for offences against a nine-year-old orphan boy at the Santa Croce Home in Kobe, is likely to lead to scrutiny of the whole position of foreign religious missions in Japan. Diet-member Osuga has already announced his intention . . .' My eyes ran on to the next paragraph. 'Finding of corpse.' '. . . Two prominent Kyoto foreign residents, English Language Literature Professor Knox and journalist-Japanologist Schneider, were the first on the scene. Both are friends of missionary Welling and knew the lovely strip-victim of what is likely to be one of the most sensational . . .' At this point, Endo-San came out from the kitchen. Having bowed low to greet me and tidied away the shoes I had just taken off in the course of my reading, he told me of three telephone calls from the Press and four separate visits from journalists. 'I say, *sensei* is out,' he concluded. 'They say, come back, come back soon.'

'Well, when they come back, come back soon, *sensei* is still out. Understand?'

He bowed.

'They go to next house.' Suddenly he abandoned English, in his unwonted excitement. Of what followed, I could get only the gist: apparently old Mrs. Furomoto had refused to talk to the journalists and when they had continued to ring the bell, hammer and scratch on the windows and shout, had asked for the assistance of the two policemen left on duty at the house. But the policemen had been either unwilling or unable to get the journalists to go away and in the end Mrs. Furomoto had been obliged to admit them. They had only just left.

At this point in Endo-San's story, I began to put on my shoes again and decided to go across to the Furomoto house. I had already called there earlier in the day, but had seen only Mrs. Furomoto, who told me that Setsuko was out and that Colethorpe was too upset to receive anyone. Mrs. Furomoto had displayed no emotion; but her skin was a peculiar saffron colour, as though she were in the final stages of jaundice, and her eyes, the right lid of which never ceased to twitch as though she were winking at me, had the appearance of being covered by some kind of yellowish film. We had talked briefly, because she had seemed to have no desire to talk at all, and then I had left. Overhead I had all the time been able to hear the sound of feet walking up and down Sanae's room and of drawers and cupboards being opened.

On this occasion it was Colethorpe, her face blotchy and her eyes raw with weeping, who came into the hall, barefooted, a kimono wrapped about her and a handkerchief clutched in a soggy ball in one of her hands. 'Oh, Mr. Knox. I was afraid that it was some more journalists—or that horrible police-officer.' She spoke almost in a whisper. 'Come in. I'll find you some slippers. Where have they got to?' She peered about the hall, bending down so that her buttocks stuck up in the air at me, the kimono caught in their cleft.

'Don't bother. I can manage with my socks. It's cooler that way. Are you sure I'm not disturbing you?'

'Oh no, come in.' She cleared her throat and repeated more audibly: 'Come in, please.'

'I wondered if I could help in any way. Sometimes a man——'

'Oh, we have plenty of men about the house at present. Two

302

policemen and a photographer and another man whose job I haven't identified.'

'I hear that the Press have been bothering you.'

She nodded and then subsided in a slack, dishevelled heap on the floor. 'Please, sit down.' I squatted by the window. 'Yes, somehow I thought that they'd—they'd be different in Japan. The newspaper-men. But they're not. Or if they are, they're only worse.'

'Newspaper-men are the same all over the world, I imagine.' The trite, soothing reply came out automatically. I was thinking of something else: of Sanae, the last time I had seen her alive, demure and radiant; exactly where Colethorpe was now sprawled, with her red eyes, the lids of which might have been skinned, fixed upwards on my face.

'You've seen what they've already started writing?'

'I've seen the *Asahi Evening News*. Yes.'

She put the soggy ball of handkerchief to her trembling lips and for an alarmed moment I thought that she was going to vomit. 'Can't they be stopped? Can't one do anything about it?'

'The libel-laws here are practically non-existent. In any case, I doubt if a foreigner like Welling would stand much of a chance in a Japanese Court of Law.'

But it was not of Welling that she was thinking; as her next remark revealed. Ignoring what I had said, she went on: 'You'd think that when someone was—was dead——' again the handkerchief was pressed to the trembling lips as though to stanch an invisible wound—'they'd be more—more careful. It's not as if she could defend herself now.'

'If she were alive she probably couldn't defend herself either.'

'They're brutes, absolute brutes. They make it sound as if she were a—a prostitute. We know that isn't true.'

'Of course we know it. But to them every strip-show girl is a prostitute. Just as every American is a millionaire, every Korean a gangster, and every Englishman a gentleman.'

'Even the police talk about her in that way.'

'You mean Ikeda-San?'

'Who?'

'The police-officer who speaks such beautiful English. Too beautiful.'

'Yes, him . . . he's a horror. I lost my temper with him. But then I spoiled it all and had a silly attack of hysterics.' She

303

giggled and I thought, for an appalling moment, that she was about to have another. 'Oh, he despised me for that. And so did Mrs. Furomoto. But you know—Sanae—Sanae and I—we——' She put a hand to her eyes exactly as though she were shielding them from the glare. Again the lip trembled.

'Yes, I know,' I said. 'You were such friends.' I felt that, if I said the worn phrase for her, she might not break down completely. I was right. She nodded, sniffed and nodded again. Tears were on her short, thick eyelashes.

'How has Setsuko taken all this?' I asked at once, eager to change the subject.

'Setsuko?' She repeated the name as though it were unknown to her.

'I haven't seen her yet. She was out when I called.'

'Out? But she hasn't been out all day. She's been in her room. Even he—the police-officer—had to see her there.'

'In her room?'

'Yes.' She nodded. 'Oh, she's allowed to be upset, it's all right for her.' Suddenly I realised, from the animosity with which she was speaking, that she did not like Setsuko and perhaps had never liked her. 'But I can't be. And if I am, I just get dirty looks from Mrs. Furomoto and that pansy with the gold-bracelet. Of course, in Setsuko's case, it's called a bilious headache. But she was crying in there for hours on end, I could hear her from my room. In the end Mrs. Furomoto went in to her and then she stopped. I daresay she's suffering from remorse,' she added with morose spite.

'Remorse?'

'For the way she treated poor Sanae.'

'I thought she was very fond of her.'

'Yes. At the beginning. But then she began to get possessive—spied on Sanae—tried to interfere . . . And Sanae hates—hated all that kind of thing. She was so—so independent.' The mouth creased downwards, the chin wobbled. 'They quarrelled terribly and then she told Sanae to go. . . . Later, she took that back, said she didn't mean it. But Sanae wasn't going to stay any longer than she could help. And nor was I. She and I—we—we always stuck together.' Her teeth fastened on a corner of the handkerchief, her head tilted sideways so that the dishevelled hair covered half of her face. There was a long, distressful silence. Then she sighed, shook herself visibly and scratched at one of her bare ankles. Tossing back her hair from her face, she looked up at me. 'Do you

304

think——?' she began; then she broke off. 'Oh, never mind.'

'Do I think what?'

'It doesn't matter.'

This kind of sticking in of hooves just before taking a fence both exasperates me and makes me the more determined to proceed. . . . 'Go on. What were you going to say?'

'Well, do you think . . . about Sanae . . . and Mr. Welling . . . ?' Again she hesitated. 'Well, do you think . . . do you think there was anything in it?'

'It depends what you mean by "anything".'

'Setsuko—I'm sure that Setsuko thinks that they are— were lovers. But that can't be so. Can it? Can it? What do you think?'

'When Ikeda-San asked me that same question a short while ago, I said that I was sure that their relationship was innocent.'

'Oh, I am glad! I am glad you think so! Sanae admired him of course—and liked him enormously. . . . Like a daughter and father. That was how it was. She was an orphan, you know that, don't you? People have such filthy minds, they always assume the worst. But you'd think that someone as educated and tolerant as Setsuko. . . . She's not usually prudish and yet it seemed to upset her so much—disgust her so much—the thought that perhaps they were. . . . You do really think that, don't you? You do really believe that they were just—just friends? Don't you, Mr. Knox?'

'One can never be wholly certain. But, as far as one can, yes, I —'

Suddenly she looked troubled, scratching again at her ankle, her thick lashes lowered and her head tilted downwards. 'If only it weren't for that photograph!'

'What photograph?'

'The photograph they found.'

'I don't understand.'

'The police. The photograph of him—of Welling. They found it among her things. Didn't you know?'

'How should I know?'

'I thought that that beastly man must have told you. . . . Among a lot of love-letters—mostly from a boy in Hiroshima, an old boy friend of hers—I knew about him. . . . Do you think that odd? I mean, having the photograph; and keeping it like that —in an attaché case, with those love-letters and other personal

305

papers, as though it were something precious. What do you think?'

'Probably she slipped it in there by chance.'

'That's what I said. But I don't think he agreed with me. And then he wanted to know how she had got hold of it—and when. As if I should know! I told him that he'd better ask Mr. Welling. I suppose that Mr. Welling must have given it to her.'

'Where was the photograph taken?'

'Well, at first I thought that it was on the beach where we all went that Sunday. But he—Ikeda-San—pointed out that it was quite another beach: at Tottori, I think. Some of the boats in the background had the name of a hotel on them.' Again she tossed away the lank blonde hair from her swollen face and looked up at me:

'You don't think it *odd*—his giving her a photograph of himself—himself like that?'

'Like what?'

'Well, on the beach. In bathing-trunks.'

'No.' But I was not yet sure whether I thought it odd or not; and she seemed to sense my doubt as she still held my gaze, her large, raw eyes glistening up under their matted lashes and the tip of her nose crimson.

I looked away. 'Do you think I can see Setsuko?'

She shrugged. 'You'd better ask Mrs. Furomoto, I suppose.' Slowly she got up and stumbled out into the hall. 'Furomoto-San! Furomoto-San!' I heard her calling; followed by the sound of slippers on the stairs. 'Mr. Knox is here and wonders if he can see Setsuko.'

Mrs. Furomoto did not reply to Colethorpe but, instead, came into me, bowing low, as I scrambled to my feet. 'Setsuko is unwell. She has been in bed all day.' It did not disconcert her that only a few hours previously she had told me that Setsuko was out. 'I think it is better not to disturb her. She is asleep at last. If she is not better tomorrow, I shall call the doctor. When she wakes, I shall tell her that you called.'

'Thank you.'

'Thank *you*, Mr. Knox.'

She continued to repeat 'Thank you' in both English and Japanese as she backed, with an incessant bowing, out of the room and into the hall.

Colethorpe returned. 'I hate all their pretence. Being out, being

306

ill. . . . Why can't they just say that she's upset and leave it at that?'

'I, too, hate the Japanese pretence.' I was thinking of Setsuko's never-ending play-acting with me and her refusal to be either truthful or true; until suddenly I felt a terrible desolation open up within me, like the actual physical rupturing of a blood-vessel or the cracking apart of a bone.

'That was where Sanae was different. She wasn't Japanese in that. She never hid anything. Never, never.' Once again she threw herself down on the *tatami*. 'And it's because of that utter truthfulness of hers that I feel so sure that if there had been— been anything of that kind between her and Welling, she would have told me, of course she would have told me.' Suddenly she jumped to her feet again and went across to the screens that separated the room from the garden. Pulling them back and forth, so that they screeched in their grooves, she looked, not at me, but into the garden, as she asked: 'But how could it have happened? How *could* it? Who would want to kill her? I don't understand. It's too terrible.' She gasped and her hands clutched at her face as though she had suffered a violent twinge of toothache. 'Such a sweet girl. . . . No enemies. . . . No one. . . . Nothing. . . .' Now she was crying, the sobs coming in one convulsive spasm after another, while her body twisted against the fragile screens with a violence that made me fear that they would splinter out-wards to precipitate her into the garden.

Suddenly the bell tinkled, and tinkled again. Then a voice called out, in Japanese: 'Excuse me —is anyone there?' It was Ikeda-San. Heavy stockinged feet clumped down the stairs and a gruff country voice said something obsequious, while Colethorpe attempted repeatedly to get herself under control. 'He's back,' she eventually said in a thin, plaintive voice, like a child's, after it has sobbed itself into a state of exhaustion. 'He said he'd be back.'

'Ah, Mr. Knox. I hardly expected to see you again so soon.' Ikeda-San's delicate head, the black, wavy hair fitting close to it as though it were lacquer, appeared around the screen-door. 'May I come in? I'm not disturbing you? Miss Colethorpe?'

Colethorpe now stood slouched against the screens, one shoulder higher than the other and her stomach thrust out. She made no reply: merely protruding her lower lip and then rubbing the back of her hand upwards against her nose.

Ikeda-San squatted on the floor, tucking his small legs beneath him. 'Please.' He extended a palm, rosy like his finger-tips. 'Please. Sit down.'

I sat; Colethorpe remained standing, her eyes averted to gaze into the garden. Ikeda-San adjusted the fan between us and then drew a handkerchief from his jacket-sleeve and proceeded to mop his forehead. 'Hot,' he said. He smiled.

'Appalling.'

'I have just come from Mr. Welling. That was hot work too. He seemed a little—disturbed. You must persuade him to be less on the defensive—more co-operative.'

'I?'

'Yes, you, Mr. Knox.'

'But I have no influence with him, I'm sure.'

'He admires you and respects you. He said something that made me certain of that.'

I should like to have asked what Welling had said, but my growing antipathy to Ikeda-San restrained me from doing so.

'I have received some interesting information,' Ikeda-San continued.

'From Welling?'

'No. Not from Mr. Welling. Though I received some interesting information from him too. From our surgeon. It confirms what I had already guessed.' He paused. 'Ogura-San was pregnant.'

Colethorpe gave a little whimper, making Ikeda-San swing round.

'Does that surprise you, Miss Colethorpe? That was what I came here to learn. It appeared to surprise Mr. Welling,' he added with a dry incredulity. 'Miss Colethorpe? Does that news surprise you?'

She turned wildly. 'It's not true. I don't believe it. It's a lie—a—mistake. How is it possible?' She appealed to me. 'It's a mistake, isn't it?'

Ikeda-San shook his head. Once again he gave his ironic smile. 'Our surgeon is completely reliable.'

Colethorpe was edging towards us; until suddenly she threw herself down beside me, huddling near to me as though for protection or warmth. She was shivering: although the sweat was streaming off my own body to make my shirt stick disagreeably to my shoulder-blades and back-bone. 'No, no,' she whimpered, a hand over her mouth. 'I don't believe it. No.'

'I'm sorry if I've upset you.' He did not bother to make it sound convincing.

Colethorpe was now crying. She gulped two or three times; then jumped to her feet again and rushed from the room. Ikeda-San raised one of his beautifully arched eyebrows; he smiled.

'I thought English women were supposed to be so—so tough and so—so phlegmatic. This girl is quite hysterical.'

'Her closest friend has been murdered less than twenty-four hours ago.'

He ignored my obvious hostility. 'At any rate her astonishment at the news of the pregnancy was more—er—plausible than Mr. Welling's.'

'You must have known about it long before this. Surely your surgeon couldn't have——'

'Oh, of course I knew about it. Even before we met this afternoon, Mr. Knox. But I wanted to keep the—the impact fresh. Fresh for Mr. Welling, I mean.'

It was only then that I realised the full gravity of Welling's situation. So far I had only feared for him as someone whom gossip would associate with Sanae; now I feared for him as someone whom gossip would associate with murder. I stared at Ikeda-San, appalled; and he seemed at once to know the reason.

'Yes, Mr. Welling is in a very dangerous position.' Ikeda-San tilted up his glasses and the small, weak eyes, deprived of that covering, gleamed, in the shuttered gloom, like molluscs without their shells. He sighed. 'Very dangerous indeed. It was madness for him to get mixed up with such trash!' The last sentence came out with a force and passion which had the effect on me of a door slamming suddenly in a quiet and empty house.

I have just come in from the garden where I have been sitting, motionless, for the gnats and mosquitoes to prey on me. Tragedy and violence bring with them not merely shock, horror and grief, but also elation: the screws are all suddenly tight, everything is in focus; one might be in the middle of a successful love-affair or writing an examination to which one knows all the answers. But now the elation has ebbed away; only those other emotions remain, a bitter residue.

Of Setsuko, about whom I have thought so much these last weeks, I have thought hardly at all: I suppose because to hear of another's grief is less painful than actually to witness it. Colethorpe—her face blotchy, the tip of her nose crimson, her eyes raw and swollen—I cannot get out of my mind. I do not believe for a moment that her feelings for Sanae were what Setsuko suspected them of being; but I am certain that though she was not in love with her, she loved her with a force far more common between two normal women than between two normal men. I remember that she once told me, to my amazement, that she had never been happier than during her stay in Japan; now Japan will be spoiled for her—a country in which the things that happen to other people happen to oneself. The extent of my pity for her now is, I suppose, proof of an affection which I never knew existed. I used to be irritated with her because she was one of those people who tended to be present when I wished Setsuko to be alone; and irritation tends to obscure, though not to destroy, more generous emotions.

And Sanae? Of her I did not wish to think; because if I did, I should see her again as I saw her last night, first hunched up at the foot of that heap of rubbish, anonymous as a discarded overcoat or jettisoned cardboard box, and then her face, swollen and pop-eyed, as it was revealed in the spurt of flame from the match clutched in Schneider's fist.

I had often enough seen death, or the undertaker's art, beautify the hideous; but now it was the beautiful which had been deformed. I had never greatly cared for her: partly because of that same resentment which I had felt against Colethorpe, for sharing in all those moments of Setsuko's life in which I had no share; and partly because that Japanese ideal of womanhood, demure, self-effacing and arch, with an inflexibility of purpose so artfully concealed that many foreigners do not suspect its existence, has never attracted me. But it was horrible to think of her terrified strugglings and swayings; of the anonymous hands thrusting her downwards to her knees (lacerated; the stockings in blood-stained, mud-defiled shreds); the gaspings and croakings to summon the aid that was not there or to plead the mercy which was not granted. Somehow her death, though it could have happened anywhere, seems to exemplify that pitiless disregard for all human life and suffering which I see daily all about me. She has joined the abandoned kittens and puppies: luckier than they, inasmuch as she died more quickly, but of not much more importance.

Finally, I thought of Welling. Was he the father of the foetus?

Possibly. Was he her murderer? No. I don't know. No. Yet: why not? All the evidence was there; and it was no use saying that he had not got it in him, because every man has more in him than we can bear to admit. What, after all, about Professor Uchiyama? This elderly man, a professor of electronics at my own University, had killed his unfaithful mistress, mutilated her and then flayed her head. Placing her skin over his own face and her hair over his own bald head, he had then hanged himself in her clothes. The case had been sensational. Yet the sad-eyed, furtive little man had no more seemed to have that grotesque deed in him, when we had met in the Common Room, than Welling Sanae's death. . . . Yes, but if I had known the Professor, known him as I know Welling——! And so I wavered between belief in his innocence and belief in his guilt; clinging to the former and yet perpetually slipping downwards to the latter.

Through all this the telephone calls and the ringings and hammerings at the door maintained a staccato rhythm, like the guns which remind one of a distant battle. Endo-San was perfect. Time and again he explained, courteously and with immense Japanese elaboration, that I was not yet back; that I was visiting in Kobe; that, no doubt, since it was getting late, I might even be staying there overnight, as was often my custom. I sat out on the darkening verandah, with the thin hum of insects in my ears and the thin scent of the tobacco-plants in my nostrils, and sipped at my glass of whisky as I listened to him.

The Furomoto house was in darkness except for the bedside lamp in Setsuko's room. What was she doing? Reading? Crying? Staring motionless at the ceiling? Sleeping perhaps? There are moments when not to know some such trivial thing seems as terrible as not to know the loved one's whereabouts. What a strange woman! Who would have guessed that the death of a girl whom she gave the appearance of despising and disliking—even so violent a death—would prostrate her so utterly? Yet the realisation of her unsuspected vulnerability afforded me a sudden hope: if she could feel Sanae's death so deeply, how might she not feel my coming absence?

'Hello, there! Hi! Mr. Knox! Hi there!' The tenuous threads of my meditation were snapped as the branches of my hedge were snapping. Someone, diminutive and green-faced in the moonlight, had tumbled into the garden. The present locked with the past and I knew, long before he approached, that this would be Mamoru

Taiichi, Big-Fat, Little-Thin, with his brief-case as worn as his shoes, his vast, yearning eyes and the nose that, snout-like, was always rooting for information. I was furious.

'Do you make it your usual practice to enter other people's houses in this fashion? I seem to remember that last time——'

'Beg pardon?' The gold-and-silver necklace glittered in the moonlight as he parted his lips in an amiable grin. 'No understand. Since I last see you, I plactise only German, not Engrish. Now I plactise with you.'

'What do you want? The last time you came those asters were wrecked and now you've wrecked them again.'

'Beg pardon? I ling and ling bell and servant say evely time that you in Kobe. But I think he lie.' He giggled. 'I think Japanese servant big liar. I want to speak to you, speak to you urgent. So I look thlough hedge and there I see Mr. Knox, sitting.' He raised his right knee, and placed his brief-case on it. 'Have you seen newspaper? Your name here. I think I meet murdered girl in this garden. Velly exciting. I meet missionaly man too. You lemember? This gives me new idea. Story of missionaly man who falls in love with stlip-girl. Stlip-girl make baby. What to do? Missionaly man flightened. So he kills stlip-girl. I like this idea. Velly lifely. Velly exciting. Maybe make good film. Maybe win plize Venice or Cannes.'

I stared at him in incredulity. All writers must, inevitably, be parasites on the sufferings of others; but this truth had never been revealed to me so crudely or so callously before.

'I call at mission, call many times. Mission lady with white hair and long nose'—(Mrs. Ambleside?)—'come out. Velly lude to me, says "Go away, you beastly little man". Beastly, beast-like? Bad language for lady. Bad language for missionaly. Newspapermen say she lude to them too. They lite bad things about her, about mission. You seen Mr. Welling yet?'

'No, I have not!' I spoke with intense annoyance.

'Maybe we go together. Maybe he see you. You Engrish, you fliend. We go together. We go now, yes?'

'Certainly not!'

'You busy?'

'Now would you please go?' The disc-like face glimmered up at me in incomprehension. 'Go! Go!' I shouted. 'And go through the front-door, not the hedge! This way!'

'Then you busy man?'

312

'Yes, very busy man. Too busy to see you even for a moment.'
I caught his arm.

'But you sit here alone.'

'That's right. Alone. And please leave me alone!'

'Ah, I understand. You leligious man! Maybe you play. Maybe
you meditate. My German friend, Zen friend, also meditate, much
meditate—sometimes we meditate together.'

'Well, we're not going to meditate together. This way! Come
along!' He stumbled up on to the floor of the sitting-room,
bewildered yet beaming. 'Now!' We were in the hall and I was
propelling him towards the door. 'It's been delightful seeing you.
Delightful. So sorry you couldn't stay. Good night. Good night.'
He was trying to say something, his Adam's apple bobbing up
and down and his mouth opening and shutting. 'Good night.
Thank you for calling. Thank you. Thank you.' Slowly I shut
the door on him.

Back in the garden I suddenly heard him shouting to me from
the road. 'Goodbye, Mr. Knox. Maybe I call tomollow!' He
sounded in the friendliest of spirits. 'Maybe tomollow, maybe
next day. I have much for discuss. You can help me. Goodbye!
Cheelio! Goodbye, Mr. Knox! I see you tomollow!'

TWENTY-TWO

I T was a long bus-ride to the foot of the hills between which
the shrine of Tanukidani was balanced and an even longer
climb up the steps, on either side of which were serried rows
of pillars bearing the names of outstanding benefactors. Sarah's
own name had once appeared, not on a pillar, but inscribed on a
square of wood, nailed up, with many others, to form a second
colonnade outside this main colonnade of stone. But that had been
long ago and it had disappeared.

In the pearly light of dawn she now clambered, crab-wise, from
step to step, an old, bilious-skinned woman, her head drawn,
tortoise-like, between her shoulders and one arthritic hand clutching a handkerchief in which she had bound up her scanty offerings. In the mission she usually wore Western dress, the discards
of Mrs. Ambleside and the other women; but she was now in
kimono and *obi*, both dingy as befitted her age and station in life.
No one else was out so early.

Suddenly she glanced up, halted in terror, and pressed herself
against the stone pillars, one arm shielding her face. A small stray
dog, trailing a length of rope, was tittuping down the steps
towards her, its ears cocked and its tail, from which the hair
appeared to have been pulled out in tufts, wagging vigorously. It
sniffed at her ankles and she gave a little moan. Then it bounced
on downwards, taking no more notice. That was bad, she thought :
a dog; at the beginning of this month; and in this place, and passing on her right. Her whole life was directed by such omens.

There were three separate shrines and at each she offered up the
food she had prepared, burned some incense and prayed. She
begged for his freedom : and by freedom she meant both his freedom from physical restraint and his freedom from the spiritual
consequences of his actions. Finally, at the largest of the shrines,
she shook from a wooden drum a bamboo stick which she handed
to the fat, sleepy priest who was yawning and scratching himself,
cross-legged on a mat; in exchange he gave her a slip of paper. This
she held very close to her small, mole's eyes, puckering the

314

brownish flesh beneath them and moving her wrinkled lips as she tried to read. Twice she shook her head, as though in an involuntary spasm. It was bad; very bad. Nothing but disaster; death; flight.

Behind the shrine there grew a hedge of privet, from the branches of which fluttered innumerable such fortunes, tied there like ribbons. She folded up her own piece of paper, with immense care, smoothing out the creases between her crooked fingers, unfolding and then folding again, until she was at last satisfied with the narrow, symmetrical spill. No less care went to the finding of a suitable branch and the tying of the bow. Then she murmured another prayer.

'Excuse me—what time could it be?' she asked the priest timidly.

He drew the long nails of his right hand down over his shaven poll and then pulled a watch out from the recesses of his robes, dangling it on the end of its silver chain so that splinters of the early morning sunlight shot hither and thither. 'Quarter-to-seven,' he intoned in the unnatural bass voice he used to impress worshippers.

She cupped one hand over an ear. Then 'Oh!' she gave a gasp, as though something had caught momentarily in her throat. 'So late!' And she began to hurry away, bowing and muttering politenesses, her body bent double and her chin on her breast.

The priest watched her as she scrambled down the steps, growing smaller and smaller as the gorge widened on either side, until she was no more than an insect, a beetle or an ant, crawling down a glittering cranny. Then the iridescent heat of the plain seemed to consume her and all at once she vanished.

He did not wish to get up; he did not even wish to look at his watch. Sarah had come in twice. On the first occasion, when she had brought his cup of tea, she had tried to talk to him, but he had turned to the wall, pulling the sheet over his head, and ignored her. On the second occasion she had shuffled and bumped around the room, setting down a tray with his breakfast on it, drawing the curtains and tidying the clothes which he had thrown haphazard around him when he had undressed the previous night. Usually so fanatical in his tidiness, he had, on this occasion, even failed to empty his pockets of money and arrange the coins one on top of each other, the biggest at the bottom, according to his usual ritual. Once again she had said something; but he had shut out the sound, merely grunting and then emitting a long-sustained sigh. Somehow he had even managed to go to sleep again after her departure. Sleep! That was all he wanted to do: to sleep, sleep, sleep, burrowing deeper and deeper into sleep, as though he were some hunted animal going to earth. But there were always people—Ikeda-San, Ambleside, even Sarah—to dig him up again.

He would have to decide about Mary. Probably, by this morning, the newspapers in Australia would carry the story; so that she would learn it, not from him as Ambleside had urged, but distorted and garbled from them. But perhaps, when he had refused to speak to her long-distance, Ambleside had then taken things into his own hands, and spoken to her himself or sent her a telegram. That would be better. When faced with an important decision Welling was one of those people who prefer to be carried along like a stick on a stream: the stream divides, the stick is swirled leftwards or rightwards, according to chance or the relative strength of the currents, with no will of its own. If he were wholly passive, like that stick, he could endure almost anything; it was choice and the action dictated by choice which he always dreaded.

So he remained where he was, in bed; as the sunlight poured more and more brightly into the room and swelled nearer and nearer. He hated the sunlight. The dark meant sleep and no-thinking and even no-being; in the dark 'They'—the police, Ambleside, the newspaper-men, his fears, his grief, his remorse—left him alone. With the coming of day they seized on him again, worrying him, snatching at him, snarling over him, as though they were beasts of prey. And how would it end? He could not stay in bed for ever: unless (the thought only then came to him) he were suddenly to be stricken with some malady—tuberculosis, a stroke, paralysis, madness even. Then he would escape them; then they could not follow, with their questionings and probings and the problems which were like so many teeth fastened in his throat. Oh, let me be ill, let me be ill! he prayed in silent agony. God, let me be ill! Over and over again he repeated the words, clutching the sheet at his waist and turning his head from side to side on the sweat-sodden pillow. In his absorption in that craving, he at last forgot Sanae.

'Mike! I say, Mike!' It was Ambleside, knocking on the door.

'Go away!'

But Ambleside entered; and it was as though he had turned up the soil and the terrified animal was blinking up into sunlight against which its pursuers were silhouetted, its mouth twisted into a snarl and its body rigid.

'It's nearly eleven o'clock, old chap. Aren't you going to get up? What's the matter? Feeling ill?'

'I feel—awful.' He nearly sobbed on the last word.

'Well, of course you do. Stands to reason.' Ambleside lowered himself heavily on the bed and placed a hand on Welling's bony shoulder. The pyjama-jacket was sticky; but Ambleside was not a fastidious man and felt no distaste. 'We've got to keep our wits about us, though. We're in a jam. All of us, not only you. But of course it's worst for you, no denying that.'

Welling merely groaned, tossing from side to side on the bed, with his eyes shut.

Ambleside was becoming rapidly exasperated. He was a man of immense physical and moral courage, as he had demonstrated in China when he had been imprisoned for weeks before his expulsion; and he had assumed that Welling was similarly endowed. To discover that he was not had, at first, merely bewildered him; but that phase had passed. His face hardened into an expression of severity as he gazed down at his colleague; and when he spoke, it was as he sometimes spoke to the servants when they did something amiss, no longer avuncular and jolly, but brutal and steel-like. 'You're not helping yourself, Welling. You're just making things worse and worse. For heaven's sake, man—show some guts! If you hide away like this, of course everyone will begin to think you guilty. Can't you see that? You've got to face up to these accusations. You can't just ignore them—run away from them.'

Run away. . . . He was scattering the sand as he raced, on and on, across the immense beach, and the terrified screams whirled out of him and away down the wind; but it was not the churning, blood-flecked waters he had to escape but the soldier revolving in that ever-widening net of scarlet, his boots clattering in one agonised spasm on another. Run away. . . . *Stop, you fool, stop!* But without his volition, his foot pressed down on the accelerator and the night, cool and obliterating, rushed up and

317

over him, a black wave which submerged and swept out of sight the woman spreadeagled in the road with the dog yapping and rearing on the end of its leash beside her. *Run away. . . . No. I'll tell you anything. Anything you want. No! Stop! No!*

Welling kicked away the sheet, swung down his legs, and jumped off the bed.

The two women had been working together for a long time in silence in the garden. They were in the shade of the hedge and had between them a pail into which they put the weeds. Colethorpe was using a knife, the bone-handle of which had broken; Setsuko a garden fork. It was the first time that Setsuko had condescended to do this job since the English girl had come to stay.

Colethorpe had first gone out, immediately after breakfast, because she could think of no other way in which to pass the long summer day ahead. The afternoon before she had tried to read and she had tried to paint, but both occupations had failed her. More than an hour later Setsuko appeared, to stand, her hands on her hips, beside the English girl, and watch her for seconds on end. Colethorpe expected the usual comments: 'Really, Aileen, there's absolutely no need to do that, you know. We have the weeding-woman and have to pay her, by agreement, whether there's weeding to do or not. Besides, you'll ruin your hands.' Sometimes Setsuko would also imply that someone unskilled in gardening was likely to do more harm than good, by pulling up valuable plants with the weeds. On this occasion, however, she merely sighed and then got down on her haunches and set to work. She did not address Colethorpe and did not even glance at her. Each behaved as people behave when they have to co-operate in an unavoidable task after they have quarrelled.

Eventually Knox came out on to his verandah, followed by Endo-San who was carrying a deck-chair for him. He looked across the garden, but neither of the women, though aware of his presence, acknowledged that he was there. He hesitated, unsure whether to call out or not—whether, perhaps, to go across; and then, guessing that they were avoiding him on purpose, lowered himself with a sigh into the chair and started to read. The news of the case was no longer at the bottom of the front-page of the paper but at the top; and he was displeased to discover that in the *Mainichi Daily News* there were not merely photographs of Welling and Sanae but also one of himself. For a while he puzzled where it had come from; and then recollected the three photographs he had had to supply to the University when he had first assumed his post. At the time he had wondered why they should be wanted: now (he supposed) he had the answer.

Suddenly Setsuko paused at her work. 'Things look bad for Welling,' she said. She used her fingers to crumble away the mud that was sticking between the prongs of her fork, still not looking up at Colethorpe.

'Yes. Worse and worse.' The English girl no longer wished to think about the case, let alone to talk about it. When she did, she felt a terrible, growing nausea, as though she had swallowed some irritant poison. 'But I—I still can't believe—I don't know— somehow—it seems to me impossible. In spite of all the evidence. The car. The envelope from the bank. The money he drew out. The photograph.'

'And the fact that she was pregnant,' Setsuko added in a tone so matter-of-fact that it chilled.

'Yes, that too.'

'Well, if he didn't do it, who did?'

'I don't know. It's all so—so odd. I thought that I knew everything about her. And now I realise that I knew nothing, nothing of any importance, nothing at all. It was this knowledge, even more than Sanae's death, which caused her the acutest anguish and made her feel that she wished to flee from Japan. She had been cheated, betrayed; the confidences had been lies, the friendship a fraud. '*Anything* could have happened really.'

'Anything? The police haven't succeeded in turning up anything else.'

'Welling said that when he met her at the station she told him that someone was following her.'

'Oh, Welling.' Setsuko flung some weeds into the pail. 'If he wanted to divert suspicion from himself he should have thought of something more effective.'

'You don't believe him then?'

'Do you?'

Colethorpe hesitated. 'Yes,' she said at last.

'Do you? Why?'

319

'I don't know. Just a feeling. A feeling that he's—he's all right. Innocent.'

'I don't imagine that the police have that feeling.'

'Then you really think that he—he's in danger?'

'Of course.'

'But that's terrible!'

'What happened to Sanae was terrible.'

'But for an innocent man to be suspected of having committed a murder——'

'Innocent?'

'Don't you believe him innocent?'

Suddenly Setsuko got off the ground. 'Really, how should I know?' she asked, dusting off her hands against each other. She still spoke in the same off-hand voice, making Colethorpe think: you're heartless, utterly heartless. But she was trembling oddly and the skin beneath her eyes and around her nose and mouth had a glistening, stretched appearance.

'He ought to leave the country,' Colethorpe suddenly said. 'Before it's too late. That's his only chance.'

'And do you think that they'd let him leave?'

'He's not under arrest, is he?'

'No. But he would be if he attempted anything like that. It would be an admission of guilt.'

'I don't see that.'

'Don't you?' Setsuko looked down at the back of the English girl's head, noticing, with distaste, the scurf which was thick at the roots of her blonde hair. Again her fingers moved between the prongs of the fork; she seemed to be undecided about something until, suddenly, she became aware that Knox was watching her. Then she shook off her hesitation. 'Well, I'm going in. I've things to do. This is the end of my sick-leave. Tomorrow I work.'

Colethorpe first watched her walk away and then called after her. 'Setsuko!'

'Yes?' The monosyllable was not encouraging.

'Isn't there anything that can be done about these newspapers? I mean—isn't there any way—anybody——? They write such filth. About Sanae, about Welling.'

'My dear Aileen, a free Press is one of the benefits which the victors conferred on this country after the war.'

'Yes, I know. But it—it nauseates me—to read such things.'

'Only because they're things about ourselves. For a change.

320

Otherwise they wouldn't nauseate us. We should lap them up. Wouldn't we?'

At that Setsuko strode off towards the house.

'Mr. Welling, I must really ask you to be more precise. At one moment you say that these—er—joy-rides ceased and the next moment you say that, on the contrary, they continued——'

'But I can't remember. I tell you, I can't remember.'

'Can't remember?'

'I—my mind is all confused. I—I've not been sleeping well.' (Sleep, sleep; if only he could sleep, through all this, right through to the end, for ever if necessary.) 'I—I can't think.'

'Perhaps you would like another cup of coffee?'

'No. No, thank you.'

'Or a cigarette?'

Welling shook his head.

'. . . Now, if you will be patient—just a little patient—I should like to go back over—over those last hours.' Welling groaned and buried his face in his arms. Ikeda-San stared down at him, on his face a curious, absorbed expression which was totally different from the expression of disgust on the face of the sergeant and the constable. 'Listen to me, Mr. Welling. Please listen to me. It is essential that you should remember exactly what——'

'Oh, leave me alone, leave me alone! ' He writhed in his chair and then suddenly burst into dry, choking sobs which rattled out of him, endlessly, on and on and on.

Ikeda-San fiddled with his gold identity bracelet and then raised his right hand to touch the back of his head. He was perched on one corner of the plain wooden table over which Welling was bowed. Slowly he exhaled his breath as though in relief. He leant forward:

'Mr. Welling. . . . Please. . . .' His voice was tender, almost maternal.

'Please—leave me—can't—can't go on——' The broken-off phrases were punctuated by the excruciating sobs.

'I should very much like to leave you. But I am afraid that we must go on. We must get this finished.'

Welling suddenly raised his dishevelled head and let out a strange kind of animal howl. All three men gazed at him in amazement.

321

'Mr. Welling—what's the matter? What's the matter with you?' Ikeda-San gave a nervous laugh. 'One might imagine that we had been trying to torture you, Mr. Welling! Please!'

'What does she want to see you about?' Lisa asked.

'How should I know?' Furomoto wished that he did know: Setsuko's call had worried him.

Lisa carefully drew in the arc of a left eyebrow. 'You never meet as a rule. She avoids you, you always say.' Furomoto continued to turn over the pages of the *Vogue* he had picked up off her bedside table, making no response. 'Isn't that so?'

'She took the other side.'

'Yes, but the old woman is prepared to be friendly with you now.'

'Perhaps Setsuko doesn't forget and forgive so easily.'

Getting up from the tapestried stool, Lisa walked slowly towards the built-in cupboards which lined a whole wall. Turning the key, she said: 'She wants something. You can be sure of that.'

'Wants something?'

'Yes. Wants something from the great Furomoto. Is that so unusual?'

'No.'

'Well, I can't wait for you. I'll go on to the club and you can follow when you've finished with her. I've never liked her anyhow. Those mannish women. . . !' She gave a theatrical shudder and wrinkled her nose.

'Mannish? Setsuko?' Suddenly he thought with a terrible mingling of passion, desolation and disgust of the fifteen-year-old body held close to his own. He gave a brief laugh. 'Mannish!'

'Why are you laughing?'

'Nothing.'

'I bet you won't be laughing by the time your interview with her is finished.'

In that she was right. When he had left the telephone, Furomoto threw himself across Lisa's bed and there, one hand dangling down to stroke the luxuriant pile of the carpet, he lay for several minutes. It was odd: Setsuko and Welling. . . . What was there between them? Still he gazed up at the ceiling, his lips slightly parted. Could they be lovers? She had been so insistent, almost hysterical; and to none of his questions had she given an answer. . . .

Well, he would do what he could. He had always done what he could for her. With a groan, he dragged himself off the bed and began to straighten first the bedspread and then his own rumpled clothes.

> ' Now the day is over,
> Night is drawing nigh,
> Shadows of the evening
> Steal across the sky.'

Standing at the back of the hideous little concrete church, Welling half-listened to the faint, straggly voices, most of them female. Miss Pinter's contralto hooted, owl-like, now below, now above them. It was strange that she had never realised that she could not carry a tune; and even stranger that the other women, so adept at hinting at each other's defects, had never made her realise it. Ambleside was taking the evening prayers and the congregation consisted almost entirely of members of the mission staff, but here and there were a few Japanese ' regulars', scrutinized at the gate before they were admitted for fear that they might be either journalists or sensation-hunters. Welling made out the diminutive eater of prayers, her shoulders only just appearing above the pew behind her, with her lank daughter, Chiyoko, on one side of her and on the other a heavily-built young man with a broad, flat nose and horn-rimmed glasses who was sharing her hymnal. She had once spoken about a son; but surely he had been killed in the war? From time to time, as she sang, she tugged at the brim of her straw-hat as though in a high wind, or broke off to lower her head to whisper to the girl and the man alternately. Not far from them Frank was standing; underneath one of the stained-glass windows, so that the late evening sunlight, filtering through a purple lozenge on to the side of his face, made it appear as if he had some terrible birthmark. He never sang, since he knew, unlike Miss Pinter, that he could not do so; but he made a show of moving his lips over the words.

' Now the day is over . . .' Soon it would be finished : the day through which he had had to drag himself, like some wounded animal, to the refuge of sleep. With what was almost a voluptuous longing he thought of his room, the drawn curtains, the light extinguished, and then of the bed enfolding him as he sank deeper and deeper into it and so into unconsciousness. But first—one of the shattered bones of the wounded animal trilled with agony—he must do something about Mary: draft an answer to her cable; or telephone; or at least write an air-letter. Ambleside had spoken to her once, but had refused to do so again; astonished and disgusted that Welling should ask it of him. 'No, old chap, I really think that you've got to speak to her yourself. She'll think it very odd—it'll upset her no end—if you give the impression of not wishing to have any contact with her.' But he did not wish to have any contact with her: not with her, not with anyone! No more with her than with anyone else could he face the recriminations and accusations and probings and explanations and excuses and pity and contempt. Why couldn't they all leave him alone?

Ambleside was now giving the blessing; and the ragged voices muttered 'Amen'. Welling turned hurriedly to escape before anyone saw him. But the prayer-eater twisted her head round at the same moment and her face contorted itself into an immediate recognition. As he fled he knew that she was pattering up the aisle in pursuit, her mottled dark-blue skirt swaying from side to side and the brim of her hat bouncing.

'Welling-San! Welling-San! Please!' She even put one of her dusty little paws on to his arm. 'I wish to speak with you. Welling-San! A moment!'

'Oh, Okada-San. . . . Good evening. . . .' He half-turned, his eyes darting hither and thither. 'You must forgive me. I'm in a hurry.'

'But Welling-San! I wish to say something. I have lead in the papers about you. I wish to say that I play for you—play for you all the time. And my daughter play. . . . Chiyoko! Come here!' The paw made a scrabbling motion in the air towards the girl, as she summoned her in Japanese. 'Here is Mr. Welling.'

The girl approached, followed by the youth. 'My daughter, Mr. Welling.' Although they had often met, her mother now appeared to be introducing her afresh. 'Chiyoko, Mr. Welling.' Welling gazed at her dumbly. 'And this is my nephew, Mr. Welling. Yoshioka-San, Mr. Welling. Velly clever boy, Mr. Welling. Doshisha University graduate.'

'Good evening, Mr. Welling.' The boy held out a plump, firm hand. 'I wanted to see you. I've been reading about this trouble of yours and I thought that maybe I'd like to have a word with you about it.' People, emerging in twos and threes from the chapel, were loitering to stare at the little group outside the door and even to whisper to each other.

'A word with me?' Welling repeated the words in a strangely dull voice.

'That's right, Mr. Welling. It might kind of help you to put your case to me. I'd be very sympathetic. My aunt here is a real friend of yours'—the prayer-eater grinned and nodded her head first at Welling and then at her nephew, tipping up her wrinkled little face in a beatific enthusiasm—'and she thought that maybe I could help you to get the—the record straight. The papers have written some terrible things about you, Mr. Welling.'

Welling was staring at him with a kind of frozen panic, his mouth half open and his eyes wide. The boy, so self-confident a moment ago, now began to falter as he pulled out his wallet and fumbled to extract his card. 'This is my card, Mr. Welling. My name's Yoshioka—in case you didn't get it. Y-O-S-H-I-O-K-A.' He spelled out the name, because it was his invariable habit to do so with foreigners. 'I work for the Asahi Press.'

'Go away.' Welling said the words in the hoarse ghost of a voice. 'Leave me alone.'

The prayer-eater ceased to gaze adoringly from one of the men to the other; she backed a little, tugging again at the brim of her straw-hat. The youth edged nearer:

'But look, Mr. Welling. . . . You're being foolish, Mr. Welling. I can help you.'

'Go away!' He repeated it louder: distorting the vowels as he did when he deliberately parodied his Australian accent to people like Knox. 'You've no business here. I've nothing to say to you.'

'But I'm a friend, Mr. Welling. I don't want to hurt you. I'm on your side. I want to see that you get a fair hearing. Don't you understand?' Even as he said these words, he was bending sideways to fish out of his aunt's enormous bag the camera he had placed there. 'Anyway, just one photograph, Mr. Welling. Outside the chapel. That's right. Hey, Mr. Welling!'

He raised the camera and at the same moment Welling struck out at it, sending it spinning in an arc to strike the gravel path and bump along it. The prayer-eater gave a little cry.

Welling was already racing towards his quarters.

TWENTY-THREE

'GOOD! So you are at home, Mr. Knox. I had heard that you were always out these days.' It was Endo-San's afternoon off and I had myself gone to the door, expecting the boy from the cleaners; but I was faced by Ikeda-San and Welling.

'The newspaper people refuse to leave me alone. I can't think what they expect to learn from me.'

'Your sufferings can't be as bad as Mr. Welling's. He no longer leaves the mission buildings, if he can help it. Do you, Mr. Welling? That's why I brought him along. He was having a word with me down at the station and then we smuggled him out through the kitchen. Those journalists must still be waiting!'

I had brought out two pairs of slippers; but Ikeda-San waved his pair aside. 'No, no. I'm not staying, thank you, Mr. Knox. I came merely to bring Mr. Welling to you. If he has any difficulty in getting away, just give us a call. You have my number?'

'No, I'm afraid not.'

'Then here is my card. Have you ever collected so many cards as in Japan—or given away so many?' He seemed to be in excellent spirits. 'There you are, Mr. Knox! Japanese one side, English the other.'

Welling preceded me into the sitting-room with a strange, shambling stiffness as though he had either taken some unaccustomed exercise or had been severely beaten. He did not sit down, but stood in the centre of the room, his head all but touching the low ceiling and his large, bony, freckled hands clasped before him. Shifting his weight from one leg to another and then back again, he gazed dreamily about the small, shabby room.

'I wanted to get in touch with you,' I said. 'In case I could be of help. I sent a message by Frank. I hope he gave it to you.'

'Yes. Thank you.'

'Do sit down.'

'Thank you.' But he still remained standing. Slowly he walked over to a Japanese doll in a glass case, which Mrs. Furomoto had given me, and stared down at it. 'Pretty,' he said, 'very pretty.'

'Yes. Too pretty. I used to like it; but now I've come to hate it. It's so—so intolerably cute.'

'Nice,' he said, lumbering away, as though I had said nothing at all. I began to feel uneasy.

'That chair's the most comfortable. Unless you prefer the *tatami*.'

He walked round the chair two or three times, and then, to my relief, lowered himself into it. 'Thanks,' he said. 'Thanks.' He raised the bony hands and drew them down his face, yawning as he did so.

'You must be going through a pretty tough time.'

'Yes. Pretty tough.' Again he yawned. 'If only I could get some more sleep.'

'Would some pills help? I've suffered from insomnia for almost all my life and I have a large collection—Nembutal, Soneryl, Quadronox, anything you care to name!'

'Thanks! It's not a question of getting *off* to sleep, actually. It's a question of time.'

'Time?'

'There don't seem to be enough hours in every twenty-four.' He shifted in the chair, making the wicker squeak. 'Always something to do . . . bothered . . . badgered.' He mumbled the last two words fretfully and then lapsed into morose silence, his hand to his chin and his gaze fixed on his shoes.

'What about a drink? I can give you a choice of Japanese gin or Japanese whisky.'

'Just a glass of water.'

When I had brought it to him, Welling sipped at the frosted tumbler with the appearance of savouring the water as though it were a vintage wine. Then he lowered it on to the floor beside him. 'I wanted to have a word with you. Wanted your advice,' he said in a peculiar, stony voice, never once raising his gaze from his shoes.

'Certainly. If my advice is going to be of any help to you.'

'You're—you're not one of our crowd. So you're outside it—if you get me—and can view things'—the bony hands seemed to reach out into the air for the word—'dispassionately. Dispassionately. And you've got a head on your shoulders. No use asking some of the people here: they've got no *nous*, no *nous* at all.' I could not remember having heard that word since my schooldays; spoken in his Australian accent, it sounded even more ugly than usual. 'So—' at last he looked up at me with a vague, twitching smile—'I decided to come to see you. Ikeda-San agreed that it was a good idea.'

'Ikeda-San?'

'The police-officer who came here with me just now.'

'Yes, I know who Ikeda-San is. But why should Ikeda-San——?'

'He's a good chap. But he's got to do his duty, like the rest of us. He's a Christian, you know.'

I nodded.

'That was a lucky break for me. His being a Christian, I mean.'

I wondered about that; but said nothing. 'Maybe I've not been playing this right,' Welling went on. He balanced one shoe on top of the other, and surveyed the result. 'Maybe. What do you think?'

'Well, if you wish me to be frank, I can't help thinking that you've been playing it all wrong.'

He gave a sigh that was almost a groan. 'They all say that.'

'You're an innocent man.' Without looking up, he gave the embarrassed yet self-congratulatory smile of a schoolboy praised before his fellows. 'But you're not acting like one. Or, at least, not like the public's idea of one.'

'You mean——?'

'You give the impression of running away. And that's the last impression you ought to give. You have nothing to hide; you have nothing of which to be ashamed: that should be your attitude. If the Press wish to see you, well, go out and see them. If the police want you for questioning, go out and be questioned. You want the murderer to be caught as much as anyone else. Don't you?'

'Yes.' It was hesitant; but then, on a confident note, he repeated. 'Yes, yes, that's how I ought to look at it.'

'What you're going through is a kind of martyrdom.'

'Martyrdom?' I could see that the word both surprised him and pleased him.

'All the anti-foreigner and anti-Christian feeling which no one has dared to express in this country for the last fifteen years has at last found an outlet. They're not getting only at you in the newspapers. They're getting at all missionaries, and even at all foreigners. You realise that, don't you?'

'Yes. Yes, of course.' But he was considering the idea as though for the first time.

'Your position is not so much different in kind from the position of those early Christians who were persecuted, tortured and executed.' Once spoken, I realised that this comparison might be tactless; I therefore quickly added: 'Though, fortunately, in this day and age, they stop at persecution. Still, you should ask yourself how those early Christians behaved and try to behave like them. If you can.'

'If I can,' he repeated slowly.

There was something abnormal about his responses: a dreamy kind of intermittency, as though his mind were slowly snapping itself free from the effects of a drug. I was beginning to get alarmed.

'Perhaps I oughtn't to give you that advice. Perhaps I have no right to give it to you. After all I'm not a Christian. And I don't approve of the missions in Japan. If I had my way, you'd all be expelled from this country as quickly as possible! Which is exactly what the Press and some of the politicians are agitating for now—thanks to this case.'

I became aware that his blue eyes were fixed on my face in a wounded astonishment. 'You're—you mean—you don't believe in Christianity?'

I shook my head. 'I'm sorry. I'd like to believe in it,' I added.

He continued to scrutinise me, his clasped hands raised before his face, with the forefingers pressing on either side of his long, bony nose and his tawny eyebrows drawn together as though in physical pain.

'A few nights ago I was reading an account by Fabre about an experiment with caterpillars. The caterpillars were placed in a ring about an earthenware pot and they immediately started walking. Round and round, round and round, ceaselessly, each following the one in front. Not one thought of breaking the chain and going off, either alone or leading his fellows, in search of the food that had been placed near the pot. And so, gradually, from exhaustion and hunger, they one by one died. . . . That, I am sorry to have to say—is how I regard Christianity.'

I did not know whether he had taken in what I had said; the eyes continued to hold my gaze and the fingers to massage the faintly-mottled sides of his nose.

'Maybe I ought to give that sermon after all,' he suddenly said.

I was bewildered by the seeming lack of connection with anything that had gone before. 'What sermon?' I asked.

Again the chair squeaked, as he shifted deeper and deeper into it. 'Tomorrow I was to preach the sermon at Evensong. But I asked—Ambleside and I agreed that he should take my place. We —we changed the announcement; the announcement on the board outside our gate. But now—now I don't know. . . . Seeing what you've advised me. I just don't know.'

In silence I watched him, aware that he was straining to reach some decision, yet reluctant to influence him in one direction or the other.

He was gnawing on his thin lower lip; again he raised the one shoe on the toe of the other. 'Those early Christians—those ones you were talking about—nothing ever stopped those chaps. . . . Witnesses for Christ. . . . They preached his word even when they were being beaten or—or stoned—or cut in pieces.' Suddenly he jumped to his feet and began walking up and down, his head all but brushing the ceiling and the floor vibrating disagreeably beneath his heavy tread. 'Let them all come. Let anyone come to the service—anyone who wishes. Maybe that's the way. And then I get up and preach. "Here I am, I've nothing to hide, what do you want? Yes. You can do what you like to me. I'm innocent. I must still bear witness, still . . ."' He halted by the window, his bony hands clasped; he stared out into the garden. 'You can see her window from here. I could see it from the road.' He turned, his face contorted. 'Sometimes I drove past. Two, three times. But Knox—there was nothing wrong—nothing bad in it! I swear! Knox, I swear!'

In my life, first at private school and then at public school, I have been obliged to listen to many sermons, all of which I have forgotten like the geometrical theorems and scientific formulae which were equally tedious to me. Many of them must have been good sermons, since they were preached by outstanding churchmen of the day. Welling's was not a good sermon; in fact, it was pitiably bad, both in content and delivery. Yet I know that I shall remember it until the day of my death.

When he left me, I could not be sure whether his decision to preach might not be a temporary whim; and I found myself half-hoping that it was, since I was, in a sense, responsible for it. It was Colethorpe who first told me of the notice on the board outside the mission gate, with the comment: 'So he's got some guts after all! After what Frank had been telling me, I was beginning to doubt it.'

'Yes. It'll take some courage to preach at this moment.'

'And Frank says that he wants everyone admitted—everyone, anyone at all. These last days they've only been letting in their regulars. And even so a man from the Asahi managed to slip in—brought by his aunt or cousin or someone.'

'Yes, I saw that in the paper. Stupid of Welling to lose his temper and damage the man's camera. That kind of thing won't help him any more than skulking in his room.'

Frank had invited Colethorpe and me to tea before the service; he had also invited Setsuko, but she had refused. 'Oh no, Frank's really too boring,' she had explained when we had attempted to make her change her mind. 'I'm sorry, Aileen, but you know how I feel about him.'

'Are you coming to the service later?'

'To the service!' My question seemed to astonish her. 'Good heavens, no! Why should I come to the service? . . . Oh, you mean because Welling is preaching. No, I haven't that kind of morbid curiosity.'

But many other people had. As we sat round the dining-room table—Frank, Colethorpe and myself at one end; Miss Rosenthal, Miss Pinter and Norah at the other; Welling alone by the window, scribbling what I presumed to be his sermon or notes for his sermon on the backs of innumerable used envelopes held together with a clip—we could hear the feet on the gravel outside: clattering if geta were worn; crunching, if shoes. It was rare for a voice to make itself audible; and this lack of speech seemed to add to the ominousness of all those unseen, unknown crowds pushing their way into the chapel to view the foreign devil-priest who was also a murderer. Surely they could not all get in, I thought: it was time for the police to shut the gates on the flood before it burst through the hideous little chapel and carried it off down the hill and into the river.

'If only we could always get such a congregation,' said Frank; and as he spoke, Mrs. Ambleside entered.

'What was that, Frank?'

'I said, if only we could always get such a congregation.'

'I think I'd prefer the smaller congregation,' I put in. 'If a larger one can only be achieved on an occasion like this.'

331

Mrs. Ambleside was pouring herself out a cup of tea. 'Oh, I don't know, Mr. Knox,' she said vaguely. 'If people begin by doing the right thing for the wrong reason, they sometimes end up by doing it for the right reason.' It was a remark which I had heard her make on more than one previous occasion. 'Don't you think?'

I fancied that she was being over-optimistic, but I did not say so. She raised her cup and sipped, still standing beside us, and then appeared to notice Welling for the first time. 'Oh, Mr. Welling, what are you up to? At work on your sermon? You've left it very late, haven't you?' She spoke as if this were an entirely ordinary occasion and the sermon a routine one. 'How can you concentrate in here?'

I myself had wondered this; and had decided that, having first sought the refuge of solitude, Welling had now come to dread it.

'Well, it's naughty of me to disturb you,' she smiled in his direction, as he still fixed on her a gaze at once startled and distraught, and then turned away. 'Rose, dear——' Miss Pinter swivelled in her chair, still masticating on the cake from which she had just taken a large bite—'that fracture-case insists on attending the service; I'm not too happy about moving her round. But if we put her in the chair. . . . What do you think? She's so tremendously keen.'

More morbid curiosity, I had no doubt; but Mrs. Ambleside seemed determined to believe that it was religious enthusiasm.

Miss Pinter gulped and then licked at the crumbs on either side of her mouth. 'If you think that there's no risk,' she said in her mournful contralto. I guessed that she rarely opposed Mrs. Ambleside even if, as on this occasion, she disagreed with her.

Frank rose, yawned, and stretched himself as though he were lifting invisible dumb-bells. 'I'd better go along and see what's happening. I told Saito-San to reserve two pews for us. But we'll be lucky if he succeeds.' Whistling 'Red Sails in the Sunset' just off key, while he jingled the coins in the pockets of his khaki trousers, he paused at Welling's chair. 'How's it going?' he asked.

Welling jerked up his head. 'Oh—er—all right, thank you.' Then he gazed down again, frowning as he continued to write with his pencil-stub on the back of yet another envelope.

At the moment that Frank swung out of the room, Mrs.

Crawley appeared and the two of them all but collided. 'Hello, Frank,' she greeted him, as he held open the door for her. 'Hello, everybody. I just dropped by before service to make my salaams and see how you all were doing. . . . Good afternoon, Mike.' She went over to Welling. 'How are things? Any news from Mary?' Like Mrs. Ambleside, she was behaving to him as she might have behaved on any other Sunday; but in her case there was an unnaturalness about the whole performance, at once over-bright and tense, which was far more embarrassing than any embarrassment she might be striving to avoid.

Welling made some mumbled answer, too low for me to catch, and she at once continued in the same artificial voice: 'Oh, good, that is good. Oh, I am glad.'

At that point, no doubt designedly, Mrs. Ambleside intervened to rescue Welling. 'Betty, dear,' she called out. 'Come and have a cup of tea before it stands any longer. I know you love your tea stewed, but this will be too strong even for you if you don't hurry. . . . Is it still three lumps, dear?'

'Three lumps!' Mrs. Crawley gave a loud, clear laugh, the girlish naturalness of which contrasted sharply with her previous artificiality. 'It's never been three! You know that, Ethel.'

Welling was getting to his feet. We all watched him surreptitiously as he first dropped his pencil and then dropped his sheaf of envelopes. Having retrieved them both, he went out without a word to any of us.

Mrs. Crawley glanced at the large man's watch which she wore on a washable linen strap around her left wrist. 'Ten minutes,' she said.

The other three women had begun to approach the end of the table where we were sitting; first Miss Rosenthal, carrying her knitting in one hand and in the other a mauve plastic bag containing her wool, so that the thread joining the two dangled to her knees; then Norah, with a book with gilt edges, presumably a Bible or prayer-book; and then Miss Pinter, panting and groaning a little as she swayed her bulk down the airless room.

'I do hope that there's not going to be any kind of demonstration,' sighed Miss Rosenthal, seating herself next to Mrs. Crawley and at once resuming her work.

'Demonstration? What do you mean?' Mrs. Ambleside asked with an astonishment which I could have sworn was genuine. 'What demonstration?'

Miss Rosenthal faltered. 'Well—I was thinking—perhaps some undesirable people—hearing that Mr. Welling——'

Mrs. Ambleside continued to point her long, fleshy nose at her, her eyes wide. Then she looked about at the rest of us: 'Do you really imagine—do you imagine there's any likelihood of—of trouble?'

'No, I'm sure not,' Mrs. Crawley said soothingly, as one might reassure a nervous patient before an operation. 'Why should anyone wish to come here to make trouble? . . . Might I just have a wee drop more?' She held out her cup to Mrs. Ambleside: an obvious diversion: 'There's nothing like tea for quenching thirst in weather like this. . . . Oh, thank you, thank you! Just half a cup.' Her hand went out: one, two, three—the lumps fell swiftly into the thick liquid. 'Miss Colethorpe, I do so want to see some of your paintings. Frank is always raving about them. They're—they're very modern in style, aren't they?'

'Well, yes, I suppose they are.'

'I sketch a little myself. When I have the time—which is not often.'

Miss Pinter raised herself from her chair, the palm of one fleshy hand pressing down on the table. She touched the sides of her nose and then her small, wobbling chin with a handkerchief which diffused a faint odour of lavender-water. 'I suppose we ought to be going along.'

We all glanced at our watches; and then with the relief of a platoon of soldiers waiting for the exact hour to advance we rose, with one accord, to our feet.

Apart from the two pews reserved for us, each guarded by a couple of policemen, there was not a seat vacant in the place; people were even crowded at the back and down the aisle from which other policemen were trying to eject them. At once, as we entered, I became conscious of being scrutinised from all sides. Is that him? Is that him? Some of them were even asking the question aloud. One woman, ancient and with her face marked with small-pox, pointed a finger at me as she turned to the child at her waist; but the knowing boy first gazed at me, and then lolled his strange, over-long, over-narrow head from side to side. No, I was not him. I could feel the tension like something at once clammy and corrosive on my skin; it even seemed to enter into my lungs, causing a strange constriction as I breathed. This, I thought, was the moment when the jury file into the court before announcing their verdict at a murder trial; or when the crowds wait, hushed and suspenseful, as one by one the crippled and dying are carried up to a shrine to be healed. 'A hymnal, Mr. Knox?' Mrs. Ambleside extended the battered, leather-covered book to me, leaning across Colethorpe and Miss Rosenthal. 'A. and M.,' she added with an arch smile.

'Thank you.'

The heat was appalling; I watched Colethorpe's hands beside me, palms upwards in her lap, with the sweat glistening in every crack and cranny.

Suddenly there was a murmur throughout the whole chapel; and Ambleside, Welling and the eight Japanese members of the choir, five women and three men, began to proceed down the aisle. Heads were turned; flash-bulbs exploded; a woman in front of me jumped on her seat, tweaking her kimono close around her knees with one hand while with the other she clutched the back of the pew; two of the policemen were tussling with a youth in an open-necked shirt as they attempted to clear the way. Ambleside seemed totally composed and unconcerned: on his face an expression of benign abstraction as he walked, eyes fixed ahead, up towards the altar. It was obvious that the members of the choir were terrified, darting glances from side to side under lowered lids, as the organ, hideously played, seemed to squeal and groan out their agony. Finally, I made myself look at Welling. I had never thought of him as a handsome man—the eyes had always seemed to me to be set too close together; the mouth was too much like a slit gashed with a razor across the narrow, bony face—but now his white features above the white surplice struck me (no doubt it was only a subjective impression) as not merely handsome but even beautiful. He held his head erect and his eyes glittered with an almost maniacal exaltation as he kept them fixed on the altar. When he had visited me, I had been shocked by his haggardness; but the face, though greenish in its pallor and even thinner than then, now radiated a kind of magnetic vigour. Every bone seemed to be distinct; and every bone seemed to be perfect in its formation—the curve of the cheek-bone; the forehead, with a hollow gouged-out above each temple; and the long, straight nose, chiselled with so much precision to balance the smooth round of the chin. His shoulders had never appeared broader; his height so great; his hands so large.

(All this, as I say, was no doubt only a subjective impression;

335

created by the tensions of that moment and in no way different from the subjective impression of the crowd which gasps of royalty: 'Oh, isn't she lovely! ')

The service began: at first to an accompaniment of shuffling, whispering, clicking and creaking which rendered even Ambleside's booming voice inaudible. Then silence expanded, like oil in ever-widening areas on water, from the place where we were seated, first to those around us, and then, ring on ring, outwards to the furthest confines of the chapel. Perhaps it was some residual respect for worship, however alien; perhaps it was the effect of Welling's motionless dignity or of Ambleside's enunciation, so like that of an actor of the old school playing a bishop or cardinal. Even the choir, growing calmer, ceased to make shrill rushes at the hymns and psalms. '. . . The darkness deepens; Lord, with me abide.' Miss Pinter sounded like one of the ancient records of Clara Butt, with the same faulty intonation and the same needle-hiss. Suddenly Mrs. Ambleside had a prolonged attack of sneezes: four, five, six. I heard her whisper to Colethorpe: 'There must be a cat somewhere. Cats always make me sneeze.'

'Perhaps someone is wearing one.' This silly exchange gave me an all but uncontrollable desire to giggle.

At last we reached the sermon; and once again, as Welling climbed slowly and stiffly up into the pulpit, the congregation shuffled, murmured and even stood up to crane at him. He waited; staring, not at them, but at something above their heads—perhaps at the ray of multi-coloured evening sunlight which slanted across the chapel from the hideous stained-glass window down on to a group of diminutive policemen who stood huddled together on one side. A flash-bulb exploded; then another and another. Until, to my astonishment, I heard people start to hush at each other; much as an audience does at a concert when prolonged applause prevents the singer from beginning an encore. Another bulb popped, somewhere close behind me, so that I had the impression for several seconds afterwards that some orange liquid had been splashed across my retina. Then there was silence.

Welling raised a bony fist to his mouth and coughed into it. Extracting a handkerchief from under his surplice, he then blew his nose. Again he coughed. Each of these actions seemed to carry the same suspense as the passes made by a conjurer and everyone watched them with an absorption which did not relax until the sermon was over. Yet, of that crowd, how many would have under-

stood what he was saying? Very few, apart from the journalists.
His voice quavered on the first words of his text and then
gathered strength:

> And as Jesus passed forth from thence, he saw a man, named
> Matthew, sitting at the receipt of custom: and he saith unto
> him, Follow me. And he arose, and followed him.
> And it came to pass, as Jesus sat at meat in the house, behold,
> many publicans and sinners came and sat down with him and
> his disciples.
> And when the Pharisees saw it, they said unto his disciples,
> Why eateth your Master with publicans and sinners?

Like many preachers, he was content to establish no more than
a verbal connection between text and sermon: in this case using
the word 'custom' as his starting-point. Much of what he said,
in a language that was a peculiar mixture of the stilted and the
colloquial, was too incoherent for its drift to be intelligible even
to me; the Japanese certainly could not have followed it. Yet
through the opaque web of jargon and slang there glowed, like a
lamp behind a frosted window, an agonised sincerity which I
found far more moving and impressive even than his breakdown
in my house. At first he read from the backs of the envelopes,
gripping the pulpit-rail, with his eyes lowered; but then, suddenly,
he jerked his head up, stared once more at that slanting, multi-
coloured ray of sunlight, and spoke without even a glance at what
he had prepared.
His theme was, predictably, unoriginal: the custom house
through which every soul must eventually pass to be asked 'Have
you anything to declare?'
'. . . Each of us here will be asked that question as we arrive
with our spiritual bits and pieces; our battered suitcases and
hold-alls and trunks. Some will have luggage marked "Not Wanted
on the Voyage" and woe to those, for they will have hidden their
talents in a napkin and their luggage shall be taken away from
them, even that they have. Others will try to get by without
declaring what they have accumulated on their earthly journey:
the sins and backslidings—dishonesties, cruelties, selfishness'—his
tongue flickered round his mouth, he swallowed—'lusts of the
flesh. But the customs-officer will know. He will not need to open
the bags and search about inside them. Those people will not get

337

by, however smooth their lyings and pretences. The customs-officer will say, "And what of this—and this—and this?" and they will be astonished that he has seen right through them, right into their luggage, yea, right into their heart of hearts. Then they will fall down and beg forgiveness and say, "Lord, Lord we have sinned. It is even as Thou sayest." Then will come others'—the eyes glittered with an extraordinary exaltation, as he leant forward, chin thrust out and hands gripping the rail—'into whose bags the children of the devil have secretly conveyed contraband goods of which they know nothing. But the customs-officer will know to whom each smuggled article belongs. He will say, "This is not yours; nor this." And he will grow mad at the others. "But these are yours," he will cry out. "And you wished to incriminate my innocent servant and to conceal your own wrong-doings, your own acts of darkness. Now I shall punish you twice over: once for the wrong-doings and once for your sins against this innocent. Yea! I shall punish thee sorely." And he will chuck them out of the custom house into the outer darkness. Then he will open the bags of the innocent man and remove all that was placed there, leaving only a few smuggled objects of no great importance. And he will say "Proceed, go on in, my friend . . ."'

I listened: at once embarrassed, appalled and moved. He was doing it so badly; and yet, at the same time, he was doing it so consummately well. Cleverness and glibness—even intelligence and eloquence—could never have had the same impact as those clumsy, trite sentences, like a schoolboy's transcript of the sermon he has just heard at Sunday chapel. If I had ever had any doubts of Welling's innocence, I could have none now. Suddenly I felt close to tears; though on any other occasion I should have been close to laughter at the absurdity of his parable.

'. . . Let us then be content to await that final custom house examination, knowing that at it no man will be able to pretend that his contraband belongs to anyone else. If, in this world, things be found in a man's luggage which do not belong to him, what does it matter? He may suffer according to this world for a brief space; but he cannot be cheated out of the life eternal. And if, in this world, someone escapes punishment by passing off his contraband on another, let us not vex ourselves. He may blind the customs-officers of this world; but the customs-officers of the next world cannot be blinded, and he will be found out and punished according to his deserts. It is enough if when that ques-

338

tion is put, "Have you anything to declare? " we can truthfully say, "Only these few small things." For not one man Jack of us will arrive at his journey's end without some objects of contraband, not one! But it will be bad for those whose luggage is heavy with it, and even worse for those who have concealed it in the luggage of others.' He stopped, as though arbitrarily, at this point; scooped up the envelope-backs, and clipped them untidily together; and then walked with a somnambulistic stiffness down the steps of the pulpit, his head still erect but the pallor of his face now relieved by two crimson spots on either cheek-bone.

When, after the blessing, he, Ambleside and the choir attempted to withdraw down the aisle, there was such a milling confusion, with the police attempting to thrust back the people who were crowding out of the pews, that eventually, at Ambleside's command, the little procession of surpliced figures retreated and made its way, with an undignified scamper, out through a side-door in the chancel. Mrs. Ambleside turned to me, outraged: 'Are these people quite mad? Have they taken leave of their senses?' Behind her two men were locked in a struggle with three policemen while a child huddled against its mother, letting out terrified squeal on squeal.

'Best to sit down and wait,' Mrs. Crawley said: and she seated herself again, to be followed by the rest of us. We none of us said anything. I think that we were all still stunned, not by the violence of the scene around us, but by the effect of the sermon: each of us fearing to ask the others what they had thought of it because we were unsure what we had thought of it ourselves. It would not be fair to say that it was dreadful; and yet, as an example of the art of the sermon, it was that. Nor would it be fair to say that it was wonderful: even though the effect of it had been so profoundly moving.

I swivelled in my seat to get a better view of the pandemonium behind me—I could not resist it, in spite of the example of the others who had tacitly agreed to ignore everything which was happening—and it was then that, to my astonishment, I saw, or imagined that I saw, Setsuko. (Later this evening she denied it.) She was wedged between a huge, rusty cast-iron stove and the wall nearest to the entrance and therefore furthest from where I was sitting, and was struggling, as everyone else was struggling, to extricate herself. 'Isn't that Setsuko over there?' I leant across to Colethorpe to whisper. But by the time I had repeated the

339

question and Colethorpe had turned, she was no more to be seen.

A hand descended down from the back of the pew and touched my shoulder. 'Mr. Knox! Was that not magnificent? Magnificent!' The 'c' in magnificent was pronounced hard, like a 'k'. 'Maybe he murder girl, maybe not. It does not matter. This speech has so—so much of dlama. And this occasion. I velly pleased.' It was Mamoru Taiichi, the necklace of gold and silver teeth brandished in turn at each of us. 'This lady I know. Good evening, Miss.' He held out a little paw to Colethorpe. 'And this lady I do not know, but I see velly often at Kabuki.' He bowed to Mrs. Crawley. 'These other ladies are mission ladies?' Not one of them seemed to feel my horror of him: even Colethorpe joined in their smiles and noddings and good evenings. 'Mr. Welling looks like film-star. Like—like Aran Radd, maybe. Velly fine, Mr. Knox'— again the little hand slid crabwise over my shoulder-blades—'this gatheling has given me many, many ideas—this serment, these people. Maybe this is good climax for me. Maybe. Now I go home and think. I like this—this scene. All this scene.' He stretched out his diminutive arms as though to embrace all he liked. 'Like velly much.'

The chapel was now clearing rapidly and I got to my feet, followed by the others. Mamoru pattered along beside me. 'Velly important to make film quickly. Here in Japan people forget quick, quick, quick. Today is intelested, tomollow——' He blew a raspberry through his bunched mouth. 'Always change. My foreign fliends say "In Japan too much always the same" but I say "in Japan too much always diffelent".' We were emerging out on the path which separated the chapel from the tennis-court. People were still waiting, dotted in small groups about the tennis-court, as though they could not believe that there was nothing more to see or hear. 'Where is Mr. Welling?'

'I have no idea.'

'Please, ladies, where is Mr. Welling?'

The women halted in their tracks behind us, their nostrils twitching at this scent of danger. It was Mrs. Ambleside who replied: 'The preacher usually likes to rest for a while after his sermon. You know, to give a sermon is a very exhausting thing. People don't always realise that.'

'But I wish to see Mr. Welling. I am fliend of Mr. Knox. Mr. Knox is old fliend. I wish to ask Mr. Welling many things.'

'Well, that must be another day, don't you think?' Mrs. Ambleside spoke kindly yet firmly, as though to an obstinate child. 'I am sure that Mr. Welling will be very pleased to see you another day. But today . . .' she gave her vague, girlish smile. 'It's been so nice seeing you, Mr.—Mr.——'

'Mamoru, Taiichi, Taiichi means Big-Fat but my fliends——'

'Mr. Mamoru. I do hope that this will be the first of many visits to our services. Matins at eleven, Evensong at five. Do come again!' She held out her hand and, bemused, Mamoru took it and bowed low, even murmuring 'Thank you, lady, thank you,' as though she had rendered him some kindness.

'I see you later, Mr. Knox. Maybe this evening, maybe tomollow. Now I go and think.' Suddenly he tweaked a beret out of his jacket pocket and pulled it, like a sock, on over his head. 'Goodbye, Miss Colethorpe . . . Goodbye, madams . . . goodbye . . . goodbye . . .' He backed away, the teeth glittering at us through the gathering dusk.

'Has that little pest been bothering you?' Frank approached.

'Oh, he seems quite a nice man, really quite nice. He's a friend of Mr. Knox,' Mrs. Ambleside said.

'He likes to say that he is,' I put in.

'He stopped me in the street yesterday—I'd never met him in my life—and started asking me a lot of questions. I soon told him to go to—to go about his business. Can you imagine a complete stranger!' I could imagine it only too easily.

We were now strolling towards the dining-hall which the staff also used as a Common Room: when Ikeda-San, accompanied by a man in uniform whom I had seen down at the station, joined us. He greeted us with his usual elaborate, yet faintly ironic, courtesy and then, in a tone of barely concealed self-congratulation, said: 'Well, that all went off as smoothly as could be expected.'

'Were you here, Ikeda-San? For the service, I mean?' Mrs. Crawley asked.

'Of course.'

'We really must congratulate you on the way your force handled everything.' Mrs. Ambleside paid him the compliment he was so obviously expecting. Ikeda-San bowed in acknowledgement. 'So many people! The chapel has never been so crowded.' She said it as if this too were cause for congratulation. 'I saw masses of people jammed at the back. Poor dears—in this heat!'

'Is Mr. Ambleside busy?'

'My husband? Oh, no. He usually likes to have a cup of tea

341

after service. Before supper. . . . There he is!' She pointed through the dining-room window which we were now passing. 'With Mr. Welling.'

The two men stood facing each other, on either side of the table, each silent and with a cup in his hand.

'I must see him for a moment. And Mr. Welling, too.'

Ikeda-San went round and in through the door into the dining-room, and said something to the men, who at once put down their cups. Ambleside gave his usual, jolly smile, put an arm round Ikeda-San's shoulder and began to propel him across the room towards the door which led to his study. Welling followed behind: his bony hands clasped and his face expressing, not that almost maniacal exaltation of an hour ago, but all the dread of a schoolboy being led off to a flogging.

TWENTY-FOUR

'**M**R. WELLING is not under arrest—at present. He is an entirely free agent, to come and go as he likes. If he likes to buy himself an air-ticket and leave this country, we cannot stop him. Not for the moment.' Ikeda-San fiddled with his identity-disc: he wished that Welling would turn round and face them, instead of staring out of the window, his shoulders hunched and his hands deep in his pockets; he had an extraordinary craving to see the expression on his face. 'But if he delays—well—it may be too late. The papers have been asking why the police are so slow in taking action: and so have some of the members of the Diet'—he gave his thin, ironic smile—'the members we should expect to do so. If Mr. Welling is still here tomorrow evening, then I think that we can safely say that he will be under arrest. Unfortunately, the nature of the evidence is such . . . You understand, Mr. Ambleside.'

Ambleside nodded, biting on the end of his pipe. He had lived long enough in the East to understand not merely what Ikeda-San had said but all that he had not said. 'And what about the possibility of extradition?' he asked; his realism in a crisis surprising Ikeda-San, as it had surprised so many people in the past.

'Yes, there is always that possibility. Of course. But I think that in this case—for one reason and another—we can rule it out.'

'But you offer no guarantee?'

'No absolute guarantee, no.'

'You see, Ikeda-San, for Welling to leave now—at this stage in the proceedings—would seem to many people—perhaps to most people in Japan—to be an admission of guilt.'

Ikeda-San nodded. 'On the other hand to be thought guilty is less—less disagreeable than to be adjudged guilty. Besides, in Mr. Welling's own country, who will care? If he had killed an Australian call-girl, that would be one thing. But a Japanese strip-girl. . . .' He shrugged. 'Mr. Welling, why don't you come and sit down with us? After all, you are the person most concerned in our discussion. Mr. Welling!'

343

Welling swung round and stared at them both with what appeared to be a total lack of recognition; then he shambled across the room and flopped into a chair, drawing his bony hands down his cheeks as he exhaled a long sigh.

'You have been following what we have been saying?' Ikeda-San queried sharply.

'Oh, yes. Yes.'

'And what do you think?'

Welling stared glumly at the empty fireplace where a vase stood containing a maladroit Japanese flower-arrangement by Mrs. Ambleside, the leaves curling and the two roses overblown.

Ambleside's teeth could be heard chewing on his pipe-stem. 'I don't like any impression of running away. I don't like it at all. Bad for Welling, bad for us.'

'The alternative could, as I say, be worse, Mr. Ambleside. If Mr. Welling were to be convicted. . . .' Welling gave another long sigh, and shook his head rapidly from side to side as though he were being troubled by flies. 'Or even if he were not convicted but had to appear on trial and give an account of his relationship with this girl.'

'Enough has been written about that already. You know that.'

'Yes. But if Mr. Welling disappears, then it will soon stop being written. After two or three weeks of excitement. On the other hand, a long period on bail or in prison; a long trial; appeals and more appeals—the whole business could last three or four years! Oh, yes, Mr. Ambleside, I am not exaggerating. Your mission— and every mission in Japan—and every Christian in Japan— would have to suffer for that whole period. I am thinking quite as much of that as of Mr. Welling when I say: Get him out of the country at once.'

Ambleside considered in silence. Ikeda-San was a Christian and a genuine one—he had no doubt of that. Being a Christian, he would wish to spare his Church and spare the mission, with which he had been for long connected, any continuation of this aggressive and often scandalous publicity. In addition, he seemed to have developed an odd kind of affection for Welling—Ambleside was perspicacious enough to notice that. But would these factors in themselves be enough to persuade him to let Welling escape, with all the consequent outcry against the inefficiency and corruption of the police in general and of himself in particular? Ambleside,

344

who knew Ikeda-San to be ambitious, doubted it—obviously there was some other, secret factor. But what?

Ikeda-San rose and stared down at the back of Welling's averted head for several seconds on end. One small hand rested on his hip. 'Well, I think it is best for you both to think about my suggestion. But remember, there is no time to lose. If Mr. Welling goes, it must be tomorrow. Otherwise, I am afraid that it will be too late for him. You understand, Mr. Welling? ' Welling nodded gloomily.

When Ambleside had shown Ikeda-San out to his car, he strolled back with the rolling, elephantine gait, head lowered on to his chest, which always indicated that he was trying to resolve a conflict. 'Well,' he said, entering the study. 'Well. . . .' He sank into the massive, leather-covered chair opposite Welling's and leant forward in it, his elbows on his knees. 'This is a poser.'

Welling still made no reply.

'Yes, it's a poser all right! There's a lot in what he says. The cards are stacked pretty heavily against you, Welling old boy. I don't mind saying it. Yes! Yes indeed! ' Again he ruminated. 'On the other hand no innocent man likes to be thought guilty by default. Because that's what everyone here will think, you can bet your bottom dollar. Yes, there's no doubt of that, no doubt at all.'

Welling raised his head, the forehead of which had been supported by one hand. 'He says that I can go? ' he said. 'That I'm free to go? '

'That's it. Free to go—to do a bunk. But you must do it now. Immediately. No shilly-shallying. . . . Well—what do you think of that little proposal of our friend Ikeda-San? '

'But would I—would I be able to get on an aeroplane—a ship? '

Ambleside was simultaneously puzzled and exasperated by this question and the vague, faintly petulant tone in which it was put.

'Ah, that's a minor point! ' he said. 'Of course, in an emergency. . . . If need be, Ikeda-San or the Embassy can intervene. Maybe we should take Embassy advice, anyway.'

'I could never come back, though? '

'No. I hardly think so.'

'I couldn't take all my things by plane. They could be sent after me, I suppose. By ship.'

'All that is quite irrelevant! ' Ambleside at last gave vent to his mounting exasperation. 'Let's consider what is important, for heaven's sake, and not waste time— —' He rose. A glance at the clock on the mantelpiece had told him that they were already ten minutes late for supper. 'Well, let's go and eat. That will give us a breather in which to think the whole thing over. I'd like to ask my wife for her opinion—if you've no objection.'

Welling raised himself slowly from the chair. 'I don't want to eat,' he said.

'Oh, come along, old man! This starvation-diet isn't going to do you any good. You've begun to look like a skeleton.' It was now the jolly, hearty Ambleside whom people usually saw : clapping Welling on the back and then thrusting him towards the door, a grin on his beefy face.

'I can't eat.'

'Nonsense! Nonsense! Some cold meat and pickles and a slice of apple-tart—what could be better for you? Won't do you any harm, no harm at all. That's the way!' The pressure of the hand on Welling's shoulder became more compulsive. 'Lead on, Macduff! On you go, old boy! I'm famished, absolutely famished.'

It was always said that Ikeda-San had not married because of his only sister, who was several years older than himself and had spent much of her life in sanatoria. Sometimes he even believed this himself. Their relationship was conducted for the most part in silence and with a formality so extreme that it surprised even their Japanese friends. Kimiko was the complete antithesis of her brother : a large, ungainly, inelegant woman with a battered prize-fighter's nose between eyes that had a slight cast in them. As a young girl she had made a small reputation with a book of poems and a *nouvelle*; but it was many years now since she had published anything.

When her brother came home, she was dusting in the 'fan-room' which he used as his study. The house was a small one, but noted for this room, the shape of a fan, with a ceiling of inlaid woods, themselves forming a fan, and fan-decorations in carving or tessera wherever one glanced. The fan opened out on to a tiny but exquisite garden through which ran an artificial stream. By an ingenious contrivance the water of this stream flowed into a bamboo drum on a pivot which as soon as it was full tipped over and then tipped back to make a resonant click on its hollow base. This sound, always punctuating the life of the house, had long since got on Kimiko's nerves, so that when she knew that her brother would be away she used to go out into the

346

garden to disconnect the drum from its pivot; but she never confessed this to Ikeda-San. The house had belonged to a famous *Kabuki* actor of the Meiji era.

As soon as he came in she backed out of the room as though she were a servant: her knees close together and her toes turned inwards, the duster held behind her. Ikeda-San had noticed at once that an Imari pot on his desk had not been replaced correctly, and he went and moved it the few centimetres to its usual position before he asked: 'Any callers?' By then Kimiko was already in the doorway.

'Kobayashi-San telephoned about an hour ago. He'll ring back.'

Ikeda-San was the owner of a small and expensive bar, frequented chiefly by foreigners and wealthy Japanese business-men; but the bar was in the name of his friend, Kobayashi, and no one knew of his connection with it. He liked to go there, to drink a glass of vin-cola or fruit-juice, as though he himself were a customer; assessing, in the process, the exact merits of each member of his staff.

'Did he say what he wanted?'

'No, he said nothing.'

Probably it was some more trouble with that bar-boy from Kyushu who alternated between insolent high spirits and depressions so profound that on one occasion he had severed the veins in one wrist with a knife.

'A glass of water, please. With plenty of ice in it.'

The house was partly in the Western, partly in the Japanese, style: with two armchairs, a sofa and a desk and some pieces of Wedgwood Blue—modern, though Ikeda-San believed them to be old—among the Japanese and Chinese pots. Ikeda-San squatted, cross-legged, on a cushion on the floor.

'Feeling all right?'

She nodded, handing him the water. 'The fever seems to have gone.'

'Good.'

He gazed out into the garden, soothed by that rhythmic click-click-click, the tinkle of the water, and the green of the foliage. Those few Western friends who were invited to visit him were astonished to find so much quiet in the heart of a city as populous at Kyoto.

Dreamily he began to wonder as he sipped at the water what

Welling would decide to do. If he stayed he would have no chance; no chance at all. Fifteen, twenty years in prison. What a fool to get himself mixed up with a slut like that! What came over people? There were times when one wondered if Welling were quite sane: one talked to him and nothing seemed to penetrate; or if it penetrated, it produced an effect totally different from the one which one expected.

A small grey bird was hopping about the garden, a snail in its beak. It jumped on to one of the five ornamental stones the arrangement of which probably gave Ikeda-San more aesthetic pleasure than anything else in the garden and tapped the snail-shell against it. Again and again it tapped, in impotent fury; the shell would not yield. . . . Ikeda-San thought of Welling, his head buried in his arms, as he sobbed out: 'Go away! Leave me alone! Oh, why can't you leave me alone?' How strange for a man seemingly so tough to lose his nerve so quickly; and in front of those two constables, mere uneducated peasants! Ikeda-San suddenly felt a renewal of the contempt and tenderness which the incident had elicited; but oddly these emotions were even stronger now in recollection than at the time of the actual break-down.

It would be much better if Welling seized the proffered opportunity and made off. He had not the stamina for a prolonged martyrdom. On trial he would cut the worst kind of figure: confused; contradicting himself; suddenly petulant and no less suddenly eager to say whatever was wanted of him; abject; despicable. Yes, despicable; despicable most of all. He would have no dignity and in Japan only dignity—the power to exact respect—would save him in the face of all that accumulated evidence. True, the sermon had had that quality: but Ikeda-San saw, with chilling clarity, that Welling could not remain for long on those heights; his was not the type. He would fall from them, inevitably he would fall; probably he had fallen from them already into that abyss where Ikeda-San had found him wallowing in panic, his body growing rigid whenever the policeman's shoe had prodded to turn him over and examine him more closely. . . .

Yet, as he wished that Welling would be 'sensible' and take the course least likely to harm himself, the mission, and the whole Christian community in Japan, Ikeda-San also found himself wishing, against his will and to his surprise, that Welling would, in fact, decide to stick it out. He did not care to analyse this ambivalence of desire too precisely; preferring to ignore it, as a habitually healthy man ignores the first symptoms of a malady which may in the end prove fatal for him. But he began to visualise what would happen if Welling refused to escape. Would he go on denying that he had strangled the girl and been her lover? Or would he (more likely) crack beneath the pressure exerted by Ikeda-San, and just as he had eventually sobbed out that yes, yes, he had loved her, she had loved him, would he sob out the rest in a bitter torrent of self-accusation? '. . . Good, Mr. Welling. I am glad that you have at last decided to tell me the whole truth. It makes it so much easier for all of us. Here—why don't you drink some of this coffee? That's right.' (A hand on the heaving shoulders; the voice soothingly tender.) 'You had provocation, you were blackmailed. We all know that. A girl of that kind stops at nothing.

'The court will take a lenient view, you may be sure. Now come—let me pour you out a little more coffee.' Staring out into the garden, which lay like some rumpled piece of embroidery, all little hillocks and indentations in the last flicker of evening, Ikeda-San saw the whole scene of surrender and reconciliation with the clarity of a hallucination. 'Please don't regard me as an enemy. I am merely the voice of society to which you wish to return; the voice of your own conscience with which you desire to make your peace.'

That telephone! On and on it rang, cutting ruthlessly through his dream of being at once son-confessor and avenger-protector. What was Kimiko doing?

'Yes?' When she at last appeared, the single monosyllable flicked out at her like a lash.

'Sorry.' She adjusted her *obi*. 'I was lying down. . . . It's Furomoto-San.'

Ikeda-San rose to his feet, making a grimace.

'Hello. Yes. This is Ikeda, here. . . . Yes. . . . Yes, I've told him that he has twenty-four hours. That's as long as we dare to give him. . . . Well, that's very kind of you. Very kind indeed. No. . . . No, no bother, no bother at all. Thank you. Thank you so much. Thank you.' He went on repeating all the meaningless phrases demanded by Japanese custom from a subordinate to a superior, until Furomoto rang off.

Returning to the room, he again squatted on the *tatami*, and then spat out into the garden, the dense green of which was now almost black. What filth! But that was how it was. If he hoped to get Tanaka's position when he retired next year, what else could he do? He listened to the click-click-click of the bamboo drum, thinking: 'What's it got to do with Furomoto? What's his connection with Welling? Why should he ask this favour?' A number of possible answers, all over-subtle, suggested themselves to him; then he gave up. Click-click went the drum; the snail-shell, empty now, gleamed up at him from the base of the nearest of the five smooth, humped stones.

Welling had been seated on the end of his bed, cutting his nails, when Sarah had hobbled in. Seeing him, she had let out a wail of horror: 'No, mister, no!' To his amazement she had then hurried forward and snatched the scissors from his hand. His mind, which had moved so sluggishly all the day, gave an infinitesimal jerk forward. Of course! The Japanese believed that it brought ill-luck to cut one's nails after sunset. Well, she had something there; he needed all the luck he could get. Sarah replaced the scissors in their green morocco-case and took out a file instead. 'Please.' She extended the file on the palm of her crooked, leathery hand. 'This good,' she said.

When she had drawn the curtains, turned down the bed and left him, it was, however, neither the scissors nor the file which he used, but his teeth. Systematically he gnawed and tore at his nails, in savage self-laceration, in many cases leaving the quick raw and oozing blood. He must decide, he must decide. . . .

All at once he jumped to his feet and began to stride up and down the room, up and down, up and down: repeating to himself phrases and even whole sentences from his sermon of that evening. 'Let us then be content to await that final custom house examination. . . . Proceed, go on in, my friend. . . . Suffer in this world for a brief space. . . . Cannot be cheated out of life eternal. . . . Life eternal. . . . Life eternal. . . . Life eternal. . . .' But it was life in this world, not the promise of life eternal, which he wanted. To be shut up for months and even years before he was brought to trial; and then after the trial? And to have to face day after day those humiliating questions and insinuations (he seemed to hear Ikeda-San's voice): 'But, Mr. Welling, this girl. . . . Your relationship . . . unorthodox, to say the least . . . in love . . . inexplicable pregnancy . . . blackmail . . . a little more explicit. . . .' Then the sentence. Death? No, no! But, no less terrible,

350

years and years in prison. How many? Fifteen? Twenty-five? He had had four years and that had been enough. Mary would die; the boy would try to forget him; and he would come out, an old man, to do—what? He covered his face with his hands; he could not tread that path any further.

Then, run, run, run! But he had always run; if he ran now, his self-contempt and self-loathing would remain glued to him for ever. That was not what those early Christians had done. With their last dying convulsions they had made the sign of the cross; with their last tortured screams they had asserted their faith. Had his sermon then been meaningless? Self-delusion? Hypocrisy? Was that the kind of man he was? In agony he tried to scramble back up onto those heights but each time he slipped backwards— lacerating himself, bruising himself—until he paused to acknowledge: No, I cannot return there. I am not the sort of person who can remain there.

Desolate, he threw himself across his bed and stared down at the floor, focusing his closely-set blue eyes on the grain of the scrubbed boards. Suddenly the idea came to him: why not confess? Confess!—— But confess what? He was innocent. Yet still the idea persisted; just as, in the past, the idea of making love to Sanae had persisted in spite of every effort he made to expel it from his consciousness. 'Yes, I killed her . . . I loved her, so I killed her . . . I had to kill her. . . . It was the only way out. . . . Yes, I did it, I did it. . . .' The words once spoken, peace, warm and tingling, invaded his whole being: a peace such as he had never known in the whole of his life. Ikeda-San was looking at him: no, not at him, but *down* at him. He was on his knees, on the floor, and Ikeda-San was above him, all-seeing, all-avenging, yet merciful. His hands touched Ikeda-San's shoes, he bowed over them. 'I did it, I did it, I did it. Forgive me. I did it.'

He twisted over on the bed as he became aware of a reiterated knocking, and rubbed his eyes with his knuckles. 'Yes?' he croaked at last. 'Yes? Who is it?'

Knox entered, smiling as he attempted to conceal his nervousness and embarrassment. 'May I come in?'

Welling sat up on the bed and gazed down between his knees, without answering.

'That was rather an impressive sermon,' Knox said. He sniffed involuntarily: hypersensitive to smells, it seemed to him as if a wild animal had been in the room.

'Thanks.'

'I think everyone found it impressive. Even those who couldn't understand any English.'

'Oh, it was a lot of rot!' Welling gripped the bed-rail with both of his hands and then laid his right cheek across the knuckles.

'No,' said Knox quietly. 'It wasn't rot.' He sat down on the bed. 'I've just been talking to the Amblesides.'

'The Amblesides?'

'Yes. . . . I'm taking a plane tomorrow evening. To Manila.' He paused. 'I want you to come with me.'

'Then you know about——?'

'Ikeda-San's offer? Yes. He came to my house to tell me about it. And so I came here.'

Welling suddenly roused himself, sat bolt upright on the bed, and turned on Knox. 'So you also want me to run away!'

'What's the alternative?' Knox asked him quietly.

'That's not the advice you gave me the last time we met.' Welling spoke with an extreme bitterness.

'No. That's true. But the situation has changed since then. Hasn't it?'

'How do you think I shall feel for the rest of my days if I make a bolt for it instead of sticking it out?'

'How will you feel if you stick it out? A long trial, probably years in jail.'

Welling banged his hand, palm downwards, on one of the brass bed-posts. 'That's not how those early missionaries of yours would have acted.'

'No. Possibly not.'

'And yet you want me to . . . ?' He looked as if he were about to punch Knox in the face.

Knox rose to his feet, and going to the window looked down on to the tennis-court. 'Those early missionaries were what we should call saints, I suppose. Are you one? I don't know. If you are—well, then—embrace your martyrdom. But if not—well, accept your limitations and be sensibly human.' He turned. 'That's all.'

'But I—I want—I wish—I must——' Welling twisted his hands around the bed-rails, squeezing them as he attempted to squeeze out the words of heroic decision which somehow would not come. 'I—I—I——' But now even the 'I' was isolated, with nothing before or after it: naked and vulnerable as a snail without a shell.

'Yes. You're right. You're right,' he said. He bowed his head over the bed-rail as though he were going to vomit. 'What—what ought I to do about a ticket?' he asked at last.

TWENTY-FIVE

I KEPT telling myself what a nuisance it was to have to leave at such short notice and how unselfish I had been in offering to accompany Welling; but this was self-deception. In fact, I was delighted. I put down roots in even the least fertile soils, and when I have to tear them up I find that a single, sudden jerk is less painful than a slow process of easing away. In the rush of getting myself off, I have no time to think that perhaps I do not wish to get myself off at all.

It was Ambleside who first hinted the proposal. When Ikeda-San told me of his offer to Welling, I suddenly felt an extraordinary eagerness to know whether he would accept it or not. Having tried, and failed, to repress my curiosity, I went across to the mission. Consciously I hoped that Welling would be reasonable and scuttle out through the hole in the bag which Ikeda-San had made for him; but unconsciously I think that I hoped he would decide to be a martyr. Why? I suppose that even the most materialistic of us would like to believe that there are people for whom material considerations are of no importance. Perhaps, also, I craved the tragic climax which we had been promised, instead of the ignominious anti-climax which now seemed more likely.

Ambleside soon drew me away from the others into his study. It was a room for which the synonym ' den ' would, for once, be appropriate. One minuscule window set high up in a wall filtered the light down on to congested leather-covered chairs and piles of old periodicals and newspapers. Through this murk Ambleside shuffled, seemingly gorged on the cold meat and pickles at which I had found him, to collapse on a couch draped, not covered, with a length of faded cretonne. The air was impregnated with what I recognised to be his special odour: an aggressively masculine blend of pipe-smoke, shoe-polish, sweat and soap.

' So Ikeda-San came across personally to tell you of his offer? '

' Yes. I really can't think why. Except that he also wanted to tell me that if Welling went, I could go too.' Ambleside was now going through all that grubby business, which I so dislike, of filling a pipe. 'Still, he could have sent one of his minions to tell me that; or at least have left it until he was sure that Welling *would* decide to go. He seems to have got the idea, God knows why, that I have some kind of influence over Welling.'

Ambleside's blunt forefinger pressed down on the tobacco in the pipe-bowl. 'Welling respects you,' he said, without looking up. Now his thumb was at work on the tobacco. 'He respects you a lot.'

'Does he?'

'You're an intellectual and he admires intellectuals. Brains.' He said this as if he did not share Welling's admiration. 'He once told me that you'd learned more Japanese in six months than he had succeeded in learning in six years.' He chuckled. 'I'm not surprised. He has no ear for languages.'

'Do you think he'll decide to go?'

Ambleside scraped a match down the side of the mammoth box he was now holding in his hand and put it to the pipe. He began to puff out smoke until the tiny, over-crowded room became dense with it. 'I hope so,' he mumbled over the stem. 'I very much hope so.'

'I've no idea what I should do if the same offer were made to me. I was thinking about it as I walked over here. I'm assuming, of course, that Welling is innocent,' I added. 'If he isn't, then obviously there's no problem at all—the sooner he gets out, the better for him.'

'Welling's innocent all right,' Ambleside said. 'Though it wouldn't surprise me if some of those hens'—he pointed his pipe out of the window in the direction of the dining-room—'secretly think that he isn't. Women have a way of crediting people with the worst kind of behaviour and yet not really thinking any less of them for it. Don't you agree?'

Ambleside frequently produces such generalisations and it is no doubt because of them that he has earned among the Japanese and even the foreign colony his reputation for 'wisdom'.

'If a man is innocent, should he run away?' It was the question I had been asking myself ever since Ikeda-San's call.

'It depends on the man.' Ambleside's small, green eyes looked shrewdly at me through the nauseating smoke that still continued to erupt from between his pouting lips. 'If a man is Welling, then he should.'

'Why do you say that?'

355

'His nerve went from the first. Not at the end of those hours of interrogation—any of us might have cracked after them—but at the beginning, right at the beginning.' I felt vaguely repelled by the clarity of this assessment. 'No, poor old Welling hasn't got the guts to face a thing like this out. And, believe me, it would need guts.'

'What about his sermon this evening? That showed—guts.' I repeated the word with the distaste I have always felt for it.

'Yes.' He was willing to acknowledge it. 'That was a fine effort, a very fine effort. It surprised me. In fact, I was surprised that he decided to preach at all. But it's one thing to produce a flash in the pan like that and another thing to keep going, day in and day out, for months and months on end. That requires something different, something Welling hasn't got. At least,' he added, 'I don't think he's got it. This whole affair has had a very peculiar effect on him.'

He went on to say that all the members of the mission, and even Welling's friends outside it, had begun to worry about his mental state. Like myself on the occasion when he had come to my house, they had noticed that all his reactions now tended to be disproportionate—either excessive to the point of hysteria or so muted that communication seemed hardly to exist. Perhaps, thought Ambleside, the 'poor chap was heading for a crack-up'. His attitude to his wife was in itself disturbing. No doubt any man would feel uneasy in such circumstances; but to refuse to talk to her on the telephone and to fail (as far as Ambleside knew) to send her any letter of explanation and reassurance seemed extraordinary conduct—especially as Welling was obviously still so fond of her. Sometimes Ambleside feared that in his present state Welling might 'do something foolish'. 'We once had a young German boy working with us in India,' he mused. 'Brilliant surgeon, really brilliant. Suddenly he became rather as Welling is now—one felt that one was slowly losing touch with him. We were busy at the time—a cholera epidemic—and I'm afraid we didn't bother much. Then, one morning, my wife went into the surgery early and found him dead, with a hypodermic in his hand. Never found the reason. But there was a lot of talk of course.' Again he began to fiddle with his pipe, like one of those neurotic packers who have no sooner crammed all their belongings into a trunk than they have to dig them out again. 'Brilliant,' he repeated. 'My wife says she's never seen any surgeon as young as

356

that who could hold a candle to him.' The fingers of his right hand were now grey with ash. 'Now, I have a nasty feeling that Welling might perhaps attempt something similar. . . . Especially on his trip back home. He's got this thing about his wife—doesn't seem even to want to talk about her, let alone get in touch with her. It—it might drive him to anything, anything at all. It's a real phobia, complex, whatever the word is.' Again the little, green eyes darted up at me through the clouds of smoke. 'When are you—er—planning to depart?'

It was in this way that he began to reveal his scheme that I should accompany Welling in the aeroplane at least as far as Manila.

Later that evening I went over to the Furomoto house to tell them the news. Only Colethorpe seemed surprised: Setsuko and her aunt gave the impression of hardly taking in what I said and of finding what they did take in of little interest to them. They were polite, because it is difficult for the Japanese not to be polite; but it was that chilling Japanese politeness which blows on one like the wind off Mount Hiei in winter and proclaims that one has given offence. What had I said, what had I done? I could not guess. Since I had both offered to pay the rent for the whole of the succeeding month and had invited them to come over to inspect any damage to either the house or the few sticks of furniture they had left in it, it could not have been that they were afraid of losing financially over the abruptness of my departure.

I took out the typed list of points I wished to raise with them and began to run through it. They nodded at each item—the packers to be let in; the milk bill; the electricity bill; Endo-San's wages—until Setsuko suddenly interrupted: 'Why don't you give the whole list and the money to Aileen? Wouldn't that be easier?'

I stopped in my reading.

'She has plenty of time on her hands now. You can deal with it all, can't you, Aileen? It won't cause you any bother?'

'Of course—if you wish. . . .' Colethorpe sounded uncomfortable.

'Good. Then you two have a word together. Arrange it between you.' She got up off the floor and smiled vaguely down at us. Her aunt rose too. There could have been no clearer indication that they were dismissing me.

357

'I'll call in tomorrow to say goodbye, of course.'

'Will you? Good.'

I scrambled to my feet, confused and annoyed. Colethorpe followed me as I began to cross the garden.

'How odd Setsuko was!' I exclaimed when I felt that I was far enough away from the house not to be overheard.

'Yes. I thought that perhaps you two had quarrelled.'

'Not that I know of.'

'She's been peculiar for some days. She's the same to me too. Very polite, very formal, very distant. . . . Oh, how wonderful these tobacco-plants smell!'

I remembered how, so short a time ago, Setsuko and I had crossed the garden together and she had picked one of the tobacco-flowers and given it to me. The dry air, crepitating with unseen cicadas, had seemed also to crepitate with my desire for her as we had walked, so close to each other and yet never daring to touch. I had been her friend; in a sense I had also been her lover. Now I had reverted to my original status of tenant. How had that come about? I might eventually discover a reason; but, since this was Japan, it would never be the real reason, of that I was sure.

'What are your own plans?' I asked.

Colethorpe shrugged, the moonlight glistening on her prominent cheek-bones and her bare arms and legs. 'I can't decide anything for the moment. I'm in that kind of state. . . . And anyway I have too little money to do anything I may decide! So why worry?'

'I could lend you some—give you some.'

'Oh no! That's awfully sweet of you. But there's no need for that, Frank wants me to work at the mission as a sort of secretary-registrar. Can you imagine? But I might do worse.' She stooped to pluck one of the tobacco-flowers. 'Silly of me to pick this. They die at once, don't they?' I nodded: I had once said something of the kind to Setsuko. 'Yes, I might do worse. It would give me a breathing-space. But can you imagine someone like me in that set-up? I ask you!'

'You'd be no more out of place than Miss Rosenthal or—or——'

'Or Welling?'

'Yes.'

Her nostrils dilated over the flower. 'I'm glad that he's clearing

358

out. And I'm glad that you're going to accompany him. Though I'm sorry to lose you.'

'Thank you.'

'He's the suicidal type, you know.'

'Who? Welling? . . . So you think that too.'

'It's obvious, isn't it? People as afraid as that tend to seek one of two refuges: death or madness.'

'Let's hope his wife will provide an alternative to those.' She giggled. 'No, I'm not being funny,' I added. 'I mean it.'

'Yes, I know you do. I'm laughing only because I find him—the whole business—so horribly sad.'

'He was in love with her, you know.'

She chucked the flower into the bushes. 'Gosh, how much he was in love with her!' she agreed.

'Why, Ikeda-San, how perfectly lovely of you to come and see us off!' The tall American girl with the snub-nose and glossy, neatly-bobbed brown hair who had just greeted Welling now swung round. 'My, but you do look elegant in that cream suit of yours. Jack! Hi, Jack! Here's Ikeda-San.'

Since she knew Welling and must, like every other foreigner in Japan, have heard his story, I wondered whether she really thought that Ikeda-San was at the airport to say goodbye to her and her husband, or was pretending to think so. Somewhere I had seen her, but I could not remember where; until she suddenly turned back to me: 'Hello there! Remember me? We met months and months ago at that dinner for the Archbishop. You were going to join our Sunday Breakfast Club. What happened to you? You never showed up. . . . Well, never mind! It's too late now, I guess. We're off to Laos.'

'And I'm off to Europe.'

At that someone distracted her: for unlike Welling and myself, who had purposely told no one of our departure, she and her husband had innumerable friends to say goodbye to them. Ikeda-San approached. 'Good evening, Mr. Knox. Good evening, Mr. Welling.' He bowed low to each of us.

'Good evening,' I replied. Welling merely stared apathetically, one bony hand fiddling with the strap of the camera he was carrying while the other rested on his knee.

'You have perfect weather for your flight. I can predict a calm passage.'

'I'm glad to hear that.'

'Mr. Welling.' Ikeda-San had sat down beside us; now he leant forward. 'Mr. Welling.' This time he repeated the name loudly.

Welling started, clutching at the camera-strap, and then answered 'Yes, yes, yes,' in a sudden rush.

'I hope that you will send me at least a postcard from Australia. I shall want to hear how you are getting on.' Even now I cannot be certain whether he was being ironical or not. 'Write to me, will you?'

Welling fixed his haggard, close-set eyes on the Japanese, blinked and then nodded.

'I am sorry that our friendship should have ended in this fashion. It was the last thing I wished. I hoped for something—different.' His voice was so soft as to be almost inaudible; yet it vibrated oddly as he added: 'Something very different.'

Welling jerked his head from side to side like a restive horse; glanced over Ikeda-San's head to where Marion and Jack were either kissing their friends or pumping their hands; and then turned to me: 'I'd like a glass of water.'

'The barman can give you one.'

But he made no move and eventually I got up and fetched it for him as though he were a child.

'Thanks.' He took one greedy gulp and then another.

'And you too, Mr. Knox. Please send me a postcard from London. A picture postcard. I should like to hear from you.' He sighed. 'Japan is so far from everywhere. One's friends leave Japan and one knows that one will never see them again.' Did he regard me also as a friend? 'Letters, or even postcards, maintain the illusion that the thread has not been snapped.'

'And will you write to me?'

'Naturally. If you write first.'

'I should like to know the end of this case. Its solution.'

'Ah that!' He gave his small ironic smile. 'I am beginning to think that it's a case which will never find an end.'

'How can you say that?' I too attempted irony. 'You have such a high reputation in the Police Force—so the papers tell me.'

'In Japan few things have a solution. And when they have a solution, it is rarely the right solution. That is sad, you know—for a police-officer like myself.'

360

The loud-speaker began to crackle over our heads and then emitted a single, prolonged shriek. A voice announced our flight.

As soon as he had unfastened his safety-belt, Welling extended his seat as far as it would go, stretched out his legs, and to my astonishment, at once went off to sleep. Behind me I could hear Marion and Jack:

'My, but look at this brooch which Mr. Tsukahara gave me! Isn't it pretty? Oh, isn't it pretty? Did you ever see anything so cute?'

'Mrs. Horibayashi was crying. Did you see that, honey?'

'Yes, wasn't that sweet of her! And so was little Noriko. Imagine that child bringing all these lovely roses. We hardly know her. . . . Oh, I could cry myself, really I could.'

Their voices faded from my consciousness as I began to think of my last minutes with Setsuko. Just before leaving I had gone over to say goodbye: having waited all day in the hopes that she would come to ask if she could be of any help to me, as Colethorpe and Frank, Mrs. Crawley and the Amblesides had done. Once again that chilling politeness had fanned my face. What time was the plane due to take off? What time would I arrive in Manila? Did I ever suffer from air-sickness? Was my packing completed? The maid, whom I had so rarely seen, had brought us bowls of frothy green tea as though to underline the ritualistic formality of the whole ceremony in which we were taking part. Then, suddenly, Setsuko turned to her aunt:

'Have you the present ready?' she asked in Japanese.

Mrs. Furomoto rose to her feet. 'I'll get it,' she said. She backed out of the room and for a few seconds we sat in silence, listening to her mount the stairs. Then all at once Setsuko rose to her knees from the floor where she was squatting and fell—I can use no other word—forward and into my arms. One hand gripped my shoulder, the other ran down my cheek to my throat; her tongue entered my mouth.

Her aunt was returning. Hurriedly she pushed me away from her: only whispering: 'That letter. I've written it. You'll find it waiting for you.'

Mrs. Furomoto shuffled in on stockinged feet, eyes lowered, and placed the present, shrouded in tissue-paper, on the floor beside me.

'What is it? I know that in Japan one shouldn't look or ask, but do tell me.'

'*Bonsai*,' said Setsuko. 'A dwarf tree. A dwarf maple-tree.'

I had once told Setsuko that I hated the Japanese custom of crippling and stunting trees; but evidently she had forgotten—hers was that kind of egotism.

'How lovely,' I said. 'Thank you so much.'

'In the autumn the leaves will turn red. Remember Japan then—and remember us then.' Few Westerners would have dared to express anything so sentimental.

'I shall forget neither.'

'I wonder.'

As we stepped out of the plane into the glare and scorching heat of Manila airport, they were all at once around us: someone —who?—must have tipped them off. 'Mr. Welling! Hi, Mr. Welling! One moment, Mr. Welling! Just a question. . . . Mr. Welling—*please*!'

Welling had escaped one martyrdom; another had started.

TWENTY-SIX

'WHERE'S Galloping Consumption? What's she doing?'
The woman who asked the question was the oldest of
the troupe: a widow, with a spastic only son to keep.
She was drawing on a cigarette in a long tortoise-shell holder, a
present from the owner of a shop for tortoise-shell goods, while
at the same time she ran a small, work-seamed hand rhythmically
through her orange hair.

'She went to meet her doctor at the stage-door.'

'That boy! What's the matter with him? Why is he so shy?
He's been here often enough before, hasn't he?'

The studious-looking girl in harlequin-glasses looked up from
buffing her nails. 'There's nothing the matter with him, if you
want my opinion. It's Skeleton Woman. She's so afraid that one
of us might waylay him.'

'What's the trouble, Okubo-San? Is it nits?' the Korean asked.

The widow continued to scratch her scalp. 'My hair always
gets dry after the rainy season ends. But it curls better,' she added.

'Try macassar oil. My scurf used to be terrible,' another girl
suggested, as she began to arrange the chairs around the table in
the centre of the dressing-room. 'Whose is this?' She picked up a
tattered American Physique Magazine from the litter of half-
empty bottles, saucers containing cigarette-stubs and soiled wads
of cotton-wool, piled sushi boxes and grubby odds and ends of
clothing. 'Mm, mm!' She goggled at a torso that might have
been Frank's.

'Kuniko brought it in. She hasn't been near a Caucasian in
weeks, so she thought it the next best thing.'

'That girl!' The widow gave her hoarse, dry laugh which was
so much like a cough. 'The things she'll do for blond hair and a
pink skin!'

No one really liked the widow, but everyone felt sorry for her.
Her husband, a peasant, had been an alcoholic, and had beaten
her up frequently before the birth of their child, thus (so everyone
believed) causing it to be a spastic. In remorse he had then left

363

the house and had wandered about the country until he had died from exposure, starvation and drink. At first her work at the theatre had filled her with loathing and remorse; but now she was inured to it, performing her tasks with the same clumsy vigour with which she had once worked on her husband's mortgaged land.

Rumi appeared: followed first by her doctor, a tall, thin youth with an intelligently cynical face pocked by acne, and then by Ikuko, the thick-ankled girl from Shikoku who was eager to get in touch with her 'Professor' during the séance.

The 'Professor' had had a haemorrhage on a platform of Osaka station while struggling to board a train, and had died a few hours later in the Casualty Ward of one of the Municipal Hospitals.

'Sorry, darlings!' Rumi drawled in her bizarre accent, half-Harlem and half-Shanghai. 'This wretched boy of mine is always late. Everything ready?'

Two girls were busy clearing the table of its débris: one in Western dress, the other in kimono and obi. Rumi bent down to stare at herself in the long blotched mirror which ran the length of one wall above the low tables littered with make-up. 'I look terrible. I wonder if it's really wise of me.' She had been ill—she was always falling ill with what she merely called 'my usual trouble', refusing to satisfy the curiosity of the other girls—and this was the first séance for many weeks. 'Do you think it's wise of me, Aki-chan?' She turned to the doctor.

'I never think it wise of you. But you insist on doing it. Some day you'll kill yourself.'

One of the girls clearing the table had found a box, buried beneath a mound of newspapers. She opened it. 'What's this? . . . Wa, it's an obi.'

The other girl peered over her shoulder: 'It's beautiful!'

The Korean joined them. 'From Ori-Dono. At least the box says Ori-Dono. Hand-woven. Whose is it?'

The girl from Hokkaido stood with her little mouth open. 'It—it used to belong to Sanae,' she said. 'I remember she showed it to me. Someone gave it to her. But she wouldn't tell me who.'

'Her missionary, I expect. . . . What ought we to do with it?'

'No one has ever collected that box of her things. It's still in Muto-San's room. I saw it there.'

364

'It'll stay there—until Muto-San begins to pick it over for his girl friends,' the widow said.

The girl from Hokkaido started to try on the *obi*; but the girl who had first found it snatched it away from her. '*Oi!* Give it back to me! I found it! I found it first!'

'You're not going to keep it, are you?' the studious girl asked.

'Wouldn't you?'

'But that's—that's . . .' She said nothing more, frowning down in disapproval at the nails she had been polishing.

'Sanae doesn't want an *obi* now. Why shouldn't I keep it?'

For a brief while the girls wrangled among themselves—some agreeing with the Hokkaido girl; some disagreeing with her; some maintaining that the *obi* should be sold and the profits shared among them—until Rumi interrupted: '*Ja*—are we going to begin our business or aren't we?' Suddenly she sounded tense: she always did just before a séance.

'Yes, come on, all! . . . Do something about that light.' The widow flopped down on to a chair, still sucking at her tortoise-shell holder although she had long since removed the cigarette-stub, and then crossed her short legs, with their knobbly knees and ankles, one over the other. 'Kumiko-chan—the light.' Kumiko, the most recent arrival, was invariably ordered about by the other girls. 'No, not like that.' The widow jumped up and snatched from the girl's hands the green silk scarf she had been binding around the bulb. 'Are you crazy? You'll start a fire. It's easy to see that they don't have electric light in your village. Round the shade, that's the way.' She began to circle the shade with the scarf as though it were a bandage.

'The music?' Rumi asked. 'Where's my record?'

'It's here.' The studious girl pointed with her buff to the gramophone which stood in one corner.

'I've such a headache,' said Rumi. She clutched at her temples, once again staring at herself, eyes wild under their thinly pencilled arcs, in the long glass. 'Terrible. Throb, throb, throb.'

'Want something for it?' the studious girl suggested.

'No good. Only upsets my stomach.' She shivered slightly, in spite of the close, steamy atmosphere. '*Ja*—let's begin!'

A battered wicker armchair, the wicker coming unwound from one of its dented arms, had been dragged into the room for her from the stage-manager's office and placed at the end of the table furthest from the shaded lamp. As she lowered herself into it, yawning and scratching under an arm, someone clicked off the overhead neon-bar. 'It'll be awful,' she muttered. 'No good at all.' Then fretfully she exclaimed: ' " The shadow has become thinner." I'm worn out.'

Kumiko, who had never been to a séance, gazed in fascination at Rumi whose bony face was now green in the light filtered across at it through the shade. 'What does she do? ' she whispered to the Hokkaido girl. 'What happens now? '

'Wait and see. It's fun. There's nothing to frighten one.'

'Come on—sit down, all.' The widow beckoned them over. 'Come on, *sensei*. You can sit next to me.' She held out a hand to the doctor who, however, merely smiled superciliously without taking it and went and placed himself beside Rumi.

Rumi put her long fingers, with their evanescent nails, up to her face, pressing the tips to her cheek-bones as she exhaled one shuddering breath after another. Her eyes were closed.

'Music,' hissed the widow.

The studious-looking girl clicked on the switch and then moved the arm of the gramophone on to the worn and slightly warped record. There was a knock, a hiss, and again a knock. She gave the arm a jolt with her forefinger. Judy Garland began to sing 'Somewhere, over the rainbow' as though Edison himself had recorded her. Everyone waited tensely, the girls hunched forward on the edges of their wooden chairs with the exception of the widow who sat back, resting her arms on her spreadeagled thighs, between which her hands dangled. Rumi grunted three or four times; whimpered; and then grunted again: strange animal grunts that seemed to come, not from her throat, but from her diaphragm. Kumiko clutched the hand of the Hokkaido girl; she was beginning to tremble. The doctor smiled: he had all sorts of medical and psychological explanations for Rumi's condition at these séances, but if he ever delivered himself of them, she was furious; on one occasion even assaulting him with her teeth and nails.

Rumi had begun to snore, her head now resting sideways on her shoulder as though the neck were dislocated, and her mouth open, with a fine thread of saliva glittering greenishly from one corner of it to her chin.

'She's already unconscious,' the widow whispered.

'She always snores just before Iori takes her,' the Hokkaido girl explained to Kumiko in a whisper.

'Who's Iori? '

366

'Sh!' someone hissed.

'Oh, make him come, make him come, make him come,' the Korean muttered to herself, as she jigged up and down in her seat with every appearance of having an urgent need to relieve herself.

Suddenly Rumi began to pipe in the voice of Iori: her elder sister (so she said) who had died so many years ago of diphtheria in Shanghai.

'Good evening, everyone. Good evening, everyone, this is Iori here. Poor Rumi is tired tonight. Very difficult for Iori to come to you. Iori tries hard to speak but . . .' The plaintive voice faded; and as it did so, terrible groans burst out of Rumi's clenched mouth. Kumiko let out a little squeal. 'Iori has some friends here.' Again the childish piping was resumed. 'She has here a man, man with glasses, man with big cut, cut all the way from . . .' Again it faded; the Shikoku girl had half-risen to her feet, teeth bared and body straining as though in an agony of thirst, while the Korean tried to restrain her. Suddenly Rumi began to whimper, tossing her head from side to side: 'But blood, blood, blood,' she wailed. 'Much blood. Covered with blood.' She arched her back; her face screwed up excruciatingly; then she slewed round and over, so that they could see only her shoulders and the glimmer of her neck under the rumpled mane of black hair. Her arms, hanging down on either side of the chair, swung back and forth with an increasing rhythm. She gasped; gasped again; and then spoke in a guttural man's voice:

'Where are they? What have you done with them? The papers you took from her desk—give them to me. Give them to me!'

The arms swung faster and faster. Her toes began a rhythmic scrabbling on the floor. Suddenly a shrill scream broke from her. 'No! Don't! I don't even understand them! I don't know what they mean! Don't! Don't! I'll give them to you! They're here! In my bag!' Some of the girls had risen to their feet; Kumiko's chair went crashing backwards into the darkness. 'No! No!' The two monosyllables came out as separate yelps.

Rumi seemed to be struggling with somebody unseen. She raised her hands and tore at the air, her body threshing from side to side and the saliva bubbling up through her lips as she seemed to be saying—What? Some girls later said 'Help'; others, 'No'. Her eyes were open and bulging from their sockets; her tongue shot out. Then her whole body all at once rose out of its chair and shot slithering across the floor into a corner as though propelled there

367

by some extraordinary force. It lay so still that not one of them imagined that she was still alive.

The widow dashed for the overhead light-switch. The fluorescent tube flickered, brightened, flickered again, and then rained its cold light down over their sweating bodies. The doctor was kneeling over Rumi, a hand to her pulse. The Korean was sobbing wildly. Kumiko had rushed out of the room.

Suddenly Rumi hiccoughed; then she hiccoughed again. Her eyes opened blearily as she hoisted herself off the floor, lifting first one shoulder and then the other, and finally raising and turning her head to gaze up at them.

'Rumi-chan!' the widow gasped. 'Your neck! What's happened to your neck!' she pointed.

But already the terrible weals were fading. Rumi sneezed. 'Get me up,' she muttered. 'Get me into a chair.'

The doctor raised her in his arms; someone pulled a chair towards her. She sank back into it. 'How was it?' she asked. No one answered. 'Well? Terrible, I suppose. And I've managed to wet myself. I knew that it would be no good. I told you all, didn't I? . . . Oi—Kumiko-chan, fetch me a drink, there's a good girl. There's half a bottle of whisky in my bag over there. Ah, I feel terrible! Like dying!' She covered her face with her hands and began to whimper: 'Like dying, like dying!'

TWENTY-SEVEN

COLETHORPE'S letter, written so long after Setsuko's, reached me in Athens only a day later. Setsuko's had gone first to my bank, then back to Japan, then to my sister's flat in London, and finally to Greece, where I had broken journey on my way home. I had planned to stay in Athens only a week-end and by then already a month had passed.

When the air-letter fell out of my sister's envelope, I felt as if a balustrade against which I had been leaning had suddenly given way. In the pleasure of being back in the city which I like more than any other and of being reunited with so many old friends, I had barely thought of Setsuko for hours, and recently even days, on end. I had written to her, of course; and when no answers had come I had a hideous sense of abandonment, until in despair I had sent Colethorpe an air-mail letter asking for news. But even at the moment when I was penning the phrases ' desperately worried . . . can think of little else . . . impossible to enjoy myself' they were already ceasing to be true.

So here was the key which Setsuko had promised to put into my hand as soon as I had left Japan ! I can never open air-letters properly, invariably having to piece them together afterwards, and on this occasion I bungled the job even worse than usual. My fingers trembled as I pushed the strips about on the breakfast table and it was many seconds before I got them right. Then at last I could read :

My dear Bill,
          Now that you are about to leave Japan and, I feel sure, will never return here—you do not really like us enough, for which I cannot blame you—I am writing to you, as I promised, to say the things I can never put into words. By now you have learned enough Japanese to know that we have very few words to express our emotions : we seldom need them. I, who am so untypical of my country, am typical in that.

I shall miss you, both as a neighbour and a friend. It was

369

reassuring at night to wake up and see, from my window, that your light was still burning and that you were busy working, so uncomfortable with that low table between your knees and your body hunched across it! It was nice during the day to know that if I had any worry or problem I could come over to you. Some of the Japanese called you hard and proud and 'insincere'—you knew that, of course—but I liked your cynical common sense in this country in which both cynicism and common sense are rare.

Most of all I shall remember our excursions together: that wonderful afternoon at Ise; the picnic before it; even the pearl-island in the rain, with all those blue-haired American women and bespectacled American men. And our swims together—I must not forget them. What fun it all was; and how sad that now it is all over.

I never make friends easily; you do. So in a way our separation will be worse for me. As I often used to tell you, I belong nowhere—neither to West nor East—and that is difficult. Perhaps I belong to the future when West and East will be one! I like to think so; it's a consolation, even if a small one.

Think of me sometimes and of the happy times we had together. I shall think of you. And please—write!

Yours ever,
Setsuko.

PS. How is our tree doing?

I read the letter again and then again: dumbfounded and dazed. I do not know exactly what kind of self-revelation I had been expecting, but this was not it. But there must be more to it, there must be! I told myself as yet again my eyes stared down at her neat script; and I continued to tell myself that for the rest of the day, drawing out the tattered strips of paper from my wallet and piecing them together as though in the hope that I should all at once hit on some new conjunction which would change everything. Then, strangely, although the words did not change and their relationships to each other did not change, I found that imperceptibly my view of Setsuko was changing. She had promised me the key, she had then failed to place it in my hand; but the lock of its own accord had slowly started to slip. Her relationship with Sanae and her relationship with Furomoto: those were the clues! Her obsessive interest in the one, her disgust for the other : I went over in my mind all the incidents in which these feelings had been revealed until I began to see that the one feeling was merely the counterpart of the other and could not exist without it. Furomoto was the man whom she had desired and then rejected in disgust and he was the prototype of all such men, myself the last of them; Sanae was the refuge on to which she cast herself just as so many years ago the horrified fifteen-year-old child had cast herself on to the refuge of her aunt. Perhaps Colethorpe had first appeared as another such refuge. Yes, I saw it all; of course, of course! How blind I had been. Slowly I placed the letter away in my wallet, feeling for her now, not that terrible intensity of longing and love, but pity, only pity. To the end, even to this last promise of truthfulness, she had been unable to do anything but lie to me, and probably to her own self as well.

The next day, Colethorpe's letter came; and yet another, and even odder and more disturbing dimension was added to the figure which was thickening in my mind.

My dear Bill,
[That was the first time she had used my Christian name.]
Your letter arrived this morning—from Greece! How I envy you!—and I'm hurrying to reply to it this evening although it's late and I'm utterly fagged out. As you can see from this address, I'm working at the mission after all. There was nothing else for it! I don't really fit in, of course, and they all hint as much and obviously disapprove of me. Even Frank's having second thoughts about marrying me—much to my relief, I need hardly add! The work's not too bad—I'm responsible for the hospital records, which were in an awful mess when I took over and are (I pride myself!) somewhat better now. Sometimes I have to help with the accounts—quite a revelation! Did you ever come to the hospital? And if so, did you ever know that it was run on Robin Hood principles, the rich (i.e. people like yourself) being overcharged to pay for the poor (i.e. Koreans who own Pachinko Parlours, brothels and bars)? Probably not! It was an eye-opener to me.

But I mustn't run on like this all about myself—and the mission—when what you want to hear about so eagerly and anxiously is Setsuko. The story is so peculiar—and vague—that I really don't know how even to begin to tell it. I certainly won't get it right, that I warn you! Anyway—a few days after you'd left Setsuko and Mrs. Furomoto announced that they were going to visit relatives in Hongkong—all quite sudden but not really surprising. I was still over at the house and they said I didn't have to hurry to move if I could look after myself. The next evening they left, giving me an address to which to forward letters. Various things began to crop up to do with the house and I wrote off but got no reply—not a word from them! Then the forwarded letters started to whizz back—'Address unknown'. That gave me a shock, I was just wondering what I ought to do—go to the police, go to Furomoto—when Ikeda-San called. Very polite; just a social call, he said. He asked how long they'd been gone, made a note of the forwarding address, put some other questions. I asked about the case and he said ' Oh, *that*! '—very much as if he'd forgotten all about it. Well, perhaps he had, like the newspapers.

The next day three men in plain-clothes—detectives—and an American turned up. They asked me the same questions and a lot more and kept asking them until I could have screamed, they seemed so stupid. Then they started to ransack the house—turned everything upside down and inside out. You should have seen the mess! Poor Setsuko would have been horrified, you know her tidiness and how she was always going on at me for leaving things around.

The next morning there was a great deal in the newspapers about the disappearance of the ' ex-wife of well-known industrialist and her niece, and a whole paragraph about Setsuko's work—assistant to Professor Something-or-other, top-secret, hush-hush, all that kind of thing. Finally there was a bit about suspected Communist sympathies and about Setsuko's knowledge of Chinese and Russian and her Russian mother—I'd never known about her myself, had you?—and the suggestion that they'd done a kind of Burgess and Maclean not a moment too soon.

I was absolutely *stunned* as you can imagine, everyone was. There was no end to the gossip, and people like Miss Pinter and Mrs. Crawley were absolutely gloating, though they kept saying that they believed not a word of it and it was all newspaper muck, like the stuff they'd printed about poor Welling. But the most peculiar thing of all was that after that first spread all over the front pages there was not another single paragraph. Can you imagine! Frank said that Furomoto had probably put a stop to it—he owns two newspapers, but would that explain the silence of the others? Or do you think that the police or the Japanese M.I.5, or the F.B.I. clamped down? I just haven't an idea, no one has.

Anyway, they've still not come back and no one has heard from them. Setsuko apparently took only one week's leave from her work and the laboratory people haven't heard either. I moved over to the mission and then some cousin of theirs from Tokyo came to pack up their things and lock up the houses. Your old servant, Endo-San, is there as caretaker, but he says he's getting bored with nothing to do and wants a real job.

So that's all I can tell you! And I know that you're going to be horribly upset and worried. Perhaps I ought not to have told you, but what good would that have been? You might write to Furomoto—you know how bad my own relationship is with him, so I can hardly beard him in his den for you! Perhaps something might come of it, but somehow I doubt it. Oh, I wish it weren't me that has to break all this to you! I'm so terribly, terribly sorry.

What other news? Well, the Welling case, as I say, already seems to be half-forgotten. Oh yes, that horrid little script-writer —Fat-Big or Big-Fat or whatever he called himself—came round looking for you and seemed sorry to hear that you had gone. He then started going on about Welling—how deeply disappointed he'd been that Welling had decided not to face the music after all. 'After his sermon,' he said, 'I think maybe this man saint. But he not saint after all, he coward'—or words to that effect. I was furious and really let fly, I can tell you! 'And what right have you to expect anyone to behave like a saint?' I demanded. Very dignified, very cold—but real nasty! He shrivelled up. Well no, actually he didn't. I can't imagine anything making him shrivel up—short of burning at the stake—can you?

Sometimes I feel that my weeks in the Furomoto house were all an extraordinary dream. And then at other times they are so real that I frighten myself by thinking of them and decide I must get out of Japan before something happens to me too. So I'm saving my pennies—I'm becoming a terrible miser!—and as soon as I have enough, well, maybe you'll climb the Acropolis one day and find me perched on top of it. A nasty surprise?!?!

When I got your letter, everyone here seemed to know who

it was from and they all wanted to know what you were doing and where you were and what you said. We sometimes envy them their lives and think that perhaps we've missed the boat; but I never realised that they sometimes envy us ours and think that perhaps they've etc. etc. Had you ever thought of that?

Well, I mustn't run on and on like this. My eyes keep closing —perhaps I ought to prop them open with matchsticks—as Miss Pinter says she used to do on night-duty in the wards in war-time! Do write again. And do tell me if there is anything I can do to help you in any way.

The only consolation for you is that you are far away from Japan. When I miss someone terribly, I find it best to go somewhere new with no shared memories and associations etc. So what could be better than Greece! I'm sure you've already found some dark-eyed maid of Athens to amuse you.

Well, so long for now!

Yours very sincerely,

Aileen Colethorpe.

I put down the letter on the desk at which I was sitting and thought about it for a long time as I suppose that I shall go on thinking about it through the days ahead. The odd thing was that I felt so little astonishment. Just as it had been possible for Setsuko to feel things and even to experience things below the trap-door of her consciousness, so also, below the trap-door of mine, I had known all this already; so that when Colethorpe now jerked the trap-door up, the shock was merely the shock of falling through it, not of finding what it concealed.

The sun was sinking and I watched it sink, staring out over the desk and down the slopes of Lycabettus. At this distance the lines of newly-erected apartment-houses looked beautiful in the deepening light, although, God knows, they are hideous enough at a close view in daytime. The bald hills opened out, hills beyond hills, a long vista at the bottom of which sparkled up the sea. In Japan one sees the sea only from the seashore. How wonderful, I thought, to have the sense of distance restored to one. I glanced at my watch. My friends would be waiting for me, but it did not really matter; they could go on waiting, sitting under the dusty plane-trees in the Plaka. I got up and yawned and stretched; and then I stared at the dwarf maple-tree—'our tree' Setsuko had called it in her letter—which stood on the desk. Poor, exquisite

374

little tree, twisted and maimed for who knows how many years, starved and stunted to make a work of art! The leaves were already crimson against the crimson sky. I put out a hand in the darkening room to pluck one from a branch, crumbling it to a fine dust as I walked the length of the corridor to the lift which would take me down into a night crowded with people.